Love
in the
Catskills

Eras of Love Series ~ Book One

by

BL Miller

ISBN: 0692479678
ISBN-13: 978-0692479674

Published by
Rose Quartz Publishing
Colonie, NY USA
www.rosequartzpublishing.com

First Edition: 2015
Rose Quartz Publishing

This is a work of fiction. Names, characters, places, and incidents are the product of the author's imagination or are used fictitiously, and any resemblance to actual persons, living or dead, businesses, companies, events, or locales is entirely coincidental.

Editing: Nat Burns

Cover Design: Ann McMan, TreeHouse Studio

Acknowledgements

This story, and indeed this whole series, is a labor of love requiring vast amounts of research. I need to thank the following people for their invaluable assistance in making the quality product you are enjoying:

Jennifer Rogel for her assistance with all things pens.
Jessie Chandler for her assistance with finding the perfect surname for Mary.
Pixiey for beta reading.
Nat for her patience and excellent editing skills.
Beth Mitchum, Carrie Carr, and Jan Carr for being cheerleaders as I reached each milestone.
Everyone on Facebook that supported me through the endless posts about this story.

Archive.org for numerous texts
NYS Library, Albany, NY for old newspapers such as the Albany Evening Journal. Also for the letters of Susan B. Anthony and Elizabeth Cady Stanton.
William K. Stanton Library, Colonie, NY, for several research books.

Dedicated to my mother, who grew wings long before I was ready for her to fly.

Chapter One

Ten year-old Mary Chandler's excitement about summering at the famous Catskill Mountain House had been at its peak when the family first stepped aboard the Hudson River Day Line back in New York City. That was nearly twelve hours ago, however, and the excitement had waned since. To make matters worse, her younger sister, Judith, succumbed to seasickness and baby brother, Daniel, snuck away from the nurse. This caused panic for the better part of half an hour as the ship's crew and passengers hunted stem to stern for the rambunctious four year-old. Now, as they rode in the large, cumbersome coach up the uneven mountain road from Catskill, it was older brother, Tobias, who attracted everyone's attention with his near constant complaints about the weather and the lack of comfort.

As they went across yet another bump, Mary wondered what Tobias had to complain about as he was sitting on one of the more comfortable end seats. She and her younger siblings were forced to sit on the center bench, a padded leather strap providing the only hint of a backrest. They had all been asked to exit the coach and walk the steeper parts of the road to ease the burden on the horses three times thus far. Her father had spoken of fresh, cool air and views guaranteed to amaze, but, thus far, all she knew was that her dress was sticking to her, her feet hurt and perspiration was rolling down her face. The constant jostling had not only thrown Daniel from his seat several times but one particularly violent jolt had sent her flying from her seat and over her sister into the frame of the coach door's open window.

Then it appeared. As the coach reached a bend in the road, Mary saw what her father had been trying to tell them about for the past few weeks. There, rising from the mountaintop in a splendor of white, was the Catskill Mountain House.

Having grown up in New York City, Mary was used to seeing grand homes and expansive buildings, yet even the greatest buildings in the city could barely compare to the beauty Mary observed. Immense Corinthian columns complemented the portico, reminding her of Grecian buildings from her picture books. It was a man-made beauty resting atop the mountain amongst the green of nature's pines and hemlocks. She easily understood now why there were several men and woman situated on the sides of the roadway with sketchbooks in hand or with canvases on easels. The sight was indeed worth being immortalized with paint and shared for others to see. Now she felt grateful for the noisy coach with its clanging and jostling, compared to the arduous task those artists must have had walking up the mountain road with their tools in hand.

The coach rounded the bend and the magnificent resort disappeared from sight. Once again, all Mary could see through the open window in the carriage door was an endless forest of hemlock and pine.

"Will it be very much longer?" she asked.

"It will if Father makes you get out and walk," Tobias said.

"You needn't wait for your father to ask," Mary's mother said. "I suspect we will all be asked to do that soon enough if this excuse of a road becomes any steeper."

Mary twisted this way and that in an attempt to see again the gleaming white of the majestic building. She saw only the shades of endless green leaves and brown bark created by Mother Nature. As she continued to fidget, she earned an admonishment from her mother.

The final minutes were sheer torture as she eagerly awaited arrival at the immense hotel. Even when the coach reached the steepest part of the trek and everyone had to yet again get out and walk, she did not mind. Walking ahead of the others, she urged them on through each inclined step. If able to, Mary would have pushed the coach from behind to make it go faster.

Time spent in Gramercy Park near her home and Sunday carriage rides to the country could never compare to the vastness of the tree canopy visible when they finally crested the mountain. The pines and hemlocks were everywhere, joined by oaks and maples to show off a series of beautiful greens that complemented a clear blue sky. A pair of lakes stretched to her right and several young people were swimming and gallivanting in them. Judith saw them, as well, and let out a squeal of delight and a request. "Mother, May I go swimming?"

"Later," her mother promised. "We have to get to the hotel and unpack first."

"Hmm, with all those trunks you brought, we shall be unpacking until right near August," her father said, drawing laughter from Tobias and a small chuckle from the gentleman seated next to him. The gentleman's wife, seated next to Mary's mother, bowed her head to hide her smile. Miss Sally, the children's nurse, also looked down.

"Only required items were brought along," her mother protested, raising her chin in challenge.

"Is that so? I am surprised we were not required to walk the entire mountain road for all the weight those four trunks have added to the carriage. I suspect not a single cricket would find room to perch within a one of them."

Mary glanced at her mother, and then looked away, recognizing the look. It was reserved for when they were in company and her mother could not say what she truly wanted to. However, it bestowed an implicit promise to give an earful when there was no one else around. Fortunately, the coach took yet another turn, leaving the lakes behind, and soon the grounds of the famed Catskill Mountain House were before them.

"Oh, Mother, it's beautiful!" Mary exclaimed, putting her hands on the edge of the window opening and stretching her head out to peer at the magnificent sight.

"Ow!" Judith protested, squished by her older sister. Mary ignored her, enthralled by the sight of the grand building.

"Mary, sit back," her mother admonished. It took a second scolding before Mary did as she was told, though even then she leaned so that she could still look out the opening.

The famed Catskill Mountain House was easily a rival to the best hotels in the city, with its four gleaming white stories, large windows, and a flurry of white uniformed servants scurrying about. Seated in the middle of the center bench, it was hard for Mary to see much beyond the hotel itself. It was only after the coach stopped and all the passengers disembarked that she was finally able to see the magical view that would never leave her.

While the hotel staff quickly carried in the heavy Saratoga trunks, filled with clothing and other essentials for the Chandler family, Mary scurried around to the east side of the hotel. There she saw the portico with the tall Grecian columns she'd caught a glimpse of during the ride up the mountain. Now able truly to view them, she found the thirteen columns held up a porch that was attached to the second story. The first story's entrance was below the portico itself. There, several white rocking chairs provided seating for those wishing to stay in the shade while the square support columns provided excellent objects for small children to run around, as they played hide and seek.

When she turned around with her back to the hotel, the view took the ten year-old's breath away. She stood but a few yards from the edge of the precipice. Moving carefully so she wouldn't get too close to the drop-off, Mary peered over the side. There, below her, treetops appeared to go on forever. Farther out spread the beautiful blue band of the Hudson River.

Looking carefully, she picked out clusters of houses and buildings, supposing them to be the town of Catskill. Geography lessons led her to believe that, beyond the river, she saw the state of Massachusetts. Never in her life had she seen so far at once. Tens, perhaps hundreds of miles were available to her eyes.

"Oh, my," she whispered reverently.

The land seemed to go on forever and she wondered, if she had in her possession a telescope, she might see the mighty Atlantic Ocean, as well. From her far left to her far right, the view simply seemed to be endless. So enthralled was she in the majestic view that she jumped, startled when she felt a hand upon her shoulder.

"Mary Elizabeth Chandler, do you hear me?"

"Oh! I'm sorry, Mother." Looking back to the vast expanse, she sighed happily. "Isn't it the most wonderful view, Mother?"

Her mother nodded. "It is very pretty, darling. Now, however, you must come to the room and change from your traveling clothes and ready yourself for supper."

"Must I?" she asked, without looking away from the enchanting landscape.

"You will have plenty of time to look out later, Mary. Right now you do as I say. And when you do come out here to look, I want you to stand farther back. They should have a railing here lest some child simply walks over the edge thinking they can walk on top of the trees," her mother added, as Mary turned to go.

Mary straightened her shoulders when she entered the dining area, taken aback by the grandness of the room. Thick heavy drapes covered most of the windows, keeping the heat out but allowing just enough light to see. Rows of tables were covered with fine white linen while colorful paintings and portraits adorned the walls. Mary wished she were barefoot so that she might feel the softness of the ornate rug beneath her toes.

Fine white plates and cups were being placed upon the tables by a flurry of servants, all dressed in an equal array of white. As her father led them to their table, Mary watched the workers. Heads down, they focused solely on their tasks, save the occasional smile to a guest or the nod in acceptance of a request. She wondered if they were allowed to enjoy the fine meals that her father spoke of or if they were only allowed to see and never taste. Mary's father spoke to one such woman, who quickly left and returned a minute later with a wooden box to put upon Daniel's chair.

"Thank you," Mary said to the servant.

Startled, the servant looked first to Mary's father, who smiled and gave a slight nod, before she answered.

"It is my pleasure, Miss." She looked back to the family patriarch. "Please excuse me, sir."

Mary took a seat next to Judith. Mirroring the seating arrangement at home, her father sat at the far end of the table while Tobias and Daniel sat on the opposite side from her. Her mother sat at the near end.

"Judith, put your silverware down until the meal is served," her mother said, while lifting Daniel onto the wooden box.

"Yes, Mother," Judith replied.

"I'm hungwy," Daniel whined.

"Daniel, we shall be dining soon enough. Mind your manners," her mother said quietly.

"We'll have none of that tomfoolery that happens at home while we are here," her father said sternly. "Mind your manners."

"Yes, Father," the three older children said in unison.

He gave a soft grunt. "The same way all of you did when my parents came to visit?"

Mary and Tobias quickly looked down at their plates.

"I suspect young Daniel will be through with school by the time they dare return," her father added.

"Let us pray," Mary's mother said.

"What?" her father said, as he unfolded his napkin.

"I believe I said let us get the prayers done now before the food is served."

"Hmm." He gave his wife a dubious look. "Quietly, to yourselves."

"Yes, Father," the children said.

Mary dared to look at her mother, who rewarded her with a quick wink. One thing the young girl was grateful for was that her grandparents rarely came for visits. She even made a point of thanking God during her silent dinner prayer for such.

The din of conversation quickly escalated as the flurry of servants dispersed the evening meal. Glasses were filled, plates placed just so. Mary found herself sitting just a little straighter in her chair as the occasion seemed to warrant it. Even the napkins felt as if they were from the most precious of linens. When the dinner was served, the aromas made her wish she could just tuck right in without having to wait for her father to take the first bite from his plate.

"See here," her father said as he scooped up potatoes with his fork. "The cost is near the same as if we have stayed at the Astor House and that fine place cannot possibly offer the air and views that we receive here."

He gestured with his hand in a wide arc at the large dining area. "Look at all the servants present to care for our needs. I might sit in a chair all day and be waited upon by a dozen men without doing more than lifting a little finger to capture their attention. Tell me, Mrs. Chandler, would the finest accommodations in Paris or London possibly compare to this?"

Mary's mother dabbed the corners of her mouth with her napkin. "The Mountain House could certainly do with a cobblestone road, Mister Chandler. Even a corduroy road would have been of more comfort than that torment we suffered through to arrive here." She paused to give her husband a small smile. "However, there is no sight in all of Europe that would compare with that just outside the door."

"Indeed," the elder Chandler said proudly, as if he alone were responsible for the breathtaking view of nature.

"Still," his wife continued. "I do wish Mister Beach had considered the safety of the children and placed some rail or fence to keep them away from the edge."

Mary's father waved his fork dismissively. "Nonsense. And ruin the beauty of the precipice? We simply must make certain that Miss Sally keeps Daniel and Judith away from the edge."

"It is so beautiful, Father," Mary said. "We can rightly see forever from here."

"So it seems," he agreed. "If good enough for Miss Jenny Lind and Mister Tyrone Power, it certainly is good enough for us." He gestured at her with his fork. "You, however, young lady, will not be spending all your days gazing out at the horizon. No, indeed."

He glanced at her mother and nodded before returning his gaze to her. "Do you not recall our discussion about your schooling and that horrid excuse which you call your penmanship?"

Mary looked down at her plate. "Yes, sir."

"While I did not feel the expense of having your tutor accompany us was necessary, nonetheless you will be studying your spelling and working on turning that scribble into something worthy of a Chandler while we are here."

She looked up at him. "But, Father—"

Silencing her with merely a look, he continued. "I have even purchased new pens and a holder for you to use. A diary, as well. I expect you to have it filled by the end of summer with whatever girls your age write about."

"So long as it is not about boys her age," her mother said.

Mary's father nodded. "Indeed, Mrs. Chandler. I am grateful she is only ten. We have but a few short years before there will be a line clear down to Fulton Street of young men coming to call upon her."

"Perish the thought," her mother said.

Mary looked from one parent to the other, not understanding what they were talking about but glad the topic seemed to have changed from her penmanship and spelling.

Her father returned his attention to her. "Every day, young lady." He gestured with his fork for emphasis. "Every day I expect you to be writing in that diary and to work on your schooling."

"Yes, sir."

"Miss Sally will be checking it and if you wish to not spend every day of this summer indoors with paper and pen, I expect to see vast improvement."

Tobias made a soft snorting sound.

"And don't think you are going to frolic about without a care in the world, Tobias Alexander Chandler."

Mary was pleased to see the smirk quickly leave Tobias' face at his father's tone.

"I note that Mister Beach has a piano in the sitting room. I expect you to practice as much here as you do at home."

"But—"

"Tobias...."

"Yes, Father."

"And what of myself, Mister Chandler?" Mary's mother asked.

"You, my dear." Mary's father smiled and reached for his fork. "You are to continue to look so radiant that the other women are positively ill with envy and the men may know that I am the luckiest and most blessed creature that God ever saw fit to place upon this earth."

Blushing, Mary's mother smiled and reached for her own utensils. "Mister Chandler, really. In front of the children?"

"I would stand and make such a proclamation that the entire room would be able to hear," he said proudly.

Mary frowned when she saw the pile of magazines and books at the bottom of the trunk. In addition, there was a bottle of ink and several pens along with an ornately carved holder. She lamented the earlier lack of effort toward her studies and penmanship that had caused the less than stellar report from her tutor. Now her time spent playing outside would have to be shared with time spent putting her studies first. Supper finished an hour before and if she had any hope of spending time outside the following day, she had no choice but to get started on her schooling. Sighing loudly, she opened the diary and stared at the blank page. Reluctantly, she dipped her pen into the ink and wrote carefully.

June 25, 1852
Father has given me this diary to write in. I do not want to. I want to go outside and play. It is not

fair that Judith and Daniel are outside playing. They read and write worse than I do. I wish I was older so I woodn't have to do any more school and Father wood not tell me what to do.

She looked up from her work and gazed out the window. From her vantage point, blue skies and green leaves offered themselves for her enjoyment. She let her mind wander for several minutes before resuming her chore.

When I am all grown up, I will not make my children do all this studying and hard work. We will play outside all the time.

Her obligation to the diary complete, Mary grumpily shoved it back into the trunk and pulled out her blue backed speller. With another sigh of lament, she opened the book and located the correct page. At that moment, Mary, certain there was no more miserable child in all of Greene County, wrote word after word, doing her best to keep the writing as neat as possible but still trying to finish as quickly as she could manage.

Later, outside, the sun was just starting to descend for its nightly nap. Orange filled the sky, treating the guests of the Catskill Mountain House with a view unrivaled. Mary walked to the table rock, the precipice of which gave way to another precipice only a small jump down. Unable to resist, she made the small jump to the lower level. Several names and dates were carved into the table rock but Mary paid them no mind as she crept closer to the edge. Below was a seemingly endless forest of trees, so dense that she swore that she might easily have stepped off the rock and walked along the treetops themselves all the way down to the town of Catskill. Beyond the small town was the water of the mighty Hudson River. Less than twenty-four hours ago, she had been trapped on the steamship, below deck in the ladies parlor with her mother. Now she could take a deep breath and inhale the sweet freshness of the pines instead of stale perfume and ripe body odor. She knelt down and placed her hands upon the flat rock. Feeling the coolness beneath her palms, she closed her eyes and let herself become one with nature for a few seconds before someone else came to break the moment.

"Stay away from that edge," a strange male voice warned.

Rising to her feet, Mary brushed off the dust and moved closer to him. "Yes, sir. I'm sorry."

"I've never had anyone fall off and I do not intend for it to happen this year," the man said. He held out his hand and helped her back to the upper precipice. "If I catch you out there again, I will tell your parents."

"Yes, sir. I won't do it again," she said.

Just then, another man came running up. "Mister Beach! Mister Beach!"

The man who had helped her up from the lower precipice looked at the man, then back to Mary. "I'm sure your mother is wondering where you are," he said. "Run along now, child."

"Yes, sir."

"Now, what is this all about?" she heard Mister Beach say as she ran back to the Mountain House. The other man's response was lost to her as she moved from earshot.

Mary found her mother on one of the sofas in the sitting area just inside the Mountain House.

"Oh, there you are," her mother said. "I wondered where you'd run off to. Here." Mary's mother held out a small wooden box, a cloth pouch, and one of Gideon Chandler's favorite pipes. "Take these to your father."

"Yes, Mother."

"Oh, yes," her mother added. "I found Judith playing with Betsy Ross." She held out Mary's doll. "You cannot yell at your sister for playing with your things if you keep leaving them lying about."

"Yes, Mother." Carefully balancing the items, along with her doll, Mary went out the front door to the portico. There she paused to absorb the panoramic view, just as awe-inspiring from the porch as it was from the edge of the table rock that jutted out above the escarpment. Wrinkling her nose at the acrid smoke from the pipe of the white haired man sitting opposite her father, Mary approached them.

"It is," her father said firmly while waving the wrinkled newspaper in his clenched fist. "And a few villains shall not change the truth more than a pebble shall dam up the mighty Hudson."

His long, slender finger poked the paper. "See here. Even the Times has said that California will not become a slave state so long as the Chinese continue to pour into the country."

The bearded gentleman sitting opposite him shook his head. "The New York Daily Times is best served as tinder in the stove."

"You would prefer more slave states, Mister West?"

"I find the very notion of slavery quite distasteful, Mister Chandler. That a man can claim ownership of another man as he would a sow or a cow ought not be part of our fine union."

He tapped his pipe against the earthen pot, emptying the spent ashes. "As it be, however, I trust not one of the purveyors of the news. The Tribune is so clearly tipped to the Whig party that Mister Greeley might well emblazon their banner across the front with portraits of Garrison and Douglass. The Charleston Mercury calls for South Carolina to secede on a daily basis. How can anyone know what to believe lest it comes from the pulpit?"

"South Carolina should...." Her father stopped when he saw Mary standing there. "Men are talking."

"Yes, Father." She held out the box and small leather satchel. "Mother said you would wish for this."

Setting the paper down on his lap, he smiled and took the items from her. Opening the box, he displayed the half dozen perfectly rolled cigars. "Now here, my good man, is some of the finest tobacco Havana has to offer." He held out a cigar for his companion before taking one for himself, putting the pouch of tobacco and the ornate pipe into his jacket pocket. "Thank you, my darling. Now run along."

"Yes, Father," she said, though she made no effort to move.

Her father pulled a small tin box from his pocket, his attention on the older gentleman.

"As I was saying...." Removing one of the wooden matches, he struck it against the side of the chair, causing a large sparking flame to form before it settled down. "South Carolina should be most grateful that the banks of New York have not called in all their debts."

He paused to light his cigar, then leaned forward and held the flame out to his companion. "Most certainly those dandies of the South would not be able to maintain those fancy plantations and grand estates without our money."

He leaned back and took a long puff, releasing a cone of smoke. "Nor would they be able to afford to purchase more slaves. We are just as much part of the problem as those plantation owners."

"And how, sir, do you reconcile that?" his companion asked. "Do you hurt your purse in the name of your principles?"

Gideon frowned. "I have changed my bank to one that does not issue slave loans and I have encouraged others to do the same," he said. "I have indeed lost business from those that support the continuation of that horrific assault of sin against man." He turned his head, spotting Mary still standing there. "Young lady, I said to run along."

"Yes, Father." This time she did as she was told. There was no need for her to continue listening anyway as she was familiar with her father's strong anti-slavery stance.

"Come along, Betsy," she said to her doll. "Let's go find someplace to play."

Mary spotted a girl who appeared to be around her age sitting on a rock near the path leading away from the Mountain House. The doll swung wildly in her hand as she ran toward the girl. "Hello."

The girl smiled. "Greetings."

"My name is Mary Chandler. What's yours?"

"I'm Hester Van Wyck. Are you staying at the Mountain House?"

Mary nodded. "Uh huh. We're summering here. Are you?"

"No. *Vader* and I live in Palenville."

"Vader?"

"My father," Hester said. "Vader is Dutch for father. He is an artist," she said proudly. "As fine as Mister Cropsey or even Mister Church himself."

"Oh. I don't know who they are. Father and Mother both like paintings. We have lots at home," Mary said. "My father buys and sells things. Where is Palenville?"

Hester pointed toward the trees behind her. "There. You have to go down the road and then back up, though. I wish there was a road right from there to here."

"Oh, the really bumpy road?" At Hester's nod, Mary continued. "We had to come up that way when we arrived."

"It's the only way to get here," Hester said.

"I saw artists on the road," Mary said. "Was your father one of those?"

"No. Those students are learning to paint. My vader has been painting for years. He has a studio where he teaches some others but he doesn't bring them up here. He paints portraits. He is doing one now for Mister Beach himself."

"Mister Beach?" Mary asked, remembering the man who had made her get back from the table rock earlier. "I met him. Is he summering here too?"

"Why, he owns the Mountain House. He's a very important man." Hester swung her legs, letting the backs of her heels slap against the rock she was perched upon. "Where do you live?"

"I live in New York City." Mary pointed in the distance to where her father was still conversing with the man with the long white beard. "That's my father. The one on the left."

"Vader has been to New York City twice already."

"Oh." The conversation lagged for a few seconds. "Do you want to see my doll?" Mary held it out for her new friend to take.

Hester turned the doll this way and that, lifting the dress to peek underneath. "She's a very pretty doll. What's her name?"

Mary giggled. "She's Betsy Ross. She used to have a flag but Daniel tore it off." She said, pointing to where a thin stitching of red material still existed in the doll's hand. "That's my little brother. He's four. He broke Mother's favorite vase and he peed on Tobias' leg when he was holding him."

Hester handed the doll back. "Your dress is pretty."

Mary smiled and smoothed out the wrinkles on her lap. "Mother bought it for me this past week. She got one for Judith too but it's not as pretty as mine," she said, shaking her head. "That's my sister. She's only six. I'm much older. I'm ten. How old are you?"

Hester straightened up. "I'm nine and almost a half."

"Do you have any brothers or sisters?"

"No. I would have had a little sister but she and my *moeder*, um, mother died when she was born."

"Oh. I'm sorry."

"I have a cousin and she is like a sister," Hester said. "Griet is thirteen."

"I have cousins too but they live far away."

"We all live together. Aunt Frances and Uncle Gerrit let us move in after Moeder died but Uncle Gerrit died last year."

"My grandmother died last year too," Mary said. "My Grandmother Chandler, not my Grandmother Franklin. She lives in New York City, too, but she doesn't visit often. I don't think she likes my father."

"There's also Hendrik and Martin but we just call them the boys. They're twelve. The youngest is Kent. He's seven."

"Wow. That's a lot of people," Mary said. "You must live in a big house."

Hester shook her head. "It doesn't seem big when we're all inside but I suppose it's big enough. I wish the bed were bigger, though. Griet kicks in her sleep all the time."

"Oh, you have to share your bed?"

Hester nodded. "Me and Griet sleep together. The boys have their own bed and then Mister Littlefield, the boarder, and his son share a bed."

"I don't share my bed," Mary said. "I have to share my bath with Judith but she has her own room. Tobias has to share his room with Daniel but they have their own beds."

"Is Tobias your brother too?"

"Yes. He's the oldest. He's fourteen." Having had enough of conversation, Mary changed the subject. "Want to play?"

Hester smiled. "Play what? Ring around the Rosey?"

"Oh, no. Mother would be upset if I got my new dress dirty." She touched her index finger to her bottom lip. "We could sing."

Tossing the doll on the ground, Mary then grabbed both of Hester's hands. "*Kittie put the kettle on, kettle on, kettle on,*" With great smiles, the girls held hands tight and twirled around in a circle, singing the popular children's song as loud as they could.

> *"Kittie put the kettle on*
> *Kettle on, kettle on*
> *Kittie put the kettle on*
> *We'll all have tea."*

The girls giggled and sang the verse repeatedly, making themselves dizzy from the spinning. When they stopped, Hester hit the ground first, providing a cushion for the unbalanced Mary to fall onto and thus keeping her new dress clean. Poor Betsy Ross was left on the ground as the girls returned to the flat rock and began an earnest series of clapping games, beginning with *Pease Porridge Hot,* continuing with games that they happily taught one another. The play ended only after an exhausting series of *Miss Mary Mack,* complete with extra verses they created in order to keep the game from ending too soon.

When Judith managed to sneak away from the nurse, Mary reluctantly allowed her little sister to join them. Then they played tag, and hide and seek, though the slower Judith often ended up on the short end of the stick in those games. By the time Miss Sally came to collect both Chandler girls, they were exhausted with play.

18

"Will you be here tomorrow?"

Hester shook her head. "I have to do Griet's and my chores tomorrow on account she did mine today. Vader must leave close on to sunup to come here and cannot wait for me."

Mary frowned. "Miss Bessie does the chores at home. Don't you have coloreds to do the washing and cleaning?"

Hester's eyes widened with surprise. "Oh, no. Only rich people have them, 'cepting those that live free like Mister John and his family does. They have a farm out past Uncle Michael's and trade with us for apples. Miss Lilly makes the prettiest dresses. Aunt Frances says no one can use a needle as well as Miss Lilly can. Vader tried once to give her a portrait in trade for a new dress for me but she said she had no use for such a thing but if he brought a deer or bear that she might. He's afraid of them bears and the deer are too quick for him, so I never did get a dress from her."

"You call your father vader and your mother…?"

"Moeder."

"Moeder but you call your uncle and aunt, uncle and aunt. Don't they have Dutch words for that?"

"They do. *Oom* is uncle and *tante* is aunt but they've always just had me say uncle and aunt. Uncle Michael does, too. I don't know why."

That explanation satisfied Mary. "When I need a new dress, Mother takes me down to the stores on Broadway and buys it or she has Miss Sally sew one. She says not to tell anyone though because if they knew how good Miss Sally did that then they'd steal her away for one of those fancy stores to be a seamstress. Father says he doesn't want her to leave and that's why he pays her so much."

"Oh, I thought she was a slave."

Mary shook her head vehemently. "Oh, no! Father and Mother are ab-ablitionist-is. They say slavery is wrong and all those southern states need to let the coloreds go free. That they's just as smart and good as the whites. Miss Sally is mighty smart too. She helps Tobias with his schooling and every day does lessons with Judith, Daniel, and me. Father said when she came to live with us first off, that she could barely read her name and now she can read and write same as anyone else."

"Miss Mary."

Mary looked to where the nursemaid was standing. "Yes, Miss Sally." She turned back to face her new friend. "I have to go." She engulfed Hester in a hug. "Come back as soon as you can."

"I will," Hester said. "As soon as I can."

"I'll look for you right here at the rock each day."

Hester picked the doll up from the ground. "Don't forget Betsy Ross."

"Thank you."

"Miss Mary."

"Remember," Mary called out as she was walking backward toward the nursemaid. "Mary Chandler. Don't forget."

"I won't. Goodbye, Mary Chandler."

"Goodbye, Hester Van Wyck."

June 28, 1852

Father wants me to write every day so I will be smart like Tobias and Miss Sally. I will be living here in at the ~~Catt~~ Catskill Mountain House all summer. It is way up on the top of the mountain. When I look over the edge, I see the tops of trees but they are too far away to touch. I think we must be a hundred miles up in the sky cause Catskill is so small when I look down at it but it was so big when we were there. I have a new friend. Her name is Hestr.

She is only 9 but taller than me. Her eyes is are blue. We played all day and she taught me new songs. I wish she had no chors so she could come play tumorr tommorrow. It is pretty here. I wish we would get to always live here.

July 6, 1852
It is sunny today. Mother said I could go swimming in the lake later but I have to finish my writing lessins. It's not fair because Judith and Daniel get to go swimming. Hestr hasn't come all week but asked her father yesterday and he said she might come tommorrow. I hope so. Every night when I say my prayers I ask for her to come. Father just called for me. I will write later.

Mary ran to her father who was sitting outside. The old man was sitting in the chair opposite him.

"Yes, Father?"

"Ah, there you are. Do you recall what I told you about that thief in mayor's clothing, Ambrose Kingsland?"

"Yes, Father."

Mary's father addressed the man sitting in the chair opposite him. "Mister Green, now see here what our fine Mister Kingsland has turned New York City into." Mary's father rattled the paper as he located the article that had him so riled up. "They called it *Trial of Speed*. Now look here. It starts:

'A very interesting exhibition took place yesterday, whether under the patronage of the American Institute or not, we cannot say.'"

He looked up. "I know that which I believe. Ahem."

"*'Which was witnessed by thousands of our citizens on Canal Street,'*" he continued. "*'The object was to show how near men could come to doing nothing, and yet keep at work. Four persons were selected for this trial of laziness*

21

by that distinguished public benefactor, Mister Perrine, celebrated as the inventor of a pavement which no human being except the Common Council has yet been found stupid enough to consider endurable.'"

He rattled the paper again, looking at his companion. "The whole of the Common Council and that Mister Davies, Esquire should all be strung up as the common criminals they are."

"Bought as easily as one would purchase a draught," his companion agreed.

"Indeed. It goes on." He took a moment to find his place in the article.

"'A stout boy would probably have done the job in a couple of hours, without inconvenience, yet to such a pitch had these experts carried their skill in making haste slowly that half the job was still undone at sundown.'"

"And yet they feel no guilt at collecting their worth," Gideon's companion said.

"They most certainly felt due a bonus, Mister Green," Mister Chandler said. "That my taxes are wasted on such frivolity is a sin no less than that of a pickpocket."

Reaching out, he put his hand around Mary's arm and gently pulled her close. "This is my oldest daughter, Mary. Mark my words, she will never be foolish enough to marry anyone whose mental capacity is as low as any of those council members."

"The forty thieves of New York," the older man said.

"Indeed," Mary's father agreed. "We would be better to open the prisons and put the criminals in office. At least then we would be clear that we were being robbed."

"Our streets would not be overrun with orphans, beggars, and those too lazy to work were the monies used in the proper manner. As it is, there shall be even more riots, I have no doubt."

Mary's father nodded. "I fear for my children, sir. I do not let Mary or her sister go outside lest it is to our park with their nursemaid. Even in Gramercy, it is no longer safe to leave children unattended."

"'Tis a sad state of affairs," the man said. "We should send those Irish back to whence they came. Only that will solve the problem."

"Too much love of the bottle and too little love of the work of an honest man," her father said. "They fight with the Negros for the jobs yet I have seen not one that is willing to work as hard as the coloreds."

"This is why they had their great potato famine," the man said. "Had they cared more for their land and less for their drink, it would not have come to pass."

Mary's father let go of her. "Perhaps we should offer them free transport to Charleston. Let them work in the fields picking cotton. They would all be on the next boats back to their island. Mary, fetch my pipe and tobacco."

"Yes, Father." She was happy to leave his company whenever he was on a tear about something he read in the paper. Far too many dinners at home were consumed with a side dish of her father's railings against the men in office.

Running to the portico, she found her mother sitting with several women, a now common sight to Mary. "Father wishes his pipe and tobacco," she told her mother. "He is mad at Mister Kingsland again."

"And the sun rises in the east," her mother said, reaching into her bag for the requested items. "What did our revered mayor do this time?"

Mary shrugged. "He hired some men to work on the road but the Times said they made haste slowly. Father said they are wasting money and picking his pocket."

"And since he has found Mister Green to join him, he has a soap box so that he might share his grievances." She handed Mary the pouch containing the tobacco along with the pipe. "Bring these back to him but tell your father that I have something for you to do."

Her mother looked out from the portico to the grassy area where her husband was sitting with Mister Green. Even from the distance, it was clear that the rant was continuing. "I'm certain you've heard quite enough about the failings of our elected officials for one day." She sighed softly. "Were it to be that he and his ilk were as concerned for the equality of women and extending us the right to vote, such problems might not exist."

"Yes, Mother."

"Certainly we would never let someone as foolhardy as Mister Kingsland and his cronies into office," Mrs. Chandler said. "Were those that were oppressed such as the colored and the women allowed to vote, there would be such great change that our country would once again return to her former glory."

"Yes, Mother."

"Rather than lining cronies' pockets with money, we would make certain the infirmed and the children were clothed and fed, not left to die on the streets of our fine cities."

"And that demon drink was no longer served," a woman sitting nearby chimed in. "Temperance is the only solution to the problem of the drunkards."

"Uh, I should get these to Father," Mary said, quickly getting away from her mother and the other woman. Her father's side dishes were not the only railings she had to listen to at dinner. As she walked away, she smiled at the thought that her parents were so similar. Where her father could not stop himself from going on about the politicians, her mother was incensed equally about women's rights.

When she reached her father, he was still going on about the City Council.

"And another thing, oh! Yes, thank you, Mary."

"Mother wishes me to come right back," she said. "She has something that I must do."

"I hope it is your schoolwork," he said. "Very well. Run along. As I was saying, Mister Green...."

As she walked back toward the portico, Mary wondered which was worse, having to listen to her father go on or to her mother. While she sat and worked on her lessons, her mother continued the conversation about why it was past time for women to have a say in politics. By the end of dinner, Mary had her fill of listening to both of them and excused herself by saying she needed to work on her journal. By the time Judith entered the room for the evening, Mary had read through all the copies of Godey's and filled two pages in her diary about the games she and Hester would play once they were together again.

Chapter Two

Mary squealed with delight and bolted from the chair when she saw Hester and Mister Van Wyck walking up the path.

"Mary!" her mother admonished. "Manners."

"Yes, Mother," Mary called back without care. "Hester! Hester!"

The girls ran toward one another for the final few yards, embracing as if long lost sisters.

"I knew you'd come back," Mary said as they twirled around in their friendly embrace.

"I was ready to go before Vader even awoke this morning," Hester said.

"She would have run all the way here if I had let her," Hester's father said.

"Oh!" Hester broke the embrace. "Vader, this is Miss Mary Chandler."

"Yes," he said. "I've heard much about you," Pieter Van Wyck said. "You're all my daughter has talked about. So, here is a question as serious as does the sun rise in the morning. Do you mind if Hester plays with you today?"

"Oh, no," Mary said in all seriousness. "I would be most pleased to spend the day with her, sir."

"That's what my daughter has been saying," he said. "Perhaps we should ask your mother?" He straightened up and removed his cap. "A pleasant morning to you, ma'am."

Mary turned to see her mother approaching. "Mother, can Hester and I go play? Please? I promise I will do my schooling later."

"It is may I, not can I, and yes you may. A pleasant morning to you, as well, sir."

"Pieter Van Wyck," he said. "I'm afraid all my child has spoken of this past week has been your daughter and how she promised to come back and play with her."

Mary's mother gave a soft laugh. "Hester has been the topic of nearly every sentence from my daughter's mouth, as well."

Mary and Hester had enough of their parents' conversation and quickly ran toward their favorite spot, the flat rock near the edge of the woods. "We can play Kittie Put the Kettle On again."

"Sure," Hester agreed. She reached into the pocket of her dress apron. "I brought my doll too. She's not as pretty as Betsy Ross but we can still play."

"I'll go get Betsy." Mary ran a few steps toward the Mountain House, then stopped and looked at Hester again. "I'll be right back. Don't go away."

"I won't," Hester promised.

Mary turned and ran as if being chased by rabid wolves, returning with the doll faster than Hester believed possible.

"I've got it," Mary said breathlessly. "Now we can play."

Protected from the June sun by the shady hemlocks, the girls played right through lunch and into the afternoon without a break. Only when Miss Sally brought them a pitcher of lemonade and sandwiches taken from the lunchtime meal did they stop. Then they only stopped playing but continued to chat between bites.

"And then Tobias' trousers fell clear down to his ankles."

Hester joined in the laughter. "This past summer, when the boys were swimming in the creek, Griet and I went down and stole all their clothes. Aunt Frances was so mad but later she told us that she and Aunt Fern did that same thing to Uncle Michael when they were around our ages." She waved her finger. "That's a secret that we're not supposed to ever tell anyone."

"I swear I won't tell," Mary said. "I won't even write it in my diary."

"You can tell me anything, too," Hester said. "I swear I'll never tell a secret you tell me."

"Uh, oh," Mary said, pointing toward the figure walking toward them. "Here comes your father."

The girls' jovial mood turned somber as he reached them.

"Hester, it's nigh time to leave."

Instantly both girls looked down and joined hands.

"Just a short while longer, Vader. Please?"

He shook his head. "I waited as long as I could for you but we shall be late for supper as it is. Come along now."

"When will you be back?" Mary asked. Hester looked to her father for an answer.

He rubbed his bearded chin. "Mister Chandler has asked me to do a family portrait for him so I shall be back in two days' time to start the sketching. If your Aunt Frances is able to spare you, I suppose you can return with me then."

"Oh, I'm sure she will," Hester said excitedly. "I shall see you then," she said to Mary.

"Yes, please," Mary said as they both rose to their feet. "I'll miss you."

"I'll miss you more," Hester replied.

"No, I'll miss you more."

"I'll miss you more than even that."

"No, you won't."

28

"Yes, I will."

"I'll miss you more than there are trees in the forest."

"Well, I'll miss you more than there are blades of grass on the ground."

"Then I'll miss you more than there are drops of water in both lakes."

"I'll miss you—"

"Girls!"

They stopped and glanced at Hester's father.

"You'll miss one another. Now say goodbye so we might get home before dark. Your Aunt Frances will have quite enough words to say to me about taking this long, as it is."

"Yes, Vader. Goodbye, Mary."

"Goodbye, Hester."

Mary watched until Hester and Mister Van Wyck were out of sight before turning and slowly walking back to the Mountain House. Even a dinner that would put their talented housekeeper to shame did nothing to improve her mood.

July 10, 1852

I am happy I got to play with Hestr today but am so sad that she had to go home. Her father said she might be able to come back the day after tomorrow but that is so away. Father said we are havng a new portret made but I wish it was just one of me and Hestr. He said no but when I am older and have lots of money, I will have Mr. Vanwyck make me a portret of us. I will put it on my wall next to my bed so I can see it all the time.

"Hester Ann, if you want to spend any time at all in the studio today, you'd best get cracking on dinner."

"Yes, Aunt Frances." She added the sliced vegetables into the cast iron pot.

The older woman wiped her hands on the cloth. "I don't know why your vader continues to fill your head with ideas about painting and being an artist. If it weren't for those other artists renting space in the studio, we'd never be able to make ends meet." She shook her head. "Certainly your vader doesn't make enough selling those portraits and signs of his."

She lifted the iron plate and placed more wood into the stove. "Hurry up, now. I haven't any more rooms to let out for someone to do your work, as well."

Hester focused on the task at hand, the reward of being able to spend time in the studio always the best motivator. It was second only to the chance to go with her father to the Mountain House so she could visit with Mary.

She felt the soft touch of her aunt's hand on her shoulder. "It looks right near time for you and Griet to have new dresses. This is barely better than a washcloth."

Hester looked up in surprise. "Aunt Frances?"

The older woman smiled. "The way you two girls are wearing out your dresses, I don't rightly believe they'll be any good by fall when you's supposed to be getting new ones made. Even your going to meeting clothes ain't right proper for Sundays. Now, it's nice enough that your vader has that Mister Chandler and Mister Beach having those portraits done but it's just not enough. If he can sell a few more soon enough, he can get into Catskill and buy some of that gingham that we saw in the window of Mister Griffen's mercantile. You need more practice with your sewing so you can most certainly help your cousin and I make them."

She wiped her hands on a nearby cloth. "Though I don't know why I bother with Griet's dress. She'll just ruin it acting like a boy playing in that mud and doing all that carrying on." A high-pitched screech caused both to look toward the main part of the house. "Those boys," Aunt Frances said, quickly moving toward the door. "Hurry up with those potatoes."

"Yes, Aunt Frances."

"Hendrik, Martin! Leave your sister alone."

Hester let the rest of the often repeated admonishments fade away. A new, pretty dress. She resolved to work extra hard on it so her new friend Mary would be able to see it before summer ended.

The door opened and a muddy creature wearing a dress appeared. Or what passed as a dress, tattered and torn from the abuse the teenaged tomboy had put it through. Hester watched with amazement at her aunt's quickness as the older woman snatched the girl, stopping the muddy mess from continuing farther into the house.

"Griet! You get down to that crick and you wash that mud off right this instant!"

Two tow-headed twelve-year old boys and their little brother Kent appeared in the doorway. "And you two!"

Aunt Frances guided the muddy thirteen-year old around them, releasing her with a slight shove. "I mean it! And bring back a bucket of water with you." She turned to face the older boys. "You two are supposed to be setting an example for Kent."

"Moeder, she started it," Hendrik said. "We were tossing the ball and she's the one who threw a mud patty at me."

"How is she going to learn to act as a girl does if you two keep treating her like a boy?"

Martin wiped ineffectually at the mud stain on his shirt. "Tell her to stop acting like one."

Aunt Frances wagged her finger. "Mind your tongue, young man. You are not too old for me to take a switch to, and you know it would be that much worse than if I had your Uncle Pieter do it."

"Yes, ma'am."

"That woodpile looks a might small, so until supper is ready you two can get working on that. I need kindling, too." The twins groaned. "Well, that's what you get for carrying on like that with her. Good Lord, but I don't know what you two are thinking most of the time."

"She started it," Hendrik tried again. "She wants to act like a boy, let her get the firewood."

"I done warned you ten times, if once," his mother snapped. "I don't give a bear's behind who started it. Now get to that firewood and I mean now."

"Yes, Moeder."

"And you." She turned to her youngest son. "All that running around is going to make that leg sorer than anything. Can't be affording to haul you off to see the doctor again anytime soon so's you need to start listening to me. Go sit on the porch and play with your whittling knife. Make me another one of those pretty dogs or horses. You know I like them."

"Yes, Moeder." The seven year-old limped out the door.

"Good Lord, I swear those children are going to be the death of me." She wiped her hands on her apron. "Well? The pickles aren't going to come out of the root cellar by themselves."

"Yes, Aunt Frances."

"Your vader said you're going to see your friend at the Mountain House again Saturday. I expect you'll do Griet's chores tomorrow so she'll do yours for you then."

"Oh, yes," Hester said excitedly as she reached for the door that led to the root cellar. "I will, Aunt Frances. I promise."

"Seems like foolishness to me," her aunt said while Hester entered the room cut into the earthen hill against the house. "Making friends with someone who is just going to leave at the end of the summer. You'll probably never even see her again after that."

"Oh, no," Hester said as she pulled the jar off the shelf. "Mary and I will be friends forever and ever," she insisted. "Until we're old and gray and even after that."

"We'll see about that," her aunt said. "Don't forget the butter."

After days of feeling little more than loneliness, Mary was treated to the sight of her friend coming up the road. Squealing with delight, Mary smiled broadly and ran across the sun-kissed field as Hester approached.

"Hester! Hester!" she shouted, waving her arm wildly. Hester smiled and returned the greeting, picking up her pace to meet her friend partway through the open area. Once again Betsy Ross hit the ground as the newfound friends embraced. "Can you stay all day?"

"Yes, Vader is doing a lady's portrait so we will be here for hours."

Mary smiled broadly. "Let's go play on the beach and make a sand castle."

Hester reached into the front pocket of her dress, pulling out a folded piece of paper. "I made this for you," she said.

Mary opened the paper, gasping in surprise at the hand drawn portrait of herself. "Oh! May I keep it?"

Hester smiled. "Of course. It's a present for you."

Mary smiled broadly, holding the drawing next to her face. "See? It looks just like me." She folded it back up and put it in her pocket. "I'm going to have Mother take me to get the finest frame to put it in when we get home. A portrait by Hester Van Wyck, the greatest nine-year old artist ever!"

"Vader said next year I can start using paints instead of just pencils. Then I'll paint your portrait just like he does the rich people."

"We'll fill up my walls with your paintings," Mary declared. "I'll even cover my window and ceiling with them."

"I'm sorry I couldn't come the day that Vader was doing your portrait," Hester said. "Aunt Frances said there were too many chores."

"I was sad," Mary said. "Mother had to keep telling me to smile for Mister Van Wyck but it was hard." She smiled and gave Hester a hug. "It's all better now that you're here."

"I was sad, too," Hester said.

"But now you're all better, right?"

"I suppose so," Hester said, smiling brightly. She pointed at a shady area near the beach. "Let's go there."

The girls giggled happily as they claimed their area away from the others frolicking at the beach. So absorbed in their play, they were completely unaware of anyone else's comings or goings. The sun danced in and out of the clouds but neither noticed as they chatted, laughed, and played together.

By the time Miss Sally found the girls down by South Lake, they were playing checkers on a board carved into the sand with a stick. Pebbles made up the tokens. Betsy Ross was lying on the ground next to the pair, completely ignored. They paused their play long enough to wash their hands in the water, then ate the sandwiches provided before returning to their play. Tears only came when Pieter came to collect his daughter. A casual offer from him to have Mary come for a visit put an end to the crying and filled both girls with excitement and anticipation. When the Chandlers were faced with the option of either accepting or putting up with their moping daughter again, the choice was simple. The date was set for the following Saturday, a week which seemed interminably long to both girls.

Chapter Three

Waving excitedly at the approaching carriage, Hester shouted. "She's here! She's here!"

"I'm not deaf," her Aunt Frances said as she came around the side of the house. "I can hear that rattletrap coming."

Hester paid her no attention as she raced to meet the slowing carriage. Mary had the door open before it came to a complete stop.

"Mary!"

The girls hugged fiercely while the driver helped Elizabeth Chandler from the carriage.

"Most pleasant to meet you," Frances said while wiping her hands on her apron. "Hester has been excited to have her friend come here. Can you stay for some iced tea?"

"That would be most appreciated," Elizabeth said, using her handkerchief to dab at her throat. "It is certainly most uncomfortable today."

Frances smiled. "Come, sit here in the shade. The wind blows most generously there." She paused long enough to tell the driver where to move the carriage so the horse could have some shade and water before she guided Mary's mother to the more comfortable area.

"Ah, there you are," Pieter said as he came around the house, his nephews following. "Hendrik, bring her bag inside. Mrs. Chandler, so nice to see you again."

"Likewise, Mister Van Wyck." Elizabeth nodded her thanks to Frances before settling into the white rocking chair. "This indeed is much cooler."

"Those are my boys," Frances said. "That there's Martin and this is Kent. Hendrik is the one that just went inside. Griet is making something special for dinner tonight since we have company."

"It is kind of you to invite her," Mary's mother said. "We shall come calling upon you the day after tomorrow to pick her up."

Pieter chuckled. "I'm sure wherever that sun is in the sky, it will be too early for those girls," he said. "Like long-lost sisters, they are."

Elizabeth took a sip of the iced tea, then nodded. "They are certainly fond of one another. I suspect it is because they are so close in age. Mary has never been like this with Judith." She turned her head toward Frances. "That's my younger daughter."

Frances nodded. "Same with Hester and Griet. Just like sisters but I never can recall her being as she is when she gets talking about Mary this and Mary that."

Elizabeth looked around. "Where are the girls?"

"I suspect they went to the studio," Pieter said. "I will go check on them."

Frances reached for the pitcher and an empty glass. "Bring that man a drink," she said. "Certainly he must be as thirsty as anyone else."

Elizabeth smiled. "I suspect he has been keeping his lips wet with the flask in his pocket," she said.

"Do not think about asking him for a sip," Frances warned her brother. "I'm not blind to how you are when you return from Michael's house."

Pieter's mouth formed a tight line but he said nothing, walking away with the glass and a quicker pace than usual. Despite her stern warning, he did indeed swap the glass of iced tea for a sip from the carriage driver's flask.

He found the girls where he expected, wandering about the old barn that had long before been converted into his art studio. "There you are."

"Hello, Vader."

"Hello, Mister Van Wyck."

"This is the studio," Hester's father said. "Here is Hester's easel. She's really quite good."

"I'll be a famous artist when I grow up," Hester said. "Then we can live together and play with dolls all the time."

Hester's father laughed and patted her shoulder. "Let's get you to make the biscuits without burning them first before you start worrying about growing up and moving away." He kissed the top of her head before stepping away. "Now, it's just too hot to stay in here all day and I'm sure Griet would love to join you two down at the creek."

Hester's eyes widened and she smiled brightly. "Oh, yes, Vader."

"I'll get the boys to get away from there and tell Griet to hurry up and finish her chores so she can join you. Don't spend much time in here. I know how you are when you get into the mood to play with your brushes."

"Yes, Vader," Hester promised. "I'll just show her some of your paintings."

"Very well," he said, giving her a loving smile before leaving them alone.

"Here," Hester said, grabbing Mary's arm and guiding her toward the largest of the artist areas. Several signs in various stages of completion were about along with a few canvases in equal levels of progress.

"Oh, that's the one of us," Mary said. "See? That's Mother there."

"I told you he was the best," Hester said. She picked up a framed canvas from where it leaned against the wall. "Here's one he finished."

Mary stepped closed and studied the landscape painting. "That's beautiful," she said. Leaning, she peered even closer at his signature in the lower right corner. "Oh! It's Van Wyck, not Vanwyck." She straightened up and shook her head. "I thought your surname was one word, not two." She glanced around. "He sure makes lots of paintings of the mountain."

"Everyone does," Hester said. She pointed another easel which sported the image of the Mountain House from the perspective of the curve in the road leading up to it. "People come from all around to draw and paint either the mountains or the Mountain House."

Mary walked to Hester's little corner. Rather than portraits or landscapes, the paintings on the walls showed flowers and fruits. "You're good, too," she said.

Hester smiled bashfully. "Not as good as Vader," she said. "Look." She picked up her sketchbook and showed her the drawing she had done. "See? That's you."

Mary smiled. "That's just like the one you gave me," she said.

"This is my first drawing," Hester said. "I drew it again to make it better before I gave it to you."

They were interrupted by Griet bursting into the studio. "Hester! Let's go! The boys are all up from the creek."

With smiles of anticipation, the three girls raced for the creek.

Frances sat on the bench next to the creek, her knitting bag holding several balls of yarn and her needles. "Now, you girls be careful," she warned. "Don't want to be having to tell Mrs. Chandler that you done went and got hurt in the creek."

"We will, Moeder," Griet said as they stripped off their clothing. "You see that rock there?" she asked Mary. "We like to jump off it."

Hester was the first to get naked. "It's fun. Like this." She took off running, jumping from the rock and tucking her legs up so she looked like a ball when she entered the water.

Mary giggled and mimicked her friend, squealing with delight in that split-second of time that she was airborne.

As the sun peeked through the trees and continued to warm the creek, the girls frolicked, splashed, and swam around. No woodland creature remained within earshot of the laughing and squealing trio. There was great disappointment when Frances announced that it was time to get out and dry off so they could return to the house and get dinner started.

"You're the guest," Frances said. "I'd no more expect you to help than I would Mister Littlefield or his son."

"Miss Harriet does the cooking at home," Mary said.

"Well, around here we do what we can do and means we do the cooking, cleaning, sewing, and washing," Frances said. "Hester, get the biscuits started."

"Yes, ma'am."

August 15, 1852
I spent the weekend with Hestr. It was fun. We swam and played and stayed up late. I wish I could live there with her. I wish we could stay here at the mountain forever. They make a desert that was so sweet and yumy. I hope Miss Bessie can make it to.

Tears streamed down Mary's face. "But I don't want to say goodbye," she sobbed. "I want to stay here forever with Hester."

"Well, you can't," her father said. "We'll be back next summer and you can see her again then."

"Vader, can't we move to New York City? Please?" Hester asked as tears rolled down her face.

"I'm afraid we cannot. I'm sorry, Mister Chandler. I know you wish to get your family on the coach."

Mary's father waved his hand dismissively. "It will wait for us," he said. "Let the girls say their goodbyes."

"Y-your new dress is very pretty," Mary said, hiccupping through her tears. "Maybe next year I'll be taller and you'll be able to wear my old dresses."

Hester sniffled. "Maybe." She used her sleeve to wipe her cheek.

"Here." Mary thrust out her arm, Betsy Ross dangling from her small fist. "I want you to keep her until I come back. She's real good with nightmares and when you play with her, you can think of me."

Hester reached into her father's satchel and pulled out her rag doll. "Here. You can hold onto mine too. That way I know you won't be lonely without Betsy Ross."

Mary took the doll. "I'll put her right on the pillow next to me," she promised.

"I will, too," Hester said. "I'll take good care of Betsy, I promise."

"I promise I'll take good care of Dolly, too."

The girls looked at one another for a moment, then both burst into new tears.

"I don't want to go," Mary cried as they embraced one final time for the summer.

"I don't want you to go either."

"You would think we were separating sisters," Mary's mother remarked before reaching down and putting her hands on her daughter's upper arms. "Come along now, Mary. Mind your manners. You will see her next summer."

Mary sniffled. "Goodbye, Hester. I'll miss you so much."

"I'll miss you more." Hester used the back of her hand to wipe at her teary face.

"More than the leaves on the trees."

"More than the stars in the sky."

"More than the grass—"

"Enough, girls," Hester's father said, giving his daughter's arm a gentle tug.

There never were two more miserable girls than at the Catskill Mountain House that day. It was two weeks before Mary would stop crying and the moping continued for a full month.

November 22, 1852

Today is my birthday. I am 11 years old. I wanted Hestr to come visit for my present but they said no. I got new dolls and dresses. When I am older, I will be an adult and I can have Hestr come visit whenever I want. When I'm all grown up and have a daughter, I'll let her have her friends come for her birthdays all the time.

Closing her diary, Mary flopped back on her bed and reached for Dolly. "I would, too. I wouldn't make her spend her whole birthday without her most special friend in the whole world."

Dolly quietly listened as Mary continued. "I wonder when her birthday is. If I knew, I would give her a big party with lots of presents." She rolled, deliberately putting her feet on the bed without removing her shoes. Sighing, she tossed the doll on the pillow. "I wouldn't make her spend her birthday all alone without me."

Chapter Four

"I swear the road is even worse than last year," Mary's mother said as the coach struck another rut and bounced the occupants around in their seats.

"Perhaps he hired Mister Perrine to design it," Mary's father said. "Though, I suspect that even he would be able to do a better job than this."

"When do you think Mister Van Wyck and Hester will be there?"

"Mary Elizabeth, if you ask that one more time," her mother warned. "They did not respond to the letter so we do not know when they will come. She has chores and he no doubt has paintings to do. They cannot drop everything to come see you."

"You drop everything to meet with Mrs. Astor and Mrs. Pike," Mary's father said. "Mary, after we are settled at the Mountain House, I will have word sent to the Van Wycks asking them to come. We could make do with a new family portrait, I suspect. If Tobias grows any taller, Mister Van Wyck will have to lengthen the canvas just to have enough room to fit his head."

Tobias smiled. "I'm almost as tall as you are, Father."

Gideon smiled. "That you are, my boy. That you are. Now if only you would concern yourself more with your studies of history and mathematics more than you do with the fairer sex, I would most certainly be a happy man." He took a moment to pack some tobacco into his pipe. "I certainly do not wish to listen to Mister Beach lecture me again this year about you and the other boys sneaking out in the middle of the night to have a hootenanny down at the lake."

Mary let the rest of the conversation around her fall to the background as she stared off at the road, wishing with all her might that a familiar face with light brown hair would come walking up to see her.

June 27, 1853

It has been three days and I have not seen or heard from Hestr. I do hope she comes soon. I miss her so much. I bought her a new doll and Mother said I can go visit again at her house. Maybe this time I can stay a whole week or even the rest of the summer. I wonder if she grew two inches ~~too to~~ also. I'll never get that right. I don't like words like that. Whoever created English should have just picked one and that's it. We shouldn't have to learn too, two, and to. I wonder if Hestr knows which one is right?

Mary wanted to write more but the candle was becoming dangerously low. She had begged her mother for a full candle but Mister Beach's rule about children having only the stubby ones was a rule that no one seemed to want to break. With a sigh, she blew out the flame. "Good night, Hester," she whispered.

"Hmm?"

"Nothing, Judith. Go to sleep."

Judith groaned and rolled. "I was trying to but you wouldn't put the candle out."

"Well, I just did, didn't I? Now go to sleep." Tucking Dolly under her chin, Mary silently prayed for tomorrow to be the day that her friend finally returned to visit her.

There were few places to go in order to have true privacy on North Mountain. The trails were often filled with guests from the Mountain House and places just off the trails such as Badman's Cave became hideouts for young lovers. It left Mary with few choices when she wanted to be alone. The far side of Ashley Falls was one of those places. It required going through Glen Mary and then crossing Ashley Creek just to end up negotiating an often wet, rocky path to an outcropping that did not even offer a view of the small falls. Instead it gave all of the noise and only the barest view of the north side of the creek. Mary's shoes, stockings, and hem of her dress were soaked. She considered it worth getting spoken to by her mother for this small bit of privacy. A week had passed since they arrived and there still had been no word received from Hester or her father. Every morning Mary would rise and wait with the women and children on the portico only to end up being disappointed. Today she needed to be by herself. With the deafening sound of the falls surrounding her, Mary opened her diary, using a pencil rather than her usual pen and ink.

> *July 1, 1853*
> *Still no Hestr today. I don't know why we can't go to her home and see her since she hasn't come here yet. What if something is wrong? Why hasn't she sent word? Why hasn't Mr. ~~Vanwyck~~ Van Wyck sent word? I miss her so much. It's lonely here without her.*

Mary trudged slowly toward the Mountain House, knowing she had to be there in time for dinner but not at all interested in being around everyone. She resolved not to be happy until she saw Hester again. A shout brought her eyes up from staring at the ground.

"Hester!" The loneliness and sadness that had been wrapped around her for so long lifted as if clouds had parted to let the sun shine. Gone was the mopey, miserable eleven year-old who saw no joy in the magnificent sights of the Mountain House and grounds. She was filled with happiness and joy again as she ran toward her friend.

"Hester! Hester!"

"Mary!"

"Oh, goodness gracious! You're here!"

Ignoring the parents and other adults, the girls ran to one of their favorite spots, a flat rock hidden through some brush.

"You're taller," Hester said, dropping her sack on the ground next to the rock.

"Well, so are you," Mary pointed out, using her hand to show the height she remembered her friend to be the previous year. "You're almost as tall as me. Oh!" She looked down. "I got you a birthday present but it's back in my room. I didn't think I'd see you today."

Hester climbed up on the rock. "Aunt Frances has been sick so Vader said we couldn't come until she felt better."

"That's all right," Mary said. "You're here now."

"I have something for you, too," Hester said. "I have only a little left." She pulled a folded paper from her pocket. "I saved it until you came back." Unfolding it, she revealed a blob of maple sugaring. She took a pinch, then held it out to her best friend. "Mmm."

Mary took an equal pinch, as well, sampling the sticky goodness. "That's better than the candies from Mister Sam's store."

"Aunt Frances says that Uncle Michael always saves more than he should for the children," Hester said.

"That he spoils my cousins and me." She took another sample. "He gives us honey candy too."

"Mother says Daniel can't have candy. He bounces around like a jackrabbit now and when he gets candies, he's worse."

Hester laughed. "Vader told me that when he was knee high to a toad he got his sweet tooth and that's where I got it from." She licked her forefinger and thumb, not wanting to waste any of the sticky goodness.

"Next year, I shall have candies packed for us," Mary promised. "Mother always takes me to Sam's for candies after we've finished our Tuesday shopping."

"You shop every Tuesday?"

"Oh, yes. Sometimes we shop on other days too but we always go on Tuesdays because the new dresses are on display."

She pointed near her thigh where a patch of worn material had been sewn onto her dress. "I got caught on the pot nail so I had to fix it. I have to wait until fall before I can get a new dress again."

Mary shrugged. "I dropped the ink bottle once on my dress. Mother told Miss Bessie to clean it but it wouldn't come out so Mother told her to use more ink to make it all black and then give it to her sister's daughter. Miss Bessie said it was the finest dress her niece ever had. Mother bought me a new dress."

"Someday I'll have a store bought dress too," Hester said firmly.

"Of course you will, silly." Mary scooted so that she was sitting cross-legged, facing her friend. "When we get all grown up and get married, we'll have lots of dresses so you'll never have to wear a homemade one again."

After slapping her thighs, Mary clapped her hands together, then held them out in front of her. Hester reacted quickly, meeting Mary's hands with her own as they repeated the motions. "*Miss Mary Mack, Mack, Mack, all dressed in black, black, black, with silver buttons, buttons, buttons, all down her back, back, back."*

Hester joined in, the pace increasing as they fell into a rhythm. *"She asked her mother, mother, mother, for fifty cents, cents, cents, to see the elephants, elephants, elephants, jump over the fence, fence, fence."*

Mary put in her own words. "When we grow up, grow up, grow up, and are married, married, married, we'll live together, together, together, until we're buried, buried, buried."

Now, it was Hester's turn. "And in our closet, closet, closet, we'll have dresses, dresses, dresses, and we'll have servants, servants, servants, to clean our messes, messes, messes."

Mary laughed and took her turn. "We'll have dolls, dolls, dolls, for the children, children, children, and they'll all have desks, desks, desks, to do their learning, learning, learning."

"And there'll be easels, easels, easels, for their paints, paints, paints, and they'll have bibles, bibles, bibles, to learn about the saints, saints, saints."

"And we'll give them chocolate, chocolate, chocolate, for their dinner, dinner, dinner, and they'll play games, games, games, where everyone is a winner, winner, winner."

It took Hester a second to come up with the next line. "And we'll have a big house, house, house, with lots of beds, beds, beds, so all the children, children, children, have a place for their heads, heads, heads."

"And every pillow, pillow, pillow will be stuffed with feathers, feathers, feathers, and there'll be so many, many, many, that no one will have to sleep together, together, together."

They continued the motions but stopped the cadences. "We'll sleep together, won't we?" Mary asked. "On account that we'll be married?"

"I think so," Hester replied. "Unless you kick in your sleep like Griet does, then I'll have to get my own bed."

"Oh. I don't think I kick, so that means we can sleep together. We'll even have Betsy Ross sleep with us on account of she sleeps with you now and she'll get real lonely if I take her home and put her in the toy box. Dolly sleeps with me every night, too, so she'll have to sleep with us, too."

"And she doesn't kick either," Hester said. "And Betsy Ross, Ross, Ross, will sleep with us, us, us, and she'll be happy, happy, happy, and will not cuss, cuss, cuss."

"And Dolly, Dolly, Dolly, will be there too, too, too, and she'll be happy, happy, happy, and not blue, blue, blue."

There were no two happier girls in all the world that afternoon than the pair singing together on a flat rock in the woods near the Catskill Mountain House.

Hester was able to return only two days later, thanks to several guests of the Mountain House requesting portraits from her father. As the season moved on, the number of guests increased. Close little nooks and hideaways were quickly overrun by those looking for hikes off the regular paths and this forced the girls to travel farther into the woods to find quiet spaces to spend their time. Neither minded as long as they were able to spend time together. On this day, no convenient flat rock was able to be found so they settled for sitting with their backs against a large rock while a carpet of fallen leaves cushioned them from the ground.

"Why did you bring that?" Hester asked when she saw Mary take a magazine from her bag.

"Father says I have to read about Abigail Adams and then tell him what I learned. We can play after."

Hester frowned. "Then, what do I do?"

"We can learn it together." She crossed her legs and opened the magazine. "We'll take turns reading."

Hester looked away. "I don't know how to read."

"Not at all?"

Hester shook her head. "I can't read nor write."

"Oh." Mary thought about it for a moment. "I'll read to you and then that way we're learning it together. How come you don't read? Don't you go to school?"

Again Hester shook her head. "Never been to one. Guess I don't have a need to. Don't need to know how to read to sew or cook or clean."

"Goodness gracious! Mother says a woman should do more than that. That we should do whatever we desire and be equal with men."

Hester shook her head and laughed. "I don't want to be doing the hunting and the chopping wood."

"Then you shan't do it," Mary said. "But there's so much more we can be. Mrs. Adams was very smart and she felt women should be equal with men too. That we should be able to vote and keep property, if we earn money, then it should be ours to do with, and not what our husbands or fathers say. Why, if Mrs. Adams was alive today, she would be with Miss Anthony and Miss Truth and all the rest that march and talk of suffrage."

"But if we're all out voting and making money, who will keep the house? The menfolk?"

"Why not?" Mary asked. "Are they not strong enough to push a broom? To wash a plate? To change linens on the bed?"

"Well, I suppose so."

Mary threw her hands in the air. "Why does it have to be women's work? Because men don't want to do it, that's why! Mother says that as long as we accept that we are not equals, we will continue to be little more than slaves."

She opened the magazine and flipped through until she found the article. "Here it is. It starts, '*In illustration of the character of this es...es-tim..es-tim-able..estimable woman.*'"

"I don't know what that word means," she said, lifting her head to glance at Hester. "'*We must be permitted to tra-tran-transcribe a few remarks on her an-anc-anc-est-ry.*'"

"Oh, I don't know what that word is either," she said, frustrated.

"'*Written by her son, the hon. John Quincy Adams.*'"

"They have a period there after hon but I don't know why," she added. "'*Abigail Adams was the daughter of William Smith, a minister of a...church at Wey-mouth,*' Weymouth. I think that's in Massachusetts. Oh, yes, see it says, '*in the colony of Massachusetts Bay.*'"

She scooted closer, pointing out where she was reading.

"I know where Massachusetts is," Hester said proudly. "When you stand in front of the Mountain House and look out, it's there past the river."

"Father took us to Boston once." Mary shook her head and made a face. "I didn't like it. I like it here much better."

"I like you here better, too," Hester said. She reached out and held one side of the magazine, allowing Mary to use her finger to keep her place as she continued reading.

The article itself only encompassed two pages but with their near constant stopping to talk about whatever came to mind, it took an hour for Mary to finish.

"'...*died of typhus fever on the twenty-eighth of October, eighteen-eighteen at the age of seventy-four, leaving her countrywomen the example of an obedient and devoted wife, a careful and tender mother, a gentle and beneficent mistress, a good neighbor, and a true and constant friend.'"*

"I don't understand," Hester said. "The story was supposed to be about her but they talked about her father, her grandfather, her great-grandfather, her husband, her son...."

"They really did, didn't they?" Mary agreed.

Hester shrugged. "They didn't say much about her. She moved, she had children, she moved again, she died, and then at the end said she was an example of all those wonderful things. I didn't learn much about her at all, 'cepting she was quite old when she died," She let go of the magazine. "I don't know no one who's that old."

"Maybe she got that old because she was so smart," Mary said. "I'm going to be real smart just like her, but I'm not going to have four children because I'm going to marry you and two girls can't make babies."

"We'll just have dolls to play with," Hester said. "Or we'll take in some of those orphans and let them live with us and pretend they're our children."

"We'll have a big house so there's plenty of room," Mary agreed. "And we can have lots and lots of orphans come live with us."

"When Aunt Katrien died," Hester said. "Cousin Will became an orphan and he went to live with Uncle Michael." She cocked her head and looked at her friend quizzically. "How come other orphans don't go live with their uncles or even their aunts?"

"I don't know. Maybe 'cause they don't know how to write so they can't tell them where they are? Or maybe all their aunts and uncles are dead, too."

"Oh, that's sad," Hester said. "I'm glad I still have uncles and aunts."

"See? So, when we get married, we'll have to have a big house so we can have room for lots of orphans." She nodded emphatically. "We'll go up to the orphanage and tell them that whoever wants to come live with us can and then they won't be orphans anymore."

Hester scooted so that she was facing Mary, then began the rhythmic clapping. "And we'll have orphans, orphans, orphans, come live in our home, home, home and they'll never, never, never, have to be alone, alone, alone."

Mary turned so they faced one another and quickly caught up with the game. "And they'll have dolls, dolls, dolls, so they can play, play, play, and won't have to work, work, work, every day, day, day."

July turned into August and while the air was cooler atop the mountain than in the valley below, even the Catskills could not escape the heat that Mother Nature sought to bring upon the land. The need to stay close to the endless pitchers of ice water, lemonade, and cold teas kept the girls near the Mountain House, often playing in the shaded area beneath the portico. Mary and Hester were quietly playing cat's cradle with some string while Hester's father, Pieter, was sketching a likeness of Mary's father upon the pad. Less than ten feet from the men, it was easy for the girls to hear their conversation.

"Well, you must read the papers, my good man," Gideon said.

Pieter gave a slight shake of his head, never looking away from his sketchpad. "Never right learned that."

Mary's father pointed the stem of his pipe at the artist. "There's no shame in that, Mister Van Wyck. Things were different when we were young. I suppose were I to live where you do, I might have never fetched a book or newspaper to read, as well. Fortunately, your daughter might be able to read the paper to you, I suspect." He smiled at his eldest daughter. "I often have Mary do the evening reading for us. Why, even young Judith is able to read the children's books mostly."

Pieter's focus never wavered from his sketching. "Hester don't know how to read either," he said. "What good would it do her?"

"What good?" Mary's father sat up in his chair. "Education of our youth is the very cornerstone of the foundation that will make this union prosper. Surely you have a subscription school within your town with which she might attend?"

"I'm afraid she's needed at home," Pieter said. "My sister, Frances, cannot handle everything on her own, least not with all her children to worry about and her husband up and dead. Subscription school for a girl?" He shook his head. "Perhaps if Hester's mother were still alive and we were city folk, Mister Chandler, but my daughter needs to learn cooking and sewing more than she needs her ABCs. Frances' daughter, Margriet, is near fourteen years and she's never spent a day inside a school. She can fix up a shirt right quick, though. That's what matters to a man looking for a wife, not iffin she can do no reading and writing."

Mary's father puffed his pipe, the blue smoke billowing around him. "Even our Miss Sally is able to read and write. She won't ever win a bee but she can read the children stories. That a woman less than three years a freed slave can read better than your own daughter, well, now...." He waved the pipe about dismissively. "That's as wrong as the spring following summer," he said. "Mary!"

"Yes, Father."

"You stop playing and go get your reader, slate, and chalk." He addressed Pieter again. "Mary will help Hester learn and she can then help the other children at home. I will send instructions with the next post for a McGuffey reader to be sent." He paused to take a puff of tobacco. "Perhaps even a complete set of the Sanders series."

"Now there's no need to go to any bother—" Pieter said, but was cut off by Gideon's raised hand.

"It's no bother at all and I fully insist," Mary's father said. "How many children are there at your home?"

Hester's father stopped sketching. "Well, let's see...the twins, Griet, Kent, my Hester...five of them, not counting the boarder's son." He scratched his chin. "I don't rightly know if he can read or not."

"Five or six children who cannot read or write? That, sir, is tantamount to a crime against the future generations and a great disservice to those boys and girls." Gideon sucked on his pipe. "Now, I shall hear no more argument about it."

He tapped his pipe on the side of the chair to empty the ash. "If Hester has to do her chores in the evening so she is free to come up with you on the days you are here, then so be it. What Mary cannot help her with, I will have Miss Sally assist. We do not leave here for another month and I guarantee you, Mister Van Wyck, by that time your daughter will know her alphabet and be able to read at least the simple sentences. You do want what is best for her, do you not?"

Pieter looked affronted. "That is a most ridiculous question, sir. I would do anything for my child."

Gideon sat back and re-lit his tobacco, a look of satisfaction on his face. "Then it is settled." He used the pipe to gesture at his daughter. "Mary Elizabeth, I believe I told you do something."

Mary scrambled to her feet. "Yes, Father."

August 25, 1853
Hestr can't read. Father said I had to take my
slate and chalk and help her learn instead of playing.

I can pretend I'm the teacher except I won't use a switch like Miss Trimble does. I'm certain Hestr will be writing and spelling better than even Judith in no time. She's real smart. She knew which leaves were poison ivy. They just look the same to me. Mother said she couldn't believe it when Father told her. She said some not nice things about Mister Van Wyck. She told me that I have to work hard and make sure Hestr learned how to read. I will work hard because I want her to be smart and then we can read stories to one another.

Mary had no doubt that what her father said would be done. It did not matter to her if she played games or played teacher if it meant that she was able to spend more time with Hester. The best part was that it meant Hester would come up to the Mountain House and visit more often. Mary filled her bag with slate, chalk, pencils, paper, and magazines for the next day in anticipation of her best friend's arrival.

Three days passed before Hester returned. With great excitement about their new adventure, Mary guided them to an area near the trees but out of the way of people walking about.

"Look what I brought for us today," Mary said as she pulled the items from her bag. "We'll have lots of fun learning together."

"What is that?" Hester asked.

"It's the new *Godey's Lady's Journal*," Mary said excitedly. "It was delivered yesterday by the post." She held the magazine out for her friend to see, opening to one of the illustrations. "Look at this."

Hester leaned close and touched the picture. "Oh, my, I right have never seen such a large building. It looks even bigger than the Mountain House itself."

"That is the Metropolitan Hotel in New York City. It's on Broadway."

"I cannot imagine how many people live there."

"Mother took me to see it when we went shopping," Mary said. "It's five stories tall."

She flipped the page. "This month's song is "Dearest, When Evening"." She looked at the sheet music, then made a face. "I don't like it. Last month it was Jenny Lind's "Bird Waltz". Oh, that was so pretty. Tobias played it on the piano for us and Father was so pleased that he called for a recital. We saw her at the Crystal Palace a year ago. She's so pretty."

Hester took the magazine and looked at the next feature. "What is this?"

Mary looked before answering. "It is about a machine called a…calico printer. Father says it's important we learn about things."

"Why learn about something you'll never do?" Hester asked. "You'll never use a calico printer so why read about it?"

"So I know," Mary said. "It's learning and Father said that learning about anything and everything will make us better people. President Jefferson did that. He read and learned about everything so he could be a great man. Father says it is a poor man indeed who has money but no knowledge and a rich man who has not a pence in his pocket but a library of reading."

She took the magazine back and showed her another article. "This is about costumes of all nations. On the other side of the ocean, there are many countries and they dress differently than we do. See?" She showed Hester a picture. "When Godey's comes, we sit together each evening after supper and Mother or Father read to us. Sometimes Tobias will read the poetry but I'm too slow to read it. I don't know enough words yet."

Hester touched the pages. "There are so many words there. I could never learn them all."

"Sure, you can," Mary said. "Here, I'll show you." She read aloud. "'*The dress worn by the better classes in most of the...the...cor...cort...courts of Europe.*'" She looked up. "That's on the other side of the ocean. Father says we'll go there someday." She resumed reading. "'*Is sw...swaa...sway-ed...swayed by the fashions of France and England.*'" She looked up again. "Those are countries in Europe. Like Palenville and New York City are cities in New York."

"Read me more," Hester said excitedly. She pointed at the picture below the paragraph. "What's that?"

"That's the way people dress in, um, H-h-hun...hung...hungry. In Hungry. Oh, Hungary. It's another country in Europe." She turned the page. "This is India. Colored people live there. Not like the colored people who live here but they're colored, too."

"Miss Mary! Miss Mary!" They turned to see Mary's nurse, Miss Sally, heading toward them. "Miss Mary! Your mother says to come right quick. You too, Miss Hester."

Once back to the hotel, they were ushered to a place under the portico where a rocking chair had been liberated from the precipice and Mary's mother was currently sitting in. Little Daniel was carefully using the chalk to mark his name on his slate. "Come, girls. It is time for you to learn your alphabet, Hester. Mary, you will help her."

The girls knelt down on the blanket that covered the wooden slats of the area beneath the portico. Miss Sally handed them each a slate and a piece of chalk.

"Thank you, Miss Sally," Mary said. Hester offered her thanks, as well.

"You are welcome, Child. Mrs. C, shall I fetch the lemonade now?"

"Yes, Miss Sally. Mary, show Hester how to draw an A."

"Yes, Mother." Using her chalk, she printed both a capital and a lower case A. "See? You go up like this, then down and across. It's easy." She handed the chalk to Hester. With slow, deliberate movements, the younger girl was able to draw a rudimentary, shaky A.

"I did it!"

Mary smiled. "You did! See? I knew you were smart."

Hester smiled. "Naw. I just did what you showed me."

"Girls, enough chattering," Mary's mother admonished.

"Yes, Mother."

"Yes, Mrs. C."

"Now, do it again."

Mary's initial belief that teaching Hester to read and write would be as fun as playing schoolhouse was quickly dashed by the reality of having adults supervising and idle chitchat forbidden. Still, it was better to spend the day learning with Hester than having the whole of North Mountain to explore without her.

August 28, 1853
Mother helped me show ~~Hestr~~ Hester ABCs and how to write her name. Tomorrow we will do it again and maybe she can learn the whole alphabet. I know she shall be able to read soon and even better than Judith.

Far too soon, that dreaded day in September arrived to herald the return to New York City. For Elizabeth Chandler, it meant returning to her favorite pastime, shopping the large stores and attending parties. For Gideon Chandler, it meant returning to the business of business, buying houses and collecting rents. Tobias and Judith looked forward to being with their friends again. Daniel was happy to return to the toys he'd been forced to leave at home, as well as the return to school. For Mary, as it had been the previous year, the day marked having to say goodbye to Hester. There was nothing the eldest Chandler girl saw to be happy about, nothing she found herself looking forward to, except the following June when they would return and she could once again spend time with the most important person in her world, outside of her family.

The arrival of the Van Wycks to the grounds of the Mountain House that day was something to both look forward to and dread. After the appropriate hellos, Mary and Hester took off to the south side of the building so they could have a few minutes alone before the carriage arrived to separate them for the next nine months.

"I wish you didn't have to go," Hester said as she set her satchel on the ground. "But I brought you something."

"You did?"

"Uh huh." Hester unrolled the small canvas, revealing a fair likeness of her dear friend. "I didn't put that cut on your nose, though."

Mary giggled. "Good. I wouldn't want to see that cut the rest of my days in my portrait."

"I reckon not." She glanced from the portrait to her friend and back again. "I didn't make your nose too big, did I?"

"No. It's just wonderful," Mary insisted, taking the canvas from her friend. "I will treasure it always. When I get home, I will have Mother take me to the finest gallery in all of New York and have it framed so I can put it up in my room." Smiling broadly, Mary gently rolled the canvas up again. "I shall put it in my trunk so it doesn't get ruined on the way home."

"I'll read every day so I can get better," Hester promised. "You'll see. When you come back, I'll be able to read to you."

"I'll save all the Godey's magazines to bring back with me," Mary promised. "We'll read them all together." She blinked, then blinked again as the tears came. "Oh, Hester! I don't want to go!"

Hester's tears followed. "I am going to miss you so much!"

Keeping the canvas out of the way, Mary hugged her friend. "When we're all grown up, we will live together and no one will make me go away anymore."

"In our big house," Hester said between sniffles.

"In our big house," Mary agreed. "Forever and ever."

"Until we go to Heaven."

Chapter Five

Eighteen Fifty-Four brought a joyous summer for Mary. Pieter Van Wyck's portraits proved to be so popular amongst the guests of the Catskill Mountain House that he was there almost daily. More often than not, he brought along Hester. While most of their time together was dictated for learning by Mary's parents, they still found plenty of time to play with their dolls or the various games girls played. Hester had indeed worked hard during the winter and spring to improve her reading, though her writing and spelling had not progressed as fast. Daniel's children's books proved to be quite helpful and with Miss Sally's help, Hester was able to quickly progress in her studies.

For Mary, there could not have been a better summer. Then came a day that Hester was expected to come but didn't. Then another. Soon it turned into a week that there was no sign of the Van Wycks. Mary was beside herself with worry when the news finally came.

August 23, 1854
Father told me that Hester and Mister Van Wyck have not come this week because her Aunt Fransis died of the collera. Mother said I cannot go visit her because she fears I may get sick as well. I said I didn't care but Father said no. I wish I was old enough to go without their permission so I could help

Hester. She must be so sad. I should be there with her.

Closing her diary, the idea that formed in Mary's head took root and grew until it became so large that she could no longer resist it. Putting the book away, she made her decision and hastened away from the Mountain House, certain she knew the route the carriages took well enough to get there on her own.

It was late afternoon when Mary reached the path that lead to Hester's family farm. The hot August sun had been beating down on her for hours. Without her fan to help cool herself, coupled with the increased humidity as she moved closer to sea level, the twelve-year old was soaked with perspiration. The dirt road seemed to go on forever and she feared that she would never reach her friend. Her shoes were not made for long hikes and her feet burned with pain. She suspected there were blisters and wondered how she would be able to handle walking back, especially when darkness would soon fall upon the Catskills.

Hester ladled the stew into one of the four bowls available. The household totaled eight people with the boarder, Mister Littlefield, and his son included. There was no extra money to waste on additional bowls or spoons, so they took turns. It was just as well, since there was not enough room at the small table for eight people to sit at the same time.

"Now Hendrik, when you're done," she said as she placed the bowl in front of him, "I want you to go help your brother fetch some water so there can be baths tonight."

"Yes, Hester."

"Hester, isn't that your friend, Miss Mary?" her father asked. Hester went to the window and saw that indeed, a dusty, disheveled Mary Chandler was approaching the house.

"Good Lord!" Hester exclaimed as she opened the door. "Mary!"

"I'm sorry about your Aunt Frances," Mary said.

"Mary, does your father know you're here?" Pieter asked.

She shook her head. "No, sir."

He scratched his bearded chin. "I right believe he's going to be cross with you when he finds out what you done." He held the door open. "Well, now, come in. Come in."

"I'm very sorry about your mother, um, moeder," Mary said to Griet and the boys.

Griet wiped her hands on her apron. "Thank you, Mary."

Hester's father gestured to the nephew who was not eating. "Martin, get up to your Uncle Michael's and fetch the cart. We can't have young Miss Mary walking back alone and we can't have her staying all night and scaring her folks half outta their minds."

"Yes, sir."

Hendrik stood up, bowl in hand, the movement not stopping him from eating his dinner. "Please," he said as he moved out of the way.

"Oh, thank you," Mary said as she moved past him and sat on the bench. "I don't want anyone to go to any fuss." She looked at Hester. "I just had to come and see if you were all right."

"Vader, couldn't she stay tonight and we take her back tomorrow?" Hester appealed to her father.

He shook his head. "This isn't like the time Will ran away from your Uncle Michael's home. There's a difference between running away to your cousin's house a mile or so down the road and coming clear away from the

Mountain House, not knowing the area and not telling anyone."

He turned his attention to Mary. "Your folks will worry like a fright when they don't know where you are. Did you even leave them a note so they wouldn't think a bear done came and hauled you off, child?"

She shook her head. "No, Mister Van Wyck, sir."

"See?" He rubbed the back of his neck. "Well, you stay and eat and when Martin comes back with the cart, I'll run you back up the mountain myself."

"Yes, sir."

"Uncle Pieter, there's someone coming," Kent said. "It's not or anyone I know."

Hester's father looked out the window. "It's from the Mountain House. Hendrik, go out there and meet them." He buttoned his shirt and smoothed his hand over his hair.

"It's your mother and Tobias," Hester said as she, too, peeked through the window.

"Please excuse us," Pieter said as Mary's family members entered the house. "We wasn't fixing to be having company."

"Our apologies," Mary's mother said. "And our deepest sympathies for the loss of your sister."

"Thank you, Mrs. Chandler."

"I'm sorry, Mother," Mary said. "But I had to come see Hester."

"We will discuss this later."

"Tobias, these are my cousins Hendrik, Griet, and Kent," Hester said. "Martin should be back right quick. He went to fetch Uncle Michael's cart so we could bring Mary home. I mean, back to the Mountain House."

Elizabeth glared at her daughter before shaking her head and giving Hester a gentle smile. "I'm afraid we cannot wait," she said. "I must get Mary back."

Walking to Griet, she took the teen's hands in her own. "I am truly sorry about your mother, child."

"Thank you, Mrs. Chandler."

"Mister Van Wyck, please accept my apologies for the intrusion."

"It's quite all right, I suppose," Pieter said. "Suppose little Miss Mary was just worried about my Hester, that's all."

"Mary, come along. Hester will no doubt come to see you in a few days."

"Um, yes," Pieter said. "I'll bring her up next week. I'll have some finished portraits to deliver anyways."

"Very well. Mary Elizabeth?"

"Yes, Mother." Mary ran and hugged Hester fiercely. "I'm sorry," she whispered. "I just had to come see you."

"I know," Hester whispered back.

Mary gave Griet a hug before being ushered out to the carriage.

"What possessed you to go wandering off like that?" Mary's mother asked her the instant the door closed on the carriage.

"I had to," she said, holding her chin up and meeting her mother's disapproving gaze. "I know it was wrong but I had to. It was for Hester, Mother. If one of my aunts died and she was near me, I know she would come see me too."

"That may well be, but you still should not have gone walking off like that." Mary's mother rubbed her own forehead. She stared out toward the studio for several seconds before speaking again. "I suppose we should have borrowed the carriage and taken you down to see her."

"I'm sorry, Mother."

Mary's mother pulled her close. "So am I," she said. "I am raising you to be a free-thinking woman. I suppose I should have expected this." She wagged her finger at Mary as the carriage moved forward. "But don't do something like this again."

"Yes, Mother."

Elizabeth pulled her gloves off and folded her hands on her lap. "I will have the butcher contacted to send them enough food to get along for a time. Those poor children shouldn't have to worry about something such as that at a time like this."

"I have almost fifty cents saved up in my room," Mary offered.

Her mother smiled and patted Mary's hand. "You have a good heart, my daughter. This is what we'll do. Tomorrow we shall ride to Catskill and after I make arrangements with the butcher, you and I will go shopping at that little mercantile. You may spend your fifty cents on things you think Hester and her family would like and we'll have them delivered."

"It was nice for you to give the boys those wooden angels," Hester said when she met up with Mary the following week. "Kent put his up on the mantle and said it will always remind him of his moeder."

"I had trouble picking something out," Mary admitted. "Mother had to help me."

"It was still very nice," Hester said. "Aunt Frances would have been happy."

To their delight, their favorite flat rock was empty. The newest issue of the *Godey's Lady's Journal* was enjoyed fully as Hester struggled through the words with Mary's help and they worked their way through the articles. A serial mystery had caught their attention and both girls were quite excited to read the new installment.

"Now, I'll have to wait until next year to find out how it ends," Hester said when they finished.

"I can ask Mother to let me send you the next issue after we're finished with it."

"I don't know if I can read it all alone. Look how much help I needed from you."

"Aw, you can do it," Mary said. "And you can write and ask me about any words you don't understand." Her eyes grew wide. "You can write to me! Oh! Goodness gracious but that's wonderful!" She reached into her bag and pulled out all of her pens, holders, and pencils. "We can write to one another!" She was so excited that she couldn't find what she was looking for and ended up dumping the contents onto the rock. "Where is my paper?"

Smiling, Hester pulled several pages from the now messy pile. "Here it is."

"I'll write to you every day and you can write to me, too, and then it won't seem like we're so far away."

"Mary, I can't afford to mail you a letter every day," Hester said.

"Once a week?"

Hester thought about it. "Perhaps once a month."

"But I can send you letters more often than you send them to me," Mary said. "You don't have to answer each one. Just write me a long letter each month and that way we won't miss one another so much."

"I'll try," Hester said.

"Here." Mary took the pencil and a piece of paper. "I'll write down my address and you can write down yours."

"I don't rightly know what the address is. I guess it's just the Voss house on the old road. But I'm sure if you put that down, they'll be able to figure it out."

"Do you think if I ask your father that he would know?"

"He still can't read anything and doesn't want to," Hester said. "Palenville is real small and I'm sure old man Sturges knows where we live. He delivers the post."

Hester started packing the items back into Mary's bag save those that she was supposed to take. "He doesn't come by very often but the next time he does, I'll ask him to write down what the proper address is so I can send it to you."

"Perhaps you'll see him before I leave?"

"I don't know. That's only a few days away."

"I know," Mary said sadly. "I hate leaving." She sat down on the rock. "I hate New York City. All the noise and smells. Oh, Hester, it stinks something awful. Not like up here where the air is so fresh and clean. There's so many people there, too. Hardly any trees 'cepting in the parks. No big lakes to go swimming in, like here, and nowhere does it look as nice as it does from the table rock. Why, I swear there isn't a place in all New York City where you can look down and see the tops of the trees like here. I don't know why Father and Mother can't just move us up here."

"Mister Beach closes the Mountain House soon after you leave," Hester said. "Then no one comes up here until clear into June. Where would you live?"

Mary shrugged. "Father could buy a house in Catskill. Then we'd be closer and I could visit all the time." She banged the heel of her shoe against the rock. "Oh, but he won't. He says he has business and we have school and all those other things that mean we have to live in that horrible place instead of here near you. It's not fair."

Hester sat down next to Mary and put her arm around her friend's shoulders. "But when we're all grown up we will live together and it won't matter where they live, right?" She gave a little squeeze. "Right?"

Mary looked at her. "Right. When we're older."

"So we just have to wait a few more years, that's all." Hester hopped off the rock. "Let's go to Ashley Falls one more time before I have to go home. We can yell as loud as we want and no one can hear us there."

Mary slid off the rock and reached for her satchel. "Maybe we'll see those people kissing there again."

Hester giggled. "They looked awfully silly, didn't they?"

Mary laughed. "All that hugging and kissing. And remember where he was touching her? I bet if her father saw that, he'd have thrown that man right down the side of the mountain."

"It was like he was petting a dog," Hester said. "I'm never going to let a boy pet me like that."

"Me either," Mary said firmly. "And no hugging, either. That's just for family and you."

"What about kissing?"

"Well," Mary thought about it. "Mother and Father kiss, but he just kisses her cheek so I suppose kissing on the cheek is all right."

"Vader always kisses me on the forehead."

Quick as can be, Mary leaned and kissed Hester's cheek. "Like that."

"Vader does it like this." Hester put her hands on either side of Mary's head and then kissed her forehead. "See?"

"Let me try." Mary mimicked Hester's actions. "Now, you kiss my cheek and we'll see which is better."

Hester kissed Mary's cheek as instructed. "I like that better," she said, doing it one more time.

Mary smiled. "I like that better, too. I think kissing on the forehead is for children. When we're all grown up, we'll just kiss people on the cheek."

"But those people at the falls were kissing on the lips. Maybe that's better."

"Mother kisses us on the lips when she says good night," Mary said. "But only once, not again and again like they were doing."

"All right," Hester said. "So when we're all grown up and have our house and all those orphans living with us, we'll kiss them just once on the lips and once on the cheek at bedtime."

"Like this," Mary agreed, kissing Hester first on the cheek, then on the lips.

Hester giggled and repeated Mary's actions. "Yes, that's what we'll do," she said. "And when we go to bed, we'll kiss one another the same way."

"Let's go now before it gets too late," Mary said, pulling the strap of her satchel over her shoulder. "If Miss Sally has to come looking for me again, Father said I won't get dessert."

They started toward the Glen Mary, which lead to the falls. "I still think dessert should come first," Hester said. Mary smiled and nodded in complete agreement.

Chapter Six

The sun shone brightly on Catskill in late June of Eighteen Fifty-Five. The Chandlers had returned to the Mountain House a full week and every day, Mary waited in a chair facing the area where the Mountain Road met the grand resort's grounds. Engrossed in her journal, she was startled by the sound of her name being shouted.

Mary excitedly dropped her journal and ran to greet her friend. "Hester! Hester! I missed you so!" They fell into a caring embrace, the long cold months of separation melting away. "Oh, my, but you've become taller."

"I shall be able to pick apples without a ladder soon, I reckon," Hester said. "Hendrik and Martin are already taller than Vader and Uncle Michael."

"Tobias is growing so fast that the britches he received for Christmas are too short. He's taller than Father now."

"Are you free today?"

"I need only put my things away and then I shall take my leave." Mary could barely contain her excitement at being near her best friend again.

Hester waited, though one could hardly call it patiently, for her friend to come back. When she did, Mary was carrying two magazines, as well as a board of slate and a small bag.

"I've been reading," Hester said proudly. "Right through all those books and magazines and even a newspaper Father brought home. Well, before it went to the outhouse."

Since it was an unusually warm day for June, the girls chose a grassy spot shaded by a good-sized maple tree.

"Father says all the Herald is good for is for use in the privy," Mary said. She handed the magazines to Hester. "I saved all the Godey's for you. I brought these two today."

"Is that serial in it? I've waiting to see what happens."

Mary nodded. "And it's the final two parts so we can read it right clear to the end," she said. "Wait until you see how they catch the murderer."

"Don't tell me," Hester said. "I want to read it for myself."

"All right. I won't tell." Mary paused. "But, it really is exciting."

"Oh, I do hope they have more embroidery patterns," Hester said. "Do you remember that pattern they showed in that magazine you gave me? Griet enjoyed making a new scarf so much and Kent took the same pattern and used his knife to carve it into the legs of the new table Uncle Michael made for us. Why, it looks as grand as one belonging in the fanciest of homes."

"I would never thought of using those patterns for carving. Kent certainly is clever."

"I cannot wait to see what he does with the magazines you've brought this year. Mister Littlefield and his son moved out but another man, Mister Grant, moved in. Griet thinks we can take in even more boarders if we fix up the house a bit. Uncle Michael is building a new set of beds and he's letting Kent help."

"Martin got a whittling knife from Uncle Michael for Christmas but I traded him my slice of pie two nights for it and then traded it to Kent for his share of the sugar. I swear he's gonna whittle down the whole forest one of these days."

Later that day, it grew cool, forcing Mary to wear her white sweater. Hester found it so pretty that she insisted on making a sketch in her new sketchpad. Mary was forced to sit this way and that until the younger girl finally decided the pose was perfect. "Now don't move," she warned.

"You could have drawn other things before I got here," Mary said.

"I know. Stay still." Hester looked up from her pad to her subject and back again, the sharpened pencil moving quickly across the paper. "I had some left in my other one and I used that until you got here. I wanted to use this one just for you."

"Are you going to put the trees and everything else in it?"

"I don't know yet. Keep your head still." Hester said. The tip of her tongue poked out from between her lips as she concentrated on the details. "All my other sketchbooks were leftovers but this one was brand new and I wanted you to be the first thing I drew in it."

Mary popped a pinch of the maple sugar into her mouth. "Mmm."

"Hold still. I have to get this just right. No, your turn your head a little more. Yes, that's it. Now stay still."

"Hester Van Wyck, the great artist."

"I'm only twelve. I can't be a great artist until I'm all grown up. At least twenty."

"I want to see."

"No. You have to stay there," Hester said, glancing up from her sketch pad.

"But I want to see." Still, Mary did as she was told, remaining on the stump.

"You will. When I'm finished."

Mary watched as Hester was the model of concentration, the young artist glancing up only occasionally while her right hand was in near constant motion putting pencil to paper. "Will it be done by the time I leave?"

"I will try," Hester said. "I hope to put the Mountain House behind you so it appears you were sitting in one of those chairs like the men do."

Mary clapped her hands together excitedly. "I shall have Mother take me to Stewarts right away when we return so I can have it properly framed and put upon my wall."

"It is only a sketch," Hester said. "I will not be able to paint again until after the harvest. You know that."

"I still want to frame it," Mary said. "Then when you paint it during the winter and I get to take it home next year, I will put the painting up next to the sketch."

"If you keep putting all that I draw for you upon the walls, there will be no room left."

"Then I will start having them placed in the other rooms," Mary said. "I'll fill the whole house with them."

"Stay still, Mary Elizabeth."

"Yes, Hester Ann."

As the day wound down and Hester returned home, Mary walked back to the Mountain House. She found her father in his usual chair near the table rock. Several boys, including Tobias, were sitting on the ground around him.

"It is a scourge worse than cholera," Gideon said, his loud voice booming with authority. "You've seen it on the streets of our fine city every day. Why, it is practically an impossibility to go to the Fulton Fish Market and back without seeing a dozen men or more lying in the gutters and smelling worse than a week-old cod."

He paused to take a puff of his pipe. "The Irish are the worst, of course, but even men born here of families that go back to our great battle for independence can be found staggering from the saloons, their pay vanished, their wives and children forced to go without food or decent clothing because their money has been left behind to slake their thirst for the bottle."

Mary enjoyed listening to her father give his speeches and indeed, the young men surrounding him were enraptured by his words.

"And what happens when those men of poor moral character finally do go home?" He banged his fist on the arm of the chair. "Violence, that's what! They strike their wives, their children cower in fear. Yet once again they will get up and repeat their actions with no concern for the welfare of their families. The Order of the Good Templars was founded, not for the occasional sip taken by our fine, upstanding citizens at their parties, but because of these men of whom I speak."

He carefully made eye contact with the boys as he continued. "The only answer, the only solution that you young men need to know, the only way this will get better and we rise to become the great union that we are, is to eliminate the evil that is alcohol once and for all from our mighty country."

One young man spoke. "But my father enjoys his wine with dinner."

"It is not the single drink by a man who has the moral character of someone such as your father that is the problem," Gideon said. "He would most certainly be quite as happy having a clean glass of water or perhaps some tea. No. Were alcohol to be wiped from our land, he would not cry or miss it one bit. As I have said, the problem is with the immigrants and those whose character is not as great as your fathers. It is for those others that we must rise up and demand that our legislature make them do what is right!"

He tapped his pipe on the chair arm for emphasis. "A man who goes to church every Sunday and takes from the sacrament is not the same as a man who goes into the saloon. Only when temperance is the order of the land and the saloons, those bastions of evil and home-wrecking, are eliminated that we will be able to walk with our ladies and children down the street without fear of seeing those drunks on the corners, in the gutters, those filthy men begging for money to replace that which they drank. Mark my words, boys, the only answer is temperance."

"A sober man works harder. Is that right, Father?" Tobias asked.

Mary thought the question odd since her father had spoken of that topic several times within their home. She could only surmise that her brother had asked it to either indicate that he was paying attention or to encourage her father to keep going. Not that her father needed any prompting to continue his rail against the sin of alcohol abuse.

"Indeed, that is most accurate," Gideon said, favoring his eldest child with a smile. "As the Washingtonians can attest. For those that have never heard of such a group, they were much as you see on the streets. They were drunkards, unable to hold down a job and if they did, they drank their money away in the saloons. Poor husbands, poor fathers, and even poorer men of society. When those men decided to say goodbye forever to the evil brew, through God's gift of prayer and by turning to one another for support, they returned as better men. They worked hard, provided for their families, returned peace and contentment to their homes."

Gideon rose from his seat and slowly walked around the circle of teens. "Marriages were saved, children regained the fathers they had thought lost forever to the bottle. These men proved that a drunkard need not take another drop of alcohol and could be a benefit, rather than a detriment, to their societies. That, you young men that are about to begin life's journey into adulthood, is the lesson you need to learn. Your fathers have worked hard to make something of themselves, to be greater than their own fathers were."

He shook his hand in the air, much like a preacher giving a rousing sermon. "They expect you to do the same. Do not fall into the temptation that so many have that alcohol is harmless. Think of the man working in your store, for example."

He pointed at one of the teens whose father owned a large mercantile on Broadway. "He is entrusted to care for the customers, to honestly handle the monies paid for the goods your father has purchased for sale. Now let's suppose he is a drunkard. He has spent his pay at the saloon and his wife and children have gone hungry. The temptation to put his hand in the till would be too great. His focus is on his home and not on his job. Is this the type of man you want working for you?"

"No," several boys answered.

"Indeed. So, tarry not to join such great organizations as the Order of the Good Templars and help to make our fine city, indeed our entire nation one where we can hold our heads high and be proud. A nation where we have overcome the demon rum."

Mary smiled and walked to the portico. She knew that by day's end, her father would have most, if not all, of those boys singing the song of temperance. She wondered what he would think if he knew that Hester's father kept a bottle of dandelion wine hidden in the studio. Certainly Pieter Van Wyck seemed a capable man and not at all like the smelly guttermen that were so prevalent in New York City. She supposed it must be because Hester's father was a man of good moral character. One thing she knew for certain, was that she would never touch any alcohol save for the sacrament. She wondered if Hester felt the same way or if she would want to keep dandelion wine in their home when they grew up.

Finding a quiet spot in the shade beneath the portico, Mary opened her diary but did not dip her pen into the ink. Instead she stared off at nothingness, thinking of the kisses she had shared with Hester before parting. They had taken turns starting the kiss until giggles forced them to stop. She decided that she liked kissing Hester and would insist upon it each time they saw one another. After all, she kissed her Grandmother Franklin each time she came for a visit and that meant that they loved one another, right? Therefore it seemed absolutely correct to her that she should kiss Hester hello and goodbye. Though, she reasoned, perhaps not again and again as they had done.

"Very well," she said aloud, though not to the level where anyone else would hear. "Just once each time. Perhaps twice."

September 22, 1854

I am home now. It was a wonderful summer and I can't wait to go back again. Hester promised that she would write and I have already started a letter to her, as well. Mother said I can only send one post per week so I will save up the pages and send them all together. Father showed me how to fold up the papers and use the glue to make sure it doesn't open until she gets it.

Hester likes to kiss me just like I like to kiss her. When we're all grown up we will kiss all the time because we love one another.

Mother says I am a woman now because I started ~~bleeding~~ *bleeding. I was scared when it happened but she said it will happen every month but I won't die from it. My stomach hurt something awful but it went away. She said that was normal and if it happens again that she shall get me a tonic to make me feel better. She said men don't bleed like that.*

They only bleed when they are cut. I don't think that's fair at all.

Chapter Seven

After one of the coldest and most miserable of winters, the Chandlers were more than ready to return to the Catskill Mountain House for the summer of Eighteen Fifty-Six. It was then, for the first time, the Chandlers accepted an invitation from Pieter to come visit the Voss/Van Wyck home for an afternoon. Mary, of course, was all for that idea as it meant she could spend more time with Hester, though she did warn her friend about her parents' views on temperance so that no dandelion wine would be served. Mother Nature sought to make the visit as pleasant as could be, with clear blue sky and a gentle wind. Mary was certain it would be a most pleasant visit.

Gideon Chandler was seated in the shade along with Michael and Pieter Van Wyck, along with the boarder, John Grant. They were enjoying cool glasses of mint tea and imported tobacco while chatting amicably on any number of topics. All the boys except Kent had doffed their clothing to enjoy a raucous time in the creek while the females gathered under a different shady tree to chat and enjoy some mint tea after spending most of the morning preparing the day's repast. Kent, refusing to join the antics at the creek since his leg was bothering him, sat alone with his whittling knife and a branch as thick as his arm.

The seven boys, along with Judith, played various games including dodge ball, hide and seek, and mumblety-peg, though Mrs. Chandler vehemently refused to let her younger daughter partake in the latter. When Judith protested, she was treated to a stern lecture about how proper girls did not play with knives and a threat to spend the rest of the afternoon in the coach if she dared open her mouth about it again. Sally gave Griet a variety of tips and time saving tricks to help her with her domestic chores. They also marveled at how well she was doing, running the house so smoothly following the loss of her mother.

Hester and Mary, meanwhile, had gone to the studio. Being so early in the season, there was only one artist boarder and he was out for the day. Mary perched herself on a stool while Hester set up a new canvas on her easel. "Father gave me this for my birthday," she said. "I've been saving it for when you came. I want to paint your portrait."

Mary smiled. "My portrait painted again by the famous artist Hester Van Wyck." She wiggled into a more comfortable position on the stool. "Will you be able to finish it today?"

"Of course not, silly." Hester pulled her finest charcoal from the glass jar which also included her brushes and palette knife. "I'm going to draw an outline, then add the paint later." A few quick slices with a sharp knife and she had a point to work with. "Now, you have to sit still or it won't look right."

"I always sit still."

Hester smiled. "No, you don't. Now, I'm doing this right on the canvas so I can't make any mistakes. Sit still."

"Did you get it yet?"

"Get what? Turn your head a little bit. No, the other way. Right there. Stay still."

"You know. It. The bleeding."

Hester colored. "Yes, I did. You know that Griet has been having it happen to her for a long time now. I knew about it when you wrote me. It just hadn't happened yet."

"It's messy."

"Yes, it is, and I went right through my rags twice."

"I don't like it."

"The good Lord saw fit to a make it happen to us so I suppose there's nothing we can do about it," Hester said.

Mary huffed. "I still don't like it."

"Good Lord, Mary, I don't like it either but complaining about it doesn't make the carrots grow any quicker. Now hold still."

They were silent for only a few seconds before Mary introduced a new topic of conversation.

"Did I tell you that I had a gentleman caller?"

That caught Hester's attention enough that she dropped her charcoal pencil and looked at her friend. "What? But you're only fourteen! Surely your father threw him down the stairs or showed him a shotgun or some such?"

Mary laughed. "It was Jacob. One of Tobias' friends. And yes, Father was quite clear with him that I was too young to have gentleman callers."

Hester gave a sigh of relief and bent down to retrieve her errant pencil. "Well, that's good." She found it and gave it a good sharpening.

"He was handsome."

"He's a boy. Boys aren't handsome. They're...." She struggled to find the right word. "They're...they're boys." A shout from outside reached them. "Do you think Hendrik and Martin are handsome?"

"Goodness gracious, no!" Mary replied. "They eat bugs."

Hester resumed her sketching. "They also drink wine but don't tell Griet. I caught them and Will sneaking into Uncle Michael's barn and getting into the bottle he keeps hidden behind the old crates."

"Oh. Oh, that's bad."

"They're boys. All boys are bad at one time or another."

"Not Tobias," Mary said vehemently. "He would never dare have any alcohol. If he did, Father would kill him and Mother would take Miss Bessie's rolling pin and hit him on the head with it." She hopped off the stool and walked to Hester. "You've never had any, have you?"

Hester sucked in her bottom lip. "Um...."

Mary's eyes grew wide. "You have!"

"Once!" Hester walked to the window to make sure no one was coming. "Twice. Just a sip. I told you that Vader keeps a bottle hidden in here." She took one more look out the window before returning to her easel. "I tried it. Tasted horrible."

"Hester Ann Van Wyck! I can't believe you did that."

"Don't you tell on me."

"I won't."

"Promise?"

"I promise."

"All right, then." Hester gestured with her pencil at the stool. "Get back there, so I can finish this before Griet calls me in to help finish with supper."

Mary went to the window. "I bet Mother and Miss Sally are helping her. Well, at least Miss Sally. Mother never goes into the kitchen unless she's telling Miss Bessie what to make. I don't see them anywhere." She returned to the stool.

"Now, sit still. I mean it."

"Yes, Hester."

"You behave or I'll make you look like a big green hen."

Mary laughed but then did as she was told and sat still until Hester finished the drawing.

"There. Now we can go in and you can help me make the pudding."

"But I never have to help with the cooking."

Hester put her pencil back in the jar. "You will this time. It'll be fun."

Mary hopped off the stool. "All right."

As they reached the door, Hester stopped. "You promise not to tell anyone about the wine?"

"I swear to God that I will not tell anyone," Mary said.

"Good." Hester paused for a second, then leaned down and gave Mary a peck on the lips. As she pulled back, Mary reached up and put her hand behind Hester's head, pulling her in for another kiss. It wasn't a simple peck, either, but rather a full blown kiss that was repeated several times before she brought her hand back.

"Promise," Mary said softly before opening the studio door and stepping outside.

June 28, 1856

Today we spent the day with Hester and her family at their house. It was great. We had lots of food that I can't even say or spell because it was Dutch but they were all yummy. Miss Sally used some of my paper to write them down so when we get home, Miss Bessie can make them for us. Mother liked the dessert to much that she had two helpings. We left so late that we have to stay in Catskill tonight because Mr. Silas said he can't drive the carriage up the mountain in the dark. Judith is sharing the bed with me. She is taking up most of the room. I have to keep pushing her over. I don't know why Mr. Beach still makes us use candles. This hotel has lamps and even Hester's house has lamps. Father said we can go back again soon for another visit.

Mary closed her diary and turned down the oil lamp.

Rolling onto her side and squeezing as much room from her sleeping sister as she could, Mary closed her eyes in anticipation of quickly falling asleep. Instead her mind replayed her time in the studio with Hester. More specifically, when they were kissing. It was more than a simple hello and goodbye kiss and while she couldn't describe what it felt like, she knew it was just something more. Something wonderful that made her smile when she thought about it. Something she hoped she and Hester would do again. Soon.

A week passed before she saw Hester again. They shared a quick kiss hello before going off on a walk in search of huckleberries. It took them far away from the other guests since few wandered to the far side of the lakes. There were no clear paths here and she was forced to carefully follow Hester to avoid prickers and poison ivy.

"Hester?"

"Hmm?"

"I had a nice time at your house."

Another twig snapped as Hester continued to make the path safer for Mary to follow. "Good. Everyone was talking about it after you all left. Uncle Michael said next time he would try to get a pig for us. He makes this sauce with vinegar and maple syrup that we enjoy."

"That's nice," Mary said distractedly. "Did you like it?"

"Watch out for this one. Here." Hester held the branch out of the way. "Of course I liked it. What a silly question." She waited until Mary was clear of the offending branch, then moved back into the lead. "There were more dishes to wash because Uncle Michael wouldn't take all of his home with him, all dirty like that, but I didn't mind. Ooh, it's muddy here. Be careful."

"I mean, did you like all of it? Like in the studio? After you stopped drawing? Before we went to be with the others?"

Hester stopped and turned to Mary. "Yes," she said softly. "I liked it." She reached out and touched Mary's long, blonde hair. "I liked it lots."

Mary breathed a sigh of relief. "Good. I liked it, too."

Hester leaned forward and brought their lips together for a quick kiss. "But I don't think we should do that in front of anyone else. They might not understand." She turned to continue their journey. "Oh! I see the clearing. I think we're almost there."

They did indeed reach a clearing, though it was not the one they were looking for. Not a single huckleberry bush was in sight.

"Oh, darn!" Hester exclaimed. "I thought this was it. It must be out past those trees there. She wagged her finger. "Don't you tell anyone I cursed. Vader gets mad enough at the boys when they do it. I don't need no getting the belt." She put her hands on her hips. "Well, don't do no good standing here."

"I bet there's no one around anywhere near here," Mary said.

"Reckon not. Who else would be foolish enough to come through all that to get a few huckleberries?"

Mary touched Hester's arm. "So, if we did something, no one would know."

She let the basket and her satchel fall to the ground, then repeated her actions in the studio days before and put her hand behind Hester's head to pull her down for a kiss.

"I think this is a better idea and hunting for huckleberries," Hester said between kisses.

With Hester's strong arms pulling her close, Mary brought her arms up around the back of the younger girl's neck, slipping into the thick brown hair.

"Much better idea," Mary murmured.

On that day, the huckleberries on North Mountain stayed safely on their bushes.

Once again, summer went by far too quickly for Mary's taste. As dolls and games gave way to long walks and many secret kisses, she found her changing body yearning for something more. When other girls her age mooned about the older boys, she found herself thinking only of Hester. How she felt when they were pressed close together. How she looked when they swam naked in the creek. How perfect it felt. They merely lay together on the grass and took an afternoon nap in the sun. As the carriage headed away from the Mountain House for another year, Mary felt as if her heart was being left behind. Promises of writing to one another during the long winter months did not hold a candle to the memory of their special moments alone in the summer sun. Moments when the rest of the world did not exist, only their long talks, tender kisses, and gentle caresses. With a sigh as the carriage hit yet another bump, Mary forced herself to remain content with the new painting given to her at the beginning of the summer and the memories acquired since then. She would need all of them to help her make it through the next nine months.

Chapter Eight

Hester stepped back from the easel, casting a critical eye upon the scene. "I need to start again."

"Nonsense," her father said as he put a gentle hand upon her right shoulder. "Why, I wish I had half the talent as you when I was fourteen. Look. Look here." He pointed at a stand of trees. "You captured the dappling of sun perfectly. Even Mister Church himself would approve."

Hester shook her head. "But Mary's face is too long. Her chin too...too...."

"It is not to look in a mirror," he said. "And you don't need to include her in every painting upon which you set to create."

"Yes, Vader."

He rubbed his chin. "It's good practice for you, I suppose. Despite what Miss Julia Hart Beers has to say, it is portraits that bring the coin. The widow Burek would not be marrying me if I only painted the Wall of Manitou or the Mountain House. You know it is portraits and signs which provide us the money we need to keep our house and the studio."

Hester set the brush down. "Vader? When they move in, might I sleep in Aunt Frances's room?"

"Mrs. Burek and I will be using that room as our own and young Thomas will have my corner. He's far too big to fit in the bed with the other boys."

Hester frowned. "Then might I sleep here?"

Her father laughed. "My dear Hester Ann. A studio is no place for a child to sleep." He put his finger on her lips to silence her objection. "Mrs. Brandt needs no further fodder for her Sunday spells. One more girl in the bed with you and Griet won't make much difference. You will share the bed with them until we have a raising in the spring. Then Michael will make a bed so little Hannah won't be sleeping with you." He tapped the tip of her nose. "But your brushes are yours alone. I suspect they'll have no cause to come into the studio. Now, mind the time and do not forget to help your cousin with dinner again."

"Yes, Vader."

That the studio she shared with her father and the few artists that paid him for use of a corner would be left alone by the younger children made Hester feel better, though the idea that even after the raising, she and Griet would have to continue to share a bed, while the younger children would have beds of their own, bothered her. Picking up her brush, she set about to fix the problem of Mary's image on the canvas. That chin that just was not quite right. Despite her intention to stop in time to go home and help Griet with the stew, it was after dark when her father returned to collect her. She was grateful for the understanding that only another artist could give about the concentration and focus the paints upon a canvas could cause. Indeed, had he not come to collect her, she would have continued painting until the lamp had burned down all of its oil.

Hester did not care about her scraped knee or palm as she watched Mary pull back the cloth cover from the pie tin.

"I'm sorry. It's ruined," she said sadly as the dessert was revealed.

"Do not fret," Mary replied as she set the fork into the mess of blueberries and crust. "I am certain it shall taste just as delicious."

"I'll make another one. Only this time I won't fall with it."

Mary leaned her shoulder against Hester's as she chewed the bite that was in her mouth. "It is as wonderful as I imagined it would be. I only wish I would be allowed into the kitchen here to make you something in kind. Miss Bessie taught me how to make those Dutch pastries with the apples in it."

"Do you mean the *appelbollen*?"

"Yes, we just call it that Dutch apple dessert." Mary put the fork to her mouth and hummed her happiness. "Oh, my, but that is good. Is that honey on the crust?"

"Uncle Michael let me have some, just for this," Hester said. "Honey on top always makes the pies better."

"Oh, yes, it does," Mary agreed, holding the fork out for Hester to take a bite. "You should come to the city and become a baker. They would line up all the way to the river for a bite."

"Careful," Hester said when some of the blueberry filling ended up on her friend's chin. "You keep doing that and I'm going to call you Mary Berry."

"You wouldn't dare."

"Mary Berry! Mary Berry!"

"If I'm Mary Berry then you're Hester Pester!"

"Mary Berry!"

"Hester Pester!"

They went back and forth until both ended in a fit of giggles. "I miss you so much when it's not summer," Hester said. "You're my dearest friend and when we grow up, we're going to live together forever and ever."

Mary stabbed the pie with the fork. "And you're going to make pies for me every night and I'll read the newspaper to you."

"Every night?"

Mary paused in her enjoyment of the pie to lean and give Hester a kiss. "Every other night?"

"If I make it every night, will you give me the good kisses?"

After a quick look around to confirm their isolation, Mary said, "Even if you never make me another pie in your whole life, I'll give you the good kisses each night." She then moved the pie tin and fork out of the way so they could do just that.

Mary opened her journal and smiled at the pressed leaf. Moving it out of the way, she recorded her thoughts for the day.

August 14, 1858

Hester brought me a pie. In my whole life, I've never tasted so wonderful a treat. Blueberries, fresh from her own home, and a crust of a quality that the finest baker in my great city would be covetous of. I did not wish to stop but my body protested having any more. Mother feared me ill at supper when I was unable to partake of more than a mere bite or two.

In a few years when we are living together in our house, I fear I shall be too big to fit through the door if she keeps making me such treats. Even if we never have any orphans to come live with us, just being able to see her every day will make me happier than anyone I know. I would give up new dresses and a fancy house without a second thought. Even wearing sackcloth and sleeping in a bed made of straw, in a shack barely able to stand the wind would be a happy choice made so we might be together.

Mary set her pen down, her mind still on Hester's kind-hearted gift. When she picked the pen up again and dipped it in the ink, a kernel of an idea had started to form.

I am going to make something for her just like she did for me. Something special. Not something from the stores like I usually do but something I make for her. Something to show her how much I love her. I don't know what yet, but it will be perfect.

Capping her inkwell, Mary wiped off the pen and put it away. Now, the problem became what to make…and how to make it. The extent of her cooking and baking ability was adding an egg or two for Miss Bessie and she had never touched a needle and thread in her life. She thought and thought, discarding one idea after another. What would Hester want? What could she need? Time passed until the dinner gong sounded and still she had no idea. Only when she sat down to eat and reached for the napkin did the answer finally come to her. When it did, there would be nothing that could stop her.

For two weeks, Mary busily worked on her gift, fretting about each imperfection and taking it apart to start again four times. During that time, there had been no word from Hester. While it gave Mary more time to work on her project, it also filled her with worry and concern. When the present was finally finished, it would be another three days before Hester would return.

Mary was practically bursting with excitement when she saw Hester coming up the road. She broke into a full run, arms outstretched to share an embrace regardless of how much road dust would end up transferring from one dress to the other. "My dear Hester. I've missed you so much."

"I've wanted to come every day," Hester said, her voice a soothing balm to Mary's ear. "Everyone's been sick, one after the other, and then Martin had a fever and we all feared the worst until this morning when it finally left him."

Mary cut off whatever else was about to be said with a kiss. She took Hester's hand in hers. "Come. It's finished."

"What's finished?"

"Your present."

"Present?"

"Yes. I learned how to sew and made you a present." She tugged Hester's hand to guide her to one of their private spots. "Well, I learned how to sew one thing and I hope I never have to touch a needle again, but I just had to make you something special."

"Really?"

"Really and truly," Mary said. "Mother took me down to Catskill and I bought some material and a needle and thread. Oh, and a thimble, too."

"You made me a dress?"

"Oh, no, something much better," Mary said as they turned off the road and into the woods. "When we get there, I'll show you."

Hester stopped, spinning Mary around to give her a resounding kiss. "Thank you."

"But you don't know what it is yet."

Hester kissed her again. "But it's something you made for me. Whatever it is, I know I'll love it." She let go and resumed following Mary up the hill.

When they reached the spot, an outcropping of several large rocks that formed a pocket on the upper side, Mary pulled the rolled up cloth from her satchel.

"It's a brush holder," Mary said, watching Hester examine every slim pocket. "I saw one at Stewarts once. I made them of different widths to accommodate your

94

brushes and here," she pointed at the shorter section. "This is where you might put those little ones. See? I sewed ties on so you won't lose them. I had enough material to put a pocket in that flap just in case you desired it. For what, I don't know but I wanted it to be special for you. I do hope I thought of everything you would need."

"It is perfect and I shall treasure it always," Hester said, her smile causing Mary's heart to sing joyously. "I have to say that I have never received such a wonderful gift. No artist, not even those whose work hangs in the finest galleries of your city, has ever had so incredible a brush holder."

Mary beamed with delight. "I wish I could give you all that you desire." She hugged Hester tightly. "I would give you enough canvas to cover the entire Mountain House. The best of easels." She waved her arm broadly. "A hundred, no, a thousand brushes! And paint of every color in the rainbow."

Hester laughed. "Where would I put all of this? Surely there is barely enough room in the house for those of us living there now and the studio is even smaller since we have two more artists taking space."

"I would buy you a house more magnificent than the finest of those in the city. So large that you would start the morning at one end and not reach the other until nightfall. With servants too numerous to count." Mary gestured grandly with her arms. "And a studio better than any artist ever had. Room for a hundred easels if you desire."

"What would I ever do with a hundred easels?"

"Make a hundred paintings, silly."

"If I did, they'd all be of you. My Mary Berry."

"And I'd make dinner for my Hester Pester."

"And all our orphans," Hester reminded her.

"And all our orphans," Mary agreed.

Hester rolled the gift up and carefully tied the ribbons surrounding it. "Thank you. I love it." She leaned and kissed Mary's cheek. "And I love you."

"I love you," Mary said. "Always and forever and ever."

Hester put her arms around Mary and pulled her close for a proper thank you kiss. It quickly escalated as their lips parted and their tongues naturally sought one another. The teens kissed and hugged longer than ever before. When they finally parted, both were breathing hard. Hester pulled Mary's head against her chest, gently stroking the soft, blonde hair.

"Tell me about your days," Hester said gently. "I've missed you so much. Tell me everything."

Chapter Nine

In the summer of Eighteen Fifty-Nine, Mary found being considered a young lady instead of a child to be more of a pain than anything else. Her mother insisted she wear white gloves whenever she was outside as befitted a proper female of her status. She was no longer allowed to wander off on her own, though fortunately going for walks with Hester was still acceptable. Her penmanship and studies had improved to the point where she was no longer required to do her studies during the summer, though she had become so accustomed to writing in her diary that she continued to take it in her satchel whenever she left the Mountain House.

Mary took her glove off and dabbled the tips of her fingers in the cool mountain lake. "I wish it were like this every day," she said happily.

The early evening boat ride had been a spontaneous but wonderful idea as far as she was concerned. Seated at the stern with Hester, she found even her elder brother's presence in the middle tolerable. After all, someone had to row the boat.

"At home the air was so thick with heat that I dare say that I could have used one of Aunt Frances' knives to cut it," Hester said. "It is as if God has blessed Pine Orchard with weather far kinder than that of the valley below."

"Are you staying for the dance tonight?" Tobias asked as he continued to move the oars in a lazy pattern, the current doing more work at moving the rowboat than he was.

"I'm afraid Mrs. V. expects me to be home before dark," Hester said. Looking at Mary, she added. "Tomorrow we shall go to Glen Mary and I will practice sketching the falls."

Mary clapped her hands twice excitedly. "Oh, yes, will you be using the new pencils?"

"I was saving them for a special scene."

"Oh, please. I do so want to see you using them before I go."

"Oh, please," Tobias mimicked. "You must use your special pencils I made mother take all day with me to find before we left the city."

Mary turned in her seat and glared at her older brother. "It was not all day," she protested. "We left after breakfast and were home before Miss Bessie had afternoon tea ready."

"And then you spent most of the evening talking while Father was trying to read the news," he said. "You would think those pencils were made of gold."

"I believe they are the most exquisite pencils I shall ever own," Hester said, giving Mary that special smile that made the city girl feel all warm inside. "If you want me to do so, I will use one tomorrow just for you."

"I do. Thank you." Mary looked around, realizing that they were now heading back toward shore. "Oh, no, Tobias. Please, just one more time around."

Smiling good-naturedly, Tobias shook his head and jerked on the oars. "I might be one of the servants for all it matters," he said. "Next time ask one of them to take you girls for a ride."

"I don't see why we couldn't have just gone by ourselves," Mary said.

Tobias laughed. "You? Row? Well, now, wouldn't that just beat all?"

Mary huffed and crossed her arms. "I could do it if I wanted," she said. "It doesn't look that hard."

"If you tried it, we'd all be swimming in the lake," her brother said.

"I would not!" Mary protested.

"I think if you wanted to do it, you'd do a wonderful job," Hester said.

"But of course you would think that," Tobias said.

"A woman can do all that a man can do," Mary said.

Tobias snorted his disagreement. "When you can vote, you can steer the boat."

Mary reached into the water and came up with a handful of water, splashing her brother in the face.

"Ignore him," Mary said. "You just wait, Tobias. It won't be long before we'll have the vote and then you'll see."

"You sound like Mother."

"Good."

"You're going to have trouble finding any man to marry who's going to let you go to all those rallies and marches like Mother does," he said. He cocked his head and looked at Hester. "Then again, I don't suppose you two are worrying about things like that."

Mary's back went ramrod straight. "What do you mean by that?"

"I just mean that no less than four of my friends have come by to call upon you and you've turned them all away as if they were guttersnipes. I don't think you're the least bit interested in marriage."

"There were five and not a brain among them," Mary said. "All so immature that they make Daniel look like an adult. And that's not what you meant."

Tobias looked around, opened his mouth, and then closed it again. "Well," he said. "I just mean that I just supposed that the way you two are so close that you'd just be, um, companions. Like Miss Standly and Miss Bracket."

"They're old maids who live together in Brooklyn," Mary said to Hester. "They come to the meetings and rallies."

"Oh," Hester said. "Two of Uncle Gerrit's sisters lived together their whole lives."

"Exactly," Tobias said. "That's what I meant."

Mary put her hands on her hips. "For your information, Tobias, not only was there not a brain among those boys that came calling, but they no doubt are just shallow, younger versions of their fathers and grandfathers. They all live in nice homes north of ours, go to the finest schools, and are supposed to be the upstanding men of the future."

She wagged her finger at him. "Future senators, bankers, men of power and influence and do you see how they act? For them, women are objects to do their dishes, raise the children." She threw her hands in the air. "Provide them with pleasure whenever they desire! If you ask them, not one cares about abolition or suffrage because they think it doesn't apply to them. All they care about is having a good time and everyone else can go to hell. I'm sorry to curse but it just gets me so angry."

"They're not all that bad," Tobias said. "Smiley likes flowers. Why, he can look at just about any flower and tell you what it is."

"And that's just so much better than helping women get the right to vote or own property or even get custody of their children in a divorce."

"Well, as I said, I don't think you are worried about getting married."

"Certainly not if that's an example of the pond of fish from which I have to choose. I'd rather be a spinster."

"Well, at least you're not wearing knickerbockers and puffing on one of father's pipes."

"I could if I wanted to," Mary said. "I'm a grown woman now and I make my own decisions. If I want to wear knickerbockers or live with Hester my whole life or even work in a saloon, I'm going to do it."

"Not me," Tobias said. "I'm going to own a bank and live in a house as big as the Astor's with a wife and five, no, six children. All boys."

"You won't be leaving your room if Father learns you've been sneaking out at night and going to those parties on the other side of the lake."

Tobias looked shocked. "How do you know about that?"

"Everyone knows about them," Mary said. "I just didn't know you were going until now."

"Hey!"

Hester giggled and shared a smile with Mary. "It's a mighty good thing the Mountain House is so far away from home or Hendrik and Martin would be there, too."

"They'd always be welcome," Tobias said. "Especially if they brought some of that wine." He looked at his sister. "Don't you dare tell Father or Mother I said that."

"I wouldn't dare," Mary said. "But you probably should bring us back now. Hester has to get home soon."

"You're the one who wanted another spin around the lake," he said good-naturedly as he turned the rowboat around. "I bet if you asked, Mister Beach would let Mister Silas drive Hester home in the carriage."

"That's quite all right," Hester said. "I would be happier walking myself. I just don't feel right having someone drive me around like that."

The conversation lagged until they reached the shore. "Tell the boys I said hello," Tobias said as the girls walked away.

"I will," Hester called back.

Mary was quiet until they were heading down the road and out of earshot of her brother. "I know you have to go soon but could we go somewhere else? Somewhere…private?"

"Come down the road a little bit more with me," Hester said. "We'll go by the big bent tree. It's not so far that you shouldn't be out by yourself and that way I won't have so far extra to walk to get home."

"I want to say good night properly."

Hester smiled. "Properly, hmm?"

"Uh huh. After all, a proper young lady should say good night properly, shouldn't she?"

"I suppose so. Being a hill girl, I wouldn't know too much about what a proper lady should do."

"I'm sure I have a book about it somewhere."

Hester reached out and took Mary's hand in hers, intertwining their fingers. "Perhaps you should show me."

"Best idea you've had all day, Miss Van Wyck."

"Why, thank you, Miss Chandler."

Another week passed before Hester was able to return. She explained that her new step-mother did not approve and as such, Hester would no longer be able to come up as often. Mary suggested going to visit Hester instead.

Mary found her mother in her usual spot on the portico. Three other women were seated around her, all fanning themselves and drinking iced tea.

"Mother, would it be acceptable to go to Hester's on Saturday?"

Mary's mother shook her head. "We have the rally in Albany on Friday. Did you forget?"

"Oh, yes. I'm sorry."

Elizabeth looked at Hester. "You would be welcome to come along. We shall return on Sunday."

"Thank you very much, Mrs. C., but I cannot be gone that long. Mrs. V., Vader's new wife, insists I have to help with her children."

Mary's mother frowned. "It seems that your step-mother is more interested in having you and your cousin raise those children, than herself. Very well, Mary is free the following Saturday should you wish for her company then."

Hester smiled. "That would be nice, Mrs. C. Thank you."

"I find it hard to believe that your husband allowed you to be able to march in that foolish parade up Broadway," Mrs. Stout said.

"Allowed?" Mrs. Chandler's voice was a shriek, though kept at a volume that did not attract attention from the others milling about the Mountain House grounds. "Allowed?"

Mary and Hester looked at one another, then quietly stepped back several paces. "Oh, my," Mary whispered.

"Were I to clarify," Mrs. Stout said.

"What is there about the word 'allowed' that requires such clarification? I do know how to read and write, lest you forget that I was *allowed* to learn such things."

"I—"

"You feel that the right of suffrage is merely a pastime? An alternative to the sewing bee or Mrs. Astor's tea parties? A dalliance to fill my day?"

"Never," Mrs. Stout said. "I completely agree with several aspects of the movement, but woman should not believe that they will ever be allowed to vote, nor hold public office. It is foolish to put such ideas into our daughters' heads."

"Foolish ideas from the foolish speeches at the foolish convention, is this what you wish to have me believe? That you wish our daughters to believe? You speak with two faces. You speak of the need for education and free-thinking, yet when we dare to think for ourselves, you call it foolish and declare that we require our husband's permission to pursue rights which should be granted to all who are born upon this land of God. Nine states, nine, have passed laws regarding property rights for women and there shall be many more. A woman might just as well be a mule or another beast of burden were she not able to read the newspaper and know that which a man does. How is it that she should be knowledgeable, yet also be considered incompetent to vote as a fair and equal citizen of this union?"

Mrs. Linder joined into the conversation. "Were I one of the legislature, Mrs. Chandler," she said, while continuing to fan herself. "I would most certainly approve any measure or bill brought by the women of the suffrage movement. But I am not, nor shall there ever be a woman of such position in Albany."

"My dear Mrs. Linder, you are most incorrect," Mary's mother said. "Just as slavery was once thought never to be outlawed within New York, so, too, shall the right to vote and hold political office be ours in time." She put her fists upon her hips. "Mark my words as surely as Mister Beach's name is marked upon the precipice, we will one day have the right to vote and be equal in all aspects to men."

"Voting," another woman scoffed. "If a woman marries well, there is no need for her to vote. Leave that to the menfolk to worry about."

"Oh, dear," Mary whispered, tugging on her friend's sleeve to get her moving. Together they quickly walked away from the escalating conversation. "Mrs. Stout and Mrs. Linder would be better off doing battle with a bear than to challenge Mother regarding the suffrage movement."

"Mrs. Chandler is rather passionate about it," Hester agreed.

"In November we went to the convention at the Tabernacle. It was no less than the most invigorating and amazing event which I have ever attended. To listen to these women speak, I would believe that it will be within my lifetime that we shall be voting and living as free and equal with men." She led them toward North Lake. "Were you to sell your paintings, would you not wish to control the money you've earned just as your father does?"

"Vader is an artist," Hester protested. "I am just—"

"You are an artist, as well," Mary interrupted. "When Mister Bryant came calling this past spring, he made comment about the portrait you gave me. The one with the flowers. He said nothing but flowering praise until Father told him that a sixteen-year-old girl did it."

"Mister Bryant himself?"

Mary nodded. "He said he'd love to see what you do when you're older."

"Perhaps I should start using my initial same as Kent does, rather than Hester Van Wyck," Hester said. "Do you know one of the men here at the Mountain House bought the cane he made for Vader for ten whole dollars?"

"Really?"

Hester nodded. "The man saw Vader with the cane and demanded to know who the artist was that carved it. He told him that it was his nephew."

Mary plucked a sprig from the hemlock tree as they passed. "If your father had proclaimed it the work of his niece, he shall have been lucky to have five dollars pressed upon him."

"I shall do it," Hester said firmly. "From now on, I shall sign my paintings as H. Van Wyck."

"And when you are as rich and famous as Mister Bryant, we shall live in our fancy house with our servants and all our orphan children."

Hester smiled and bumped her upper arm against Mary's shoulder. "I think I will need to sell quite a few paintings before that will happen."

"You would get more done if that crabapple of a step-mother would leave you to the studio rather than nursemaiding her children," Mary said.

"I do not see why they should be allowed to eat before everyone else, nor why her daughter is allowed new dresses twice a year while Griet and I have to wait until after the harvest for money from Uncle Michael to buy material. I believe if Griet were not so handy with needle and thread, she and I would most certainly be running around in mere sacks."

"May she have long corns and short shoes," Mary said.

"Very long corns," Hester added, causing them both to laugh.

"Just a few more years," Mary said. "I will have Father buy us a house and I will take you away from that woman."

"May the good Lord see it so," Hester said. "Were it not for Vader, I would have moved to live with Uncle Michael and Will the moment she moved in." Hester stopped. "Where are we going?"

"I thought we might go down the road a spell and perhaps go into the woods?"

A knowing smile crossed Hester's face. "I reckon not to read the new issue of Godey's?"

Mary smiled. "I suspect I might have a better idea than that," she said. "After all, it is practically the end of July already."

"I believe it is the eighteenth."

"Exactly. More than half the month is already gone. I need to, um, what's the term? Oh, yes, I need to stock up for those long winter months when we will be apart."

Hester put her arm across Mary's shoulders. "Miss Chandler, I do believe if I were to kiss you from sunrise to sunset every day, it would not be enough to make you happy from the end of September until the end of June next year."

"Quite true," Mary said. "But we most certainly could make the attempt."

Hester laughed. "Not too far down the road. I saw many artists set up at the bend this morning when I came. I would rather they drew the Mountain House rather than us."

"I think a portrait of us kissing would be quite nice to have. In fact, I believe we should practice such a pose right away," Mary said. Hester wholeheartedly agreed.

Chapter Ten

There was a noticeable chill in the air. If mid-October was anything to go by, Mary was certain the winter would be most brutal indeed. Entering the parlor, she mentally went through the events of the past week in a desperate attempt to determine what she had done to warrant her parents calling a private meeting with her rather than discussing what they wanted during breakfast. "Father. Mother."

Her father gestured at the empty settee. "We would like to speak with you, Mary Elizabeth. Sit down."

"Yes, sir." She breathed deeply. It was never a good sign when her father used both names. "Is anything the matter?"

"I believe your father told you to sit," her mother said.

"Yes, Mother."

Her anxiety rose as her father waited until she was seated and then for a few seconds longer before speaking.

"Now tell us, as if we did not know, what would you like for your birthday?"

She relaxed, relieved that she was not in any trouble. However, having been turned down the previous six years, Mary held no hope that her request would be granted. Still she had to try anyway. "I wish very much for Hester to come visit."

Mary's father looked at her mother, a smirk crossing his face. "One of these days she'll have a mind to walk all the way to the mountain if we keep saying no."

"We're lucky our eldest daughter deigns to come home with us each September," her mother said. "I half expect her to declare herself an artist just so she might request board at the Voss house."

Mister Chandler chuckled. "Do not give the child thoughts, Mrs. Chandler."

He looked back at Mary. "Now then, we were discussing having your friend come for a visit." Mary could not stop the smile on her face as she felt the glimmer of hope that her dream might this time come true.

"But there is a problem with that," her mother said, dashing her hopes. "Where would she sleep?"

"Oh, there's lots of room in my bed," Mary said excitedly, having anticipated their questions many times before in the preceding years. "She'll be no bother, I swear to it."

"Indeed? And how would she get here? It's a mighty long walk from Palenville."

"Oh, Father, she'll ride the steamship or the train. Wait!" She rose from the settee and dashed into her room far quicker than propriety dictated. She returned with a small leather moneybag.

"I can pay for her ticket," she said, opening the drawstring and letting a pile of various coins drop noisily onto the table. "It's five dollars and fifty cents from the Oak Hill Station in Catskill to the city, is it not?"

"Where did you get so much money?" her mother asked. "Whenever I take you shopping, there is not so much as a three-cent pence in your reticule."

"I've been saving it," Mary replied. "Just in case. Having Hester come visit is worth so much more than any candy or a new comb. Please, Father and Mother. I'll never ask for another thing my whole entire life. Please, oh, please, let her come."

Her father rose from his chair and peered at the coins on the low table. "Mary Elizabeth Chandler. You have gold dollars, half dollars, quarter eagles...." He moved the coins around to better see them. "A couple of half eagles, some nickel pence, and even some silver dollars. Why, there must be more than twenty dollars there."

"Twenty-two and a half dollars," she said proudly. "Oh, and six pence. That's enough for Hester to come, isn't it?"

Her parents smiled at one another before her father addressed her. "Yes, Mary. It's enough for her to come. You go make haste and write her a letter of invitation for the fortnight around your birthday if it shall be of convenience for her family. I'll put it in the post tomorrow."

Mary squealed with delight. "Oh, thank you, Father. Thank you, Mother." She practically jumped from the settee and hugged both of them. "Oh, this shall be the best present I've ever had. Thank you." As she started to head to the writing desk, her father stopped her.

"Mary."

"Yes, Father?"

"You forgot your money." He scooped it up and placed it back in the pouch. "You'll need it to take your friend places while she's here. We'll take care of the tickets. It's part of your birthday present."

She gave out another squeal of delight and thanked them profusely. She was so excited that she almost spilled the bottle of ink trying to remove the cork stopper, quite a feat indeed considering the flared base of the small bottle. Forcing herself to calm down and go carefully, she poured some of the black liquid into the inkwell, then penned the message to Hester.

An hour and three drafts later, she finally ended up with the invitation written just the way she wanted it. With that task completed, all that remained was to stare at the clock and calendar waiting for word that the offer was accepted and, beyond that, Hester's arrival in mid-November. The waiting for the reply would be an interminable burden for Mary. It would prove even more interminable for her family as she pestered them each day about whether a reply had come and offered endless suggestions about what they would do and see once Hester arrived.

Hester read the first part of the note aloud.

"*My dearest Hester, Father said that I may have anything I wanted for my birthday and I once again asked if you could come visit. This time he said yes as he is tired of my asking each year. Mother fears you have too much work to do, but that if you are able, it would be acceptable to her. I have enclosed some money so that you might use the telegraph to respond.*'"

She looked up at her father, step-mother, and cousins. "The city of New York, Vader! Oh, please! Please, might I go?"

"That is such a long way to go," her step-mother said. "And by yourself? An unattended young woman?"

"I think it's wonderful," Griet said. "New York? With all those people and buildings? Why, it must be a place most magical. Please, let her go, Uncle Pieter."

"A place of sin and riots," her step-mother proclaimed.

Hester's father scratched his bearded chin before speaking. "Now, Mother, I very much doubt that Mister Chandler would allow Hester to get involved in a riot or any other such nonsense."

Hester's eyes grew wide with excitement as she began to believe that he would say yes.

"Griet and Kent, you would have to do her chores, as well as your own 'cepting for what the young'uns could help with," he said.

"They certainly will not," his wife said. "It is not for my children to do her chores."

"I will," Griet said. "Oh, I wish I could go with you, Hester."

"I'll do it, as well," Kent said. "I'll even carve you a fancy comb so you can look as pretty as all those ten percent ladies do."

"Whatever would you wear?" Hester's step-mother asked. "Even your going to meeting dress is not good enough for socialites like the Chandlers. They supper with the Astors, for goodness' sake." She shook her head. "No. I think it is utter nonsense."

Crestfallen, Hester's smile faded. It was indeed true that compared to the fancy store-bought dresses that Mary wore, Hester's homespun clothing, even the new dress she received just a month ago, looked like little more than rags in comparison. "But I have nothing better to wear," she said sadly.

Her father came to her rescue. "Were they concerned more for her clothing than the child herself, they would not have extended such a generous invitation," he said. "Certainly they know she has nothing better than the two dresses they've seen this past summer and wouldn't expect her new fall dress to be much more."

"And you would have her wear those amongst the upper ten?" His wife shook her head again. "It is not as if she or Griet can make a decent enough dress for such a thing."

"Perhaps Miss Lilly could make one," Griet said. "If we can buy her the material."

Hester's eyes widened when she saw the look on her father's face.

"I fear there is no money for such a thing," he said. "With all of the Mountain House folks gone, there are none wanting portraits. I hoped to sell some of my landscapes, but with so many artists creating the same, I was unable."

He glanced in Hester's direction but his eyes would not come up to meet hers. "If a new artist rents space in the studio soon...." He let the sentence hang.

Kent spoke up. "I can give the money for cloth, Uncle Pieter."

"And I have enough to help pay Miss Lilly to make it," Griet added. "She will make it as fine as any sold on Broadway."

"But you were saving your money for a new saw," Hester said.

Kent shrugged. "I reckon I can just keep borrowing Uncle Michael's a spell longer, that's all. I can make a chair with the same saw grandfather and uncle used, just as well as if I had a fancy new one."

Hester's step-mother threw her hands in the air. "It seems everyone here is set on her going." She looked at Hester. "I must say the thought of you traveling unescorted from here to the city?" She wrung her hands together on her apron. "That I do not like."

"She's sixteen now, Mother," her father said. "We will pray to the Lord to protect and watch her."

"A Bible is little protection these days, especially in that den of sin and sorrow."

"She could take Martin's hunting knife with her for protection," Kent offered.

"Young ladies do not run around with hunting knives," Hester's step-mother said. "What would the Chandlers say?" She shook her head. "Nonsense. Complete and utter nonsense letting her go off like that. If she were my child, I would never allow such foolishness."

Her father wagged his finger at Hester. "I don't want you to getting to liking it so much there that you go and end up staying, do you hear me?"

"Oh, I won't, Vader, I promise," Hester said as she crossed the room and gave him a hug. "Thank you. Thank you so much."

"There, it's settled," he said, gracing his only child with a smile. A quick glance at his wife showed her scowl of disapproval, but it mattered not to the happy teen. She was going to New York City and she was going to get to see Mary again. Tattered dresses, scuffed shoes, even the ratty carpetbag to hold her clothes mattered nothing at that point. She ran to give Griet and Kent hugs and thank them.

"Now don't you let them go puttin' any of those fancy ideas about women into your head," her step-mother admonished. "All that votin' and having a say in men's things might be fine for those city folk, but it don't get the butter churned here. You understand?"

"Yes, ma'am."

"That woman coming here and talking all about freedoms and 'pression and such nonsense." Mrs. Van Wyck waved her hand dismissively. "Honestly, Pieter. I don't know why you let them put such ideas into your daughter's head. It's a wonder she's not wearing britches and expecting the men to cook the dinners. Bad enough they's got her reading like she's a smart one."

"Now, Mother, I was against her learning to read and write but it has turned out for the best. Why, her and Griet have learned all sorts of new things to make for dinner and look at all the things Kent has been able to make, once she taught him how to read those magazines with the fancy furniture and what not in them." He patted the sideboard. "We wouldn't have this one with all those drawers and such that you fancy if it weren't for her bringing home one of them Godey's magazines and showing it to him."

114

"Still utter nonsense if you ask me," she said. "I never learned to do no reading and writing and I am just as happy for not knowing. It certainly hasn't helped her one bit with her sewing. That's what be important, Pieter Van Wyck. Not paintin' and reading. No man's wanting a woman acting smarter than he is and there ain't a one that be wanting her to sit around reading no magazine and playing with paint and brushes when she should be fixing his britches or making his supper."

She wagged her finger at Hester. "When you git back, you'll best be working on that sewing of yours instead of fooling around in that studio." She gave Pieter a sour look. "Ain't no money to be made there."

Kent stood up. "I'll go to Uncle Michael's and have him bring the cart," he said. "You can send that telly-gram today if we get there soon enough."

"I'll go," Griet said. "You know going all that way hurts your leg too much."

"Then I'll go get some wood to make that comb," he said. "I'll make it so pretty for you that them high-fallooting ladies will all wish they had one so nice."

Chapter Eleven

Mary could barely contain her excitement as the carriage pulled up at the upper city station at Thirty-Fourth Street. "Is she here yet, Father?"

"Soon," he said, disembarking and then holding his hand out to assist first her, followed by her mother. "She shall be here soon."

Mary tried not to fidget but was unable to keep all the pent up energy inside. Without realizing it, she started pacing, looking up at the large clock frequently as if she could will time, and the train, to move faster. She watched her father walk up to the ticket booth, then return moments later.

"There has been significant snowfall just outside of Catskill. It has caused a delay."

"A delay? Goodness gracious." She looked up the track, then resumed her pacing.

Her father chuckled. "Mary Elizabeth Chandler. If determination and impatience were as efficient as coal, the Hudson River Railroad would need only place you in the engine car. You should sit before you wear a hole plumb through those boards."

She scowled at him. "You are without humor, Father," she said, which only caused him to chuckle. "Are you certain the train is coming? Pray tell it did not meet with an accident?"

Thanks to her growth spurt, Mary was now the same height as her father. Reaching out to stop her frenetic

116

pacing, he gently cupped both sides of her head, then tilted her down for a peck on the brow. "My dear daughter. There has been no accident. Merely a slight delay."

"Delay." Mary said the word in the same tone as her younger brother said oatmeal. "They should throw more coal on and make it go faster to make up that 'delay.' Don't they realize people are waiting?"

She huffed with displeasure and went to the bench. She could tolerate less than a minute before she was back on her feet, resuming her pacing. Never had a clock moved so slow as the one she continually stared at while walking back and forth. She silently cursed Mother Nature, the Hudson River Railroad, even the manufacturer of the clock as the minutes slowly ticked by.

Almost an hour passed before a distant whistle sounded.

"Is that it?" Mary asked excitedly.

"I believe so," her father answered. Mary broke into a run, ignoring her mother's call to walk like a lady as she raced to the platform.

If waiting for the train was difficult, watching stranger after stranger disembark, with no sign of Hester, was pure torture. "Where is she?"

Elizabeth put her hands on Mary's shoulders. "Look."

Finally, after weeks of waiting and anticipation, the one person Mary wished to see above all else stepped from the train.

"Hester! Hester!" Mary waved frantically and ran to her. "Oh, Hester! You're here! You're finally here!"

"I'm here," Hester said, returning the fierce hug.

"Hello, Hester," Gideon said when the pair finally separated. "Is this all of your bags?"

"Yes, sir."

Mary's father picked up the tattered carpetbag and waved for his coachman. "Mrs. Chandler, I do believe at some point in your many shopping trips, a new bag properly befitting a young lady might be acquired."

Mrs. Chandler cast a disapproving eye at her guest. "Is that your going to meeting dress, child?"

"Yes, Mrs. C." Hester tugged on her sleeve self-consciously. "I was going to get a new dress made but Miss Lilly took ill. Griet and I can make an everyday dress but not a going to meeting one, I'm afraid."

"Very well," Elizabeth said as the coachman took the carpetbag. "You are a little tall for Mary's clothes, but, nonetheless, you will wear something appropriate of hers tomorrow and we shall simply have to go shopping at Rothmeyer's. It will not do for our guest to appear as a guttersnipe. I am certain that we can find a new dress or two for you." She clapped her hands together. "It is decided."

"Thank you, Mrs. C." Hester said, uncertain what else to say.

"No trouble at all," Mary's mother said. "Now, however, we should make haste to the telegraph office so that word may be sent to your family of your safe arrival. Come along." She walked toward the line of carriages.

"It's all right," Mary said, giving Hester's forearm a gentle squeeze as they followed. "We will have fun shopping together. Mother and I will take you to the finest stores in all the city."

Hester gave an embarrassed smile. "Other than a few trips with Vader to the mercantile in Palenville and one trip with Mother Van Wyck to Catskill, I have not gone to a store. Certainly not those as fancy as here."

Her eyes grew wide at the line of hackney coaches outside the train station and wider still when they approached the ornately decorated carriage that was to be their transport. "Oh, my." She touched the polished black lacquer door trimmed in golden paint. "I have never seen such a beautiful carriage."

"It arrived just this past week," Gideon said. "Far more comfortable than the previous one, though Mrs. Chandler does most of the traveling in it. By the time you leave, I'm sure you will have seen every store the Empire City has to offer."

"Mister Chandler!" Mary's mother scolded, earning a chuckle from her husband.

"I would suspect the horses know their way to the stores so well that I could dispense with a coachman were there not the need for someone to carry the parcels from the store to the carriage and then into the house," he said.

As the coachman opened the door, Gideon held out his hand. "If I may, Mrs. Chandler." He repeated the action until all three women were in the carriage, then climbed in himself.

"I trust your journey was acceptable and without incident?" he asked once settled.

"Oh, yes, sir. Uncle Michael had business, so he took me to Catskill and waited until I boarded that most wonderful ferry to cross the river. I was but a short time at Oak Hill when the train arrived. Oh, my what a wonderful trip it was! It went so fast that I could scarcely believe it. My seat allowed me to see the river and I watched as town after town came and went along the way."

"This was your first time upon a train, was it not?" Mary's mother asked.

"Yes, ma'am. What a most wonderful creation." She looked at Mary and smiled. "A might noisy, though. I could scarcely hear my own thoughts above the clamor."

"It is a most helpful product of locomotion," the older woman agreed. "I recall when the only transports were sloops with huge sails. Barely faster than walking, they were, though indeed they were beautiful to gaze upon.

Now trains move nearly as rapid as the bird. Soon there will be tracks everywhere, perhaps even to your very door."

Hester laughed. "To my very door, Mrs. C?"

"They are building rails up the roads of our city, even as we speak," Mary's mother said. "Those iron horses are going everywhere. Soon there will be little place for us to walk upon as those rails are laid down endlessly."

"I dare say that we will probably see the end of the horse and buggy in New York City within just a few years at the rate things are changing," Gideon said.

"Certainly it would improve the odor," Elizabeth said. "There is little more distasteful than the smell of a horse putting droppings in their buckets. Unless you include those that do not use buckets but rather let the beasts deposit wherever they wish."

"We are going to have so much fun," Mary said excitedly. "We'll go to the museums and the stores and even the galleries so you can see all the great works of art that we have here."

"I don't wish to put you to any trouble," Hester said.

"It's no trouble at all," Gideon replied. "Mrs. Chandler loves to shop and any excuse will do." He chuckled at the look given by his wife. "Why, I would venture that you will probably see some of the same stores two or perhaps three times before you leave."

"Oh, Mary!" Hester exclaimed as she looked out the window. "Isn't that the hotel we saw in Godey's?"

"Yes," Mary said. "The Metropolitan."

"There are far better hotels to see," Mary's mother said. "When we are out tomorrow, we will take a tour of the city so you may see some of the best buildings we have."

"Thank you, Mrs. C."

After experiencing her first visit to a restaurant, the rest of the ride to the Chandler's brownstone in Gramercy

Park was spent listening to Mary excitedly talk about all the places they were going to visit and the things they were going to do. By the time they arrived, Hester was exhausted just thinking about it.

Hester's first thought when she entered Mary's bedroom was white. Everything was white. The chest of drawers, the dressing table with matching chair, even the curtains and canopy were the most vibrant white she had ever seen.

"It is beautiful," she said.

The only places that showed color were the framed drawings and paintings upon the wall, all done by Hester's own hand. One in particular captured her attention and approached to touch the beautiful wooden frame.

"I told you that I would have it framed as soon as we returned," Mary said, coming up from behind and wrapping her arms around Hester's middle. "Cherry wood. Mother let me pick it out myself."

"It's perfect," Hester said, running her fingertip across the rich grain. Her other hand rested on Mary's. "Absolutely perfect."

"Do you see? There is plenty of room for you to paint more for me," Mary said. "I want to fill the whole room with your paintings." She kissed Hester's back through the dress. "Are you tired?"

"Oh, yes," Hester said. "I was so excited this morning that I was awake and dressed well before the morning chores." She turned in Mary's arms and put hers around the older teen's neck. "All I could think about was that I would be seeing you today. I've missed you so much."

"You're really here," Mary whispered. "Really and truly here."

121

"I am," Hester whispered back before bringing her lips down to meet Mary's mouth. All the time spent waiting for their reunion was worth it as they spoke with their hearts rather than words about how much they meant to one another.

"W-we should get ready for bed," Mary said breathlessly when they finally parted.

Hester silently agreed, crossing the room to open her bag in search of her nightgown.

"You may have either side," Mary said as she changed. "You're the guest."

"I don't mind either side," Hester said as she pulled off her dress and donned the nightclothes. "Usually Griet has the side by the wall and I take the outside but your bed is in the middle so there is no wall side."

Mary climbed into the bed, scooting to make room. "I'm sure..." She interrupted herself with a yawn. "Oh, pardon me. I'm sure we'll be comfortable, no matter what."

"It seems I'm not the only one who is tired," Hester said as she made her way under the covers.

Mary extinguished the oil lamp. "Mother is very happy," she whispered, propping herself up on one elbow to look down at Hester, the moon casting a soft glow into the room. "She loves to shop. I suspect it is more of a joy to her than even the finest meal would be. We shall have great enjoyment tomorrow."

Hester squeezed Mary's hand. "I have never owned a store-bought dress before. Whatever will I do with it when I go home?"

"Wear it, silly."

"Oh, no. It will be far too fine for home. If I wear it, it'll be ruined."

Mary laid back down, resting her cheek against Hester's upper arm. "Use it as your going to meeting dress and you'll be the prettiest girl in all of Palenville."

"This bed is so very soft," Hester whispered.

"It is filled with the finest of feathers, as are the pillows, but it does get lumpy sometimes when the feathers bunch up. When I grow up, I'm going to have a new mattress made for you filled with feathers even finer than mine." Mary kissed the underside of Hester's chin. "And a pillow, no, two pillows to match."

"Even though we cannot be married?"

"Even so," Mary promised.

"Griet should be most pleased with the extra room in the bed while I am here."

"I wish you could stay forever," Mary said before giving a soft yawn. Her arm snaked across Hester's belly. "You're softer than any feather."

Hester covered the gentle hand with her own. "So are you. I wish we lived together now so we could always sleep in the same bed."

Mary's fingers moved in small circles along Hester's tummy. Hester raised her hand up above her head, giving Mary full access. For several long moments there were no sounds save that of their breathing as Mary continued to let her fingers and hand roam across Hester's middle.

"I wish we could be married," Hester whispered.

"Me, too," Mary said softly, her right leg draping itself across Hester's. "Sometimes I wish I was a man so I could marry you."

Hester lifted her head so she could reach the top of Mary's and placed a soft kiss on the thick, blonde hair. "Yes," she agreed. "I also wish that, many times." She buried her fingers in the softness of Mary's hair, guiding her friend to rest against her breast. "I love you, forever and ever, Mary." She was rewarded with a gentle squeeze.

"I love you, forever and ever, too."

It took only the slightest nudge to get Mary to move up so they could kiss. Hester let her hands roam freely on the older teen's back, enjoying the softness and warmth.

Mary shifted until she was completely on top and their kisses quickly went from gentle to heated. Their tongues brushed across one another and soft moans were muffled by their mouths. Mindful not to make too much noise, they nonetheless took great pleasure in not having to share the bed with Griet. Hester gasped when Mary kissed her neck.

"Oh! Oh, my darling," she whispered, putting her hand on the back of Mary's head to keep her there as this new and most wonderful sensation took her reason away. She felt lost in a sea of pleasure as Mary's hands squeezed her shoulders and her body reacted to the soft lips and tongue caressing her neck.

"I love you," Mary whispered, sliding down to kiss Hester's breastbone.

"I love you, too." The feelings became scary in their intensity and Hester finally had to put her hands on Mary's shoulders and gently push her back. Both were breathing hard.

"That felt so good," Hester whispered. "I've never...." She swallowed. "I've never felt anything like that."

Mary's fingertips touched her cheeks and it took only the slightest urging for Hester to take the lead, rolling onto Mary and using her own mouth to blaze a trail across the older teen's chin and to her soft throat. The answering moan seemed so loud to Hester that she feared someone might have heard but Mary gave no indication of being concerned.

"I love you," she whispered, brushing her cheek against the gown-covered inside of Mary's breast. She heard the rapid heartbeat against her ear and thought it was the most wonderful sound in all of creation. She smiled as gentle fingers slid through her hair, down to caress her cheek, then back again.

"I love you," Mary said softly. "I wish we could stay like this forever."

"Hmm." Closing her eyes, Hester luxuriated in the feeling of Mary's body beneath her.

"Come here."

Hester allowed herself to be rolled onto her back, smiling when she felt Mary curl up against her, their positions now reversed.

"I could sleep just like this," Mary said. "I love it when you hold me."

Hester let her fingers play with Mary's hair in a gentle, slow rhythm. "I love holding you." She lifted her head just enough to put a kiss on Mary's crown. "Go to sleep, my Mary Berry."

The older teen hummed in contentment and settled even closer. "Good night, my Hester Pester. I'm so glad you're here."

"Me, too."

Chapter Twelve

Hester watched the morning sun slowly rise and illuminate the room. Her entire right side was pinned and despite the slowly growing urgency of her bladder, she was loathe to move and disturb her sleeping friend. Finally it became too much and she had no choice but to gently shift and wake Mary.

"Good morning."

Mary groaned and lifted her head. "Good morning."

Blinking sleepily, Mary yawned, then set her head back down upon Hester's breast. "I don't want to get up," she mumbled.

"I don't either but I have to," Hester said. "I need to use the…you know."

"Oh." Mary rolled onto her back, releasing Hester's bladder from the pressure of a knee being on it. "Me, too. You go first. Miss Bessie put some fresh cloths in there last night. They're next to the wash basin."

"So nice not to have to run outdoors or squat over a pot," Hester said as she left the bed.

"Yes," Mary agreed. "I much prefer our chamber pots to your outhouse or that pan."

Hester opened the door, separating Mary's bedroom from the washroom, barely getting the lid up on the seat before her bladder insisted on being released. She made a mental note to sketch the commode and have Kent make it as his next project.

"I'm so happy you are here," Mary said after she finished in the washroom. "Oh, dear, you can't wear that today. Mother is taking us shopping. Here. Take that off and I'll find one of mine for you."

It was one of the few times that Hester felt ashamed of her situation. Removing her dress, she put it into her bag while Mary hummed and looked through the rack of dresses in the closet. She dutifully tried on three before Mary finally declared one to be as close as they were going to get. It was a bit high in the waist and a good two inches above her ankles. She thought it then drew attention to her scuffed and worn shoes.

"Don't worry," Mary said as she helped fasten the buttons up the back. "Mother will get you new shoes, too."

"I don't feel right having your mother spend so much money on me." She felt a soft kiss against her back and loving arms encircle her waist.

"She wants to do this for you," Mary said softly. "I want to do this for you." She squeezed, then let go. "Please, Hester. It would make both of us happy."

She came around so that they were facing one another. "Don't worry about the money. I've wanted you to come here for so long." She stepped up on her toes and gave Hester a soft kiss. "Please, let's just enjoy it."

"It just doesn't feel right." She stepped to the full length mirror and turned this way and that. "This is very pretty," she admitted, running her hands along the soft material.

"You look prettier in it than I do."

They were interrupted by a knock on the door. "Girls? It's time for breakfast."

"Yes, Mother," Mary answered.

The other family members were entering the dining room as Mary and Hester arrived.

"Here," Mary said, pulling out the chair to her right. "You sit next to me."

"But that's my seat," Judith protested.

"Judith," Gideon said sternly. "Hester is Mary's guest. You most certainly are capable of moving over one seat. You can see we had another chair put out."

Mary's younger sister groaned but did as she was told.

"Good morning, Hester," Daniel said sweetly.

Hester smiled at him. "Good morning, Daniel."

"Yes," Tobias said. "Good morning, Hester."

"Good morning."

Elizabeth entered the room, taking her seat at the opposite end from her husband. "I trust you slept well, Hester?"

"Yes, Mrs. C. Quite well, thank you."

"I'm surprised Mary didn't keep you awake half the night," Gideon said as he poured coffee into his cup. "After all, she hasn't seen you in six weeks. I was certain she was saving everything up to tell you." He smirked. "How the weather has been, how many days before we return to the Mountain House, how many leaves have fallen."

"And how Miss Bessie was sick," Hester said, causing light laughter from the family. "Is she better?"

"You may ask her yourself," Gideon said as the swinging door opened and a large black woman carrying a tray laden with food entered. "Miss Bessie, young Miss Hester here wishes to know if you are feeling better."

The cook smiled broadly. "So this is the famous Hester, is it? Well, child, I am feeling as fit as can be." She placed the tray on a sideboard and set plates, laden with breads, fruits, and containers of jam in the center of the table.

"She did worry us for a time," Elizabeth said. "Tobias, please pass the coffee before your father drinks it all."

The Chandler children all reached for the food only to be stopped by their father's admonishment. "We have a guest. Mind your manners. Hester, please help yourself."

"Is there tea, Miss Bessie?" Mary asked.

"Just about ready, Miss Mary. Miss Hester, is there anything else you would like?"

Hester shook her head. "Oh, no, Miss Bessie. This is all wonderful. Thank you."

"I will bring the rest out," Bessie said before disappearing behind the swinging door.

"We're going to have so much fun today," Mary said. "Mother, may we leave as soon as we're finished eating?"

Gideon chuckled. "She's just a little excited."

Elizabeth smiled. "I think within the hour is certainly soon enough."

"I want to go," Judith said.

"We've spoken of this before," her mother said. "You may come along tomorrow but today is just for Mary and Hester. Your sister has been waiting so very long for her to come visit."

"And on Friday evening, I think a nice family outing is in order," Gideon said. "Mister Astor tells me the new restaurant near the Lyceum has some of the finest steaks in the city." He smirked and pointed his fork in the direction of his wife. "I presume the seamstresses will be most busy this week."

"I would have appreciated more notice, Mister Chandler," Elizabeth said as she reached for her delicate china cup. "You know I need to plan for such outings."

"Mother will need a new dress," Mary whispered to Hester.

"I'll need a new suit," Tobias said. "My trousers are almost to my knees."

"If you would stop growing, you wouldn't need a new suit," Gideon said.

"Goodness. I haven't the time to take you, Tobias," their mother said.

"The boy is certainly old enough to go by himself and have a suit made," their father answered. "Tobias, go today and make certain they know it must be ready for Friday. Have them put it on my account."

"Yes, Father."

"Take your brother with you. Everyone else is getting new clothes."

"Remember, no candies for him," Elizabeth said.

Miss Bessie returned with another heavy tray. This time it contained more food for breakfast than Hester and Griet had ever made for an entire day. More breads, a mountain of ham, a silver tureen filled with a white gravy, and so many other foods that it made Hester feel full just looking at it. Despite Mary's dress feeling loose on her now, she was certain she would be popping the seams by the time the meal was finished.

At Mister Chandler's insistence, Hester tried the coffee and deemed it far superior to the one that Michael would occasionally bring to the Voss homestead. Mrs. Chandler then encouraged her to try the tea, which also tasted finer than any Hester had tried before.

After so many brisk days, New York City seemed to welcome its newest visitor with mild temperatures, bright sun, and little wind. Mary and Hester had gone outside to await Old Jack, the family's groomsman. Mary pointed out the park across the street, explaining that only people who lived in Gramercy Park were allowed to use it. It seemed odd to Hester, for whom fences were only meant to keep animals in, not people out.

Hester colored when a very unladylike belch escaped. "Oh, good Lord! I'm so sorry. Excuse me."

Mary laughed. "It's better to come out there than the other place."

"If breakfast is like that every morning, I won't be able to fit on the train to return home."

"Well, then, you would just have to stay here, wouldn't you?"

Hester smiled and shook her head. "I wouldn't know how to live in this big city. Certainly Vader would never wish to live here. And who would help Griet take care of the boys?" She stared at one of the trees behind the wrought iron fence. "No. I'm sure it's very nice for you but I'm happy in Palenville."

The front door opened and Mrs. Chandler stepped out, dressed in such finery that she rivaled those that appeared in the drawings of Godey's. "Old Jack isn't here yet?"

Mary put her hand on her brow to block the sun as she looked down the street. "Here he comes."

"Wonderful," Elizabeth said. "It will be a busy day for us, girls."

"It will be a busier day for those stores," Mary said under her breath. Hester turned her head, so Mary's mother could not see her smile.

"Well, my dear," Elizabeth said once they were settled in the carriage and it was making its way toward the shopping district. "Since your father is an artist, I thought perhaps when we are done with the dressmakers, you would enjoy visiting some of our best galleries to see art that comes from all around the world."

Hester's eyes widened. "Oh, yes, Mrs. C. That would be most wonderful."

"Very well, then. Today we shall purchase clothes, have our lunch, then visit the Abbot's Egyptian Museum, and Mister Bryant's works at the American Art Union. If there is enough time we shall see Dusseldorf Gallery. Tomorrow we will visit the Gallery of Scandinavian

Paintings and the National American Historical Paintings, as they are in the same building."

She opened her reticule and referred to a piece of paper. "I believe you will benefit from a visit to see our great city library, as well as the Lyceum of Natural History. I first brought Mary there when she was a little girl, barely six if I properly recall. Was it six?"

"I think so, Mother."

"She so enjoyed seeing all those rocks and shells. I don't believe she appreciated the history I was trying to instill upon her then, but now she does and we've attended several lectures there."

"Yes," Mary agreed. "Tobias always has the most comfortable naps when we go."

"Mary!" Her mother feigned outrage, then smiled. "We've learned to leave him at home the past few times. Incorrigible."

"I would like to see it," Hester said. "I've never been to any museum or art gallery."

"Wonderful." Mary's mother glanced at the note again. "Perhaps if there is time while you are here, Hester, we shall also visit the New York Historical Society. I believe they even have some information about the area where you live."

Hester wondered how they would have the time to visit all the places Mrs. Chandler had listed, especially since Mary warned her that dress shopping was a lengthy affair.

The carriage turned a corner, bringing several larger buildings of the business district into view.

"Mother!" Mary pointed at the large building they were passing. "Oh, Mother, please could we? Just one?"

Hester craned her neck to look through the window, seeing several brownstone buildings but uncertain what her friend was so excited about. "What is it?"

"Oh, it's a studio," Mary said. "We could get our photograph taken together and then I would be able to see you even when we're apart. Wouldn't that be wonderful?"

Mary's mother smiled. "I believe that to be a most enchanting idea," she said. "When we are finished with our shopping, we shall retire at once to Mister Brady's studio and have photographs taken. I don't understand all the different methods by which they make the photographs now, but I have seen several. We will have to ask Mister Brady which one will be best suited for us."

"Oh, thank you, Mother. Thank you." Mary reached out and grabbed Hester's hands in hers. "This is the best present I've ever had. I wish you could stay forever."

"It does no good to wish for things that cannot be," her mother said. "It is better to enjoy the time you have together now and you shall see her again when we return to the Mountain House to summer there. Hester, is there any place you wish to see while you are here?"

Hester licked her lips hesitantly before answering. "I have heard so much of Mister Barnum's museum, Mrs. C. Perhaps, if it is acceptable, we shall be able to visit there?"

"Oh, yes," Mary said. "That would be most entertaining. He has so many things there that you just cannot see anywhere else in the world. Please, Mother?"

"I have heard more 'please mother' since Hester's arrival than since you first learned to speak, my child." She smiled indulgently. "Yes, Hester. We shall make plans to visit Mister Barnum's establishment. Perhaps the day after tomorrow. I am certain you will find great enjoyment there."

"Thank you, Mrs. C."

"It is my pleasure indeed. Now, we have special plans for this weekend. The children will be staying home. Mister Chandler and I, along with Tobias and you girls, will be going to the Broadway Theater."

Hester's eyes widened. "The theater?"

"Oh, Mother! Thank you."

Mrs. Chandler gave a small laugh. "I do say that I enjoy hearing that more often, as well." She reached out and patted her daughter's hand. "We should have done this for you last year instead of that trip to Boston. I dare say that while Mister Chandler and I enjoyed it, my daughter found it to be the equivalent of having teeth pulled."

"It would have been better if Hester had been with us," Mary said.

Her mother laughed. "I am not surprised you would think such a thing," she said. "Everything would be better if Hester were there."

"It's true," Mary said.

While Hester had been warned that it was Mrs. Chandler who took a long time when it came to dress shopping, it was Mary who caused them to have to cancel most of the museum and gallery trips for the day. One dress after another was considered and rejected as Hester dutifully stood there, feeling much like a doll being dressed and undressed repeatedly. Twice she had tried to tell Mary that what had been suggested for her by the store clerks was perfectly acceptable and both times her friend went on about how it wasn't perfect at all and insisted that Hester try on another one.

Mrs. Chandler had already selected shoes, gloves, hats, and even a reticule for Hester but as the morning turned into afternoon, the finest dress shop in New York City still could not produce a single garment that Mary deemed worthy for Hester. It was only when Mrs. Chandler put her foot down, did Mary grudgingly agree and allow the seamstress to do the pinning required. In contrast, Mary tried on only two dresses before making a selection. Old Jack loaded the carriage with the various boxes, doing his best to leave enough room for the three ladies to still fit inside.

Chapter Thirteen

Mary's mother stood before a large mirror, turning her head this way and that to admire the feathered hat. "Hmm. Mary? What do you think?"

The teenager scrunched her nose and shook her head. "The blue one was better."

"Hester?"

Hester hesitated before answering. "I believe you look beautiful in all of the hats you have tried, Mrs. C."

Elizabeth gave her a small smile. "Child, there is a difference between being polite and being honest. I would prefer honesty. Politely, of course."

They all gave a short laugh at the joke.

"I think that simple white one you tried on first was the best, Mrs. C."

"Is that so?" Mrs. Chandler turned to the young women attending to them. "The white one and find it in the appropriate sizes for both girls." She reached up to remove the plumed hat. "We shall have to find dresses to match now, you realize."

"Would the new dress you've selected for me not do, Mrs. C.?"

"I suppose it would, Hester. However, I do not believe you will suffer with having more than one or two new dresses." She reached and put her hand on Hester's shoulder. "If your mother were alive and had the means, I believe she would wish to see you pampered this way. You tarry so much at home and ask for so little. Allow me to do this for you."

Hester nodded, touched by the gesture. "Yes, Mrs. C. Thank you so much."

"There. Then it is settled. Now, let us find appropriate dresses for the theater to match those hats. Certainly your usual theater dress is a bit tight around the middle now, Mary."

She waved her hand dismissively. "You have inherited your figure from your father's side of the family. No one would accuse any of their husbands of failing to provide enough meals for them. Come along now."

"That's Mother's way of saying they're all as big as a horse," Mary whispered as they were led past the rack of furs to a display of dresses.

"Hester, do you have a warm coat for the winter?"

"Yes, Mrs. C."

Elizabeth looked at her and raised one elegant eyebrow. "Hmm. Very well. If you decide otherwise, you have but to speak up."

"Yes, Mrs. C," Hester said, knowing full well that even if she did find her coat to be less than ideal, she would not ask for a new one. She wondered how she was going to get all the things already ordered or purchased for her back home. Certainly, three of her carpetbags would not be enough at this point.

Barnum's Emporium was a most magical place and the girls oohed and ahhed at everything they saw. But it held not a single candle to the wonder of Mister Brady's photography studio. It was the first time Hester had ever seen a camera and was surprised to see it mounted on a wooden tripod with several large lamps and mirrors positioned behind it. With great excitement, Mary and Hester posed together for two photographs, then a suggestion from the photographer resulted in one of Mary with her mother and a final image of the three of them together. With the promise that the images would be framed and ready by the next week, it was off to the enchanting world of Abbot's Egyptian Museum.

For Hester, it was stepping into another world. Golden figurines and items from a land far away filled her with wonder. She listened with rapt attention as the curator regaled them with stories about the amazing land and its people.

If that weren't enough to overload her teenaged mind, they managed to squeeze in two different art galleries that afternoon. Mary tried her best not to look bored as Hester flitted from one painting to the next, standing as close as she dared and absorbing it all with an artist's eye. She wished she had one of Mister Brady's cameras to capture the paintings that she knew she would never see again. She always thought her father to be a great artist but now she realized why he painted portraits for the people on holiday and made signs for the local merchants rather than having a gallery filled with his work. The men, and a few women, who created these works of art were so extraordinarily talented that Hester wept at their greatness.

The final stop of the day was Stewart's, where Mrs. Chandler found it necessary to purchase a variety of brushes, tubes of paint, and another sketching pad for Hester. The young teen wanted to protest such lavishness being thrust upon her but she found it impossible to do so when she saw the joy it gave Mary's mother to buy the items.

After the packages were given to Old Jack, an impulsive request from Mary put them in the store next door. There, a rainbow of colorful candies, fruity drinks, and seemingly endless varieties of chocolates and fudges tempted everyone's sweet tooth.

While Mrs. Chandler was busy chatting with an acquaintance who had also stopped in, Hester slipped several of the candies to Mary.

The older teen quickly put one into her mouth. "Thank you."

"I have too many," Hester said. "But I could not tell your mother no."

"I know," Mary said. "That's all right. You always give me treats."

"I hope Uncle Michael gets a better sugaring season next year. We didn't get hardly any candy from him."

"Really?" Mary's eyes narrowed. "But you had some when I came up this summer."

Hester smiled and took one of the candies for herself. "I always put some aside for you," she said. "Even if it means I don't get any for myself." She shrugged. "This year I didn't have enough for both of us, so I just kept it for you."

Mary moved closer, making certain only Hester could hear her. "If we were alone, I would kiss you."

"Next year, I will make sure to put it all aside for you, no matter how much Uncle Michael gives me."

"We'll share it," Mary said, popping another treat into her mouth.

Hester leaned closer. "Will I still get all my kisses?"

Mary smiled. "I'm sure we'll share lots of those, as well."

"I will never be able to fit all these new clothes into my bag," Hester said two nights later while carefully removing her new dress.

"Oh. Mother is giving you one of the old trunks to carry your things back in," Mary said. "I heard her speaking with Father about it." She stepped closer, offering a hand for Hester to steady herself with. "He warned her that you were only going home with a new carpetbag and one trunk and that she needed to control herself," she added with a laugh.

Smiling, Hester finished slipping out of the dress. "Your mother certainly enjoys shopping."

"The way the sun enjoys rising each morning," Mary said. "It gives her great pleasure to spend Father's money. I suspect that she will bring Judith along with us tomorrow. She has not been to the Lyceum yet."

"I'm very excited," Hester said as she finished removing her clothing. "To see all those paintings at the other museums? And the library?"

"I cannot see how the library would be exciting," Mary said. "Oh, wait! I wanted you to wear one of my nightgowns instead. Here. It will be short on you but much warmer than yours." She rubbed her arms. "There certainly is a chill in the air tonight."

"Thank you," Hester said as she took the offered garment. "But I think I will be quite warm enough between that thick quilt of yours and the way you sleep almost on top of me."

"You're more comfortable than the bed," Mary said, reaching for her own nightgown. "I wish I was as tall as you." She looked down at her bosom. "And I was smaller about the top."

"I think you are beautiful just as you are," Hester said. "I am too thin."

Mary reached from behind and wrapped her arms around her friend's middle. "No," she whispered, pressing the side of her face against Hester's bare back. "You are perfect."

Hester rested her hand atop the pair joined about her middle. "I wish I could live with you always, Mary."

"So do I." Mary gave a quick squeeze before stepping back. "Let's get to bed. At least we have this time together."

"Yes," Hester agreed. It took only a few minutes for both to finish dressing for bed and then get under the covers. As they had every night before, Hester took position on her back while Mary curled up over and around her, one leg draped as if to keep her from leaving the bed. They shared gentle touches, then tender and sometimes passionate kisses before finally settling down. Two more contented teens could not be found in the Empire City that night. Hester gently stroked Mary's hair until they both fell asleep.

"It is quite pleasant to see someone who appreciates their food," Mary's mother said. She gave each of her children a pointed look.

"I don't like peas," Daniel protested.

"There are starving Indians on those reservations out west that would be grateful for those peas," his father said. "Hester, would you like some more?"

"Oh, yes, please." Before anyone else could react, Mary stood up and leaned to fetch the serving dish.

"Mary Elizabeth," her father scolded. "You know better than to reach such as that. Sit down and ask your brother to pass the peas."

"But I was getting them for Hester."

"It is no matter. You still need to mind your manners."

"Why should today be different from any other time?" Tobias asked.

"What did I say to all of you about behaving while Mary's guest is with us?"

"Yes, Father," the children said in unison.

Elizabeth demurely sliced through her beef. "My mother has sent word that she will unable to join us for Thanksgiving dinner."

"Why? Are they refusing to let her out of Bloomingdale?"

She glared at the family patriarch. "Mister Chandler! We have company!" She addressed Hester. "My mother is not insane, child." She looked back at her husband. "And she has never been a patient at Bloomingdale."

Gideon smirked and speared a piece of his food. "If there was ever one deserving of an apartment above Asylum Road, it is Mother Franklin. The woman is as sane as Mayor Tiemann is honest."

Mary's mother dabbed the corners of her mouth. "If you persist with this, Mister Chandler, your next address will be at Bellevue recovering from an unfortunate meeting with Miss Bessie's best rolling pin."

The older children muffled their laughter at the exchange.

"I am sorry, Mrs. Chandler." He shared a conspiratorial look with his eldest son before continuing. "Hester, did you know Mary's mother's family descends from royalty?"

"Truly?"

"Indeed. Why, there is even a wonderful family resemblance."

"Mister Chandler," Mary's mother said in a low, warning tone.

"Mother Franklin looks just like Henry the Eighth."

Tobias, who had been taking a drink at the time, broke into a fit of coughing mixed with laughing. Mary used her hand to cup Hester's ear and whispered what the late monarch looked like, which caused the young guest to use her napkin to hide her smile.

"Even bears a remarkable resemblance to that great statesman, Benjamin Franklin," Gideon added. "Are you certain you're not also related to him, Mrs. Chandler?"

"Later," came the warning to Mary's father from his irritated wife, though she then gave a small smile. "My mother does have the most unfortunate affliction of having whiskers on her chin." She looked at her husband. "However, she does not have a beard," she admonished.

"Mrs. V also has hairs on her chin," Hester said. "Perhaps I should ask her if she is related to King Henry?"

There was a slight pause as the adults tried to maintain their composure before they and the older children, laughed.

"I would not suggest such a thing," Mrs. Chandler said, her eyes twinkling with merriment.

"And if you do," Mary's father said. "Do not indicate that you received the suggestion from us. Your step-mother barely tolerates us now."

"She should not have said that women were put upon this earth to serve men," Elizabeth said, raising her chin haughtily. "I did nothing wrong by correcting her."

"Yes, Mrs. C."

"I'm not certain calling her a backward relic from before man could read and write helped the situation," Gideon said.

"I was being honest," Mary's mother said. "The woman is a poor influence on Hester, Griet, and that daughter of hers." She reached for her glass. "Never believe any of the nonsense that woman tells you, Hester."

"I won't, Mrs. C."

After the fine meal, they retired to the drawing room. Mary guided Hester to the settee, then promptly joined her on the narrow furnishing.

Mary's father turned up the lamps, casting a golden light throughout the room. Mary's mother sat on a cushioned chair with a table filled with magazines and newspapers to the side. Picking one up, she settled in to read. Eleven year-old Daniel opened the wooden box situated in the corner and pulled out a cloth bag. "I want to play dominos," he announced.

"So do I," Judith chimed in.

"I don't want to," Mary said. "Mother, Hester and I are too old to play those children's games."

Mary's mother smiled. "You played with your brother and sister just last week."

"That was different," Mary said, pointedly ignoring the snort from her father. "We should like to play The Mansion of Happiness."

"I've not played that game," Hester said.

Daniel threw the bag of dominos back into the toy box. "I'll get it," he said, scrambling to his feet and tearing across the room to the shelf where the board games were kept.

"It's easy," Judith said, racing back to the parlor to claim her seat at the table. Hester followed Mary and took the seat her friend indicated. She expected the four of them to sit on different sides but Mary had pulled out the chair next to hers. "It'll be easier if I show you," she said by way of explanation. Daniel set the folding game board up on the table along with the ivory teetotum and octagonal plate.

Mary pulled tokens from the box. "I'll be green and you can be blue."

Daniel quickly took the red counter while Judith claimed the yellow wooden playing piece. Despite being the youngest, eleven year-old Daniel was all arms and legs, able to easily reach the teetotum positioned between Judith and the older girls.

The Chandlers being as competitive as they were, had to spin the top-like teetotum to see who would go second, all agreeing their guest should go first. Hester gave the teetotum a spin. "Two," she said when the ivory top stopped. She moved her token to the second octagonal image, which showed a young boy kneeling in prayer next to his bed. "Pie-pie...."

"Piety," Daniel said. "It means being good."

"You get to move ahead six spaces," Judith offered helpfully. Hester did so, putting her piece on a plain green octagon.

"My turn," Daniel announced, spinning the teetotum with far more effort than necessary. When it finally settled down, the number showing was a six. "Water! I move forward to number ten." He slid his piece to the green octagonal space.

"See?" Judith said as she reached for the teetotum. "It's fun."

"As long as you land correctly," Mary said, waiting until her sister reached the third space, a plain green octagonal, before taking the teetotum and giving it a spin. "Four. Honesty. I get to go ahead six spaces."

Hester's next roll put her on the poverty space. "What's that mean?"

Judith answered before her older sister could. "Nothing, because you weren't sent there." She snatched the folded paper from the box and opened it up to read directly from the rules.

"'*Poverty, the Whipping Post, House of Correction, the Pillory, the Stocks, Prison and Ruin are to be considered as blanks in your progress to the Mansion for it would be cruel to punish a person for merely passing such a place; therefore, till one is found guilty of a crime, he cannot be sent to either.*'"

She tossed the paper back in the box. "Your turn, Daniel."

"Four. Oh, no! I landed on passion." Judith and Mary started laughing.

"What happens now?"

This time Mary was the quicker sister, pulling the rule sheet to her bosom before Judith could get hold of it. Making certain her parents were not watching from their chairs in the other room, she stuck her tongue out at her younger sister before reading the rule.

"'*Whoever gets in a Passion must be taken to the Water and have a ducking to cool him.*' Back you go, Daniel."

And so, the game continued. Back and forth they went, virtues moving them forward, sins back. Landing on an already occupied space caused the first person to be sent back to the beginning, an event that caused raucous laughter all three times it happened to Daniel. The one time Hester did that to Mary's green wooden piece, she was treated to a shoulder bump and a whisper. "Just you wait, Hester Pester. I'll get you yet."

Twice Mary ended up in the house of correction and once in the prison but somehow she still managed to make it past ingratitude and the summit of dissipation to land at the sixty-seventh space, the mansion of happiness. "I win," she crowed.

"I wanna play again," Daniel said, grabbing for the tokens and setting them all back at the start position.

"Me, too," Judith said.

"Play by yourselves," Mary said, pushing her chair back from the table. "Hester and I want to play something else."

"What shall we play?" Hester asked.

"Dominoes," Daniel said.

Mary grudgingly agreed and for the next two hours the quartet played hand after hand of the tiled game. There was so much laughter amongst them, that twice the patriarch of the home had to order them to quiet down. Hester had many fond memories of playing games with her cousins, mostly outside, and was certain they would also enjoy dominoes. She decided that when she finally sold her first painting, she would use the money to purchase the game for the family.

Bedtime brought another round of cuddling and kissing. When Hester finally broke for air, both teens were breathing heavily.

"If life truly were like that game," Hester said. "We would most certainly spend all of our time being dunked in the water."

"It would be worth it," Mary said, her hand roaming Hester's middle. "Don't you believe so, too?"

Hester smiled, then gave her answer in the form of another passionate kiss.

Chapter Fourteen

The smile that had been on Mary's face throughout her birthday party was still there when she and Hester retired to the bedroom for the night. "Wasn't it grand?"

Hester nodded. "I've never been to such a party. We've made cakes and had our favorite dinners but oh, my, Mary, it was nothing like yours. I've never even seen a cake so big."

"Mother does so enjoy a party." Flopping onto the bed, she held her feet straight out. "Would you mind? These shoes are so tight."

Hester dutifully knelt down and removed the white shoes. "Why do you wear them if they are uncomfortable?"

"They matched my dress, silly. Oh, but they do make my feet hurt something awful."

"I'm sure Mrs. C. would be quite happy to buy you new ones." As she would do occasionally to her own feet, Hester rubbed the areas she presumed to be sore.

"Oh, my, but that feels so wonderful," Mary said. "Please do go on."

Hands made strong from a life of working about the homestead pressed and massaged to the answering groans of pleasure. "You have soft feet."

Mary laughed and patted her belly. "I have soft everything, Hester." She propped herself up on her elbows, then flopped back down. "And I had far too much cake."

"Miss Bessie made a most wonderful cake."

"Oh, she didn't make it. Mother ordered it from the baker. After all, it is my birthday." She wiggled her right foot. "Do the other one, please."

"As you wish, birthday girl."

"It is too bad your birthday is in February," Mary said. "If it were summer, I would arrange for the finest baker in Catskill to make you such a cake and I would make sure you had even more presents than I received."

Hester shook her head. "There is barely enough room in the house for everyone and everything now. I had hoped with the raising that we would have more room but Mrs. V...."

"The witch."

"That's not nice, Mary."

"But true. She's absolutely dreadful. I don't know how you put up with her." Mary sat up. "That extra room was supposed to be for you girls to have, not that mean little son and horrid daughter of hers. Why should he have a room all of his own when Hendrik, Martin, and Kent are all nearly grown and still share the same bed?"

"There was much yelling about it, but Mrs. V. certainly yells louder than anyone. If Vader had not agreed, she would still be yelling."

"I don't know why he married her, Hester. After all, you and Griet were doing just fine taking care of the house and the boys. Why, you've told me that she doesn't even bother to help with most of the meals. Just stands there and says 'clean this' and 'pick up that' as if you were slaves."

Hester switched back to the left foot. "Let us not become upset about things we cannot change," she said. "I would much rather think about your wonderful birthday. Did you get everything you'd hoped?"

"That's enough," Mary said, gently pulling her foot away. "Come here."

Hester climbed on the bed, sprawling out alongside the birthday girl.

"I wanted only one present for my birthday," Mary said, reaching out and cupping Hester's cheek. "You. I didn't care about a fancy dinner in a fancy restaurant or a party with all those upper crust snobs and their parents." Her thumb strayed to caress Hester's lips. "All I wanted was for you to be here with me. I would have been happy with broth and not one other present otherwise. You are what made my birthday special, Hester. Just you." Their lips met in the most tender of kisses. "Just you."

"I'm so happy to be here, too." They kissed again. "And I'm happy you like your present."

"I love my present," Mary corrected. "The perfume smells so wonderful and the bottle is beautiful. I shall think of you every time I wear it."

Hester gently stroked the soft, blonde hair. "I remember the first time we met," she said softly. "You were all smiles and the sun made your hair just shine. You've grown up into a beautiful woman."

"So have you."

A gentle knock broke through their moment. "Girls?" Elizabeth called. "Time to turn down the lamps and go to sleep."

"Yes, Mother."

Hester stood up first, then held a hand out to pull Mary upright. "Help me with the buttons?"

"I will if you help me with mine."

Hester turned around. "I think it's silly to have buttons up the back. How is anyone supposed to reach them?"

Mary undid the top button. "Because women of my station have people who help us get dressed and undressed. If you weren't here, Miss Sally would be helping me. Some people have servants who do nothing but help their ladies get dressed."

"Griet would pitch a fit if she had to help me get dressed every day."

"I wouldn't mind," Mary said, undoing another button, then kissing the bare skin exposed. Another button, another kiss. "I would do it every night and never complain." With each button opened, she took advantage of the opening to kiss along Hester's backbone. "There."

"Thank you." When Hester turned around, she pulled Mary into her arms and kissed her slowly, gently, pouring her emotions into the moment. "Now, let me help you."

"But you're not out of your dress yet." With that, Mary gently tugged on the sleeves until Hester's arms were freed. The action also exposed the younger teen's breasts, which Mary stared at for several seconds before finishing her task.

Now nude, Hester stepped behind Mary and performed the same ritual, accentuating each button opening with a kiss, plus one on each of the bared shoulders for good measure. When both were naked, Mary blew out the far lamp. The one on the nightstand, she lowered the wick significantly but did not extinguish it.

Hester reached for her nightgown, then stopped when she saw Mary reach for the turned down corner and pull the covers back.

"Come to bed," Mary said softly. "We'll be warm enough."

With the exception of bath time and swimming in the creek, Hester never remained nude for more than the time it took to change clothes. The idea of sleeping without any clothing at once seemed both strange and wonderful. She joined Mary beneath the sheet and quilts, enjoying the sensation of their naked bodies touching.

"Shall I put out the lamp?"

Mary shook her head. "Not yet." Her eyes seemed larger, darker than usual as the dim light cast a soft orange glow on her face. She slid her hand over Hester's middle in slow, lazy circles.

"I love you, Hester."

Hester licked her lips, Mary's hand causing the most wonderful sensations to race through her body. "I love you, too. Always and forever."

Now, when Mary climbed half on top of her, their breasts were not encumbered by layers of material. Mary's full breasts pressed against her own, practically flat ones.

"This feels so nice," Mary murmured.

"Yes."

They pressed together, softness against softness and when they kissed, Hester's hand moved of its own volition to rest against the side of the older teen's ample bosom.

Love and desire, mixed with teenage hormones, took control, telling them without words that what was happening was right, wanted, needed. The kisses became more heated, hands gently squeezed, hips rocked against thighs as they enjoyed the sensations.

"I don't care that we can't be married," Mary whispered, her breath hot against Hester's ear. "I love you the same way a man loves a woman and I know you do, too."

"Yes," Hester whispered, letting her hands slide down to caress Mary's buttocks. She arched her neck at the sensation of warm lips touching her throat. "Yes, Mary. Yes." She was forced to give up her hold on the soft rear when the older teen slid down, their legs intertwining. Her body was on fire with feeling, every inch of skin feeling far more sensitive than ever before.

"Oh, Hester."

Hester could only gasp when Mary's lips closed around her nipple, worrying it into a hardened tip. She believed there could be no greater pleasure, no more exquisite feeling. Certainly she could no longer be on the bed but had to be floating in the air as she lost all sense of thought and could only feel. She repeated Mary's name again and again, unaware of the way her hips were rocking or that her hands were clasping and releasing her love's shoulders.

She knew that any second she was going to die and float away to heaven. Every place that Mary touched, kissed, or licked felt like nothing else Hester had experienced before. Her rare experimentations alone were nothing compared to the inexplicable joy that Mary was giving her. She barely had the presence to put the pillow over her face to muffle the endless litany of sounds that escaped her throat. Her heart was pounding so hard that she swore it could be heard throughout the house. When she was certain she could go no higher, Mary's touch did just that and more, sending her over the edge in cascading waves of joy.

Hester had no control over her body. Her chest was heaving, her heart refusing to slow down, her mouth so dry that she found it impossible to swallow. She could only lie there helplessly, unaware of the tears leaking from the sides of her eyes.

"What's wrong? Did I do something wrong? Hester? Oh, please, don't cry. I'm sorry. Shh, it's all right."

Unable to find her voice, Hester could only shake her head and grasp blindly for her love. It seemed forever that she cuddled in Mary's arms, listening to the rapid heartbeat beneath her ear before she finally regained enough control to speak. "I love you."

She felt Mary's hand wiping the tears from her cheeks. "I love you, too. Why were you crying?"

Pressing her face against Mary's bosom, Hester shook her head. "I don't know."

She took a couple of breaths before continuing. "It was…wonderful. No. Not wonderful. More than wonderful." She felt Mary kiss her forehead. "So much more than wonderful."

Mary gently guided Hester's back onto the bed, then knelt above her. "I love you. And I loved touching you," she added, kissing her gently.

"Come here," Hester whispered, using her arms to pull Mary's body flat against hers. For several minutes they shared gentle kisses, simply enjoying the feeling of their bodies together. Soon enough, the kisses weren't enough and Hester's desire to give the woman she loved the same pleasure she had just received became too great. Their kisses became more passionate, hands moved more purposefully. Mary thrilled at Hester's touch, whispering words of approval at every touch, every action. Hester found herself acting on instinct, seeming to know what would please her lover. They made love twice again before their bodies demanded sleep.

Entering the washroom, they were careful to be quiet so as not to disturb Judith, whose room was on the other side of the far door. After returning to Mary's room and donning their nightgowns, they cuddled together until finally falling asleep in one another's arms.

Turkey, pumpkin, baked goods galore. Hester had never seen so much food at one time in her life, especially for such a small family. She tried to take small portions, but Mary and her father would have none of that. Mister Chandler insisted that it was unacceptable to be able to see any of the plate itself when it came time for the Thanksgiving meal, happily adding yet another slice of the fine bird upon the guest's plate. Platters of food lined not only the table, but a side table, as well.

Hester was certain that Tobias' plate would break under the weight of all that he placed upon it and she could only smile when Mrs. Chandler admonished the younger children to eat their vegetables and meat, as well as the sweet desserts that were served alongside the main dishes.

"Now, Hester, before we each eat enough food to feed half of the city," Gideon said. "We like to go around the table and have each person tell us what they are most thankful for. Tobias, please start us out."

"I'm grateful for my family and all this food," he said.

Seated next to his older brother, Daniel decided the usual oldest to youngest didn't apply and went next. "I'm thankful we haven't had any oatmeal since Hester came to visit." Everyone laughed. "And for Mother and Father."

"What about your brother and sisters?" their mother asked.

"Oh, sure. Them, too."

Elizabeth smiled and shook her head. "I am grateful for my wonderful husband and children, this beautiful home that we live in, that everyone is healthy, and that we had Hester come visit us this year." She smiled at Hester. "I feel as though I have three daughters."

"Don't go having any ideas," Gideon said, causing more laughter. "Judith?"

"I'm thankful for my family and that Grandmother Franklin isn't here to yell at Father."

"Judith!" Elizabeth hissed.

"But it's true!"

"You've taught her to speak her mind," Gideon said to his wife. "Hester?"

"I am thankful for so many things that I don't know where to begin. I'm thankful for my family and that everyone is healthy, of course, and I am very thankful that you were so kind as to invite me here. Thank you for all the wonderful clothes and all the supplies so that I can paint more and for taking me to all those places. Thank you for coming to the Mountain House each year so I can see Mary."

She looked at Mary. "I'm most thankful for Mary. She's like a sister to me and I just can't imagine my life without her."

"That was nice," Elizabeth said.

"I'm thankful for my family," Mary said. "I'm thankful you let Hester come and give me the best birthday present I ever had. And I'm very thankful for Hester."

Gideon finished the thanks giving with the appropriate appreciation for his children and wife, then added in a louder voice that he was grateful to Miss Bessie for making such a wonderful meal. With that, he led them in grace and the feeding frenzy was on.

Hester was amazed and quite touched that both *appeltaart* and appelbollen were served. She made certain to compliment Bessie on not only the wonderful meal, but on perfectly recreating the Dutch desserts. She and Mary quickly became engrossed in a detailed explanation of both the differences and the similarities of their holiday meals. Mrs. Chandler asked Hester to share more recipes with Miss Bessie, which the teen happily obliged.

As happened every fall at the Mountain House, the time to part came far too soon. Despite Mary's attempts to prolong the visit, her parents insisted that Hester had to return to Palenville.

Hester and Mary hugged fiercely as Old Jack struggled to remove the Saratoga trunk from the back of the carriage. Tobias ended up having to help him so it didn't fall.

"I don't want you to go," Mary said.

"I don't want to go either, but we'll see one another again in June," Hester promised. "And I will have that new portrait done by the time you arrive."

"That's so far away."

Hester took Mary's hands in hers. "We'll send posts and you know I will think of you often," she said.

"It won't be the same," Mary replied. "I became used to having you here."

Gideon put his hands on his eldest daughter's shoulders. "Mary Elizabeth. You are no longer a child. It's time for Hester to return home and you have to accept that. Hester, we enjoyed your company tremendously. I hope you will be able to come again for another visit."

"Thank you, Mister Chandler." She let go of Mary's hands and turned to face Elizabeth. "Thank you so very much for the clothes and everything, Mrs. C."

Mary's mother smiled indulgently at Hester. "It was a true pleasure to have you visit with us. I wish we had allowed Mary to have you come earlier."

"You will come visit again next year, perhaps," Mary's father said. Two porters arrived and reached for the shiny new trunk. "Now, be careful with that."

"Griet is going to be so surprised when she sees all that new cloth," Hester said. "Thank you again."

"As I've said before, I believe that were your mother still alive and capable of doing the same for her daughter's most special friend, she would without a moment's concern. I would not show those writings from Miss Anthony and Miss Truth to your step-mother, however. I suspect she would prefer those to become fuel for the stove than to be read."

"Or the outhouse," Gideon added.

"Yes, Mrs. C."

Mary's mother reached into her reticule, pulling out a small pile of coins wrapped in cloth. "Now, Hester, you must promise that when you arrive, you shall go directly to the telegraph office and send word."

"I will not be able to stop my daughter from wearing a hole in the carpet otherwise," Mary's father said.

"I will."

"There is a little extra in there should you and your uncle wish to dine in Catskill before returning home," Elizabeth said. "Your uncle is picking you up, is he not?"

"I believe so," Hester said. "If not him, it will be Kent or one of the boys. They know when to expect my return."

"Very well. You show Kent that book Mister Chandler purchased for him and make certain he understands that an improvement in his penmanship and reading is expected by next summer."

"Yes, Mrs. C."

The conductor announced that it was time to board.

"I wish you weren't leaving," Mary said as she pulled Hester into one final hug. "I wish you would stay forever."

"I wish I could, too," Hester said, squeezing back just as fiercely. "I'll see you in June."

"June twenty-fifth," Mary reminded her.

"June twenty-fifth. I'll be there. I promise."

They looked at one another for several seconds, silently conveying the words they could not say with Mary's parents standing so near. Reluctantly, Hester turned and stepped into the train.

Once she found her seat, she looked out the window, watching as Mary was being led back to the carriage. She didn't need to see the older teen's face to know she was crying. Tears rolled down Hester's cheeks as the train left the station. It was a long, lonely ride back to Catskill.

Chapter Fifteen

Hester passed the time waiting by doing what so many other artists had done during the past thirty years, sketching a picture of the grand Catskill Mountain House. The white, wide-brimmed hat Mrs. Chandler had purchased her the previous fall helped keep the sun from her eyes and the new sketchpad, with its firm cardboard backing, made the perfect medium to draw the first day of the season for the famed resort.

Despite keeping busy with her work, the day seemed to move far too slowly before the welcoming sound of the carriage reached her ears. By the time it came up the drive, Hester had her pencils and pad back in her bag and was concentrating on not running up to the coach.

Mary was the first one out, ignoring all manner of protocol, running to Hester. They shared a perfectly acceptable kiss between good friends, careful not to allow it to go beyond propriety.

"I've missed you so much," Hester said.

"I've missed you more."

They had to stay outside for a little bit while the trunks were taken inside and Mister Chandler registered them for the season. It gave Hester time to hug Mary's mother and Judith, as well as say hello to Sally, who was no longer a nursemaid but had been kept on by the family in the capacity of being Mrs. Chandler's maid and lady-in-waiting.

Finally Gideon came out and announced which room Mary and Judith were going to be sharing. A quick excuse about wanting to show Hester a new magazine allowed the girls to make their escape and go into the Mountain House.

Once in the privacy of the room, Hester hugged Mary gently, moving her hands up and down the warm back covered with only a thin layer of muslin. "I love you," she whispered into Mary's neck.

"I love you, too," Mary said, pulling her head back so she could look into Hester's eyes. For several seconds they looked into one another's eyes, seeing and revealing their souls. The silent agreement made, Mary hesitated no more in bringing their lips together. Seven months of physical separation melted away as they kissed.

Even being on the third floor of the Mountain House was not a guarantee of privacy from the outdoors. As they continued to express their feelings through their caresses and kisses, both made certain to keep from being in a position to be seen through the window.

"Well, now," Mary said breathlessly when they finally separated. "That's the best welcome I've ever had."

"It's a welcome I'm happy to give."

Their private time was interrupted by the sound of the rest of the family coming up the hall. Judith came in, prattling on about how unfair it was that this was their ninth summer at the Mountain House and she was still forced to share a room. When Mary pointed out that Tobias and Daniel were still sharing a room, it did nothing to assuage the younger girl's indignation. Not interested in hearing anymore about how unfair life was to the disgruntled fourteen-year-old, Hester and Mary left the room in search of another place to be alone together.

But it was not to be. While few people were there for opening day, there were still enough members of New York's elite that Elizabeth insisted Mary had to come and politely socialize. It seemed every time Mary would finish talking with one, another was there. Much to the eighteen - year-old's consternation, several had sons whom, according to their mothers, were the cream of the crop and perfect candidates to court Mary. As much as she wanted to tell these mothers that she already knew their boys, most being friends of Tobias, and what dullards they were, propriety dictated that she simply smile and nod. There were also other young debutantes who ran in the Chandler's social circle, casual friends of Mary, and they had much to talk about. Mostly, it was about the opposite sex, of course.

When they finally broke away, it was time for Hester to leave. They walked down the mountain road to the big bent tree, one of their favorite private spots. There they managed a few kisses and a promise from Hester to return as soon as she was able.

When Hester returned home, she was shocked to see her trunk, the Saratoga trunk given to her by the Chandlers and containing her private belongings, wide open with her things scattered across the bed. "What is going on?"

"I tried to stop her," Griet said apologetically.

Her step-mother crossed her arms and glared at Hester. "I thought it was high time I took a look at what you've been hiding in there." She grabbed the lacy dress Hester had been given to wear to the theater. The dress that Mrs. Chandler herself had fawned over and said looked so beautiful. The dress that matched the hat that Hester currently was wearing.

"That's mine."

"You don't wear it," her step-mother said, tossing the garment back onto the bed. "Too fancy for these parts, anyhow. Better to give it to Miss Lilly to cut up and make somethin' more appropriate. She might even throw in something extra, just for getting such fanciness."

"No! That's mine and I'm saving it for a special occasion." Hester walked past her nemesis and collected her things to put back in the trunk.

When she picked up the beaded reticule, it felt far too light. A quick shake told her why. She whirled to face the older woman. "Where's my money? What did you do with it? Give it back! You had no right nor cause to take it!"

"You had no right nor cause to be hiding that money! Pret' nigh four dollars there." She wagged her pudgy finger at Hester. "Now, I don't get to have no say about those cousins of yours, but I'm your mother. What I say goes."

"You are not my moeder!" Hester screamed, her feeling about having her privacy violated rising above any thought of respect for an adult. "You're just a mean, rotten woman who married my vader and does nothing that a true moeder would do around here. Griet and I are more moeders in this family than you ever were."

"You horrible, horrible child!" Before Hester could react, Mrs. Van Wyck snatched the framed photograph of Hester and Mary and sent it hurling at the fireplace. "This is all because you spend your time with that rich girl and her family! No more! I forbid you to see them again."

The door opened and Kent hobbled in. "What's going on?"

"You just mind your business," Mrs. Van Wyck said to him.

Shocked, Hester picked up the treasured photograph. The glass had shattered and to her horror, the force of the impact against the stone left a small gouge on Mary's image. Tears sprang to her eyes as the years of putting up with her step-mother finally became too much.

"She stole my money," she said to Kent. She held the photograph out angrily. "Look what you did! You're a mean, rotten woman and I'm not going to stay here any longer."

"Why you...." The older woman slapped Hester just as Hendrik and Martin reached the doorway.

Hendrik moved first, stepping between his cousin and her step-mother. "What's wrong?"

"I've had enough of her and her attitude," his aunt said.

Tears streaming down her face, Hester moved from behind him and carefully placed the photograph in her trunk. Martin came in and formed a second human barrier between her and her step-mother. With the twins turning twenty, they were big and burly enough to form an intimidating pair. They also shared their cousin's dislike for the woman.

Hester threw her belongings into her trunk, including her nightgown and other daily dress. Her carpetbag, the new, gaily colored carpetbag that Mrs. Chandler had so carefully picked out for her, was also opened so she shoved items into it. "Would one of you please go to Uncle Michael's and have him bring his buggy?"

"I'll get Uncle Pieter," Kent said before limping off toward the studio.

"You're leaving?" Martin asked.

Hester sniffled. "I can't take it anymore," she said. "She went through my things and stole all the money I've been saving."

"Give her back her money," Hendrik said.

"No! She has no business having that much money and keeping it from us."

"It's hers," he said.

"Not anymore. If she wants to leave, all the better. Always disrespecting me and acting all special because of that rich girl being her friend. I'll not have it any longer.

Girl her age should be married, not playing with paints and running off to visit her friend all the time."

Hester tossed her satchel in the trunk, then closed the latches.

Griet ran to the doorway. "Uncle Pieter! She took Hester's money and broke Hester's photograph. Hester wants to move to Uncle Michael's."

"What? No one's moving anywhere." Pieter entered the house. "Mrs. Van Wyck, now you had no reason to take that money. Give it back to her."

"No! And don't you go taking her side again. I'm your wife and she's supposed to be honoring her mother and father just like the Bible says. This is all your fault, putting those fool ideas in her head about being an artist and letting her have that rich girl as a friend."

"They've been friends since Hester was a little girl," he said. "Hester, honey, please stop crying."

Hester sniffled and wiped at her face. "I can't stay here anymore with her, Vader. I just can't."

Martin put his hand on his cousin's shoulder. "I'll help Hendrik take your trunk outside and then I'll go get Uncle Michael."

"Boys, just don't be going and doing nothing right now," Pieter said. "Let's…let's just sit down and talk about this."

"She wants to go, go!" Mrs. Van Wyck said. "You want to choose playing with your foolish brushes and pretending to be rich like your friend, then go! Puttin' those foolish ideas about women having rights and such into my daughter's head. Why, it just goes right against God, that's what. Right against God."

"Vader." Hester wiped her eyes. "Do you think, if I stay, that things will ever get better or will it always be like this?" They looked at one another silently for a moment before she lowered her head. "Boys, please take my trunk outside. I'm finished."

Griet hugged her cousin. "Oh, Hester, I wish you wouldn't go."

"I have to," Hester said, wiping ineffectually at her tears. "I just have to."

She turned to face her step-mother. "You want my money so much?" she asked. "Then keep it. It's worth every pence to know I'll never have to see you again."

With Hendrik and Martin carrying the trunk and leading the way, and Griet and Kent behind her, Hester exited the house.

The boys carried the trunk to the studio. While Hester filled it with her art supplies and as many of her canvases as she could roll and fit inside the trunk, Martin took off at a run to his uncle's house a mile up the road. Even from across the yard, the shouts from inside the house carried to them, mostly Mrs. Van Wyck's shrill voice, though occasionally they could hear Pieter speaking back at her.

"I wish I could go with you," Griet said. "God have mercy on me, but I hate that woman."

"Me, too," Hendrik said.

"Remember when I lost that bag of coins I had?" Kent asked. "Why, I probably didn't lose it at all. I reckon she took it. After that, I started hiding my money under that rock on the back side of the studio and ain't never lost any more since then."

Hester nodded. "I reckon you're right about that," she said.

Pieter came out from the house and walked to them. The Voss family decided to wait by the road, giving Hester and her father some time alone.

"I wish you wouldn't go," he said.

Hester nodded. "I know, Vader. But I have to."

He looked down. "I know. I suppose I knew you'd have to leave someday but I never thought it would be 'cause of her."

"You can always come up and visit," she said.

"I will," he replied. "I'm sure Michael will let you have one of those empty rooms for a studio of your very own."

Painting was the last thing on her mind but she nodded in agreement anyway. "They…they could use a woman's touch. The good Lord knows the last time they gave that house a proper cleaning."

"If I had known how she really was…." He shook his head and looked away. "Lord, forgive me for saying this, but I wished I'd never married her." He put his hand on her shoulder. "I thought you needed a mother after Frances died. I never thought…." He shook his head again. "I never thought she'd be like this. That she would cause you to leave."

"I'll just be up at Uncle Michael's," she said. "I'm not going off to the city."

"If you did, you'd have your paintings in a gallery in no time, I just know it. Find yourself a good man who'd put you in a nice house and take care of you the way I wish I could."

"I love you, Vader." The tears came as they hugged, not letting go until Will arrived with Martin in the buggy. Hester hugged her cousins, who all promised to come visit as often as they could. Kent even offered to move with her, but Griet said she needed him to stay with her.

Not one member of the Voss family spoke to their aunt for the better part of a week after Hester left. Even then it was always a short, clipped answer belying the tension that permeated through their home.

Once Michael heard Hester's side of the story, and that her father approved of her moving out, he was more than happy to have his niece live with him and Will. There were several empty rooms within his old farmhouse, though he lacked any sort of a mattress for her to sleep on.

Will offered his bed to her, but she refused, insisting she would not make her older cousin sleep on the sofa or with their uncle. Michael and Will gathered as many blankets and quilts as they could, even throwing an old bearskin rug into the pile to make a soft place for her to sleep until a trip to the mercantile could be made to purchase a mattress.

A corner room upstairs provided plenty of light once she washed the windows and became her own private studio. The back room, as it was called, was a catch-all for furniture that wasn't good enough to be sold but was too good to be turned into kindling. Thus Hester ended up with her own chest of drawers and a wobbly dressing table. A copy of Godey's wedged under one leg solved that problem.

While Michael was too old-fashioned to approve of women voting or having equal rights to men, he and Will had lived without a female in the house for more than a decade and, while they didn't keep the cleanest house in Palenville, they'd managed to get by. Thus it was worked out that it was just as easy for the three of them to split up chores that normally would have all fallen to Hester. For the cooking, washing of the dishes, and sweeping the floors, that was fine. However, once she saw how they handled washing their clothes, or rather, how they dunked their clothes into the water and then hung them on the line to dry, she insisted on taking that chore upon herself alone.

When Griet came to visit, she brought along the requested needle and thread so they could spend an afternoon mending their cousin and uncle's garments. By the end of that first week, Hester was happier than she had been in a long time, though she still missed her father and the Voss family.

The biggest advantage to moving in with Michael and Will was having easy access to the buggy. Rather than having to walk three miles down the road, another mile to the Mountain Road, and then three miles up to the

Mountain House, she only had to pay the toll and Will was able to drive her up in a fraction of the time. The money for the toll came as a gift to her from Kent, who would stop by regularly and keep her updated on the goings on at the Voss household.

Mary was furious. "How dare she!" She was so mad that she took the side of her fist and pounded the square railing supporting the portico. "She took your money?"

Hester nodded. She had never seen Mary's face so red, nor heard such a litany of vile and imaginative insults hurled with more venom than a rattlesnake.

"If I was there, I would have taken a frying pan to her head. How dare she do such a thing!"

"But it's better now," Hester said. "I love living with Uncle Michael and Will. They even take turns with me, doing the cooking and dishes." She took a step closer and lowered her voice. "And I have my own room now."

Mary was too angry to follow that statement to the obvious conclusion. "She just bumped you out. From your own home!"

"No. I chose to leave. She didn't make me."

"Goodness gracious, but she most certainly did!"

"What is all this yelling about?" Mrs. Chandler said as she came down the front steps. "I can hear you clear to the far side, Mary."

"That shriveled up old witch went into Hester's things and stole her money," Mary said. "She even tried to throw our photograph into the fire."

"There was no fire," Hester explained. "She threw it against the fireplace and broke the glass."

"Why would she do a thing like that?"

"Because she's a shriveled up old witch, that's why," Mary snarled. "Hester had to go move in with her Uncle."

"What? Child, tell me what happened."

Hester explained, again leaving out the detail of the slap. "But it's real nice at Uncle Michael's. I have my own room now, plus another one to use as a studio."

"That wretched woman," Elizabeth said. "Mary, go fetch my coin purse. How much money did she take from you?"

"I had more than four dollars saved up," Hester said.

"Where did you get so much money?" Mrs. Chandler asked as Mary went into the Mountain House.

Hester gave an embarrassed smile. "When you sent the money for my ferry and train tickets, you gave me too much and told me to keep it, remember? And then, when I went home and had that extra money that you said to go out to dinner, we didn't go, so I put that away, too. I was saving it to buy Mary another present this year for her birthday."

Elizabeth took the teen's hand in hers. "You are such a precious girl, Hester. Your mother would be so proud of you."

Hester wasn't sure what to say to that. "Thank you, Mrs. C."

"Now then, you mustn't worry about the money. I will replace it." She held up her hand to forestall any protest. "Mister Chandler and I gave you that money and we certainly don't take kindly to someone stealing it. Do you need anything else?"

Hester looked away, thinking of the blankets she was using as a makeshift bed. "No, Mrs. C. I am quite comfortable."

"I have known you since you were younger than Daniel is now and I can tell you are hiding something," Elizabeth said.

"Uncle Michael has been most generous with me," Hester said. "Truly, I do not need anything."

"Hmm."

Hester knew Mrs. Chandler did not believe her, but hoped the older woman would not pursue it. She was grateful for all that her uncle had done to make her feel welcome and was loathe to do anything to that would make him feel otherwise.

"I will have Mister Chandler ask Mister Beach to allow one of his coaches to take you home tonight."

"Oh, no, Mrs. C. My cousin Will is going to come pick me up near four o'clock. Uncle Michael has the buggy and horse."

"Oh, yes, that he does. Very well. Ah, here she is. Give me that, Mary." Elizabeth opened her reticule and removed several bills. "Here, now, take this. Tut tut tut, It is a gift, child. You do know that it is considered impolite to refuse a gift."

"Yes, Mrs. C." Hester took the money, realizing even as she was putting it into her pocket that it was more than she had lost. "Thank you most kindly, Mrs. C."

Elizabeth smiled. "It is my pleasure. Now if you will excuse me, I need to speak with Mister Chandler. Mary Elizabeth, no more of those outbursts. People will talk."

"Yes, Mother. Come along, Hester. I want to show you something in my room."

The second the door was closed, they were kissing. "I'm still mad at that old witch," Mary said when they parted. "But I am very happy you are away from her. She's such a dreadful creature."

Hester held Mary in a loose embrace. "I am, too."

Mary cocked her head. "Did you say you have your own room?"

"Yes. Upstairs. Will and Uncle Michael have their rooms downstairs. I have my own studio room now, too."

"Your own room." A slow smile spread across Mary's face. "I can't wait to come for a visit."

Hester returned the smile. "I think it will be more enjoyable than sharing a bed with Griet."

Mary kissed Hester's chin, then her throat. "I certainly hope so."

"But I should tell you that I don't have a bed yet. Just a bunch of blankets and quilts. Oh, and a big bear rug on the bottom."

"So, I'll buy you the best bed Catskill has to offer."

Hester shook her head. "No. Your mother gave me money to replace what I had lost. I was saving it for something special but I think there's enough for me to buy my own bed now. Uncle Michael would have bought me one once he was paid for the order at the mill, anyway. You needn't worry."

"Speaking of beds." Mary kissed her, then guided her away from the wall and to the bed. Once they were sprawled on the soft covers, they continued to kiss some more before Mary propped herself on one elbow and rested her head against her hand. "So tell me everything again. I promise not to hit anything this time."

Hester retold the story, but quickly learned it was not Mary's indignation she had to worry about but rather the older teen's roving hand, which was touching her in a most delightful way through the thin material of the homemade dress. Soon any discussion about the recent events was discarded in favor of continuing the fun they'd had the previous fall. Careful to remain fully clothed in case Judith arrived, they still managed to arouse one another significantly before they agreed to stop before they went too far.

"You are a temptress," Hester said breathlessly, sitting up and adjusting her dress.

"Oh? I'm sorry. Was that my hand that went down the front of my dress and was touching my—"

"All right," Hester smiled. "But I couldn't resist. They were right there." She leaned, gave Mary a quick kiss, then sat up again. "Tell me about your winter and spring. Did you do anything interesting?"

"Not since you left," Mary said, sitting up, as well. "Father is focused on the election and with the South threatening to secede. Don't ask him about either or he'll go into one of his sermons."

"I doubt anyone in my family knows who Mister Lincoln is."

"Oh! Did I tell you that old man Batchelder brought a case of wine with him this year? He shared some with some other men and they were singing so loudly in the dining room that Mister Beach himself had to come down and tell them to be quiet. You know how he feels about spirits."

"Did your father see them?"

"He didn't see them but he heard them. We were all treated to a temperance lecture this morning after breakfast. I'm sure Mister Batchelder barricaded himself in his room lest someone break in and destroy whatever he still has. The way he was singing last night, I doubt he could have much left."

"Uncle Michael enjoys his wine but he never starts singing." Hester shook her head. "I've heard him at Christmas though and I'm glad he only does it once a year."

"Tobias sings very nicely, but Daniel sounds like someone rocked on his foot with the rocking chair." Mary shrugged. "Judith and I sing well, I suppose."

"You did when we were little girls," Hester said. "How many hours did we spend singing *Kittie Put the Kettle On*?"

Mary laughed. "Not as much as when we played *Miss Mary Mack*."

"Whatever happened to Betsy Ross?"

"I gave her to Judith and I think after that Miss Bessie gave it to her granddaughter. I'm not sure."

As the day moved on, the teens continued to lounge on the bed and chat about whatever came to mind. They also made sure to take the time to share kisses and sometimes risqué touches. Before they wanted it, four o'clock arrived. They said their reluctant goodbyes with Hester promising to return in a few days.

Hester stepped back from the canvas and studied it with a practiced eye. She was convinced her father would be pleased with the effort. The Mountain House gleamed with white except where shadows cast a gray tint. However, rather than the typical image highlighting the splendor of the grand resort, Hester concentrated on the bastion of the women, the portico.

Between the Grecian columns, several women decked out in a sea of white finery were chatting and holding fans. Below the stairs and always shaded by the decking, children played with jacks and blocks while others were reading. She made sure to include the nursemaids who watched the children while their mothers discussed everything from the latest fashions to, in the case of Mary's mother, temperance, suffrage, and emancipation. Hester had tried to work an image of Mary into the painting but in the end decided that her love deserved to always be the centerpiece of the art, not just another character within a sea of people.

Dipping her brush into the black paint, she added "H. Van Wyck" to the bottom right corner, then cleaned her brushes.

She was just finishing up when she heard the carriage come up the road. Looking down from the open window, she was surprised to see that it was one of the coaches from the Mountain House. Then she spied the familiar blonde head inside. "Mary."

"Mary's here," she announced as she raced down the steps. Upon receiving no answer, she remembered that

Michael and Will were spending the day with Kent in the woodshop. A quick run of her fingers through her hair and smoothing the front of her dress were required before she opened the door.

To her surprise, all the Chandler women, even Sally, had come. "Hello. Welcome."

She and Mary exchanged hugs and a friendly kiss before Hester shared hugs with Mrs. Chandler and Judith. "Please, come in."

"I wished to see for myself what your situation was like," Elizabeth said as she entered the house. Removing her hat, she handed it to Miss Sally, who put it on the rack next to the door. Mary was more casual, tossing hers, along with her gloves, onto the counter. Judith mimicked her sister, though since she did not have gloves to worry about, only had to remove her hat.

"May I offer some cider or perhaps cold tea?"

"I believe the cider would do quite nicely," Elizabeth said. "It is dreadfully hot today and I must say that my tolerance for the Mountain Road grows thinner each year, if it is indeed possible to dislike that poor excuse for a route any more than I do already."

Hester pulled out the chairs surrounding the birch table, gesturing for the four women to sit.

"Thank you, but I prefer to stand," Elizabeth said, then gestured at Sally. "My dear, please do not stand on formality. I'm certain you are just as much, if not more so, uncomfortable than I after that ride. You would think with all the money Mister Beach has, that he could put in a decent road."

"Thank you, Mrs. C.," Sally said, gratefully taking the closest chair and sitting down.

Hester handed her the first glass, then served Mary, Mrs. Chandler and Judith. It was a deliberate act on her part , since she had seen, during her visit to the Chandlers, that the servants always ate after the family. Even in the

174

previous years when the Chandlers had come to visit the Voss household, Sally and the coachman, usually Silas, took their plates to go eat out of sight of the others.

"It certainly is bright and airy," Elizabeth said, slowly moving about the kitchen. She opened one cabinet, then another. "Plenty of dishes for everyone to eat at once. I never did understand why you had so few plates at the other house."

"Just never seemed necessary to get more," Hester said. "We just took turns."

Elizabeth arched an eyebrow and continued her inspection. "You cook on this stove?"

"Yes, Mrs. C."

"I suppose it serves the purpose," she said, eyeing the utensils, then the glasses. "Still, it does indeed seem an improvement on the other house."

"Mother didn't like going inside your old home," Judith added helpfully. "Just like she didn't like Mrs. Van Wyck."

"I suspect that is a sentiment shared by many," her mother said.

After declaring that it was clear that the home lacked a woman's touch, Elizabeth insisted on seeing Hester's room. There, no amount of protestations from Hester would appease the older woman from the opinion that it was unfit for a young lady.

"But I am going to have Uncle Michael purchase me a bed when he goes to town the day after next."

"And what about curtains? Those rags on the windows have no doubt been there since the war of independence. I understand your uncle is trying, but he would have no better idea what curtains to purchase than he would which parasol is in style."

"I suppose I will get them in time," Hester said.

"Nonsense. Miss Sally, make a list. Come. We'll start with her bedroom." The servant dutifully followed while a flabbergasted Hester returned to the kitchen with Mary and Judith.

"Don't bother trying to stop her," Judith said. "She has a bee in her bonnet."

"More like a hornet," Mary said. "You should have heard what she had to say when we went past the Voss home. I'm surprised she didn't have Mister Silas stop so she could get out and tell your step-mother what she thought of her."

"Oh! Mister Silas!" Hester had completely forgotten about him. She quickly took one of Michael's largest glasses and filled it with cold tea. "Excuse me."

After giving the grateful coachman the drink, she took the teens on a tour of the house. Everyone liked her newest painting. Mrs. Chandler even indicated that it would go well in the parlor at their home so she could look at in the winter months and remember how nice Catskill was.

Hester excused herself to go tell her uncle and cousins of the Chandler's arrival. The men stopped their work and came into the house, at which point Mrs. Chandler went on about how pleasant it was that he had taken his niece in after the incident but that if he didn't mind, she would like to purchase just a few things to make Hester's room a bit more comfortable, such as some perfumed soaps and things that a woman of Hester's age ought to have.

Always the gentleman, Michael agreed and thanked her most wholeheartedly for her generosity. He insisted they stay for an early supper before returning to the Mountain House. The table held six, so Kent offered to eat in the parlor with Miss Sally and Mister Silas.

As soon as they were finished eating, Mary asked if Hester would show her the studio again.

"You know Mother will not stop with curtains and soaps," she said once the door closed and they were alone.

"I know, but how can I tell her no?"

Mary smiled and moved closer, putting her arms around Hester's neck. "You do seem to have that problem with Chandler women, don't you?"

Hester smiled, putting her arms around Mary's back. "At least one particular Chandler," she said before bringing their lips together.

"As soon as you have a bed, I'm going to insist on being able to come up for a few days," Mary said, putting gentle kisses along the line of Hester's jaw. "And nights," she whispered.

"I love you, my Mary Berry."

"I love you, too, my Hester Pester."

They remained in their loving embrace for a few more seconds before silently acknowledging that they had to return downstairs. Far too soon, the carriage pulled away.

"She's a good woman," Michael said, his hands deep into the soapy water. "It's nice to see someone who cares about you so much."

"Yes," Hester agreed. "Mary is the best friend I could ever ask for."

"Mary? I was talking about Mrs. Chandler," he said.

"Oh, yes. She is wonderful."

"If I didn't know any better, I'd reckon you were one of her own kin, the way she treats you." He put the final dish on the rack. "Here, get the door for me, please."

"Yes, Uncle." Watching him carry the heavy bucket of water out to dump it rather than making her do it, Hester smiled. As much as she missed her father and cousins, despite them visiting regularly, she knew she had made the right decision. Thinking about what the privacy of her own room gave her, she knew, without a doubt, that she would never move back to the Voss home.

Three days later, Hester was again in her studio when she heard an approaching wagon. She heard it long before she saw it and quickly realized there was too much clanging noise coming from it to be one of the sturdy coaches from the Mountain House. It sounded much more like one of the traveling purveyors of wares that occasionally would come around to sell rural folk various housewares. Putting her brush into the jar of water to keep the paint from drying, she removed her smock and headed downstairs.

The wagon was from the mercantile and to her surprise, the twins were sitting on the back. Martin jumped off first.

"Mister Griffin thought you still lived with us and that the address was wrong because the order said to go to the Van Wyck farm," he said.

Hendrik stood up and pushed wooden crates to the back. "Hey, Hester! This is quite the load here. We figured we'd better come and help Mister Griffin get it all in."

"How much is there?" she asked as the boys unloaded three wooden crates filled with items. Over the side walls of the wagon, she could easily see a mattress but couldn't make out what the other items were.

"I think she bought out the whole mercantile," Martin said. "Mister Griffin said some of this is from the mill, too."

"Hoo wee, but this smells awful pretty," Hendrik said, stopping in front of her to show her the contents of the crate in his hands. "All those pretty soaps and oils and even those powder puff things."

"Put them on the table, please," she said.

Will and Michael came out from the barn and joined them.

"Looks like Mrs. Chandler done bought you a whole house worth," Michael said. "Will, go help your cousins."

"I-I can't believe it," she said. Mister Griffin was more than happy to stand by and let the strapping young men do all the hard work. "Mister Griffin, this is all from Mrs. Chandler? For me?"

The portly man looked down at his paper. "For Miss Hester Van Wyck from Mrs. Gideon Chandler. Deliver to the Van Wyck Farm. That's you, that's her, and that's here."

Martin climbed back into the wagon. "Will, give me a hand with this."

Michael reached into the wagon and pulled out one of the crates. "Come on, boys, let's get her things out of there so Johan can finish his deliveries."

"What deliveries?" Johan said. "This is all for her." He gestured at the wagon. "All that cloth, those sewing notions, even those fancy copper pots."

"Oh, no!" Hester exclaimed. "This is too much. Just too much."

"Ha!" Hendrik said. "You should have seen Mrs. V's face when he pulled up. Kent told him that you lived with Uncle Michael now and everything had to go up here. She was so mad. I bet Uncle Pieter got a talking to."

"Hendrik, help us," Will said. Together, the three young men hoisted the trundle bed from the wagon.

"Wait until Kent sees this," Martin said. "You know he's gonna want to make one for himself so he doesn't have to sleep with us anymore."

Michael nodded. "I wouldn't mind learning how to make those myself."

"You do and give me a better price than I get in Albany and I'll buy it from you," Mister Griffin said. "I've sold four of these already this year. Wouldn't have thought there'd be as much call as this."

Hester was shocked by the transformation. Her pile of blankets were neatly stacked in the corner and a gleaming new bed was in their place. The smell of the soaps was overpowering. Two had caused her to sneeze

BL Miller

repeatedly so she put those in one of the unused rooms. There was more than enough material to make both light and heavy curtains for several rooms and with the wicker basket full of sewing notions, she was certain she would never again want for a needle or thread.

For the first time in her life, Hester sat on a new bed. A bed that was purchased just for her. No straw, grass, or old rags filled it. Only soft feathers plumped near to overstuffing. She ran her hand over the soft quilt. A new one had come with the bed but she preferred the one Michael had given her, made with love by her great-grandmother. Unbidden, tears came to her eyes as the feelings became overwhelming.

When she went to the Mountain House the next day, the tears started again. No matter how many times Mrs. Chandler tried to tell her that it was all right, that all the gifts were just a little something for her, Hester could not stop thanking her and repeating how grateful she was.

When the Chandlers came as a family to visit the following week, Hester broke out the new pots, spending most of the morning in the kitchen with Griet to make sure that there was plenty of food for everyone.

The Voss family came, followed later by Pieter, willing to incur his wife's wrath for the pleasure of spending time with family and friends.

Gideon surprised the men with a box of fine cigars, causing much coughing among the younger men and an admonishment from Elizabeth that twelve year-old Daniel was still too young for such things. However, since she was inside most of the time, the pre-teen was able to sneak a few puffs from his older brother and their friends.

The creek was wider and deeper behind the farm and a large branch that hung out above the water provided the perfect location for a rope swing. The six boys made enough noise splashing and yelling that it easily reached the house and Mrs. Chandler swore they could probably have been heard all the way to Catskill.

A delightfully cool breeze allowed Hester, Griet, and Sally to work comfortably in the kitchen with the windows open, while the Chandler women sat around the table. The bowl of biscuits quickly disappeared as the conversation flowed. Miss Sally insisted on helping with the second batch, showing the girls an old southern recipe she had learned from her mother. Griet insisted it would become part of the Voss family diet from that point onward.

Keeping in mind Gideon Chandler's feelings about temperance, the Voss and Van Wyck men took turns slipping into the barn for a nip from a jug hidden within. Even Silas managed to sneak in there a time or three.

The Chandler women and Miss Sally all agreed that Hester's redecorated bedroom was wonderful and the curtains she and Griet had made were just as nice as any found in the stores of New York City. Hester admitted that they had help when Miss Lilly up the road heard about the delivery and that they never would have thought to add the ruffles, were it not for her.

Mary and Hester even found time to be alone despite the gaggle of people milling about. There was a slide lock on the bedroom door but they dared not use it lest someone come up and ask why they had locked themselves in. Instead, they contented themselves with heated kisses, a few caresses, and a promise from Mary that she would come stay for a few days very soon.

Since the table was too small in the kitchen to seat everyone and even sending some to the parlor would not work, Michael and Pieter set up two old doors on sawhorses to use as makeshift tables. Wooden crates worked quite handily for seats while the older people used the chairs. Michael, who cared nothing about propriety or stations in life, insisted that there was plenty of room for everyone and that Mister Silas and Miss Sally join them. There was no prim and proper eating. The conversation was loud and sometimes raucous. The teen boys playfully insulted and elbowed one another in attempts to snare the final piece of this or the last spoonful of that. Mild admonishments to behave from the adults did nothing. Despite protestations of being too full to eat another bite, appetites returned when the desserts were presented.

Only when Mister Silas announced that the hour had grown late, and they had to leave in order to return to the Mountain House by dark, did the party finally break up. Gideon left the remaining cigars with Michael to divvy up between him and Pieter while the Palenville teens and Mister Silas all made final trips into the barn.

Griet and Will helped with the dishes while the Voss boys helped their uncle clean up the makeshift tables and douse the fire. Pieter and his daughter hugged and talked until it, too, was time for him to leave. As he and the Voss family walked down the road, their voices carried back to the Van Wyck farm long after they had disappeared from sight.

When Mary made her journal entry that night, details about the party stretched for three pages. There was no doubt that another such gathering would happen before summer's end.

Chapter Sixteen

While they saw one another every few days, it was two weeks before Mary and Hester managed to be alone again. As soon as Hester closed the door, Mary was against her, their bodies thumping back against the wood.

"I waited so long for this," the older teen whispered between kisses. Her hands could not seem to get enough as they roamed across Hester's sides, shoulders, and neck. "I thought Judith would never go swimming."

"I wish...mmm...this door...locked."

"I wish I could nail it shut and keep you here with me" Mary said, sinking her fingers into Hester's light brown locks. "I love you, my Hester Pester."

"And I love you, my Mary Berry."

Careful to keep her voice soft enough to not carry through the door or the thin walls, Mary continued to murmur words of love and affection as she kissed Hester's lips, jaw, and neck. Moaning softly when she felt her breast being covered, she returned the touch, cupping the younger woman's bosom and gently squeezing. "Hester. Oh, Hester."

A familiar voice in the hallway broke the moment, giving them only a few seconds warning before their privacy was shattered. It was enough so that when Judith opened the door a few seconds later, Mary and Hester were sitting on the bed, a copy of Harper's between them. "Hello, Judith. Were you not going swimming?"

"The boys were dunking and splashing everyone, so we decided to come here and um, play with the paper dolls." She gestured to the two girls standing behind her. "This is Sarah and Susan. It's their first summer here."

Mary and Hester exchanged greetings with the newcomers while Judith walked to the large Saratoga trunk and opened it. "I thought Hester and you already read that one."

"I-I liked this article and wanted to read it again," Hester said, holding up the magazine. "Yes, see? It's about the battle of New Orleans."

Mary stood up. "I think we'll go outside and read it on the portico. Come on, Hester."

Once they were downstairs, they began giggling. "Paper dolls?" Mary said. "Judith hasn't played with paper dolls in years. I don't even think she packed them."

"What do you think they were going to do?"

"I don't know. Perhaps she managed to steal some of our father's tobacco and one of his pipes." Mary shrugged. "We did that when we were that age."

"That's true," Hester said. "Do you remember when we played with paper dolls?"

Mary leaned closer. "Now, we just play with one another."

Hester smiled and ducked her head. "You stop that," she said playfully. She knew that her cheeks were turning red.

"But it's true."

"Yes, it is." She looked toward the table rock. "Uh, oh. Your father is giving a sermon again."

"When is he not giving a sermon?" Mary asked. "He should have become a preacher. Can you hear what he's talking about this time?"

"No. Let's get closer."

"My good man, the people need fear not that Mister Lincoln will free the slaves or ban it throughout the union. Why, just look right here. It says '*Mister Lincoln's position is eminently conservative and that his election will by no means involve a triumph of the anti-slavery element of the Northern and Eastern States*'. It also says that he has said," Mister Chandler rattled the paper for emphasis. "And I quote, that he is '*not now, nor ever, been in favor of repeal of the fugitive slave law*'. He is just too conservative."

One of the preeminent bankers spoke up. "And there you go, with your attempts to disguise what that abolitionist in hiding's true intents are. You cannot fool me, Mister Chandler. The papers were quite clear on his speech at Cooper Union. He rides the same train that Mister Garrison of Boston and that Frederick Douglass take seats upon. Mark my words, sir. If he is put into office, there will be no rest until he has reached in and usurped control of honest men's property with the stroke of a pen."

"They are human beings, sir. Living, breathing, human beings. No man should ever be able to claim ownership of another."

Standing several yards behind Mary's father, so as not to attract his attention, Mary and Hester listened intently to the gentlemen arguing.

"I hope he does," Mary said. "Win, I mean."

"Do you think he'll free the slaves?"

"I don't know. I know he doesn't want to let slavery into the territories, but he wants to let the southern states keep their slaves."

"Then why do they want to leave the union if he's elected? They'll still be able to keep their slaves."

"I guess they're worried that if more new states are made and they don't allow slavery, that one day it will be changed in the constitution and no state can have them anymore."

"But did you hear what your father just said? That Mister Lincoln is against repealing the fugitive slave law?"

Mary held her hands out and shrugged her shoulders. "I don't rightly understand it all, but it has to do with the way the laws are and the constitution. Unless it's changed, it's still the law."

Hester crossed her arms. "If women were able to vote, they could change those laws. I don't know a woman alive that thinks slavery is right."

"I guess that's why they don't let the women vote," Mary said. "We'd change too many things to make them better."

Hester took a quick look around, then leaned in and lowered her voice so only Mary could hear. "If I could vote, I'd make it so we could be married."

Mary smiled. "As would I. And we could own property, keep all of our money, and have a proper say in things."

"I hope it won't be much longer and we'll be able to vote."

"It won't be," Mary said. "Every year the rallies get larger and the women become more vocal. Why, I'm certain that, within five years, we'll be voting and having equal say with the men."

"Are you sure you'll be able to come tomorrow night?"

Mary smiled and led them away from where the men were talking. "Even if it rained so hard that Noah started building an ark, I will be there," she said. "Are you certain your uncle or cousin won't find out that you slipped out?"

"I'm sure," Hester said. "They never come upstairs and I know which boards creak."

They smiled at their clandestine plan, both wishing it was tomorrow night already.

The moon was high in the night sky when Mary slipped out of the Mountain House. Following the path she knew so well, it took less than half an hour to reach Newman's Ledge. There, silhouetted by the moonlight, was Hester.

"I thought you might not come," she said.

Mary knelt down next to her, quickly wrapping Hester up in a lover's embrace. "I had to wait for Judith to fall asleep and she wanted to talk tonight."

Her lips found the edge of Hester's jaw and worked their way up to her ear. "I thought about this all day."

"As did I," Hester said, her head moving to give Mary more room to explore. Her hand slid up Mary's side until she encountered the soft swell of her friend's breast. "I wish we had our own house here. A place where we would not fear someone coming upon us. It will be so nice when you come to visit next week."

"I like this," Mary whispered, leaning into her lover's hand. "When I'm alone, I imagine you doing this to me. I've gone for walks into the woods and…brought myself to pleasure thinking of you."

"I do, as well," Hester said. "It is another reason I enjoy having a room and a bed to myself."

"I love you, my Hester Pester."

"And I love you, my Mary Berry." Hester moved her hand from Mary's breast so they could embrace.

Mary shifted until she was half on top of Hester, then rested her head against the younger woman's chest.

"I find myself doing so at nearly every opportunity," she admitted. "At home, when the moon is bright enough to light my room, I hold our picture with one hand and touch myself with the other. I pretend it is you who brings me to that special place." She covered Hester's breast with her hand. "Always, it is you."

Hester reached behind Mary and undid the buttons that held the older teen's dress closed. "In my room, we'll be able to be as we were on your birthday."

"Just us, no clothes and no one else," Mary said. They parted long enough for Hester to tug on the sleeves, leaving the dress open and her love's breasts exposed to the pale moonlight.

"You're so beautiful, Mary. So very beautiful."

Hester's dress had no such buttons, designed to be pulled on and off over the head. Their solution was to simply hike the garment up while the petticoats were pushed down. It wasn't the perfect solution but it did allow access while remaining able to redress quickly should someone else decide to take a midnight stroll. Their desire had been building for so long that it took little for them to bring one another to their initial peaks. They made love again, slowly, wanting their special time to never end. The hours passed yet it seemed far too soon that they had to redress and return to the Mountain House. They shared one final, heated kiss before Hester turned and walked down the Mountain Road. Mary watched her go, longing for the time when they would never have to part company.

Luck was with her that night as she was able to sneak back into the Mountain House and then her room just as easily and unnoticed as she had slipped out hours before.

Chapter Seventeen

Hester led the way into the root cellar. The way the Van Wyck farmhouse had been built against the small rise, similar to the Voss House, it had been easy during the years for Michael to expand the cool area until it was nearly half again the size of the house. Wooden shelves held several glass jars with tin lids sealed with wax to keep the food inside fresh. In the furthest corner were the blocks of ice covered with straw.

"The jam is here," Hester said, quickly pulling one of the jars from the shelf. When she turned around, Mary was closing the door. "We can't stay long," she warned.

"Long enough," Mary said, moving in close and stealing a kiss. "It is so very difficult to be near you and not be able to touch you."

"I hate September," Hester said, her face visible from the slits of light coming through the gaps in the boards of the cellar door. "It always means you're leaving soon."

"Then we shall endeavor to make the most of our remaining time," Mary said, slipping her hands around Hester's waist. "I need more memories to help me through the next nine months until I can see you again." They kissed several more times before time became an issue.

"We have to return to the others," Hester said as she stepped back. "Besides, you'll be staying tonight."

Mary smiled. "Two whole days," she said. "Whatever shall we do with ourselves?"

Hester reached for the door. "I do believe that won't be a problem."

"Show me your studio again later," Mary said, moving forward quickly to capture one last kiss. "And perhaps we'll need more jam."

"Or pickles," Hester offered as she opened the door. "Some jerky, ice…."

"Mint," Mary added. "Peaches…."

Hester smiled, deciding this was the most wonderful way to ever wake up. Mary was curled up against her with not a stitch of clothing separating their bodies. Slipping out so as not to wake the sleeping blonde, Hester quietly opened the door, slipped across the hall to the room where the commode had been set up, then returned to the warmth of the thick quilt and even warmer body. She kissed Mary's shoulder. "Mary, my darling, it's time to wake up."

"No," Mary mumbled a reply. "You kept me up too late."

Undaunted, Hester let her hand slip around to brush across Mary's breast. "If you wake up now," she said softly, "We'll have some time before I need to go down and make breakfast."

"Hmm?" A lazy smile crossed Mary's face as she rolled onto her back. "Yes?"

"Yes." Pushing the covers down, Hester leaned and kissed the now fully exposed nipple. "But, of course, if you want to sleep some more…." Her answer was a firm hand pressing against the back of her head.

"Don't you dare stop," Mary said. Hester could only chuckle as they started their day off in the best way possible.

By the time the teens managed to make their way down the stairs, the house was filling with the smell of breakfast cooking. They entered the kitchen to find Will at the stove and Michael seated at the table.

"Good morning," Michael said. "The coffee is ready."

"Oh, thank you, Uncle Michael." Hester reached for two of the heavy mugs. "But I thought it was my day to make breakfast."

"We figured you girls would be up late talking," Will said. "And I didn't want to wait any longer. I'm starving."

Michael chuckled. "Yes, doesn't it look like I starve my nephew?"

Will patted his protruding belly. Like his cousins Martin and Hendrik, he was big, strapping, and looked as though he had never missed a meal. "I got the eggs for you, too," he said. "But only because I needed them so I could make this."

Michael held out his mug. "I'll take some more if you don't mind. Miss Mary, please sit wherever you'd like."

Hester set the two mugs next to one another on the table, then took her uncle's mug and filled it. "It smells wonderful, Will."

"You can make breakfast tomorrow," Michael said to Hester. "I assume you girls are going to be up in your room or in the studio most of the day?"

"Yes. I was hoping to do another sketch or two of Mary before she leaves and I need to get the canvases ready for her to take home."

"That sounds right fine to me," he said. "Will and I need to get that table done for Miss Lilly and then we have that chicken coop to finish for old man Brant before we can start on building a trundle bed for old man Griffin." He paused to take a sip of coffee. "Just make sure to call us for dinner lest we go and work right through it."

"I will." Hester and Mary shared a knowing smile. The house was going to be theirs for the whole day. While she did honestly have to get the canvases ready, there was little doubt what else they were going to do. After all, Mary left next week to return to the city and it would be nine months before they would see one another again.

Hester had hoped to be able to visit for Mary's birthday but fear about possible riots if Mister Lincoln won the election had put an end to that idea. They would have to content themselves with the time they had remaining and thanks to her cousin and uncle's busy workload, they would have more privacy than expected.

"What are you so happy about?" Will asked as he lifted the cast iron pan from the stove and headed for the table.

"I just believe it is going to be a wonderful day," Hester said. "Oh, that looks wonderful."

"Yes, it does," Mary agreed as Will filled her plate with the mixture of potatoes, eggs, onions, bacon, and greens. Leftover biscuits from the night before were perfect to sop up the grease and the fresh honey was an added bonus. Mary declared that she had never had such a wonderful breakfast, which earned her being given the last biscuit by Will.

After a second pot of coffee was made for the boys to take to the barn, Hester, with unexpected help from Mary, took care of the dishes. Then it was a laughter filled trip upstairs where they spent more time in the bed than out, filling their day with pleasurable memories to keep them during their long separation.

When the coach arrived with Elizabeth and Tobias to take Mary back, Michael presented Mary with a gift he had been working on and just finished. A hinged, rectangular, long wooden box that was the perfect size to transport the rolled up canvases. "Can't have my niece's hard work ruined on the way back to your big city," he said as he presented it to her.

Hester included the painting she had been working on earlier in the summer, the one Mrs. Chandler had admired so much, along with two more paintings for Mary. Michael gave her a jar of honey with a playful warning to Elizabeth not to let her daughter eat it all at once. As was the annual tradition, the girls hugged and cried as they said their goodbyes, separating only when Michael put his hands on Hester's shoulders and Mary's mother all but pushed her daughter into the coach. The long waiting period for June had now started.

Chapter Eighteen

It seemed like any typical spring day when Mary sat down at the table for supper. She had received a letter from Hester that afternoon and was looking forward to writing a response as soon as she finished her meal.

As they ate, she noticed Tobias looking from one parent to another, then back at his plate. Clearly, there was something on his mind. She thought perhaps he had finally found a girl worth courting more than two weeks or had decided which business career he intended to pursue. She never would have guessed what did finally come from his mouth.

"I joined the union army today."

Mary's father rose from his chair. The vein on the side of his temple bulged prominently. "You did what?"

Tobias looked up. "I went to Fort Schuyler and joined the fifth volunteers," he said. "Some of the other men from my class went, as well. We're Zouaves."

Mary's fork stopped in midair. "What?"

She was shocked by the announcement. Certainly her elder brother had been a vocal supporter of President Lincoln and even louder in his disgust at South Carolina seceding from the union, but to go and join up? "Tobias, you're joking, right?"

"I'm not," he said.

It was several seconds but might as well have been minutes for how interminably long the silence felt before her mother spoke. "You are not going to join the army."

Mary saw a concern in her mother's face that she had not seen since Daniel had suffered through smallpox.

Her mother shook her head. "If Mister Lincoln wants men to fight his war, let him find someone else's son. Tomorrow you will go down there and tell them that you've changed your mind."

"I will not," Tobias said firmly, slapping his fork on the table.

"I will not have my son killed," Elizabeth said, her voice rising to a level never heard at the supper table. "Gideon, tell him this is not going to be."

When her mother used his given name rather than Mister Chandler, it was always a sign that she was extremely upset. Mary set her fork down and looked at Judith, who appeared equally concerned. In fact, her younger sister looked as though she were about to cry.

"I want you to finish your education," Mary's father said firmly. "Your career will not be helped at all by serving in the army."

Tobias wiped his mouth and threw his napkin on the plate. "My career? Father, it is not my career that I am concerned about. It is the good of our country. Did you not read to me exactly what President Lincoln said?"

"Mister Lincoln can rot!" his mother shrieked. "The country can rot! I want my son alive and safe!"

"It's done," Tobias said. "I'm not changing my mind."

"Tearing my heart out! You are tearing my heart out as surely as if you used a knife to open my chest and reached in with your own hands, Tobias." Their mother wiped at the tears coming from the corners of her eyes. "We did not raise you to be so disrespectful to your mother."

"It is not being disrespectful to you, Mother," he said. "It's being respectful to my country, to the union. Is that not how you raised me, Mother? Is that not why great-grandfather died during the war for independence? For our country? Would it not be disrespectful to him for me to stay home and do nothing while the country he died for is torn asunder by those southern traitors?"

"Then be disrespectful to him!" Elizabeth cried. "Be disrespectful but be alive! Finish your schooling and be as Mister Garrison or Mister Greeley and do battle with words. Let others wage war with the weapons and the blood."

Tobias looked down and shook his head. "Mother, I am no longer your little boy, but a man and I have to do as a man must."

"Tobias, that is enough," his father quietly warned. "Mrs. Chandler—"

"No!" she cried. "No! I care not if you have gray hair and grandchildren of your own," she said to her eldest son. "You will always be my little boy. You will always be that baby that I stayed up with for three days when you were colicky. The one I fed soup to when sick." She placed her elbow on the table and supported her head with her hand upon her brow, hiding her teary eyes from her children. "You will always be my little boy, Tobias. Please, do not do this."

"I am sorry, Mother. I truly am," he said softly. "Still, I will not change my mind on this."

"May we be excused, Father?" Mary asked. Without waiting for an answer, she rose from her seat and motioned to her younger siblings to follow her.

"Son," his father said. "This war will be through in a matter of months. By then you will have missed the rest of the year's schooling. You must reconsider."

"He's not going!" Elizabeth said, now fully sobbing. "Dear God, no."

Closing the pocket doors to the parlor did nothing to temper the volume coming from the dining area. The younger Chandlers heard every word as their parents continued to argue with Tobias. Tears ran down Judith's face and Daniel looked as though he were not far behind.

"Come here," Mary said, pulling the younger teens close. They all jumped when they heard a dish smash against the wall. Their perfect world where the unrest between the north and south was only relayed to them in newspaper stories had now been shattered. Never again would their family be the same.

April 25, 1861
Tobias announced that he joined the union army today. Mother won't stop crying and Father is smoking his pipe without pause. If they were not so against alcohol, I suspect both would be drinking now. It's terrible. How could he do this? I don't think he has been in a fight since he was younger than Daniel and he's never held a gun. Perhaps his part of the army will stay here in the city where we won't have to worry about him. Certainly those other boys he goes to school with don't know anything about fighting a war. How could they possibly go up against those men from the south? I fear if Mother doesn't stop crying that we will have to call the doctor for her. I'm so worried about her. I'm worried about him. I wish now that Mr. Lincoln had never won the election. I can only hope and pray that it will be finished soon and that Tobias stays safe.

Despite Mary's hopes and her parents' protests, the fifth infantry left New York less than a month later. The unit paraded through the city on their way out, met with thousands of cheering supporters and dozens of sobbing mothers.

They had taken Tobias to Mister Brady's studio the week before and now her mother clutched the framed photograph in her hands, refusing to let it go even as she wiped her eyes. As dashing as her brother looked in his bright red pants and blue wool coat, Mary couldn't help but fear that she would never see him again. How much fighting could they have possibly learned in only four weeks' time?

Far too soon, the parade was done and people returned to their homes. Mary did her best to comfort her mother, but she knew that only when the photograph could be exchanged for the real Tobias would Elizabeth Chandler find any comfort.

While the war waged on, described in all its gory glory in the papers, another war brewed at home. Grandmother Franklin arrived for an unannounced visit and learned of her eldest grandson's actions. Immediate and scathing blame was placed on Mary's father for allowing it to happen and Mary found herself trying to play peacemaker between the adults while her mother continued to weep and clutch Tobias' picture. In the end, her grandmother left, having done nothing but make the situation worse.

Chapter Nineteen

Hugging fiercely, Mary felt the loneliness of the past nine months slip away, replaced with the comfort of feeling Hester in her arms again. "I've missed you so very much."

"Not as much as I've missed you," Hester said. "I've just about worn your letters out rereading them."

"I kiss our photograph each night." She pressed her lips to the side of Hester's neck. "Every night."

"As do I," Hester said. "I worry as much for you being there in the city as I do for Tobias. I do so hope the South comes to its senses and this war ends quickly. Have you heard anything new?"

Mary shook her head, slowly breaking the embrace. "Nothing. Father checks the post each day and we all look through the newspapers. He's even taken to having the boy bring the Sun just in case they have any news that the Times and the Tribune doesn't."

Hester's eyes widened. "The Sun? Your father would sooner set that paper on fire as to read it."

"He also has the boy bring the Herald." She gave a small smile. "He has Mother or I read it for him, lest he break something."

"Break something?"

"The last time he read the Herald, Father became so angry that he broke Mother's favorite vase."

"Hendrik and Martin speak of joining, but Vader, Griet, and I keep asking them to stay. I don't know how Griet would manage without them and it is so very dangerous."

"What about Will?"

"Uncle Michael needs him too much. He's spoken about wanting to join once in a while but I don't think he will."

"Tobias wrote that he was not hurt at his first battle, a place called Big Bethel, but Mother is so very terrified for him. Father tells her we need to just keep praying, but she asked if those boys that died at Big Bethel didn't have anyone praying for them? She worries so much for him."

Mary shook her head. "I worry so much for her. She barely eats, barely talks. She just mostly sits in the chair and cries." She squeezed Hester's hands. "I'm afraid to come for a visit because I don't want to leave her alone that long."

"I understand," Hester said softly. "Come, let's go sit with her for a while. I'm sure Mrs. C. would like that."

Three weeks later, with Judith's promise to stay with their mother, Mary took the afternoon off to spend with Hester. The went through Glen Mary, past Ashley Falls and even over the peak of North Mountain, but their final destination was still a secret to Mary. Whenever she asked, Hester would only say that it was a surprise and they needed to keep going.

It took the better part of two hours trudging through the woods for them to reach the spot that Hester had selected. "How are we to get back up from here?" Mary asked as she dropped to the lower ledge. Once there, she discovered that the upper ledge formed an overhang, giving the lower one a cave like appearance.

"We don't," Hester said as she made the jump down. "We have to climb down those rocks there and then follow the creek for about two miles before we get back near any of the trails. It should only take little more than an hour for you to get back to the Mountain House."

She dusted her hands together and smiled. "I'm glad I found it. None of the tourists know about it. I doubt even Mister Beach himself knows of this since it's so far off his property." She put her hands on Mary's shoulders. "There's no good view from here, nothing to attract those city folk to come this way at all."

"Well, there's something to attract this city folk," Mary said, turning to face the younger woman. "I am glad you found this place, too." She drew her finger down the side of Hester's cheek. "To be able to touch you without worry or fear. This is worth a journey ten times as long."

"I do love you so," Hester said, sliding her hands down to reach the small of Mary's back and pulling her so close that their bodies pressed together. "And how can the great Lord Almighty disapprove of love?" She brushed their lips together. "If He does, then let it be Him who judges and punishes me. It is not for man to say how my heart feels."

Mary's fingers sank into the long straight tresses of Hester's hair. "I wish that we could stay here forever. Just you and me, free to touch without concern."

With a tug, she pulled Hester's face to hers, kissing her passionately. The privacy emboldened her to be more daring, her lips parting of their own volition to find an equal response, soft moans of pleasure reaching their ears only.

They dared to remove all of their clothes, putting them in a pile to cushion their bodies from the hard rock. Their hands roamed, finding all the places that brought pleasure.

Long after their lovemaking was through and they had dressed, the couple cuddled together, listening to the sounds of wildlife and just enjoying the feeling of being together.

"I have to go home soon," Hester said softly. "Will will probably be waiting for me by the time we get back."

"I know. I need to get back to Mother."

"I'll come back in a couple of days." She kissed Mary's temple. "I'll even bake you a pie."

Mary smiled and brought their joined hands up for a kiss. "You don't have to do that."

"I'll make one for Mrs. C., too."

"She'd like that."

Pulling her hand free, Hester cupped Mary's cheek and brought their lips together for one last kiss. "We need to go."

Mary reluctantly nodded, hating for their special time together to end but knowing that they needed to return. As Hester had predicted, Will was waiting for her when they returned. She quickly left and Mary turned her attention to her daily task since Tobias walked out of the city, reading all the newspapers in search of any news about the Fifth Infantry.

Never had a summer at the Catskill Mountain House dragged on so long. There was no play for Mary on the days that Hester did not visit. She spent most of her time with her mother, whose desolate mood showed no signs of improving. Only three times did letters arrive from Tobias, mostly talk about life about camp and how he was safe. When Mary was not with her mother or Hester, she was with her father, listening to the news reports and his speculation about how the war was going.

Mary was grateful that Judith had several friends to spend time with, as did Daniel. She much preferred them to be enjoying their time at the Mountain House, having fun rather than worrying about their elder brother. Certainly she and her mother were doing enough worrying for everyone.

Despite Hester's invitation for the Chandlers to come to the Van Wyck farm for a visit, it did not happen. Elizabeth had stopped all of her work with the suffrage and abolitionist movements. Instead, she spent her days at the Mountain House sitting in the chair, waiting for the next letter to arrive. As much as Mary hated to be so far away from Hester, she was nonetheless glad to return to the city at the end of September, since at least then her mother would be around her social circle and hopefully would start to come out of the dark shell she had withdrawn into.

Chapter Twenty

But that was not to be. Gideon was forced to attend holiday functions on his own or with Mary as his companion. Her mother no longer wanted to hear the news accounts, unless they specifically had to do with the fifth infantry. Sally and Bessie, both fiercely worried for Elizabeth, seldom left her side during the day. At night, Mary kept her company until her mother retired at an early hour, then the eighteen year-old would write in her journal, work on her studies, or write letters to Hester.

Shopping, once her mother's favorite pastime, became Mary's job. She was forced to purchase the presents for her siblings, father, and the servants. For her own gift, she simply chose more ink, paper, and a new diary as hers was almost full. They decorated the tree but only Daniel seemed to take any pleasure from it. Gideon kept himself surrounded with newspapers, admitting to his oldest daughter that he had no idea what to do to help bring his wife back from the dark morass. Sadly, Mary didn't either.

One cool day in late April, Mary ventured out to purchase some paper and powdered ink for her brother, who had written that he and other men were in desperate need of these items. She added several of these items to her order, then wondered what else the men might need. Pens and pen holders were added. As she left the store, she noticed a tobacco shop across the street, recognizing it as the one her father frequented. Indicating the stop to Old Jack, she went in search of pipes and tobacco to send along.

Wrinkling her nose at the strong smell as she entered, Mary looked around.

"Might I be of some assistance, Miss?"

"Yes. I am in need of pipes and tobacco."

The bald salesman rubbed his chin. "Is this for your husband? It would be better if he were to come in and select what he wanted himself."

"It's for my brother and the other boys risking their lives for the union," she said.

"Oh!" The salesman's attitude changed. "Please allow me to show you what we have to offer. Now these pipe bowls are some of the best that can be found. Ivory. Hand carved. Exquisite detail."

Looking at the ornate pipe bowl, then its price, she realized she could buy a dozen of the less expensive plain wooden ones for the same cost. "I shall take two dozen of these," she said, pointing to the sturdy but cheaper pipe bowls. "Along with an equal number of stems and ten pounds of tobacco." She also selected an equal number of cloth bags capable of holding both the pipes and some tobacco. "Please add this to Mister Gideon Chandler's account. I'm his daughter, Mary."

"Yes, Miss Chandler. I will make arrangements to have it included with his next delivery."

She waved her gloved hand dismissively. "There is no need. My coach is outside."

The salesman looked through the window. "Oh, yes. I shall have your order ready for Old Jack in just a few minutes."

Mary nodded and left the store. After a few words with Old Jack, she decided to take a short walk while waiting. She had only gone a few doors down when she saw a sign taped to the window of an empty storefront proclaiming it to be the Woman's Central Association of Relief. Curious, she went inside.

"Miss Sally! Miss Bessie!" Mary called as she entered the house. "Please clear the table. Everything. I need it."

"Yes, Miss Mary," Bessie said.

Mary turned and moved out of the way as Old Jack entered, his arms laden with a stack of boxes. "On the table, please."

"Yes, Miss Mary."

Elizabeth rose from her chair. "Mary? What is this?"

"It's for Tobias."

"All this?"

"I'll go get the rest, Miss Mary," Old Jack said.

"The rest? Mary Elizabeth. He cannot possibly carry all this around with him. What were you thinking?"

"It's not all for him, Mother," she said as Miss Sally relieved her of her coat. "For him and the other boys in his unit. I have pens and paper and tobacco and pipes and…oh, you'll see. Miss Bessie, I need help putting these into twelve bundles. Mother, where's the letter where Tobias wrote the names of his tent mate and some of his friends?"

"I have it by the chair with all of his other letters," Elizabeth said.

"Would you please fetch it? I need to make sure these are labeled for each. Oh, goodness gracious, I hope I have enough." She pulled items from the boxes. "Here, Miss Sally, help me get everything out so we can start putting each bundle together."

"Yes, Miss Mary."

"Miss Bessie, we need a knife. These soap bars need to be cut down into four. Mother, I need you to write down everyone's name so we know who we're sending these to."

Mary expected an argument or an excuse about not feeling well, but to her surprise, her mother went to the secretary and pulled out some paper. Mary showed the others the brochure she had taken from the Woman's Central Association of Relief. It listed items the men needed, as well as general items that would be appreciated.

Miss Bessie directed Old Jack to start putting things on the sideboard as she and Miss Sally sorted through everything.

To everyone's surprise, Elizabeth sat at her usual place at the dinner table, quickly looking at the sundry items being stacked about.

"I'll make Tobias'," she said, putting a large piece of the brown paper wrapping in front of her. "Mary, you said there are going to be twelve bundles?"

"Yes," Mary said, shocked that her mother was showing signs of life after so many months being depressed and uncommunicative. "There's four of us, so I think we can each make three bundles. Um, what do you think, Mother?"

Elizabeth carefully placed one of the pipe bowls and stems into their slots in the tobacco pouch, then took the pipe bowl back out. "Get one of your father's pipes," she said. "I think Tobias would like that."

"Yes, Mother."

"Miss Bessie, you sit in Judith's seat. Miss Sally, take Daniel's. Mary, you can sit in your father's chair."

The servants looked at the matriarch of the household, then at Mary for confirmation. Blinking in surprise, Mary nodded. "Yes, I think that would be easier. Splendid idea, Mother."

"Old Jack, open those other boxes and packages for us. You should help until it is time to fetch Mister Chandler."

"Yes, Mrs. Chandler," Old Jack said.

In a scene that would send Elizabeth Chandler's peers into apoplexy, the women of the house sat at the same table as the servants and worked together to create the twelve bundles.

"Whatever is all that material for?" Elizabeth asked, nodding her thanks as Miss Bessie handed her one of the quartered bars of soap.

"Some will be cut down to make bandages, which I'll send to the Woman's Central Association of Relief. They'll send it on to the U.S. Sanitary Commission, which will distribute it to the field hospitals that are tending to the wounded. The woman I spoke with today said they're always running out of clean bandages and that infection is killing just as many union soldiers as the battles are. The other material is for making socks and uniform shirts. The boys' uniforms are getting torn and then there's just not enough to replace them."

"Mister Lincoln should be doing more to help them," Elizabeth said.

"That's why there are these groups, Mother. I think even Mrs. Astor belongs to one. I'm sure she doesn't do this but she must give money."

"Money won't give these boys a way to write home to their mothers," Elizabeth said. "No. This is a splendid idea, Mary. This is better than just giving money. Miss Bessie, would you fetch us all some tea?"

"Yes, Mrs. Chandler."

As Mary worked, she couldn't help but smile as the transformation. She prayed this would be what would help her mother come back from grieving for a son that was still alive.

June 15, 1862

Next week we leave to go back to the Mountain House. Mother said she is looking forward to it and went out shopping yesterday. I hope we get a letter from Tobias soon, so we know if he and the others received their presents. Mother is already making new ones and wants to know how many boys are in his unit so she can make certain everyone gets something. As sad as she has been this past year, she now is determined. She joined three groups that send packages to the soldiers and help with the medical supplies for the hospitals. She hugged all of us last night and I didn't realize until then just how long it had been since she had done that. She still doesn't laugh or smile often but I'm certain once she receives a letter from Tobias, she will.

I don't have to stay with her all the time now, so I'm certain I will be able to spend some days with Hester at her uncle's house. I'm certain she will laugh when I tell her how many dullards have come calling to ask Father if they could call upon me. One even came calling for Judith. I thought Father was simply going to throw him down the stairs. If he knew that Judith was kissing that Jack Mansfield from next door, I'm certain his head would explode. I think Father still believes she is six years old.

I read some of my old diaries. How funny that Hester and I used to make mud pies and kiss frogs. When we're all old and gray, I am going to show her the diaries so we can laugh at how silly we were as little girls. I'm glad Father made me start writing. When I have children, I will make them write in diaries, too.

Chapter Twenty-One

Hugging fiercely, Mary and Hester shared a quick, friendly kiss.

"I have missed you so much," Mary whispered, her face buried in Hester's light brown hair.

"Not as much as I have missed you," Hester replied. She took Mary's hand in hers. "Come, we'll sit here in the shade."

"I have been sitting for so long that I wish to go for a walk instead." Mary looked at her mother. "We shan't be gone long, Mother."

"Make certain you are back in time for supper," her mother said. "You know Mister Beach does not appreciate people arriving late, which you are frequently, when you two go wandering."

"Yes, Mother."

"Mrs. C. does seem much better," Hester said once they were out of earshot from Mary's family.

"I wish I had known about those groups when the war first started," Mary said. "She's even been talking to her friends and getting many of them to join."

She gestured at the far side of North Lake. "Let's go to Glen Mary. I know she was hoping for a letter from Tobias before we left but there's still been no word if he and his unit received those bundles I wrote you about."

"It's been more than a month since Vader received a letter from the boys. Will keeps saying that he wants to join up, but I hope he doesn't."

"Kent's not old enough yet, is he?"

"No. He's only sixteen but with that left leg shorter than the right, I doubt they'd take him anyway."

"I've heard stories that boys as young as fourteen are lying about their age and joining."

"Fourteen is far too young to be killing other men, no matter the cause. The Bible itself says thou shalt not kill. It doesn't say thou shalt not kill unless the president says it's all right."

"Is there ever a good age for that, Hester?"

"No. I wish they'd all just put down their guns and find some other way to resolve this."

"I agree," Mary said. "I truly swear that if women were in control, there would be no wars."

"No wars and no children going hungry in the streets of our cities."

"It's so sad to see them. There's just not enough orphanages. Again, if women were in charge...."

"I wonder, if women were in charge, would we still have to hide how we really feel?" Hester asked.

"I suspect it's something we'll always have to hide," Mary said, taking Hester's hand in hers. You truly must stop growing. I barely come to your shoulder now." She rubbed her thumb across the back of Hester's hand. "I shall require a ladder in order to kiss you soon." She patted her own stomach. "I must stop growing. My dresses barely fit me now."

Hester smiled. "I reckon Griet might be able to help let them out," she said. "She truly does quite well with the sewing. It is clear that my skill resides with a brush, not a needle."

"You have skills far more than just painting," Mary said as the approached the trail to Glen Mary. "I fully intend to help you practice that this summer." She gave their joined hands a quick squeeze. "Several times."

"Miss Chandler," Hester said, feigning shock.

"I need practice with that particular skill myself."

Hester smiled and nodded at a couple passing in the opposite direction. It was only a few minutes' walk to reach the point where Ashley Falls was quite loud, helping to drown out their conversation from other guests' ears. "I suspect, my Mary Berry, that you had plenty of practice with that particular skill all by yourself."

Mary ducked her head and blushed. "I have indeed," she admitted. "Almost nightly."

"There are certain advantages to having a bedroom on the second floor," Hester said. "And a bed to myself."

Mary smiled slyly. "Have you been practicing, Miss Van Wyck?"

"I would say almost as much as you have, Miss Chandler."

"I wish we could practice right now."

Hester smiled and shook her head. "We can't go behind Ashley Falls today. They're so strong that the spray completely covers the log and we would most surely fall in."

"I'm certain Mother is feeling well enough to allow me to come for a visit," Mary said. "Oh! I brought back that box your uncle made so we can use it again this year to bring the paintings home."

Hester smiled. "Is that so? What makes you think I am painting anything for you this year?"

Mary bumped up against her. "Because you make me paintings every year."

"Perhaps I should be as those painters in Europe and start painting nudes."

"While I would certainly be willing to be your muse, I cannot believe that Mother and Father would approve of a nude hanging in my room."

Hester grinned. "If I were to paint you as a nude, it would hang in my room."

They looked at one another for just a moment before bursting into laughter.

"I think it best that we just keep with me at the lake or in front of the Mountain House," Mary said.

"That doesn't mean that you cannot still pose for me."

"True."

"Soon."

"Oh, yes, my Hester Pester. Soon."

Intimacy was the last thing on Hester's mind the day Mary was due to arrive. She had spent the morning trying to comfort her uncle, bereft upon discovering the nephew he considered a son of his own had slipped away the previous afternoon to join the union army.

"It will be all right, Uncle Michael," Hester said, rubbing the older man's back as he slumped in his chair, his elbows on his knees and his head bent down.

"Of all the foolhardy things that boy has ever done," he said, shaking his head. "How will I ever be able to get a good night's rest again? Martin and Hendrik and now Will? I swear if Kent breathes so much as one word about joining, I'm going to tie him to that old oak until after the war is through."

Hester nodded, fully understanding her uncle's dismay. She looked up, toward the window. "I hear the coach."

Michael stood up and rubbed his face. "I suppose we should get out there and greet your guest, then."

"I brought one of the letters that Tobias wrote," Mary said as she exited the coach. "He saw Hendrik."

"Yes, Hendrik sent a note home, as well, but read yours. I would enjoy hearing it. Good afternoon, Mrs. C."

"Good afternoon, Child," Elizabeth said, opening her arms to receive a hug. "I kept meaning to thank you for the painting."

"Oh, yes," Mary said. "I forgot to tell you. Mother had it hung in the parlor. When the sun shines on it, it looks as if the sun is shining in the painting."

She unfolded the letter. "Here. Mother wants to take it back with her, so let me read it to you now. He wrote it three weeks ago, but we didn't get it until just last week."

"'Dearest family of mine, how I miss you so. Thank you for the gifts. We were so pleased to get the soap and tobacco. If you shall send matches next time, we would most certainly appreciate it. Some playing cards, as well, though I know Mother would not approve. The homesickness is unbearable at times, especially when I am lying on the ground at night with but a single blanket to use as I try to keep warm. Often my tent mate and I will share our blankets, so that we might make it through without shivering. He is my third tent mate as the other two have been killed. I fear he will not be the last, just as I fear I am not his last. I did receive a most wonderful gift here during the Siege of Yorktown. I was playing cards when a soldier came to me and knocked off my cap. When I arose to defend myself, what joy to find it was none other than Hendrik Voss. He has grown a beard so thick that I did not recognize him at first. His unit had arrived only the day before and they too have seen too much blood and battle. I know it to be my duty, but I do wonder how God can forgive such a sin as I have continued to repeat with each battle. I try to say that they are just rebs, but nowhere in the great book did it say that it was all right to kill rebs. Are they not, too, the sons of God? I see their faces in my dreams and I fear they shall haunt me the rest of my days. Please, keep sending me letters and papers as I share them with the others. I shared all my pens and ink with those* *who did not receive a bundle from Mother and so need new pens and ink. If you spare me some of Miss Bessie's apple pie, that would be wonderful, too. It has been too long since we have enjoyed anything that resembles good food. I miss you all and pray each night that this rebellion will end soon. Your loving son, Tobias.'"*

"That is nice," Hester said as Mary handed the letter to her mother. "I am afraid that Vader has Hendrik's letter but I am sure if you stop by, he will be glad to show it to you."

"I am pleased that you have heard from him," Mrs. Chandler said. "I suspect my temperament is not such that I should face your step-mother at this time. Perhaps you can bring it the next time you come to the Mountain House."

Hester nodded. "Yes, Mrs. C. I will do just that."

"How is Martin?"

"He wrote only twice, but says that he is fine. He says his horse is finer than any he has ever seen before and faster than the wind. He misses home but has been making friends. He says the fifth cavalry is the finest unit and will chase the rebs back all the way to Charleston."

"I most certainly pray so," Mary said.

"I should return," Elizabeth said. "Mister Van Wyck, it is always pleasant to see you."

"And you, as well, Mrs. Chandler."

Silas held the door open with one hand, using the other to help Mary's mother into the coach. They were quickly on their way.

"Come inside, Mary," Michael said. "I'm afraid I can't offer you any of Will's fine cooking, but I'm sure Hester will make something you'll enjoy."

"Oh? Is he ill?"

"He said he was going for a walk yesterday," Hester said. "He told Kent when he went by the house that he'd joined up."

"Oh, no! Goodness gracious!"

Michael shook his head and went back inside.

"Uncle Michael is upset."

"I understand. Why didn't he leave a note?"

"He never learned to read and write," Hester said. "Uncle Michael walked down to the house last night after Will had been gone for a few hours and that's when Kent said Will told him not to tell anyone until morning."

She opened the door. "As soon as it was daylight, Uncle Michael took the wagon down to Catskill but he was already gone. The man at the ferry said a bunch of soldiers left early this morning but he wasn't sure if they were going to Albany or New York City."

Mary shook her head as she followed Hester inside. "That's so terrible."

Michael was nowhere in sight. Hester pulled out one of the copper pots given to her by Mrs. Chandler the previous year and set it on the counter. "I think a soup would be best," she said.

"I shall help."

Hester smiled. "I've seen you try to peel carrots when you stayed with me at the house. More carrot went in the slop pile for the pigs than ended up in the pot."

She opened the drawer and pulled out two small knives. "I will peel and you can cut them up." Setting the knives down, she walked to the oil lamp sitting on the far counter and lit it. "We'll need three carrots, an onion, and oh, there's some pork belly in there."

Mary opened the door to the root cellar for her. Once inside, Hester hung the lamp, then whirled around and pulled Mary into her arms.

"I need you to hold me," she said, sighing happily when she felt Mary's arms tighten around her.

"Always," Mary said. "As long as you need."

For several minutes they stayed like that, one offering comfort and the other gratefully accepting it.

Michael joined them for the meal, though beyond inquiring about Tobias, he said little. After supper was finished, he said he had work to do and retreated to the barn. Together, the women washed the dishes and tossed the peelings into the pig trough. Less than an hour after they had finished eating, they were upstairs and stripping off their dresses.

"This war has gone on too long already and I do not know if the damage will ever be repaired," Mary said quietly.

Hester's arms went around her. "I pray for the boys several times a day. They will be safe."

Mary leaned into the embrace. "I feel dreadful for your uncle. At least Tobias and the twins let people know before they left."

"I know. Kent is so good with making things from wood but he has his own chores to do at home. I don't know how much he'll be able to help Uncle Michael."

"If I knew how to make furniture, I would help him."

Hester smiled and kissed the top of Mary's head. "I reckon you would. You've always had a kind heart."

"I love you."

"And I love you."

Mary let out a most unladylike yawn. "Oh, pardon me."

"Should we go to bed?"

Mary rubbed her cheek against Hester's chest. "I had planned on something else but..." She yawned again. "Oh, my."

"Come. It is just as enjoyable to have you sleeping next to me." Hester released the embrace and turned down the blanket.

"I suspect that is not quite true."

Smiling, Hester slid between the covers, then patted the empty space next to her. "Turn down the lamp. And it is true. I do enjoy holding you."

In moments, they were snuggled together, sharing the same pillow.

"Mary?"

"Hmm?"

"Perhaps we won't have the big house and all the orphan children we wanted when we were little girls, but this house is nice. I'm sure we could live here."

Mary put her hand over Hester's, pressing them against her own belly. "I do not believe Mother and Father would approve."

There was a long pause before she spoke again. "But I would live in an outhouse if it meant we were together." She felt Hester's lips against the back of her head.

"No. You are right. They didn't raise you to live in Palenville with the chickens and pigs. You deserve the finery of the city. I just don't know how we'll ever be able to do it."

"I think it's best we not worry about it until after the war is done and everyone is home safe," Mary said, patting the hand holding her.

"I just can't leave Uncle Michael. Not now."

Rolling, Mary put her hand on Hester's cheek, then kissed her gently. "It may not be the way we imagined when we were children, but it will happen. I swear to God that someday, we will live together." She shifted onto her back. "Come here. I wish to hold you tonight."

Hester slipped deeper into the covers and snuggled close. "Thank you."

Mary kissed the top of Hester's head. "I love you."

"I love you, too."

Chapter Twenty-Two

June 30, 1862
I cannot tell Mother and Father of my fears
for they have so many of their own. Today when I
was helping Hester with breakfast, I cried for my
brother, for her cousins, for my uncles and their sons.
As if a mighty dam burst forth, I could not stop crying
in Hester's arms. Even when the food was burned,
she cared to hold me as a mother would a child,
forsaking the food so that we had to throw it to the
pigs and start again. How I wish that she were my
sister. That when the summer ended, and the leaves
changed to reds and golds, she would come home
with me. I miss her so when we are apart. She said I
deserve the finery of the city but I would give it all up
to live with her. We agreed to wait until after the war
to talk about it again. Perhaps then we will be able to
live the way we dreamed of for so many years.

Despite his initial protestations, Michael ended up
letting the girls come help him in the barn after the
breakfast chores were finished. "But only until Kent comes
up to help me," he said.

Since Mary's clothes were too fancy to risk getting
sullied with either linseed oil or stain, Hester took on that
task while her guest carefully brought the smaller pieces of
wood that Michael needed. By the time Kent arrived, it was
close to mid-afternoon. The women excused themselves to

the kitchen, again insisting over Michael's protests that even though it was his turn to cook that they would take care of it.

"Is this too much flour?"

Hester wiped her hands on the small towel and peeked into the mixing bowl. "Not if we were feeding the entire union army."

Using a spoon, she scooped out as much of the dry flour as she could. "We'll just have to add more eggs and butter. Kent can take the extra home to the family."

She reached for an additional pan. "I should make you do the dishes since you're causing me to use extra pots and pans."

Mary laughed, giving Hester a hip bump as she went by. "I'll get the butter."

"More potatoes, too," Hester said as she reached for the basket of eggs on the counter.

"You know, Father pays Miss Bessie for doing our cooking. What are you going to pay me?"

Hester turned and wrapped her arms around Mary, catching her before she could move away. "You want to be paid? Hmm, and just how much are you going to charge, Miss Chandler?"

Mary laughed, putting her arms around the taller woman's neck. "I'll have to think about that."

"I haven't much coin. Perhaps I can pay you in another way?"

"Perhaps," Mary teased, a knowing smile on her lips. "It would depend on what you're offering."

"Whatever could I offer?"

"I'm certain we could work something out."

Food forgotten, they kissed. They were so focused on one another that they forgot about their surroundings until the kitchen door opened. Bolting apart, they stared in surprise as Kent came in.

"Kent! Um, we were, uh, we...."

"Eggs and butter," Mary said, quickly crossing the room to reach the door to the root cellar.

"Yes, that's it. We need more eggs and butter. Um, did you need something?"

"I wanted to take a pitcher of tea out to Uncle Michael."

Hester handed the glass pitcher to him. "You'll have to chip the ice. I just made a pot yesterday, so there should be plenty in there."

"Thanks." Kent followed Mary into the root cellar.

"Whew." Hester leaned back against the counter. There would have been a great deal of explaining to do if Kent had come in just a second earlier. She turned around and busied herself mixing ingredients and mentally calculating how much extra she would need to make to compensate for the excess flour Mary had put in the bowl.

"Did he say anything to you?" Mary asked once Kent left.

Hester shook her head. "I don't think he saw. Did he say anything to you?"

"Not about that. Just that he wished the root cellar at his home was as full as yours. He asked about Tobias."

"Good." Once she was satisfied that the food was cooking nicely, Hester turned to face Mary. "We have to be more careful."

"I know. I thought I was going to have a heart attack when the door opened."

Hester gave Mary's hand a quick squeeze. "As least we have the rest of today and part of tomorrow."

"It's a beautiful day. Perhaps we can go sit near the creek?"

"I'd like that. I'll bring my sketchbook. I've not drawn you near the creek before."

Letting go of Mary's hand, Hester picked up the wooden spoon and stirred the contents of the two pans, then lifted the lid and checked on the soup.

"Oh, he did say that he heard at church last Sunday about Mother and her friends going into Catskill and buying up half the mercantile. Did I tell you that she and some of her friends who are also in the W.C.A.F. have been having bundling parties up at the Mountain House?"

"No. That's wonderful. I truly am happy that Mrs. C. is feeling better."

"So am I," Mary said. "I was worried about her. You should come and help with the bundling. I'm sure you would enjoy helping out."

"We have something similar at church, but we make bundles to help the women who are suffering because their husbands or sons have gone off to fight. Usually, we provide food."

"I didn't consider the ones left behind. It must be hard for Griet having both boys gone."

"At least Kent and Vader are there to help. Mrs. V. kicked out the last boarder a month ago."

"She did? Why?"

"Vader said she didn't like him and you know how she is when she's not happy. I truly am grateful to the good Lord that I live here now."

"With Will gone, will you still be able to come visit me?"

"I hope so. I can't take Uncle Michael away from his work to help me and I'm not sure he can spare Kent, either. I'll have to ask Vader to bring me or I'll just walk."

"You can't take the wagon yourself?"

"I don't think Uncle Michael would allow that. I've never driven one before."

"You should learn," Mary said, taking the wooden spoon and sampling the soup. "Oh, that's hot."

"This is why your mother has Miss Bessie in the kitchen and not you," Hester said with a smile as she took the spoon away. "I should. I'll ask Uncle Michael about it." She shrugged. "I know Aunt Frances knew how to drive a wagon and most of the women around here do, too. I guess it's just because we've always had the men and the boys around to do it for us."

"Just like voting," Mary said.

Hester held up her hand to forestall a suffrage sermon. "I will ask."

"Don't ask. Tell him that you're going to learn to drive the buggy."

"Darling…."

"I mean it. Stand up for yourself, Hester. You're nineteen now, not nine. You're a grown woman. Why, in your grandmother's time, I'm certain you'd already be married with four children by now."

"And carrying a fifth," Hester said. "My Grandmother Van Wyck had eight children before she was twenty-five."

"Goodness gracious! Eight? I cannot imagine eight children. Especially without a nursemaid to help."

Hester smirked. "You cannot imagine making dinner without Miss Bessie." She handed Mary the wooden spoon. "Stir everything."

"Yes, m'lady." Mary did as instructed. "I happen to think I cook quite well…in the bedroom."

Hester blushed and smiled. "You most certainly do, my love. You need no assistance there."

Chapter Twenty-Three

As had become the custom, Mary's family gathered around her father as he folded the newspaper, just so, and quickly scanned the front page. A quick flip to see the bottom half of the page, then he returned to the beginning and cleared his throat. She knew from the sight of the large map taking up so much of the page that there had been a mighty battle. "It seems that General McClellan has sent our boys into a battle for which they were ill prepared. The article begins,

'Camp before Richmond, Saturday, June twenty-eighth, eighteen sixty-two. The army of the Potomac no longer needs to complain of inactivity, for the comparative quiet of the past month have given place to three days of as desperate, determined, and bloody work as the fiercest clamorer for active movements could desire.'"

"Harumpf." He scowled. "The only people clamoring for battle are those who don't have sons looking down the barrel of a musket rifle."

He quickly scanned the article.

"'*Losses for the union estimated to be…fifteen hundred.'"*

Her mother gasped and Miss Sally asked God for mercy.

"'*Those engaged in the repulse of Stonewall Jackson represent his route to be most quick and disastrous. He came down upon them expecting a surprise but found them all momentarily expecting his approach, having been informed by General McClellan two days previous that he was coming upon them. Instead of a surprise, the enemy received the first shot, and after two hours fight retreated in confusion. "'* He paused.

"'The wounded from the fight, which immediately ensued, represented it to have been a most terrific encounter, the enemy coming out from Richmond upon them in such dense masses that the shell and grape poured into them as they advanced, made great gaps in their lines, which were immediately filled up and they moved forward most determinedly. Their artillery was so poorly served that the damage to our ranks was light in proportion. They still moved on and exchanged showers of minie-balls which were destructive on both sides, but when General Porter ordered a bayonet charge, they retreated in double-quick, though General Porter pursued them but a short distance. "'

He dared to give a small smile, which disappeared as he read the next paragraph.

"'The enemy again rallied and approached our lines a second time, when the same terrible slaughter ensued, this time their artillery, being better served, was more effective in the ranks of our men'."

He shook his head and scanned the column.

"'Again for the fourth time, General Porter fell back to his first position when an order was received from General McClellan to continue his retrograde movement slowly and in order. As soon as it became apparent to the enemy that it was the purpose of General Porter to retire, the enemy again pushed forward most boldly and bravely, when their advance was checked by the entire reserve force, consisting of the New York Fifth, Lieutenant-Colonel Duryea—'"

"By the Lord above, that's Tobias' unit," Elizabeth said.

Mary was surprised at how tightly her mother squeezed her hand as they continued to listen to her father speak.

"*'The enemy made a fierce attack on the reserve, but cannon were posted at various points of the route by which they were retiring toward the Chickahominy, which occasionally poured in shot and shell upon them and checked their movements and enabled the troops to move back in the most admirable order. At one time, in this retrograde movement, the reserve force of General Sykes charged on the enemy with the bayonet and drove him back nearly a mile. In this charge the gallant New York Fifth and Colonel Bendix's New York Tenth drew forth the plaudits of the army, for their steadiness and bravery, in which they, however, lost about a hundred of their numbers.'"*

For the first time in Mary's life, she heard her father's deep, resonating voice choke on words.

"*'Whose bodies it was necessary to leave...to leave on the field.'"*

Mary's mother covered her mouth. "Lord, no. Oh, please, no."

Gideon quickly turned the pages until he reached the last one and scanned the list of killed and wounded. "No, Mrs. Chandler," he said. "His name is not among the list of those injured or killed."

He held the paper out for her to see. "See? There are others from his unit but not him. Our boy is still safe."

Elizabeth took the paper from him and stared long and hard at the list before nodding. "He's not there," she agreed, falling back into her chair and letting the paper hit the ground. Mary picked it up and scanned the names herself. Her eyes widened. "Mother."

Elizabeth was dabbing her eyes. "What?"

Folding the paper, Mary handed it to her, pointing out the name she wanted her mother to notice.

"Oh, no!" Elizabeth rose and turned around. "Mrs. Murray, is Frank in company G?"

"Yes. He was just transferred there last month."

It took less than a second for the wealthy woman to turn pale, her mouth opening and closing with no sound coming forth. The other women quickly scurried around Mrs. Murray, all understanding whose name had appeared on the list.

The mournful wail that finally came forth broke the hearts of all around her. Mary hugged Judith, noting that her father and several other men were heading inside the Mountain House to look for Mister Murray. Mary remembered Frank's name being one of those to whom a care bundle had been sent that first day she had come home with a coach full of sundries and a thought to help. Letting go of Judith, she now went and joined the other women who were offering comfort to a mother who would never see her child again.

As happened every day, the majority of the patrons of the Mountain House were waiting when the coach arrived, its various hanging pieces of metal clanging like bells to announce its approach. Mary stood on the periphery, seeing her mother near the driver. She hoped for a magazine forwarded on from home or better still, one of the rare letters from Tobias as it was now the middle of July and they had not heard from him since late May. Seeing a letter being handed to her mother, Mary smiled and walked to her.

"It's from him," her mother said happily as she opened it.

"*Dear Father and Mother, I wish this post was bringing you good news but I fear it is not. We were ambushed three days ago by the rebs. I am in a field hospital but fear the lack of supplies and doctors leaves me far worse than if I were home. I cannot feel my right leg, which the knee seems twice as large as it should be. When I touch it, it is hotter than any stove.'"*

"Was that the Battle of Gaines Mills?" Mary asked. "What date did he put on the letter?"

"I believe so," her mother said. "He doesn't date it but mentions that he hopes we will enjoy the fireworks of Catskill as we have every year, so it must have been before the fourth of July."

"But his name wasn't in the paper," Mary said. "You know Father checks it every day. He wasn't listed."

Elizabeth shook her head. "I do not know, Mary. Oh!" She held the letter to her breast. "I want to go to him and bring one of the finest doctors from the city with me. My little boy!"

"All right, Mother." Mary put her arm around her mother's shoulders. "Let's go tell Father, Judith, and Daniel. Perhaps Father can arrange for a doctor to go to him."

"I just want to bring him home," Elizabeth sobbed. "Just bring my boy home alive."

As she escorted her mother inside, Mary explained to the other women looking on with concern about what had happened. Miss Sally, who had been mending a torn knee in one of Daniel's knickerbockers, took the crying woman the rest of the way. Mary turned around and went in search of her father. She had planned on asking to go spend time with Hester but knew now that was not an option. Her mother needed her and Mary knew her own desires had to come second. She also knew that Hester would understand.

Chapter Twenty-Four

"Well, see here," her father said. "Our former President, Mister Martin Van Buren has died." He shook his head. "I can recall when he was first elected Governor of our fine state. Why, he had not even warmed his seat in Albany when he was whisked away by Jackson to be secretary of state. Your Grandfather Chandler said right then that it would not be long before he would be president and he was correct."

"Didn't he live near here, Father?"

"Yes, Mary. In Kinderhook. I'm not certain how far from here, but certainly close enough to be considered local. I suspect many black buntings will be draped throughout Catskill this day." He rattled the paper. "I am pleased that he lived long enough to see Washington, D.C. abolish slavery."

"It's a shame he didn't live long enough to see the end of this terrible war," Mary said. "Is there any news about the fifth?"

"Not that I've seen yet," her father said. "I can only pray that they are resting up after those terrible battles." He folded the paper to better read the columns on the right hand side of the page. "You said the boys were in the Seventy-Second New York and the Fifth New York Cavalry, correct?"

"Yes. No one knows what unit Will is in yet."

"I haven't seen anything about the fifth cavalry since the battle near the Orange courthouse last week. I'm not sure when I last saw something about the other unit."

"You've been checking the names every day?"

"Yes, Mary. No Van Wyck or Voss and yes, I have looked under the V's and the W's just in case someone made a mistake."

"Thank you, Father."

He slid the paper down between his thigh and the chair, then reached into his pocket for his pipe. "I dare say you should be getting packing right about now."

"Packing? For what?"

"I do believe that is has been a month since you have seen Hester, has it not?"

"Yes but, oh, Father, I cannot leave Mother now. Not without news from Tobias."

"It was her idea," he said. "Though rather than have her escort you, I feel the need to leave here for a few hours and will accompany you myself."

"Oh, Father, thank you!" She squeezed his hand, knowing he would not want her to hug him in such a public setting. "Oh, but I do have to pack. Yes. I will be back in just a few minutes."

"Harumph." He sucked on his pipe, exhaling a blue cloud of smoke. "I know what a few minutes means to you when you're packing. Make haste or I shall have Mister Silas leave without you."

Mary's arrival was a surprise to Hester, who had missed her dear friend terribly. Not in any apparent hurry to leave, Gideon sat down with Michael in the large wooden chairs positioned under the shady hemlock and indulged in talk about the war and generously shared his cigars. Mister Silas whiled away the time by making trips to the barn, careful not to be seen by the temperance preaching Mister Chandler.

"Come with me," Hester said. "It's almost finished."

"My painting?"

"Yes. Come and see." Taking Mary's hand, Hester led her up the stairs.

There, on the easel, rested what Mary could only describe as Hester's best work yet. It portrayed Mary in her ruffled white dress, sitting on a stump with the creek running in the background. "Oh, Hester. It's beautiful. It belongs in a museum."

"I want to keep this one," Hester said. "I will have Uncle Michael mount it and then have Kent make me the most ornate frame possible. I want it in my room, so when I wake up in the morning, I can see you smiling down at me with the sun kissing your hair."

Still admiring the painting, Mary put her arm around Hester's waist. "It truly is remarkable."

"I am pleased with it."

"You should be. As fine any I've seen in the museums, I'll swear to it." She reached out, careful not to touch the canvas. "See how the sun just, um, dapples through the leaves of the trees? How that bird looks ready to just jump off that branch and fly away? I love it."

She turned to face Hester. "And I love you."

"I love you, too."

"Always and forever."

Hester smiled. "And ever and ever, after that."

An early supper allowed Mary's father and Mister Silas to partake before leaving, though clearly both the coachman and Mister Chandler were uncomfortable with sharing a meal at the same table. A party outdoors, set up on makeshift tables is one thing. Sitting down at a kitchen table was something else entirely. Still they made the best of it, if the conversation was a bit stilted. Mister Silas was, after all, under the employ of Mister Charles Beach himself and there were certain standards the owner of the Catskill

Mountain House expected those in his employ to adhere to. Asking one of New York City's upper crust to pass the salt was not one of them.

Amused by the tableau, Mary wondered who was the more relieved when the meal was finished.

"Oh, my goodness," Michael laughed as the coach pulled away. "I don't suppose it was such a smart idea to ask Silas to join us?"

"Goodness gracious," Mary said. "Poor Mister Silas. Why, he practically ran to the door when he was finished."

"Next time we'll sit them right next to one another," Hester said, joining in the merriment.

"Oh, dear, but wouldn't that be amusing?" Mary reached for her glass. "I think it's good for Father. He spends so little time with anyone not of his station."

Michael scratched his dark beard. "For someone who doesn't spend time with people below his station, he certainly seemed to enjoy talking with me today. He said he has a friend in the government that he is going send word to try to find out where Will is."

"Oh, that would be wonderful!" Hester said.

"Yes, it would," Mary said. "I wish I had thought to ask him to do that before."

"He may be my nephew, but I think of him as my son. I can't imagine my brother or his wife's souls are at rest with him out there in all that fighting. Frances and Gerrit's, too." He drained his glass. "I'll have to work twice as hard tomorrow to make up for the work I didn't get done today." He patted his shirt pocket, where four fat cigars were peeking out. "If you ladies will excuse me, I think I'll go enjoy one of these generous gifts from your father and then get some work before the sun goes down."

"All right, Uncle Michael. Mary and I will clean up here and then retire to the studio for the evening."

"You're a grown woman and I got no rights to be telling you what to do, but I've heard you walking across that floor in your studio at all hours of the night lately. Mary, I trust with you here, that she'll get herself to bed at a decent time."

"I'll make sure of it, Mister Van Wyck."

Michael smiled. "Good night, girls."

"Good night."

"Good night, Uncle Michael."

The smirk that started on Mary's face the instant Michael closed the door grew and grew. "You heard him," she said. "He wants me to make sure you get to bed at a decent time. He said nothing about letting you sleep."

Hester laughed and stood up. "I'm sure he didn't mean it the way you're taking it."

Mary chuckled, thoroughly amused with herself. "I'll clear the table."

"I'll go feed the pig, then I'll get the water heating for dishes."

"Would you like to take a bath tonight?"

Hester gave her a knowing smile. "The last thing you let me do in the tub is bathe myself."

"Is that a complaint?"

Hester stopped at the door and smirked. "Not at all."

Chapter Twenty-Five

Gideon Chandler read the single line in the casualty list again, then handed the newspaper to one of his companions and strode to his wife. "Mrs. Chandler, if I might have a word."

Once she was away from the other women, he told her the news. "The paper says that a Willem Van Wyck was shot in the leg…bad."

"Good Lord!"

"I'm going to ride down with the coach and send a telegram to Washington. I'll find out all that I can and then I'll hire a carriage to take me to the Van Wyck farm."

"Whatever you have to do," she said. "Make certain Mary stays with Hester."

"I will. She isn't due to be picked up until tomorrow and I would venture no one up there knows."

"Oh, this is just terrible." She clutched the lapel on her husband's white suit coat. "Please, Gideon. See if you can find out more about our boy."

"I've asked twice but I will ask again," he promised.

Michael was running across the yard as Hester and Mary came from the kitchen, all responding to shouts from Kent from inside the carriage.

"Will's been hurt!" Kent said as he exited the coach. Pieter Van Wyck exited next, followed by Mary's father.

"What happened?" Michael asked, looking from his brother to Mary's father for an explanation.

"He took some grapeshot to the leg," Gideon said, holding his arm out to embrace his daughter. "He's in a hospital in Washington, D.C." He held up his hand. "Now I've arranged for the finest medical care possible for him and they will send word to the telegraph station in Catskill as soon as there's any further news."

"I-I should go to him," Michael said, more lost than Hester had ever seen him.

"Yes, I think that's best," Mister Chandler said. He turned his head to look at his daughter. "Tobias is fine," he said quietly. "He was returned to his unit last week."

Michael wiped his hands on his pant legs. "I need to change. I need, um, to pack something. I don't know. Pieter, do you have any money for train fare?"

"I will take care of all that," Gideon said. "When we get to Catskill, I will send word ahead and locate proper lodging as close to the hospital as possible for as long as you need."

"I'll pack some things for you while you get your going to meeting clothes," Hester said.

Michael took several steps toward the house, then stopped. "Kent, there's an order for old man Griffin that I have to have finished for Friday. He'll be coming to pick it up."

"I'll take care of it, Uncle Michael."

"And um…" Michael rubbed his forehead. "And the beans and blackberries are ready. When they come, tell them I want the beans done first."

"Go," Pieter said. "Hester can tell us what else needs to be done."

Gideon put his hand on his daughter's shoulder. "Mary?"

"Yes, Father?"

"I trust you will stay here with Hester. I must admit I know little about farms and I'm certain you do not, as well, but two sets of hands are better than one. You're her friend and she will need you to step in and help her."

"Of course I will," Mary said. "Whatever she needs."

He smiled and kissed the top of her head. "You've grown into a fine woman, Mary. Some day when you settle down, you'll make some man a wonderful wife."

"I think I shall become an old maid," Mary said. "I should go see if Hester requires help."

"Someday," her father said as she walked away.

Mary awoke to find herself alone in the bed. When calling out did not turn up Hester, she dressed and went outside. "Hester? Hester?"

"In the barn," Hester called back.

Mary walked in the barn, seeing all the woodworking tools and materials but no sign of the younger woman. "Where are you?"

"Go through the door. I'm with the cows."

"Why are you with the cows?" Mary opened the door and received her answer. "Oh!"

Hester was sitting on a stool and rhythmically milking one of the two cows. "This has to get done first, then the other chores."

"That looks painful," Mary said. "Don't ever try to milk me."

Hester turned her head and grinned. "Yours are much more fun to play with."

Mary stood behind Hester, putting her hands on the younger woman's shoulders. "I'm pleased about that. Why didn't you wake me?"

"I needed to get out here and it's not like you know how to milk a cow."

"I could learn. I knew that's where milk came from." She grimaced. "I just didn't realize it was done that way."

"Usually Will or Uncle Michael does this." Hester stood up. "I'll show you how to do it and then I'll go do Stubborn."

"Stubborn?"

Hester gestured at the other cow, who let out a resounding moo. "She's stubborn. How she earned her name. I can't rightly recall what it used to be, but Stubborn sure fits her."

Mary gingerly sat down on the low stool. "You have to do this every morning?"

"Twice a day," Hester said. "Kent or Griet will be up to get one of the pails. The other is for us. Since it's just you and me for now, we'll keep some and use the rest to make butter and cream. Usually we only do that every other day but if we don't, the milk will go to waste. If we get too much before Uncle Michael gets back, we'll give it to the Voss'."

She squatted down. "Now grab her like this and you just squeeze and pull, squeeze and pull. Nice and steady."

"We have to make butter? Like in the magazines— where they use a butter churn?"

Hester laughed. "If you want butter for your biscuits, and just about anything else I make for breakfast and supper, we sure do. Now, you try it."

Within minutes, Mary had gotten the rhythm down and was comfortable enough that Hester could move on to the other cow.

"Your turn, Stubborn," Mary heard the younger woman say. "No, I don't want any kisses today. No. What did I say? Yes, you're a good girl. Now, let me have some milk."

"This isn't so terrible," Mary said. "I shall help with this every day."

"Good. After we finish milking them, we have to clean them and then let them out in the pasture. Then we have to feed the horses and let them out, then clean the barn. After that, we can make breakfast."

"Goodness gracious! All that? Before breakfast? Every day?"

Hester chuckled. "City girl."

It took far longer than Mary had anticipated to finish with the animals. Her stomach grumbled loudly as breakfast was cooking, then again when she reached for the plates.

"We'd better feed that before it yells again," Hester said. "Do you want coffee or tea?" She lifted the lid on the canisters. "We have more tea."

"Tea."

Together they finished filling the plates and sat down. "I won't be able to do any painting today. Everyone's coming."

"Everyone?"

"Uncle Michael said the beans and the blackberries are ready. Many of the neighbors will come and do the harvesting, but we'll have to take the full pails and give them empty ones."

Hester paused to take a sip of tea. "And we have to keep bringing out tea and water for them. It gets mighty hot out there doing all that work under the sun. And today's fixing to be a burning one."

"What are we going to do with all those beans and berries?"

Hester chuckled. "We don't get all of them," she said. "The folks that come take home most of it. We'll have plenty for ourselves and for down the road. In fact, I think we still have some blackberry jam from last year."

"I don't understand. Why do all that planting if they're going to get most of it?"

"They come and do the planting and then come back again for the weeding and finally for the harvest. That's why they get most of it. We do it for all the crops. Uncle Michael has all this land and lots of these folks don't have so much. It helps the land because this way it gets used. It helps them because this way they get some things they wouldn't get otherwise and it helps us because if it was just Uncle Michael, Will, and me, we wouldn't be able to farm all this land by ourselves. You've seen how small the Voss home is. Just those few acres. They'd never be able to raise enough food to feed everyone there. All those maple treats you enjoy? It takes a mighty lot of sap to make just a little syrup and sugar. Even with all the boys helping, Uncle Michael would never be able to get all those trees done in time."

Mary picked up her cup. "So the neighbors help and in return he helps them by giving them food."

"Well, it's not giving, really," Hester said. "They earn it for all their work."

She paused to take a sip. "Just like Miss Lilly used to make all our dresses and the boy's clothes in exchange for things like butter and apples. Even when Uncle Gerrit was alive and we were all living there, I reckon we couldn't have eaten all those apples."

"So you help them and they help you."

"It's what neighbors should do," Hester said. "It's the same when someone needs a raising. Everyone comes and helps because when they need help, the others will come and help them."

"Certainly is different than life in the city," Mary said.

Draining her cup, Hester stood and reached for her plate. "That's why no one up here in Palenville, at least up here on the hill, starves or goes without things they truly need and your city has people, even children, starving in the streets."

She scraped the remains from her plate into the slop pail. "We need to get back to work. The folks will be here soon and I'm sure Kent will be along to help take care of Uncle Michael's orders."

Mary was exhausted by the time night fell. She fell asleep as soon as her head hit the pillow and struggled to wake up when Hester did. She disliked the milking but preferred it rather than the task of raking and shoveling the stalls. She was relieved when Hester stopped having her do it, though the blisters on her hands were what put an end to that.

Mrs. Chandler, Miss Sally, and Judith came to visit after a week. By then, the dress Mary wore every day was stained and had enough rips that Miss Sally declared it unsalvageable. Mary declared it worth it to be able to help Hester and understood now why Hester never wore the dresses that had been given to her three years prior.

Judith was happy to enjoy biscuits with blackberry jam and fresh butter but absolutely refused to take the slop pail out to feed the pig. It was a simple chore but one Mary disliked, finding the pigs to be noisy and smelly even if they always seemed happy to see her arrive with the pail.

Three weeks passed before Michael returned. Old man Griffin brought him and Will up from Catskill in his delivery wagon, stopping at the Voss home to pick up Pieter, Kent, and Griet.

Hester sobbed as soon as Pieter and Michael carried Will from the cargo area.

"It's all right," Will said groggily. His eyes were unfocused and sweat covered his forehead while several days' worth of growth covered his face. "It doesn't hurt right now."

"It's all right, son," Michael said. "We'll get you inside and you can rest."

Will smiled and shook his head. "Not like I'm going to walk away, I reckon." The blanket that covered his lower body clearly revealed a void where the bottom half of his right leg should have been.

Hester followed the rest of her family into the house. Mary thanked old man Griffin, then wondered what she could do to help. Entering the kitchen, she decided to make a pot of coffee, then went into the root cellar and brought out the large pot of stew that she and Hester had been having for supper the past two nights.

"God bless you," Michael said as he reached for the pot. He sniffed the air. "That smells wonderful."

"It's um, hotspot."

"Huspot," Michael corrected as he filled a mug with coffee.

"It's almost warmed up," Mary said, mentally calculating how many people were there and pulling down the proper number of bowls from the shelf.

Michael took a sip of the hot brew, then grimaced. "Oh!"

"Is it too strong? I wasn't sure how much to use. Hester usually makes the coffee for us."

Michael smiled, though Mary was certain it was simply for politeness. "Just a little," he said, pouring half into an empty cup, then adding water to his own. He stirred it, took a sip and nodded with approval. "That's better."

Pieter entered the room, followed by Griet.

"There's coffee," Michael said. "Mary made it."

"It's too strong," Mary told Griet. The older woman smiled and patted her shoulder, much as Hester often did.

"I'll fix it," Griet said. She took a sip from the half-full cup. "Oh, my!"

"I thought I was supposed to fill the basket."

Griet smiled and dumped the contents of the basket into the slop pail. "Only halfway," she said. "There'll be grounds at the bottom of the pot now. Won't hurt anyone." She added water to the remaining coffee in the pot, as well as the cup.

"I'll get the stew," Mary said. "Hester made most of it."

"I'll take some," Michael said.

"Me, too," Pieter said.

Kent entered the room. "Can he have some more medicine? I think it's wearing off. He's cursing something awful."

"Two spoons," Michael said, then shook his head. "Give him three. It'll help him sleep."

Kent nodded, then left the room.

"I can't believe it," Pieter said. "He's so young."

"Crippled for life," Michael said, looking up when Mary handed him the bowl. "Thank you, Mary."

Mary returned to the stove, wondering about Tobias and his leg injury. She decided that if he was returned to duty than it must mean that he had healed completely.

"His first battle," Michael said. "First time he runs into the rebs and he almost dies." He spooned out a cube of meat from the stew. "Have you heard from the boys?"

Pieter shook his head, taking the bowl offered to him by Mary. "Thank you. Not a word since you left," he said to his brother.

Michael set his spoon down, lowered his head, then pounded his fist once on the table. "This damn war!"

He looked up. "I'm sorry, girls."

"It's all right, Uncle Michael," Griet said.

"Yes," Mary agreed. "We understand." She set the pot on the trivet. "We'll go see if Hester needs any help."

It was rare that Mary saw Hester cry but that night, alone in the privacy of their bedroom, she held the younger woman tight as racking sobs shook her. She whispered nonsense words and rocked Hester in her arms, gently stroking the dark hair, doing whatever she could to provide comfort. When Hester finally cried herself to sleep, Mary stayed awake a while longer, watching over her love and silently praying for the war to end and all the soldiers to come home safely, until exhaustion finally claimed her.

Mary was milking Stubborn when Michael entered the barn.

"I can do that," he said.

"I don't mind," she said, despite truly disliking the chore. "She's not so bad once you get to know her."

"That cow has kicked over more pails of milk than I care to count," Michael said. "I'll take care of the horses, then. Um, Mary, I wanted to thank you."

Mary smiled. "You're welcome, Mister Van Wyck."

"I mean, I'm most grateful for you spending so much time here helping Kent and Hester."

"I'm most pleased to help." Stubborn lifted her tail and dropped a steaming pile on the ground. "Mister Van Wyck? Perhaps after I finish milking her, I might go help Hester with breakfast?"

"Of course," he said. "I'll finish the rest of the chores out here."

"Thank you."

The coach from the Mountain House arrived about midday to fetch Mary back. Climbing into the coach and sitting down next to her mother, Mary looked down at her ruined dress and frowned. "I understand why Hester never wears the good dresses except when she goes to church."

Her mother reached out and touched Mary's hair. "After you take a long bath and put proper clothes on, give that to Miss Sally to pack away. Perhaps Miss Bessie will be able to use some of the material to make a dress for that new granddaughter of hers. You certainly will never wear it again. What is that on your hand?"

Mary held them out for her mother to see. "Blisters. They hurt."

"You poor dear. It is a considerate thing you did, helping Hester. I do hope, however, that it has not caused you to long for life on a farm."

"Oh, no, Mother," Mary readily agreed. "I enjoyed helping with the cooking and even making preserves and jams but the animals smell and there is a terrible amount of work to do each day. I don't know how Hester does it."

"She was raised that way," Elizabeth said. "And you were raised to live in a fine city and have other people do those menial tasks."

As Mary looked at her rough and blistered hands, she agreed. If she and Hester were to live together, it would have to be in the city. Mary had milked her last cow and fed her last pig. Certainly she had no intention of ever shoveling up after an animal again.

Late August finally brought the desperately desired letter from Tobias. Mary was the one to fetch it from the noon coach, racing to deliver it where her mother was sitting on the portico trying to stay in the shade.

"Another letter!" Mary exclaimed. "And this one has a picture in it." Before looking at the letter, she noted that there were two CDV cards surrounded by the letter. It took only a second to recognize the images. "Oh, my! It's Tobias, with Hendrik and Martin."

Her mother took the cardstock images. "Read the letter, Mary."

"Yes, Mother. He says,

Dearest family, I have made it through another month safely, save for one minor injury which I will not share lest it upset my beloved mother. The Battle of

Manassas, which they are also calling the Battle of Bull Run, was worse than anything you have read in the newsprint. I pray it is the worst of the fighting that I will ever have to endure. The only good thing of it was that the Ira Harris unit of the cavalry was called in for support and Hendrik was able to see his brother again. Both are well and send their regards. Mathew Brady's men are here with their strange instruments taking photographs of the dead as well as the living. Another gent with a cart showed up and asked if we would like to have pictures taken to send home. There were four taken but I have chosen to keep one as did Martin. The other two are enclosed and I ask that you give one to Hendrik's sister Griet. We are all grateful for the supplies that you sent as I have shared them with as much generosity as I could spare. I must say that my holder has broken and thus while I have many pens, I have nothing to hold them so that they might be used. Hendrik has let me borrow the one that Kent made him and I must ask that if you were able to secure one of those for me, I would be most grateful. I tried to offer him most of my possessions in exchange but he would not part with it. My love forever, your son, Tobias.'"

Mary folded the letter. "Hester is not coming again until next Saturday. I shall send word to her straight off and ask her to have Kent make him a new holder for his pens."

"Yes," her mother agreed. "Send word and ask for two holders, to be sure. I do not wish him to miss a letter to me for want of a way to write."

"Yes, Mother."

Her mother moved the Harper's magazine from her lap, tucking the pair of photo cards into her bag. "I will need to make him another package of supplies then," she said, the desire to avoid exertion during the mid-day heat apparently forgotten as she rose to her feet. "Please take the letter to your father and ask him to have Mister Beach arrange for us to accompany the coach back to Catskill this afternoon. We have some shopping to do."

Hester handed her two hand-carved pen holders. "Kent has made a few for both Hendrik and Martin and was not sure which one your brother had preferred. This one is from hemlock and this one pine."

Mary took the holders, smiling as she turned them in her hands. "They are most beautiful. It is no wonder that he wished for one of his own from him. Oh!"

She reached into the front pocket of her dress, pulling out the photo. "I forgot. Tobias sent this along to give to your family."

Hester's eyes grew wide as did her smile. "Oh, my! Hendrik and Martin and Tobias all together? What a blessing from the good Lord above." Her fingers traced the images of her cousins. "Look at those beards."

"When they return home, we shall hire one of those traveling photographers to come and take another photograph of them just like this but dressed in their finest suits," Mary said. "We can display them side by side upon the mantels."

"We should have a new photograph of ourselves together," Hester said. "We've both grown so much since the one we took at Mister Brady's."

"Yes, indeed," Mary agreed. "You've become more beautiful." She glanced around to make sure no one was within earshot or paying any attention to them. "I wish we could go for one of our long walks right now."

Hester smiled. "I wish we could, as well. It has been too long since we've had such pleasure."

"I would be happy with a place to hold and kiss you right now," Mary said. "Perhaps I might show you a new magazine up in my room?"

Hester smiled. "I would most enjoy seeing a new magazine up in your room, Miss Chandler."

"Oh, I almost forgot. Mother is taking me next weekend to Ellenville to hear Miss Anthony speak. I told her that you might wish to come."

"I can't," Hester said. "There is just too much work to do at home. I couldn't possibly leave Uncle Michael and Will alone that long."

"Could Griet not come up and care for him?"

"No. She has her own home to care for. I'm sorry, Mary."

"Very well. Another time."

"Let me say hello to your mother and then you can show me this new magazine."

"Just the magazine?"

Hester smiled. "It would be nice if you showed me more than that."

"I'm certain that can be arranged."

Chapter Twenty-Six

Gideon was startled to see a wagon racing across the open lawn. "Mister Chandler! Mister Chandler!"

"Kent? Have you lost your senses, boy?"

Others came running from the Mountain House to see what the commotion was about.

Kent jumped off the cart and removed his hat. "Excuse me, Mister Chandler."

"Kent, lad, Mister Beach will stripe your hide if he knew you were driving across the field as such. What has you so fired up?" He looked at his passenger. "Griet?"

The young woman's face was red and tear-stained, a handkerchief balled up in her fist. "I-is Mary here?"

"Mister Chandler, it is my Uncle Pieter."

Mary came running, quickly going to Griet's side of the wagon.

"What happened? Is it Will?"

Griet shook her head. "Uncle Pieter."

Gideon looked at the growing crowd. "Daniel! Help her down. Kent, you get these horses and this wagon back to the stables before Mister Beach sees this."

As soon as Daniel helped Griet down, Mary took the older woman into her arms. "All right," she said softly. "It's all right. What happened?"

"He-he...." Griet sniffled and wiped at her face. "He's dead."

"Oh, dear," Mary's mother said.

Mary looked at her father. "Father, I must go to Hester. She needs me."

"He was walking back from Uncle Michael's and fell dead in the road," Griet said. "Just fell, dead."

Mary's father reached into his jacket and removed several dollars. "Mrs. Chandler, perhaps you should ask the kitchen for a basket to take with you. I'm certain Miss Sally will be able to care for Daniel and Judith for a number of days. Hester needs someone to mother her now."

"Certainly," Elizabeth said. By then Judith had joined the group. "Judith, run in and ask the kitchen for a basket. Tell them what is going on and that they should make haste."

"I shall take just a moment to pack some clothes," Mary said, wiping the tears from her eyes.

"Yes," Elizabeth said. "Please pack a bag for myself, as well." She took Mary's place, holding the sobbing woman tight.

"Shall I ask Mister Beach for the use of a coach, Mother?" Daniel asked.

Mrs. Chandler raised her head and watched as Kent limped across the field, wiping his eyes. "I believe we can manage one trip in their wagon," she said. "Miss Sally?" she looked around. "Where is Miss Sally?"

"She went to help your daughter," one of the women said. "The poor dear."

"You, there." Elizabeth gestured for one of the Mountain House staff. "Please find two, no, three blankets that I might take along."

"Yes, Mrs. Chandler."

No member of polite society would ever be seen riding on a pile of blankets in the back of an old work wagon, but that was where Elizabeth and Mary Chandler were, their backs pressed against the wooden side and Griet sandwiched between them. The Palenville woman was still weeping, but the uncontrollable sobs had stopped.

As they approached the Voss house, Mary asked, "Mother? Should we stop and pay our respects to Mrs. Van Wyck?"

"That would normally be appropriate," Elizabeth said. "But I do believe that woman would rather have a visit from Satan himself than to see me." She rubbed the back of Griet's head. "When she returns home, I'm certain she will extend our condolences."

Griet nodded.

"Kent?"

"Yes, Mrs. Chandler?"

"Please continue on to your uncle's home."

When they arrived, they found Will siting at the kitchen table with his uncle. Both men rose when the women entered, though Will had to lean heavily on the table and sat down quickly.

"Where is she?" Mary asked.

"Up in her room," Will said.

"I'm going to go upstairs," Mary said. "Excuse me."

"Hello, Mrs. Chandler."

"It is good to see you feeling better, Will," Elizabeth said, giving his shoulder a quick squeeze on her way to the stove. Opening the stove door, she tossed in some kindling.

"Oh, I should do that," Michael said.

"No need," Mrs. Chandler said as she added water to the pot, then placed it on the stove. "When did this happen?"

"Last night," Michael said. "He had come to visit with Hester." Michael returned to his seat. "Everything was fine. He complained about his arm hurting a bit but that was all." He shook his head. "He left and we went to bed. It must have been close on to midnight when Kent came and told us."

"I wondered why he was so late coming home," Kent said. "And Mrs. V. told me to go get him." He pulled out a chair and sat down. "I found him just lying in the road."

"It was awful," Griet said as she opened the canisters to show Mrs. Chandler the tea and coffee. "Everyone came down to the house and Mrs. V. just started screaming at Hester that it was all her fault."

"Goodness, what a dreadful thing to do," Elizabeth said. "His own daughter."

"It was horrible," Griet agreed. "Hester was so upset. She...that woman wouldn't even let Hester give her father a kiss goodbye. Just awful."

"I should go down and see if she needs help getting his going to meeting clothes on him," Michael said. "Kent?"

"I don't want to go back there," the youngest Voss said. "I'd right tell that woman just what I think of her for doing that."

"Kent, remember what we're taught on Sundays. We have to be charitable to others." Griet reached for the tea balls. "Even if she isn't."

"He was her husband," Elizabeth said.

"Come on, son," Michael said. "We'll come back here after and you can help me make his coffin."

Kent reluctantly followed his uncle out.

"Would you prefer tea or coffee, Will?"

"Coffee, please, Mrs. Chandler."

"Have you made coffee before, Mrs. Chandler?" Griet asked.

"I have a servant at home to do that," Elizabeth said. "However, I have made tea and it certainly cannot be so different."

Griet reached for the coffee pot. "I'll make it. You should ask Mary sometime about the first time she made coffee."

"Uncle Michael said he could have used it to varnish wood," Will said.

"Willem!" his cousin hissed. "Manners!"

Griet smiled at Mrs. Chandler. "She meant well."

"Is there a tray that I might bring the tea upstairs?"

"Um, yes. I think so," Will said. "Griet, check in the back of that far cupboard. I think *grootmoeder's* old tray is back there."

Soon Griet was carrying the tray up the stairs while Mrs. Chandler followed. They found the younger women sitting on the edge of the bed, Mary gently rubbing Hester's back.

"We thought you might like some tea," Griet said.

Hester looked up, saw Mary's mother, and quickly moved into her caring embrace. "I can't believe it."

"I know, child. I know."

"What am I going to do?" Hester sobbed.

Mary cleared off the small nightstand to make room for the tray laden with tea and cups. She busied herself with pouring the tea while her mother continued to comfort Hester.

"H-has anyone contacted Domine Van Vlecq?" Hester asked.

"No," Griet said. "After they get back, I'll ask Kent to go to the church and fetch him and let the neighbors know."

Hester sniffled and stepped back from Mrs. Chandler. "Where did they go?"

"Uncle Michael and Kent went down…to the house to take care of things."

"Oh." Hester looked around. "I think I'm supposed to be doing something."

"What you should be doing is sitting down and having some tea," Elizabeth said as she gently pushed on Hester's shoulders. "We're all here and so is the rest of your family. You let us help you." She took the cup being offered from Mary. "Drink this."

By the time the sun dropped low in the sky, word of Pieter's death had spread through the small Dutch community. Most who knew the family, mostly through the church, went to the Voss homestead while those with a closer relationship and those that lived on the northern part of the road came to the Van Wyck Farm.

While Michael and Kent worked on the coffin, neighboring men toiled in the family cemetery to dig the grave. Will stayed at the table inside while the women filled the kitchen and parlor. Hester came downstairs to receive their respects and did her best not to break down into tears. Some of the older women spoke so much Dutch that Mary had no idea what they were saying but nodded anyway. When Griet was not in the kitchen, she helped translate and introduced Mary and her mother as friends of the family.

As much as Griet and Kent did not want to return to their home, to deal with their step-aunt and because their uncle was lying in state in the parlor, nonetheless they took their leave after Griet had made up the sofa for her Uncle Michael and placed clean sheets on his bed for Elizabeth to sleep in. Mary, of course, slept with Hester, though the younger woman had a fitful, poor rest.

It was a beautiful day, just the kind that Hester thought her father would enjoy as the crowd gathered around his grave. She even made the effort to be civil to her step-mother, who countered by ignoring her. The Catskill Mountain House coach brought Gideon and his other two children to attend. Minister Van Vlecq gave a traditional sermon in a blend of English and Dutch. Everything was calm until the service was finished and the crowd had dispersed. With just the Van Wyck, Voss, and Chandler families left, Mrs. Van Wyck turned to face Griet and Kent.

"I am sure your uncle will allow you to borrow his cart so you can move your things as soon as possible."

Kent's eyebrows rose halfway up his forehead. "What? We're not going anywhere."

"Nonsense. It's my home now and you two are leaving."

"Mrs. V., it's our home," Griet said.

"It belongs to us," Kent said. "It was our father's, not Uncle Pieter's."

Anger shone in the older woman's eyes. "You can't fool me. That house belonged to my husband and now it's mine."

"It's theirs," Hester said. "It belonged to Uncle Gerrit, their father."

"That's not true! It was Pieter's."

"That's why everyone called it the Voss house," Kent said. "Voss! V-O-S-S!   Voss!"

Will pushed up from the chair, grabbing Kent's arm for support. "They're right," he said. "The house belongs to Hendrik, Martin, Griet, and Kent. Not you."

Michael, excusing himself from his conversation with Gideon, joined the fray. "I have the deed with my late sister's papers. The house belonged to her husband's family and it was left to him. When she died, it went to their children. Pieter never owned it. Frances let him and Hester move in there after his wife passed back in forty-four."

"I don't believe you."

"Mrs. Van Wyck, I will be happy to go get the deed and show you."

"And before you get any idea about it," Will said. "*Grootvader* Van Wyck left this to Uncle Michael and my father. Uncle Pieter had his own house."

"Vader sold our house when we moved in with Uncle Gerrit and Aunt Frances," Hester said.

Mrs. Van Wyck glared at her step-daughter. "Then where's that money? He must have given some to them for living there and that means that house is mine!"

Hester looked at her uncle, uncertain of the answer.

"As I recall," Michael said. "He purchased two cows, a pig, and everything he needed to turn the old barn into a studio. The cows and pig are long dead and gone and the barn is still theirs."

The conversation deteriorated from there. In the end, Mrs. Van Wyck stormed off down the road with her children in tow. Michael, Griet, and Kent jumped into the wagon and followed.

Gideon gave a small smile. "Reminds me of when my father passed away," he said.

Hester looked at him with tears in her eyes. "Mister Chandler? Does that mean that she will take Vader's paintings? Everything in the studio?"

"I don't rightly know," he said. "Perhaps when she calms down, things will be better."

"And perhaps we'll get an honest mayor in the city," Elizabeth said. She put her arm around Hester's shoulders. "Come, child, let's get you inside."

"But his paintings," Hester cried as she was led away.

Mary went to her father's side. "Father? Is there nothing you can do?"

"It's not that far of a walk, is it?"

"About twenty minutes or so."

"Very well." He turned to his son. "Daniel, help Will inside. I'll be back soon." With that he started down the road.

"Yes, Father," the youngest Chandler said. Mary followed them, carrying the kitchen chair that had been brought out for Will to use. Silently she prayed her father would be able to do something to help Hester get her father's paintings.

The coach from the Mountain House had been waiting half an hour when Michael's wagon returned. To Hester's great delight, several of her father's paintings, mostly landscapes, were in the back. She and Daniel carried them inside, all the while thanking Gideon profusely.

"Thank you, Father," Mary said.

"I assume you had to purchase them?" Elizabeth asked.

"To keep that...woman from hurting Hester more by selling them or even destroying them? It was money well spent. Mary, go help your brother. I'm certain old Mister Silas is tired of waiting for us."

While the rest of the Chandler family returned to the Mountain House, Mary stayed on for another week. Though grief-stricken, Hester was finally returning to normal and swore she would be all right.

Two days after Mary's return, the Chandlers left the Mountain House to return home to the city.

Chapter Twenty-Seven

Mary was happy on that final Monday in June of Eighteen Sixty-Three. A letter had arrived from Tobias the previous week telling of his promotion to corporal and he seemed positive that the war would soon be done, despite President Lincoln's call for a draft. The train ride from New York City to Catskill was peaceful and the entire family seemed enthusiastic about returning to the Mountain House.

Best of all, Hester was waiting there when the coach pulled in. After a few minutes of visiting with the family, they were off for a walk to one of their favorite spots.

"Have you started painting again?"

Hester looked ahead as they followed the familiar path through Glen Mary en route to Ashley Falls. "I tried to pick up a brush last week but it is so hard to without thinking of Vader." She shook her head. "He was always so proud of my painting. I just can't imagine doing it knowing that he'll never see it."

Touching Hester's forearm to stop their progress, Mary moved closer and put her arms around her beloved's waist. "I know it's hard, my darling."

"Yes," Hester agreed. "Very hard."

Mary gently stroked Hester's back. "At least that step-mother of yours is gone."

Hester nodded. "Less than two weeks after Vader was buried. Moved back with her family in Coxsackie."

"Best place for her," Mary said. "Not to speak ill of anyone but that woman was more sour than a crab apple."

Hester gave a small chuckle of agreement. "She was that."

"I cannot believe she took the Voss' to court to make them prove the house belonged to them." Mary shook her head. "Just as well she didn't want anything to do with your father's paintings and was willing to sell them to Father."

"She sold off all of his brushes and easels," Hester said. "Never went in there the entire time she was there." Hester shook her head. "He's barely buried and she's in there trying to get whatever money she could."

"At least you have those paintings now."

"Yes," Hester agreed. "I still have several of his landscapes to treasure."

Mary rubbed Hester's back. "You'll paint again," she said.

"I don't know. Right now it feels like I won't, ever again."

"In your letter, you said Will was doing better?"

"Oh, yes! Kent made him an artificial leg. Can you believe that? It's not as though his leg is back but he can walk around now without assistance beyond the cane. No more hopping or using those crutches."

"That's wonderful."

"He's even back to doing all of his own chores at the farm and working with Uncle Michael on the furniture. He and Kent have been making these chairs that are just selling as fast as can be, to the mill and even to old man Griffin at the mercantile."

Hester held out her hand to help Mary cross a fallen log. "Oh, and did I tell you that after Kent made that leg, he got the idea to put some wood on the bottom of his left shoe and now he can stand straight up and doesn't have hardly any limp at all? He can even walk from his house to the farm without his knee hurting anymore. The good Lord smiled on them both."

"I'm pleased to hear it," Mary said.

"It means I can come see you more often again. Perhaps even if there is another rally, I might be able to go with you this time."

Mary smiled. "That is good news."

"And last week? A letter from both Hendrik and Martin arrived on the same day!" Hester smiled. "They're both doing well. Well, as well as can be expected in a war."

As they approached Ashley Falls, a gentle breeze kept them company and for that moment in time, all seemed right in their worlds.

Chapter Twenty-Eight

The morning of July fourteenth started as any other at the Catskill Mountain House. The family ate their usual breakfast, chatting about the various and sundry things that all families do. Elizabeth took her usual spot on the portico, surrounded by her friends, where they shared their usual talks about all matters inconsequential.

Judith disappeared immediately following the meal, off to spend the day at South Lake frolicking with her friends.

Daniel, armed with one of his father's pipes and a small amount of tobacco, took off into the woods with his friends.

Mary had the newest issue of Godey's to look through and found herself an empty chair by her father near the table rock. Upon arrival of the early coach, Gideon sat down with the day's copy of the New York Times.

"Anything interesting?" her father asked as he folded the paper into reading position.

"Not yet," Mary replied, adjusting her bonnet.

Gideon read for a few minutes, then sat up straight, his eyes widening. "What? Oh, sweet Lord, no."

Mary straightened up. "Father, what is it?"

His eyes never left the paper. "Mary Elizabeth, go fetch your mother and make haste about it. Oh, this is terrible. Simply terrible."

Mary ran as fast as she could, to the shady area on the south side of the Mountain House. By the time they returned, her father was reading an article to a crowd of men gathered around him. Even the nearby servants had stopped their tasks to listen to him.

"*Upper part of the building was occupied by families, who were terrified beyond measure at the smashing of the windows, doors and furniture. Following these missiles, the mob rushed furiously into the office on the first floor, where the draft was going on, seizing the books, papers, records, lists, etcetera, all of which they destroyed, except those contained in a large iron safe. The drafting officers were set upon with stones and clubs, and with the reporters for the press and others, had to make a hasty exit through the rear.*"

"Oh, dear," one of the men exclaimed. "I can scarcely believe it. A riot in the city? A crazed mob?"

"They set fire to the building," Mary's father said, pausing to find his place in the column. "And then attacked the Deputy Provost-Marshall. It says he was beaten so badly that there is little hope of his recovery."

"Was that Edward Vanderpoel?" another man asked. "I've dealt with him before. A fine and honorable fellow."

"The same. Listen to this," Mister Chandler said, his deep voice commanding attention.

"*The Orphan'...*" He closed his eyes briefly. "Dear Lord." Opening them, he cleared his throat and resumed reading for the crowd.

"*The Orphan Asylum for Colored Children was visited by the mob about four o'clock.*"

Several of the women gasped. Mary noticed that the group surrounding her father grew larger as word spread about what was in the paper. He continued.

"*Hundreds and perhaps thousands of rioters, the majority of whom were women and children, entered the premises and in the most excited and violent manner they*

261

ransacked and plundered the building from cellar to garret.'''

"Women and children?" one woman exclaimed. "Against orphans?"

Mary's father continued.

"'*When it became evident that the crowd designed to destroy it, a flag of truce appeared on the walk opposite, and the principals of the establishment made an appeal to the excited populace, but in vain.'''*

He paused again to scan the article. When he raised his head, Mary saw the glistening in his eyes. "They burned the orphanage down. The Times says scarcely a brick was left upon another." He let the paper drop from his hands to the ground and sat down, burying his face in his hands. Never had Mary seen her father so distraught.

Another man reached down and retrieved the paper, relaying the key points. "The mob attacked the Tribune, every colored person they found…set men on fire, hung men…burned homes, killed the firemen's horses to keep them from being able to reach the fires, burned the postmaster's home, the Bull's Head Hotel, an entire block on Broadway."

Tears streamed freely down his face. "The police were completely overrun. There's a list of officers killed. The destruction just fills the page. Private homes, businesses, it just goes on."

He handed the paper to another man and walked away, his handkerchief coming from his pocket and going to his eyes.

For several long moments, there was a stunned silence as the crowd absorbed the unbelievable news. Finally Mister Chandler rose, scanning the crowd until he found the person he was looking for. "Mister Beach! Mister Beach! I require a coach at once, sir. I must return home."

"Oh, no, Gideon," Mary's mother exclaimed. "You cannot! It is not safe!"

"I have to," he said. "Miss Bessie is there. Old Jack is there to mind the horses. I need to go make sure they are safe. Our home may be in ruins." He looked around, then raised his voice. "Mister Beach!"

"I will go, as well," another man said.

"Yes," yet another said. "I need to make sure my counting house is in working order."

"My factory," said another.

"I shall need the telegraph."

"The telegraph was destroyed," the man who had taken the paper from the ground said. "Even the Armory was set afire. We shall be lucky if the city is anything more than a smoldering pile of rubble."

"I cannot understand," one of the women said. "How could man do this to another man?"

"And women," another woman said. "To orphans. Colored orphans. What could they have done to deserve this?"

"It's Mister Lincoln's fault," one of the men said. "He freed the slaves and brought the war of the rebellion upon us."

"He should never have freed the slaves," another man said.

"Good God, man! If you had your way, the whole union would be a slave state."

"Better than the anarchy happening now. Did you see how many of our fine young men were killed at Gettysburg? Gettysburg? Tens of thousands. For what? For the coloreds?"

"It's not for the Negros," someone else said. "It's to keep our union together. Do you think if the South wins and gets to keep the confederacy that they're going to leave us alone? They'll take everything we have and make us slaves as surely as they do the Negros. Do you want them to come take everything you have of any value and then burn your homes? Take our women? They'll do that. Our women and daughters. That's how those rebs are."

Voices raised as several of the men engaged in a heated argument about emancipation, secession, and the costs of war. Unable to take it anymore, Mary walked away from the crowd, away from the Mountain House. Though she knew to never leave without an escort, without telling anyone, with only her bonnet to protect her head, she took to the toll road and headed down the mountain.

"Hester!" Griet's raised voice pulled her from her reading of the previous week's newspaper. "Hester, Mary is here."

"What?" Hester rose and quickly smoothed her hair and dress. "What do you mean she's here? I don't hear any carriage."

"She's walking up the road."

"Walk…" Hester moved to the window and looked out. "Oh, dear!" She raced out of the Voss home and into the road. "Mary! What are you doing here?"

Mary ran into Hester's arms. "Oh, Hester, it's so horrible."

Hester held her fiercely. "What is wrong? Don't worry, I am here. Whatever it is, I will make it better." She gently guided Mary into the house.

Buried in Hester's embrace, Mary shook her head. "No. It's too horrible. They are rioting in the city. Hanging people…burning the orphanage."

"What? Burning an orphanage? You're not making any sense. Whatever are you speaking of?"

"Here," Griet said, pulling out a chair from the table. "Sit her down."

Hester nodded and guided her distraught friend to the chair, tossing the bonnet onto the table. "Please, Griet, some water for her."

Tears rolled down Mary's face. "They...they burned the orphanage for the colored children. They've all gone mad."

"I don't understand," Hester said. "Who?"

Mary shook her head. "I don't know. The Irish? They started with the draft office and then just went through the city. They're chasing the coloreds, killing them, setting fires. They had to take those poor children out on a barge to keep the mob from killing them. Can you imagine? Trying to kill little children? Children?"

Hester took the water from her cousin and placed the glass in Mary's hands. "You must drink this. I cannot imagine such a horrible sin. Where did you hear such a thing?"

"It was all through the newspaper today," Mary said before taking a sip of the water. "Father is going to head back home and make sure Miss Bessie and Old Jack are safe." She leaned her head against Hester's waist. "It's just so horrible."

Griet handed Hester a wet cloth. "Thank you." Using the cloth, Hester gently wiped Mary's face, trying to cool her down after the long, hot walk.

"There now, it will be better," she whispered as she daubed her love's hot skin. A slight pull on the neckline showed the true extent of the angry red sunburn on the back of Mary's neck where the bonnet had failed to provide shade. Hester hissed at the sight. "Oh, Mary, you are badly burned." Pushing the blonde hair back, a similar redness shown on her lower face.

"I'll get the vinegar," Griet said.

"It's just so awful," Mary mumbled.

"Yes." Hester said the word but cared not a whit for what was happening in the city. Her world centered Mary and relieving the pain she was feeling. "My love, you should take care not to be so long in the sun."

Mary sniffled. "I had to come see you. I…I needed you."

Hester bent down and kissed Mary's forehead. "I am here, dearest. I am here." She gently tugged on the back of the dress, pleased to see that the bonnet had protected part of Mary's neck.

"Hester, the boarders are coming," Griet said. "Perhaps you should take Mary to the root cellar? You'll have privacy there to tend to her burns."

"Yes, that is a good idea," Hester said. She gently tugged on Mary's elbow. "Come now. I'll take care of that sunburn and then we'll get you something to eat."

"Boarders?"

"After Mrs. V. left, Griet took in two boarders. Come with me."

Entering the root cellar, Hester set the lamp on the shelf, then closed the door. The gaps in the vertical slats gave little strips of light but it was the golden glow of the wick that illuminated the earthen room. She quickly found herself enveloped in a fierce embrace, Mary's head buried into her neck.

"Oh, my Mary," she whispered, gently rocking the sobbing woman in her arms. "My Mary, there, there. I have you. It will be all right. There, there."

Mary was unresponsive to the phrases, helplessly bawling as if a small child. Hester continued to offer a soft tone and gentle words of comfort. Time passed this way until Mary was finally out of tears and able to bring herself into composure.

"I love you," Hester said, kissing Mary's forehead as the tight embrace ended.

"I love you, too." The sound of men's voices and chairs scraping against the wooden floor filtered into the root cellar. "You should go help your cousin."

"No. She can handle it and I'm sure Kent will be home soon. I only came down for a visit. You are more important." She brought her hands to the buttons on the back of Mary's dress. "Here, let's get you out of this so I can put the vinegar on your sunburn."

Despite her intention of treating the sunburn, the moment Mary's shoulder was bared, Hester could not stop herself from leaning and giving it a gentle kiss. "Mary."

"Please," Mary whispered, turning as her arm was freed from the white dress. She helped pull the other arm free, then push the dress to the ground. Now the sunburn stood out even more. The bottom of Mary's face and her neck were a deep red tone against the paleness of her arms and shoulders. She put her arms around Hester's neck, pulling her in for a kiss. "Please, Hester."

"Here?" Still, despite her protests, Hester's hands were far from idle, moving restlessly across Mary's chemise covered back and sides. "What if Griet comes down here? Or Kent?"

She covered Mary's lips with her own, moaning softly when they parted to let their tongues touch. She gasped into Mary's mouth when the hands she longed to touch her did just that, squeezing one of her breasts and brushing over the hardened nipple. "Oh, dear Lord."

"Hester, my Hester."

Unable to resist, Hester stepped back. "Wait." She moved to the corner and picked up a firkin of butter, placing the cask against the door. She added a crate half filled with gourds from the previous harvest, creating the best barricade she could, to afford them privacy. "There is no blanket or covering I can use to keep the dirt from us," she said.

"What about the potato sack?"

"That's barely better than the ground itself," Hester said, though she went to the canvas bag and emptied its contents on the dirt. "We have to be quiet."

Just then one of the men gave a raucous laugh. "I doubt they would hear us even if we screamed," Mary said, stepping the rest of the way from her dress.

"I am not the one who screamed that night on Newman's Ledge," Hester pointed out as she laid the sack on the ground. She closed her eyes and smiled when soft hands closed around her middle from behind.

"That was because you sent me to heaven, itself," Mary said, giving a gentle squeeze before bringing her hands to the front buttons of Hester's dress. "Please?"

It took only a slight nod from Hester before she was reduced to just her shoes while Mary wore the same with only her chemise still on her body.

"That burn looks so painful."

Mary shook her head, kneeling down on the sack. "I don't feel it. I don't feel anything except sadness." Reaching up, she took Hester's hand in hers and gave a gentle tug. "Please, my love, please help me feel something else."

Kneeling down, Hester slipped her fingers under the strap of the chemise. "I love you so very much," she whispered. "My Mary Berry."

Mary and Hester were cuddled together, now clothed and enjoying the intimacy that followed their lovemaking, when Griet's voice came through the door. "She's putting vinegar on Mary's sunburn and they're talking. I'm sure they'll be out in a few minutes."

"The vinegar," Hester said, scrambling to her feet.

"Wait, we need to put everything back," Mary said as she, too, stood up.

"Vinegar first. Thus it has time to dry while we put things back. That way it doesn't seem like we just did it." She poured vinegar on the cloth. "Oh, my, but that burns the eyes."

"Just as well," Mary said, turning her back so Hester could reach the worst part of the burn on her neck. "They will think I have still been crying."

"Will you stay the night?"

"I should have left a note for Mother and Father. They will no doubt be worried."

"I suspect they will assume you have come here, as you did before, or up to the farm." She gently urged Mary to turn around. "It is getting late. If you left now, it would be dark before you were halfway back to the Mountain House."

"We could borrow your Uncle Michael's wagon?"

"It would still be dark before we could reach the Mountain House and then whoever drove you would have to try to come home in the dark. It is only a quarter moon tonight. Not enough to safely see the roads." Hester shook her head. "You'll have to come back to the farm with me tonight and we'll have Kent or Uncle Michael drive you back tomorrow."

"I don't want to leave you."

"You won't. At least not tonight. Now, chin up." She carefully daubed the vinegar laden cloth on Mary's face, being as gentle as possible. After finishing the task on the sunburned shoulders and neck, the couple put everything back.

Within minutes they said a quick hello to Kent, went out the door, and headed for the farmhouse. There, at supper, Mary relayed in a more comprehensible manner about the goings on in the city. Will and Michael were both shocked and outraged, though Will pointed out that allowing people to buy their way from the draft might not have been the best idea since only the people with wealth could afford to do so. It led to a lengthy discussion about the haves and have nots and the ways that it might have contributed to the riots. By the time the trio was done talking, it was quite late. Hester and Mary went to bed but both found sleep hard to achieve.

Gideon returned three days later.

"Come, let us talk," he said as he ushered his wife and Mary toward an unoccupied area near the rear of the Mountain House.

"Pray tell, is Miss Bessie all right? The house? We've been reading such awful things."

"We thought the Bread Riot back in fifty-seven was the worst it could be." He shook his head. "This is on a scale that defies comprehension."

"Oh, dearest Lord," her mother whispered, bringing her hand to her mouth.

"The mob has taken control in every way that I can see," he said. "When the telegraph lines are repaired, they cut them again. The police move in to protect someone, and the mob chases them away. No black man is safe. Some of the fifth volunteers that came home are organizing to try to protect people."

"Tobias?"

Her father shook his head. "No. They have not called in the union army yet, despite repeated requests to do so. I fear Mister Lincoln doesn't know what to do."

He reached out and put his hand on his wife's shoulder. "They burned the livery. I'm afraid your carriage is gone. Miss Bessie and Old Jack are safe. He is staying at the house. He's afraid to go back to his apartment because no black man is safe on the streets right now. I told him to stay there with her until I send word that it is safe for him to return home."

"Our home? It is safe?"

He gave a small smile. "It is well. It was when I left, though I cannot say if it will still be that way when this insanity is through. I gave Old Jack grandfather's gun, just in case."

"Whatever shall we do?"

Gideon shook his head. "We do as we always do. We stay, live our lives, and let things go back to normal. It will happen. The police are starting to regain order and the fire department is back to putting out fires. The people will calm down, Mrs. Chandler. They always do. There's already word that some of the banks will issue draft loans to those that show employment and have letters from their employers."

"What about those who don't?"

"As long as there is a draft, there truly isn't much anyone can do beyond what has already been done. We can only pray for a quick end to the madness tearing our union apart."

He reached into his pocket for his pipe and tobacco. "Ah, if you will excuse me. I have to share the news with the others."

Mary waited until he was out of earshot. "Thank you for not telling him."

"You are an adult now," Elizabeth said. "However, I am still cross with you about leaving without a note."

"It won't happen again."

Elizabeth adjusted her hat. "Well, at least I knew where you had most likely ventured off to. I cannot say the same for your brother. Daniel disappears so often that sometimes I wonder if he came along this summer or not. As for your sister, a young man so much as takes a step and her head turns as fast as a windmill."

"She is at that age, Mother."

"Harumph. I don't recall you acting as such. I suppose I should be grateful that she only shows interest in the young men from good families."

"Yes, Mother." Mary wisely did not point out that since Judith only saw boys from their neighborhood and here at the Mountain House, they were the only ones the teen could show interest in. She had no doubt that if her younger sister saw a burly boy working at a mercantile or sawmill, she would be equally as attentive.

"I too, have things to do," her mother said. "Since the new materials arrived today, we will be having a bundling party tomorrow as soon as the staff clears the tables from breakfast. I expect you will be there."

"Of course," Mary said.

"Very well."

As Elizabeth walked away, something she said stuck with Mary and an idea formed. Now if she could only pull it off, and more importantly, get Hester to agree.

Chapter Twenty-Nine

"You want to do what?" Hester crossed her arms. "We'll be caught as surely as an ant gets caught in molasses."

"It's perfect," Mary said. "You said Will is back to doing his share and that you would be able to come if Mother wanted to take us to a rally for a few days."

"A rally," Hester pointed out. "And with your mother."

"This is almost the same."

Hester raised her eyebrow at the fallacy of Mary's statement. "No rally and no mother. How is that almost the same?"

"Hester Ann Van Wyck, you are twenty years old. Other than the one and only trip to the city, have you ever been farther than Catskill?"

"That is not the point."

"That's exactly the point."

"Why can't you just come to the farm?"

"It's not the same."

"It is the same," Hester said, tossing Mary's words back at her. "We're alone on the second floor. Why risk it?"

"It will be fun." Mary took the younger woman's hands in her own. "We can go places, do things, enjoy our time together."

"I thought we already enjoyed our time together?"

"We do, but this will be better." She leaned up on her tiptoes and gave Hester a kiss. "Trust me."

"I trust that we will be caught and your parents, and Uncle Michael, will be furious with us. Worse, they'll find out what we've been doing."

"We're adults now, Hester. We're grown women who are free to make our own decisions."

"Then why not tell them?"

Mary let go of Hester's hands and folded her arms across her chest. "Because Father and Mother would never let me go."

"Exactly!"

"Please? Just this one time?" She stepped forward and put her arms around Hester. "Just for the weekend. No one will ever find out, I swear it."

Hester sighed. "Are you sure?"

"Positive." She rested her head against Hester's chest. "I love you." She smiled when she felt a kiss on the top of her head.

"I love you, too."

"Is that a yes?"

"Yes but if we get caught, it's all your fault."

"I'll take full responsibility," Mary said. "Mother would know it was my idea, anyway. You're not devious enough to come up with an idea like this."

"Devious?"

"Sneaky."

"Oh. You're right about that," Hester said. "You are very sneaky."

Despite Hester's objections, Mary's cajoling won and a week later, the plan was put into action.

"Do you have everything you need?"

"Yes, Mother." Mary tried hard to keep her excitement from showing as she handed the driver her bag. So far her plan was going off perfectly but she knew that one simple slip of the tongue could spell ruin to all her hard effort.

"Extend my regards to her family," Mary's mother said as the coachman opened the carriage door.

"I will, Mother." Mary gave her mother a quick peck on the cheek. "I will see you in three days." Turning her head to hide her smile, she climbed into the coach. She patted her reticule full of coins and bills, grateful that she'd had the foresight to bring her stash of money with her when they left New York City for summering at the Mountain House. Now all of her careful saving would pay off handsomely with this most special of trips.

"Remember, if they have any of that huckleberry jam left, see about bringing back a jar."

"Yes, Mother. Goodbye. I love you. I will see you on Tuesday."

As the coach moved, she settled back into the leather seat. Her smile grew broader as the coach took her away from the Mountain House and to her secret rendezvous.

Will wrapped a piece of cloth around an apple. "Are you sure you have everything?" he asked as he handed her the fruit.

"I am only going to spend three days at the Mountain House with Mary," Hester said. "I am not traveling to the Washington territory."

"Other than your trip to visit Mary, I don't believe you've been away for three days since you and Uncle Pieter first moved in with Uncle Gerrit and Aunt Frances," Will said. "Perhaps some extra handkerchiefs?"

"No, thank you. If I need another, I'm sure Mary will loan me one of hers." She ran her hands down the front of her lacy white dress. It was the dress Mrs. Chandler had bought her four years' previous to wear to the theater.

Hester was certain the two inches she had grown since then did not matter as it still draped to her ankles.

"Are you sure you don't want me to wait with you until the late coach arrives at Catskill Landing?" Kent asked, hooking his thumb over his belt. "I don't mind driving home at night."

Hester shook her head. "No. Mary is going to meet me in Catskill and we will do some walking about before taking the stage back." She put the covered apple into her carpetbag. "You know how her family is about shopping."

"I'm surprised old man Griffin's mercantile ever has anything left by the end of the summer," Michael said. "Mrs. Chandler is most happy when she is making purchases."

"Yes," Hester agreed, not caring a whit about Mary's mother's shopping habits and eager to get going before she made a mistake and let the secret slip out. "Kent, are you ready?"

"The new chairs for the mercantile and the bench for Mister Mower at the mill are already loaded." He hefted the worn carpetbag containing Hester's other change of clothes and the few personal items she had packed.

"Oh, I hope they both buy your furniture," Hester said. "Can you imagine if Mister Griffin starts selling your chairs along with his own pieces? Why, you might just be able to buy Griet one of those fancy sewing machines I saw in the newspaper. Then she would be able to make dresses as fine as those store bought or made by Miss Lilly."

Kent shrugged. "He bought the first ones I showed him. Don't rightly see why he wouldn't buy these." He reached for the door. "Long as we make them chairs as good as any man, people buy them."

"You're right," Hester agreed. "Thank you for all your help. I will see you in a few days."

Catskill Landing was bustling with the latest arrivals from New York City and Albany. Most had landed at Oak Hill Station across the river, then taken the ferry across. Hester and Mary blended in with the crowd, each carrying their single bag of clothing for their three-day excursion. Sharing knowing smiles, they walked past Beach's coach, bound for the Mountain House.

"I don't know why we didn't think of this before," Mary said as they approached the ferry.

"Because your parents would most certainly take a switch to you if they knew what we were doing," Hester said, looking around to make certain no one she knew saw them.

"You must trust me. Mine are far too worried about that young man that has been hovering over Judith, as if he were a moth and she the brightest candle, to worry about me spending a few days with my dearest of friends." She walked closer so as to bump their upper arms together. "Please do not worry, Hester. I have thought this through completely. Ah look, here we are."

"Good afternoon, ladies," the ticket master said as he rose to his feet and touched the brim of his cap. "How might I be of service?"

"Two tickets on the Hudson River Line to Albany, please," Mary said. "My sister and I are visiting our dear brother who is quite ill."

"Certainly, Miss. You'll find our ladies car to be of the utmost in style and quality for your trip. Your total is four dollars and fifty cents, please."

Mary opened her reticule, sharing a smile with Hester as she pulled out the proper amount of coinage for the fare.

"It is a most beautiful day for traveling," the ticket master said as he took the coins from Mary.

"Indeed," Mary responded. "How long shall we expect this journey to take, sir?"

"The train will arrive in Albany by six-thirty," he said, placing the money into a box and retrieving the appropriate tickets.

Hester was too nervous to speak, leaving it to Mary to thank the ticket master and to lead them away.

"Oh, I am so excited," Mary said as they strolled toward the ferry landing.

Hester smiled. "I am, as well."

"Three days." Mary lifted her face toward the sun and smiled. "Three days, Hester. Just you and me, far away from our families."

"I do not believe I could possibly be happier," Hester said. "I do hope we have pleasant weather with which to explore."

Mary stopped basking in the sun's rays and turned her head to look at Hester. "I care not a whit if it were to pour the most violent of rains, so long as I am with you."

Smiling softly, Hester gave Mary's free hand a squeeze with her own. "Ahh, were you a man, able to truly court me."

"It is a most unjust turn of fate," Mary said. "No man shall ever make my heart feel as you do."

Reaching the landing, they followed the signs for the ferry. "Nor I," Hester agreed. She shook her head as if to ward off the sad thought. "Enough of this," she said. "We are going to Albany!"

Within half an hour, they were being taken across the Hudson River by the ferry to the Oak Hill Station, where shortly thereafter they were aboard the late afternoon train heading north to Albany.

"I just hope no one recognizes either of us," Hester said, leaning so only her companion could hear.

Mary waved her hand dismissively. "The only people who know me are at the Mountain House and the only people who know you would never go to Albany. We're perfectly safe."

Since they were alone in their seats, Hester reached and covered Mary's hand with her own. "Please understand that I am most pleased to spend this time with you, but I do worry that we lied to our families."

"We shall be back to them this Tuesday and no one shall be the wiser." She entwined Hester's fingers with her own and gave a little squeeze. "Worry not, my dear one."

"I do worry," Hester admitted. "But I am also quite excited. I have never been to Albany before. Is it as grand a city as New York?"

"It is different," Mary said. "The capitol is quite beautiful as are many of the buildings, but there are less people milling about. Certainly far less Irish. When Mother and I were here for the suffragist rally, we enjoyed a most amusing play. I am certain we shall be able to find something of equal entertainment."

"I would be happy to see those beautiful buildings."

"We shall hire a coach to take us about and see whatever you wish," Mary said. "There are more parks but fewer theaters. Still we will find many things to see and enjoy during our stay." Releasing Hester's hand, Mary took a step back. "Now, shall we join the other ladies for tea?"

"You will like the Stanwix Hall Hotel," Mary said as they left the train station. "Mother and I stayed there when we went for the suffragist rally back in Eighteen Sixty-One. I am certain it is just as grand."

Hester smiled at her. "I would care not if we slept out in a park with nothing but our clothes to keep us warm," she said. "I am happy to just be with you. Where we sleep is of no consequence."

Mary smiled. "The things you say to me. How could any man hope to compare?"

"I am speaking only the truth."

Entering their room, the ladies set their bags down, then turned to face one another. "It feels so long since we were able to sleep together," Hester said.

"Yes, it does," Mary replied, stepping closer and putting her arms around the younger woman's waist. "I love you, my Hester Pester."

Hester's fingers sank into the long, blonde tresses. "And I love you so very much, my Mary Berry."

"Then show me," Mary said, reaching up to undo the buttons on the back of Hester's dress. "I wish for you to show me once." She brought their lips together for a quick kiss. "Then again." Another kiss. "And then again after that."

"And again after that," Hester promised, her own fingers working on divesting her lover of her dress.

"And I will show you," Mary promised. "You said you did not care where we slept. I'm sure you also meant that you did not care *if* we slept."

"I would wish to never sleep again if it meant I could stay with you alone in this room forever." She cupped Mary's cheek. "Your smile makes my heart skip a beat."

"And yours makes my heart feel as though it shall burst forth from my chest," Mary said. "I go to sleep each night holding you in my dreams and wake up with you as the first of my thoughts."

She slid the dress off Hester's shoulders. "I want to kiss every freckle, touch every inch of your skin." She proved her point by placing a gentle kiss on the now bare collarbone, smiling when she felt Hester's hands grip her shoulders tightly.

"Must we ever leave here?" Hester asked.

"Were it possible to remain here until we were old and gray, I could never have a moment of regret."

"Nor I," Hester agreed. She gave a little shimmy to help with the removal of her dress. "Perhaps we will not see any of Albany, save for the train station and this hotel."

Mary turned around to give access to the buttons at the back of her dress. "There is always next time," she said. "It is not as if the statuary will suddenly leave the city."

"Next time?"

"Oh, yes," Mary said. "If we cannot stay here forever, then we must plan to return again." She slipped her shoulder from the dress. "It truly is a beautiful city."

Hester kissed the nape of Mary's neck. "Beautiful. Yes. More beautiful than anyone I have ever seen." She kissed the soft skin again. "More beautiful than the most golden of sunsets over the mountains, the most glorious of sunrises."

Chapter Thirty

Hester smiled and burrowed closer, believing it to be the most glorious morning of her life. Her nude body was pressed against Mary's equally naked form and though the sun declared it time to be awake, she was certain they had achieved only a scant few minutes of sleep. Kissing the bare back before her only served to rekindle her desire.

"Mmm, if you keep doing that, I fear we shall never leave this bed," Mary said, covering Hester's now roaming hand with her own. "We would die of starvation."

"But I would die happy," Hester said. "Being in your arms is heaven to me."

She kissed Mary's bare skin again. "Truly the good Lord has blessed me to have this, to share this, with you. In all my born years and all those ever after, never shall I be this happy."

Mary brought their joined hands to her lips and kissed Hester's knuckles.

"I will treasure the memory of this trip for the rest of my life," she said. "I wish we were able to go away even farther, to leave New York and this world we live in." She brushed her cheek over their joined hands. "Some place far away where we could be together as we dreamed of when we were children."

Hester gently tugged until Mary was back against the mattress. "I dream of that, as well," she said, separating their hands so she could run her fingers through the blonde hair as she looked down upon her love. "I love you with all that I am, my sweet Mary. I will always love you, even when I am old and gray."

"Love me now, my Hester Pester," Mary said, reaching up to caress the side of the younger woman's breast. "Touch me in the way that only you may do. Make me feel what only you can."

"And what of breakfast?"

Mary smiled at the gentle teasing. "We shall have a large lunch instead."

Hester smiled. "Or perhaps an even larger supper?"

"Perhaps." Locking her arms behind Hester's neck, she gave a gentle tug, encouraging their mouths to engage in some non-verbal communication.

From the moment Hester's hand started to drift downward, Mary knew she was lost. Her legs parted quickly in anticipation of that most magical of touches. She could do little more than moan and repeat Hester's name while her body reacted in the most wanton of ways. Her hips moved of their own volition, rising up hard to meet the two, then three fingers sliding into her, the calloused thumb brushing repeatedly on that special spot. Forcing herself to control her volume when she wanted to scream with pleasure, she quickly slid over the precipice with a shuddering release. There was no time to recover as Hester quickly took her again, then a third time. Breakfast was completely forgotten as they let their passions take control.

The carriage jostled and jolted the couple as it made its way along the Old State Road from Albany to Schenectady. Hester used a fan borrowed from Mary to move the air about her face.

"I swear it never becomes this hot at home."

Mary was rapidly fanning herself with a fan showing a motif of flowers and birds. "It does in the city," she said. "It does always seem much cooler upon your mountains."

"There is much to be said for living in the mountains," Hester said.

"But you also have cows. Cows that make the most unpleasant odor."

"Cows that give milk and butter and cream," Hester countered.

"And unpleasant odors."

Hester stared out the window. Her smile faded away.

"My darling, what's wrong?"

"Another time."

Mary put her hand on the younger woman's arm. "No. I can see that something is upsetting you. What is it?"

Hester turned her head to look at Mary. "You were such help to me on the farm last year and I was, and am, truly grateful for all the hard work you did." She took Mary's hand in hers. "But I know that you would never be truly happy living there."

"So you'll just have to move to the city."

"And leave my family?"

"Yes. You can always return for visits. Married women often move away from their families. Oh, Hester, think about it. There's so much to do in a city, so much to see."

"So much noise, so many carriages going back and forth. Always so busy."

Mary pulled their hands up for a kiss. "You wouldn't be happy in the city."

"And you wouldn't be happy on the mountain."

"So what do we do?"

Aware that the coachman could not see them from his position outside the carriage, Hester leaned and kissed Mary passionately.

"We keep loving one another," Hester said. "We have our summers and our stolen moments and special trips like this." She cupped Mary's cheek. "And we keep loving one another."

"I will always love you, Hester Ann Van Wyck. Always."

They stared into one another's eyes.

"And we enjoy every moment we have together, just as we always have," Hester said. "Now tell me more about where we're going."

"You've heard of Schenectady."

"I've heard of it but I don't know anything about it."

"It's small."

"Smaller than Catskill or smaller than New York City?"

"Smaller than Albany. Bigger than Catskill. I'll tell you what I learned when Mother and I were here."

Hester settled back in her seat and put her arm across the back, inviting Mary to cuddle against her. "Tell me everything."

"Mind your step," Mary warned as Hester moved closer to the high edge of the riverbank.

"Mary Chandler, while you have been walking on those flat, paved streets of New York City, I have spent my life walking along streams and kills." She wrapped her hand around a thick branch to steady herself as she moved along. "I do believe the mighty Mohawk River will not swallow me whole today."

Mary's response was to pick up a pine cone and toss it at her companion. "If it did, I suspect it would find you sour and spit you back out."

Hester held onto the tree and used her momentum to come half a turn so she was facing Mary. "I do not believe sour was the term you used to describe my taste last night."

Mary flushed a bright red. "Hester Ann Van Wyck!" she admonished, though she was smiling through her embarrassment. "A proper woman does not speak of such things."

"A proper woman does not run off with another woman to do improper things." She reached out and pulled Mary into her arms. "It is a joy indeed to not be a proper woman."

"Indeed," Mary agreed just as they kissed.

The sadness and seriousness of their carriage ride had faded away as both resolved to put the dark thoughts aside and concentrate instead of enjoying their holiday.

Having spent much time taking long walks in the woods of the Catskill Mountains in their efforts to be alone, following the high banks of the Mohawk River was rather simple for the pair. The coach Mary had hired for the day was parked a mile upstream from their location. The tall pines provided much in the way of seclusion while the water scouring the rocks gave a melodic background noise to their conversation.

"We do need to be careful not to stain our dresses," Hester warned. "We are not able to wash them before our return."

"It would be hard to explain such a thing," Mary agreed, though her hands were roaming on Hester's body in a manner that gave every indication that their bodies would soon be on the soft, moist ground. "It is one thing to explain grass stains upon the back of my dress when I am ten and quite another to do so when I am twenty-one."

"We should then return to our hotel room," Hester suggested, stopping the hands that were caressing her breasts through her clothes. "For the sake of our dresses."

"Yes, for the sake of our dresses," Mary agreed. Still they remained pressed against the tall pine, kissing and caressing one another for several more minutes before finally separating.

As they walked back toward the coach, they came upon a downed tree that while lower than they would have liked still served as an acceptable place to sit down for a short time.

"See the squirrels playing on the other bank?" Hester asked, pointing at the pair of furry critters scampering about the trees and rocks of the western side of the Mohawk. She took Mary's hand in her own. "I remember when we were so young and carefree."

"Before this horrible war," Mary said.

"When all that mattered each summer day was if I was going to be able to go with Vader to the Mountain House to see you." She pulled their joined hands to her lips to kiss Mary's soft skin. "When all that mattered each winter day was how soon the summer would come again. Sketching and painting helped, but not much."

Mary mimicked the gesture, pressing her lips to the back of Hester's hand. "During my time away from you, I would talk to the picture of us that you drew." Leaning her head against Hester's shoulder, she continued. "Now, it is that photograph of us that accompanies me to sleep at night and greets me each morning."

"As it does with me," Hester said, tilting her head so her cheek could rest upon Mary's soft, blonde hair. "I wish we had one of us right now. Something to help us remember this special time we have shared. I love you so much, my Mary Berry."

"I love you, my Hester Pester. I'm certain they have a photography studio in Albany but how would we ever explain it?" She looked around. "We'll have to find something else to remember this trip. Something simple…something no one would question. Hmm. I have it."

She walked to the edge of the grassy area. Two feet below was a sandy riverbank.

"Here, help me down there."

"What are you doing?" Hester asked.

"I have to get something." Mary held out her hand. "Let me down."

"Mary…." Nonetheless, Hester used one hand to hold onto a stout sapling and the other to help Mary down the sandy drop off.

"There," Mary said triumphantly as she let go and stepped to the water's edge. "Now, let me see."

Hester watched as her friend looked down at the shallow water of the riverbank. "Please be careful."

"Ah, here we go." Water splashed upon the hem of Mary's dress as she took a couple of steps into the water.

"Mary, please. Your dress. The currents. This river is much faster than the creek behind the farm."

"I'll be safe." Bending down, Mary pulled two small stones from the water, then stood and returned to grasp Hester's outstretched hand.

"I thought we were trying to keep our dresses clean?" Hester admonished, kneeling down to wring out the hem of Mary's dress.

"I will simply tell Mother than you and I were playing near the stream," Mary said, holding out her hand to show Hester the two stones. "Pick one. These will be our mementoes for this trip."

"Pebbles from the river?"

"Yes. Do you not see? If Judith or Mother asks, I can simply say that it is a stone from your stream that I took as a souvenir of this weekend and should anyone ask you, you could say that it came from South Lake. When we see them, it will remind us of this day when we were able to spend the day walking along the Mohawk River without thought or care for anyone else."

Hester smiled and took one of the stones from Mary's hand. She kissed it, then put it back. "That one is yours," she said as she claimed the other stone.

"Wait." Mary took the stone from her and put it to her lips. "There. Now whenever either of us needs a kiss from the other, it is there in the special pebble."

"How could there ever be a more perfect day?" Hester asked as she placed the pebble into the side pocket of her dress.

"There could not," Mary agreed. "Now. I am famished. We should return to Albany and enjoy the finest that the capitol has to offer."

"Did you enjoy yourself today?"

Hester set her spoon down and dabbed at her lips with the napkin, appearing every bit the well-mannered young woman out for supper with her sister. "Most certainly. The Shakers are a most remarkable people and the Cahoes Falls were nice."

"Certainly not as spectacular as the Kaaterskill Falls."

Hester nodded in agreement. "Nothing is as wondrous a sight as our own falls. Still it was nice to see a different one."

"Did you enjoy the show?"

"Oh, I did indeed. Those dancers were most delicate. What was that called?"

"Ballet. I hear that they have performed in all the major cities." Mary paused to slice into her chicken. "That woman with the rope, what was her name?"

"Rosita. Rosita, queen of the rope and her cloud swing."

"I did not believe a body could move in such a manner."

Hester smiled and lowered her head, her shoulders shaking with mirth.

"What?" When Hester would not look up, Mary reached out and gently poked her with the fork. "What? What has you so amused?"

"If you were to see yourself at…certain moments, my Mary Berry, you would indeed believe that a body could move in such a manner."

Mary felt the heat rise in her cheeks as she returned the smile. "Miss Van Wyck." She glanced around to make certain no one was near enough to hear them. "When we return to our room, I shall have to see if I can make you move in such a manner."

"That is a challenge I would be most willing to participate in, Miss Chandler."

The next afternoon, Mary and Hester smiled broadly as they, along with several others, walked along the shady paths of the Albany Rural Cemetery. A portly man with a booming voice acted as a guide of sorts, pointing out with great panache the grave of one of Albany's elite or the ornate statuary that made the graveyard so famous.

"Oh, my," Mary exclaimed. "I swear that angel looks as though he were about to take flight."

"Most of the markers in our little burial area are either wooden or just a rock that someone chipped on," Hester said. "Kent carved up a nice piece for Vader but it has already split from the weather just like grootvader's did." She walked and touched the marble stone. "I've never seen one of this beauty."

"My grandfather has a large stone," Mary said. "With flowers and shields. I suspect had he seen these…." She pointed at the various statues within their view. "He would have wanted one, as well."

"With all these carriages, there is scarcely room to walk," Hester said. She gave an appropriate smile in response to a man touching the tip of his brim as he and his wife walked past. I would like to see those geese and swans about the pond but I see no empty benches. So many people."

"They are making memories," Mary said. "When the husband has passed onto heaven, the wife can come and visit his grave, then come down here to the pond and relive the memories of the times they were here together."

She stopped their forward motion and turned to look directly at Hester. "They are no different than we, my Hester Pester. We treat our time together as something more precious than the finest of jewels. Moments to be treasured, remembered and relived again and again to help us through those times when we are apart."

"Would it be possible, I would wish to be buried next to you," Hester said.

Mary squeezed Hester's hand, then turned to watch the couples walking along the shaded path. "If I could make such an event possible, I certainly would," she said. "Oh, look! I do believe that is Archangel Michael. Let's take a closer look."

"Did you enjoy your visit?" Kent asked while setting Hester's bag in the back of the cart.

"Very much so. How are things at home?"

Kent smiled. "Nothing changed in three days, Hester. How was it at the Mountain House?"

Hester grabbed the sides of the cart and placed her foot on the wide step Kent had installed. "As it usually is."

"So the fire didn't bother you?"

"Fire?" Hester took a deep breath, her mind racing as Kent climbed up on the cart, then reached to help pull her up. "Oh, well, I suppose with all the excitement, it just left my mind."

"Mm hmm." He reached for the reins. "You, my dear cousin, are a terrible liar."

"I, I, I—"

Kent laughed. "I know you did not go to the Mountain House. I saw Mary leaving the afternoon coach with a bag of her own. Certainly, she would not need to pack clothing for herself if you two were simply returning there."

"Oh." Caught, Hester had no idea what to do. Lie? Evade? Beg for mercy? "Does Uncle Michael know?"

Kent shook his head and with a snap of the reins sent the horse into motion. "I said nothing to him or Will. As it was, there was no fire. You have nothing to worry about."

"Thank you. Truly." She felt her pounding heart start to calm down.

"So where did you two go?"

Hester hesitated before deciding to trust her cousin with the truth. "Albany."

Kent let out a low whistle. "Well, now, that certainly is daring. Did her family know?"

"No. She told them that she was coming to Palenville to visit with me."

"So you told us you were going there and she told them that she was coming here and then the two of you took off to Albany?"

"Yes."

Kent laughed and stamped his foot on the floorboard. "If that don't beat all. Good for you two. I'm glad you got away. Even if it was just for three days."

Unsure what else to say, Hester simply said, "Thank you."

They road along for a while without talking about much more than the weather and how much Kent had made from selling his chairs to the owners of both the mercantile and the sawmill. They were out of Catskill and on the quiet road to Palenville when Hester finally summoned up the courage to broach a subject she had often wondered about but never asked. "Kent?"

"Hmm?"

"You truly will not say anything?"

Still looking forward, he smiled. "I know there are dandies that fancy other men." He turned his eyes in a quick glance at her before looking forward again. "And I suspect there are women who fancy other women?"

Hester looked down. "I think…I believe God would not allow something as wonderful as love to be a sin, no matter who it is with."

Kent nodded. "And for you, it is Mary." He paused. "I saw you kissing her once. In the kitchen at Uncle Michael's."

The snort of the horse and the clopping of the hooves upon the ground was the only sound for several moments before she took a deep breath, raised her head, and answered her cousin with the secret she had kept inside for so long. "It is."

She pulled the handkerchief from her pocket as she felt the sting in her eyes. "There will come a time when she will have to marry and make a family of her own, but it will never change how my heart feels for her."

"It doesn't have to be," Kent said. "She could move in with us, let others think she is a cousin. You two could move away somewhere no one knows you and pretend to be sisters. Become teachers or a seamstress or even open up your own boarding house."

Hester dabbed at her eyes. "Mary needs finery and family. Certainly her parents will never allow such a life for her as to be one who cleans and cares for strangers. I would not want that for her, either."

"So what happens? You simply let her marry some man? Perhaps marry one yourself?"

"Perhaps. There are worse lives, Kent. As we feel for one another, we both know it is not to be. We can only take these moments together. A few hours here, an evening there, a weekend at the farm. This secret trip." A sob caught in her throat. "These memories to hold us when we are apart."

He reached and patted her hand. "I am glad you had this trip, then," he said. "If you wish to plan another in the future, I will be most happy to help you." He squeezed her hand. "I am sorry, Hester. So sorry. I'll never tell. I swear."

"Thank you."

"So tell me about Albany. I want to hear everything."

Hester smiled, feeling a great weight lift from her shoulders. The rest of the ride was spent regaling her cousin with the details of her trip. The details that did not involve the things they did in their room at the Stanwix, of course.

Chapter Thirty-One

The brutal winter of Eighteen Sixty-Three finally gave way to the Spring of Eighteen Sixty-Four. It seemed the war would not end and every day was spent reading the news or waiting for the post with the hope of a letter from the boys fighting for their country.

As agreed in their letters, the day the Chandlers returned, Hester would be waiting in their special spot near Ashley Falls. Mary made quick excuses to her family about wanting to go for a walk and quickly left the Mountain House.

Mary looked at the sky, noting the sun directly overhead. She quickened her pace through Glen Mary, turning when she reached the falls. She made certain to smile at everyone who approached on their strolls but made no effort to talk to them, intent on reaching her destination. Years of walking through the woods had taught her well, and she knew where to cross the stream so that only her shoes and ankles became wet. It took only a few minutes to be so far off the trail that she would not be noticed by the others. She was glistening with perspiration by the time she reached the set of rocks that stood as tall as she, where Hester was waiting for her.

"I am free until supper."

Hester smiled. "Wonderful."

She held a hand out to help Mary to the woolen blanket laid upon the ground. "I brought some sandwiches and apples to keep us this afternoon." She sat down next to Mary. "You look wonderful."

Mary smiled. "It is Miss Bessie's cooking. I cannot fit into any of my old dresses. You are as thin as ever. You need to eat more."

Hester laughed as she took Mary's hand in hers. "I eat more than enough," she assured her. She kissed Mary's palm. "I've missed you so."

"I swear the winters and springs are getting longer," Mary said. "This cold spring did not help at all. Father was talking about not coming up until July."

"Oh, no! That would have been horrible."

"Exactly," Mary agreed. "That's why I pitched a fit until he gave in."

"Mary Elizabeth Chandler!"

Mary laughed. "I would have come upon my own and I told him such. I've missed you so much."

As they usually did when in the woods, a cautious glance around was given before they dared to kiss. As their last kiss had been nine months previously, it was no surprise to either when that first kiss led to another, then another, then the parting of lips to better share their mutual expression of love, desire, and longing. While their location was fairly safe, it was not safe enough to dare divest themselves of any clothing, limiting the couple to kisses and the squeezing of breasts through their dresses.

"Soon," Hester promised, adding a soft moan as Mary's wandering fingers located the hardened nipple pressing against the cotton.

"Tonight?" Mary's breath was hot against Hester's ear.

"I can't. Come up this weekend, or even tomorrow."

"I miss you so much, my Hester Pester."

"And I miss you even more, my Mary Berry." Hester's fingers found Mary's nipples and gave them pinches. "So very much."

"I wish you could have visited me this winter."

"By the time Griet was better, Kent was sick. Then there was Griet's wedding and by then the snows were too high for me to travel anywhere."

"I know, but I still wanted to see you." She kissed Hester's hand. "At least you found time to paint again. I'm so happy about that."

"I am, too. I hadn't realized how much I missed it."

"Your family had best remain healthy this summer," Mary warned playfully.

"I sold two paintings to a young student of Mister Church. I should be able to pay for half of the train fare."

"I will pay the entire cost if it means I can see you during the fall. Perhaps two trips before next summer?"

"Mary, it is only June. Could we wait until September before we start getting upset about the end of summer and being separated again?"

"I never want to be separated from you," Mary said. "Never. When I am old and gray, I wish you to be by my side. Right until I take my final breath."

"As I wish with you," Hester said before they engaged in a series of heated kisses and roaming hands.

"If you keep this up," Mary warned. "We will need to go to the other side of Ashley Falls."

Hester smiled and kissed Mary again. "I have no objection," she said.

"It is a fine thing indeed that we cannot get one another pregnant," Mary said. "If I were a man, I would never be able to refrain from touching you before marriage."

"It seems that Griet felt the same way about her new husband." Hester leaned back.

"How is she?"

"Quite uncomfortable. She is most certainly not the glowing picture of happiness that we have read pregnant women to be."

"Has your uncle calmed down?"

Hester smiled. "Uncle Michael is pleased to soon be a great-uncle but he does not like Sten and I suspect will continue to feel such until the good Lord comes to take him away."

"If it had been Judith suddenly with child and requiring a wedding, I am certain Father would have done the same thing your uncle did."

"Sten is lucky it was only a good thrashing with a switch. Uncle Michael felt he deserved far worse than that. If Aunt Frances were still alive, she would have beaten him with a belt until he was within an inch of his life."

Mary reached for an apple. "It truly is a beautiful day. Tell me about the paintings you sold. Were they new ones?"

"Yes. I made them during the winter."

As the sun moved through the sky, the lovers relaxed and enjoyed their time together. Conversations moved from the paintings to the war to everything that was happening with their families. As usual, it ended far too soon for their liking, though Mary promised to arrange a trip to the farm for a visit within the next few days. When they parted, they had no idea their next meeting would be so far removed from what they had envisioned.

Chapter Thirty-Two

The next morning, Mary carried her cup of tea for herself and a cup of coffee for her father across the lawn area to where he was sitting in his usual chair. "Thank you, Mary."

Mary glanced over his shoulder at the paper. "Has Jefferson Davis surrendered yet?"

"Let us hope it is he and not President Lincoln who surrenders," her father said. "The casualty list for Cold Harbor takes up far too much of the page. He squinted. "Is that? Oh, no!"

"What is it?"

"Oh, no!" Gideon pulled the newspaper closer to his face, peering intently at the small print.

"Father?"

He shook his head. "It is the list of men buried at the Eighteenth Army Corp Hospital Burying Ground." He looked up at her. "Martin is on it."

Mary swayed, reaching out to grab the back of her father's chair to steady herself. "Are you certain, Father?"

"Martin Voss, fifth cavalry, New York." He shook his head. "That poor boy."

Seeing Michael's wagon at the Voss home, Mary and her mother stopped there. Hester and the rest of her family were inside, sitting around the table.

"I'm so sorry," Mary said as Hester ran into her embrace.

"It is a sad, sad way to find out about a death," Hester said. "Mister Mower from the sawmill drove up here this morning with the newspaper to tell us."

"Father saw it in the paper, as well," Mary said. She turned and embraced Griet. "I'm sorry."

"We received no word, n-no...."

"I know," Mary said gently, stroking the older woman's back.

"How could the Army do this?" Kent asked, his tear-streaked face revealing pent up anger. "He deserved better!"

"Yes."

"He deserved to have a telegram sent. Even a simple letter!" Turning away, he pounded his fist against the counter. "We deserved it! He sacrificed his life for this country and all he gets is a simple burial and a single line in a bottom column of the newspaper? It's wrong, Mary! It's just wrong!"

Hester gestured at the blond man standing next to Griet. "Mrs. C., Mary, this is not the way we expected you to meet Griet's husband but this is Sten. Sten, this is my dear friend, Mary Chandler and her mother."

"Pleased to meet you," he said.

"You should sit down," Elizabeth said to Griet, who was rubbing her protruding belly.

"I was hoping the war would be finished before the baby came," Griet said as she took a seat. "The boys would have been so happy to be uncles."

"Hendrik probably doesn't even know," Kent said.

Hester nodded in agreement. "I will send a letter," she said.

"I should do it," Griet said. "Oh, please excuse me, Mrs. C.. Would you like some tea or...or something?"

"I'll get it," Hester said. "I'll make enough for everyone. I think it will be a long day."

Mrs. Chandler left a short while later, informing Mary that the coach would come to the Van Wyck farm to pick her up in three days. The rest of the day was spent reminiscing about Martin and praying for Hendrik to return safely. It was nearly nightfall when Michael drove Will, Hester, and Mary to the farmhouse.

Though they had long since retired for the evening, Mary and Hester found sleep elusive. Both tossed and turned, nightmares about receiving similar news for Tobias and Hendrik plagued them. By the time morning came, neither could say that they had any reasonable amount of rest.

The following day was busy as everyone gathered at the Voss home to receive the neighbors coming to pay their respects. Mary busied herself making tea for the guests that wanted it while Hester offered up glasses of wine and cider for the others. In mid-afternoon, a shriek from Griet changed the somber tone into one of excitement. Her water broke, sending the men outside and the women into action as the contractions started only minutes later.

It was fortunate that not one but two of the neighbors who had come were midwives. One had even helped Frances deliver all four of the Voss children and now as Griet screamed and pushed, a new child was about to enter the family. Mary, who had only a vague recollection of her Mother giving birth to Daniel and none for Judith, thought the process would go quickly. She was shocked when the hours went on and still no baby made an appearance. It was morning when Erik Martin Emanuelson finally arrived.

As Griet enjoyed some well-deserved sleep, Mary leaned over the wooden cradle and stroked Erik's cheek. She felt a gentle hand on her shoulder and turned her head to see Hester's face mere inches from her own. To her surprise, Hester gave her a gentle kiss before sitting down next to her.

"Kent and Sten are doing the morning chores," Hester said. She glanced at her sleeping cousin. "I doubt Griet will wake anytime soon."

Mary yawned. "I certainly understand. I'm exhausted and I was just watching."

"I don't know how grootmoeder had so many," Hester said. "I can't imagine Griet wanted to go through that again."

"I don't remember Mother screaming such," Mary said. "And she certainly didn't use such language."

Hester chuckled, then gently stroked the infant's soft blond hair. "Look how much hair he has. He's so perfect."

She looked at Griet, then back to the baby. "I believe that for this blessing from the good Lord, she would say that he was worth all the pain."

There had been several times, when she was younger, that Mary had wished she were a man so she would be able to wed Hester. Seeing the longing as the younger woman gazed upon the infant, she again wished she was a man so she could give Hester the one thing that all the Chandler money would never be able to buy, a child of her own.

Chapter Thirty-Three

Mary looked around the studio, noting that the latest painting of her was still only half-finished and now no longer was on the main easel but perched on a smaller one pushed back into the far corner. On the main easel sat a new painting mostly completed. It was of Erik, resting in his mother's arms while Sten sat next to them. "It's beautiful."

"Thank you. I had such trouble capturing his eyes. They're not the same blue as yours and I kept wanting to darken them to match." Hester picked up her brush. "I'm so used to doing yours."

"You'll get used to his," Mary said. "It's good that you did this. It won't be long before he is growing and without any photographs, this will be the only way they'll be able to look back at how he appeared as a baby."

"I'll finish yours before the end of September," Hester said.

"I'm not concerned. I understand." Mary walked to the window and stared out at the yard. "It's your family."

She heard the brush being put down and then felt Hester's arms encircle her from behind. "What's wrong?"

Mary shook her head. "I didn't say anything was the matter."

"This is not the first time you've said that my family comes first to me. Not even the first time this week. Something is bothering you."

303

Mary bowed her head. "I keep thinking about the future. Our future."

"Oh." Hester let go and moved to stand next to her. "It's not as simple as when we were little girls." She too stared out the window, leaning her hands against the sill. "We'll never have that big house with children."

Mary glanced at her, seeing the same pain on Hester's face that she was feeling. "Please understand that I am so extraordinarily happy when I am with you. Truly I am."

Hester gave a small smile that quickly faded. "But the farmer's life is not for you any more than the city is for me."

Mary felt the sting of tears. "Things are changing so quickly. How did we go from being little girls to grown women? So very different?"

"We've always been different, Mary." Hester looked at her, then looked away. "You enjoy the parties and riding around in coaches. All the shopping and those committees you and your mother are on. The rallies and the speeches, the trips to London and Paris. I enjoy making dinner for the family. Holding Erik, spending hours alone in the studio painting or an afternoon by the creek sketching and drinking wine."

"And the pigs and the cows."

"Yes, and the pigs and the cows. And the cats and the goats." Hester pointed out the window. "You see that tree? When we were children, we'd all come up here after our chores were done and climb it. The boys could go higher than Griet and I could, but we still did it. *overgrootvader* Van Wyck planted that tree himself when he and my *overgrootmoeder* first moved here."

"That's your grandfather?"

"Great-grandfather. This farm used to belong to his wife's family and when they married, this land was given to them. He built the main part of this house himself. There weren't any neighbors on the north part of the road back then. Someday Erik will play on that very same tree and then after that, his children and grandchildren." She shook her head. "Even with us always talking about living in a big house and all, I always used to picture it here. Orphan children or my own children, it didn't matter. I just always believed that there would be children that would climb that tree someday and be calling me moeder or even mother."

"And I always saw us in a large brownstone house with a sidewalk and parks and theaters to go to."

"If I want a park, I just have to step outside. There are trees everywhere." She walked back to the easel. "Your family comes here three months a year to escape the city." She picked up the brush, then set it down. "But then you always return."

"You're correct," Mary said as she too walked to the easel. "We do escape up here. But we escape the noise and heat, not the rest of it. We don't milk cows or sweep floors or even make beds. The Mountain House gives us trees and fresh air and two lakes to play in but it also gives us a large staff of people to bring our food and do the cleaning. In the evening, there's someone who plays the piano or one of the ladies gives a recitation or sometimes there is a dance or even a play. People from all around the world come here but mostly it's the same men and women that my parents socialize with back home. Other than your family, I don't believe Daniel and Judith even know anyone who lives in the area."

She took Hester's hand in hers. "I know if I asked, Father would buy a nice home in the city, but that would not make you happy."

Hester nodded. "If I asked, I'm sure Uncle Michael would let you live here, but that would not make you happy."

"We love one another, but we also love our own lives. We wouldn't be content otherwise."

"So we're in the same place we were a year ago," Hester said. "Just be happy with the time we do have together and the rest of the time, be happy with the lives we lead."

"My heart will always belong to you, Hester. I could never love another the way I do you. I know it."

"You are my heart, Mary. I think of you first in the morning and last before I go to sleep. No one else will ever make me feel the way you do." Reaching out, she used the back of her hand to caress Mary's cheek. "So, we have our summers."

"Yes," Mary said softly. "And other times. You can come visit. The trains are getting faster every year. In no time at all, traveling from Catskill to the city will be just as quick as a carriage ride from here down the hill to Catskill is now."

Hester embraced her, then lowered her head until their lips met, kissing Mary softly. "Then let's be happy with what we have."

"Yes," Mary agreed. "Very happy."

The Van Wycks and Kent waved as Mary's coach moved down the road.

"When did you say you would make a trip out to the Mountain House?" Michael asked.

"Next Friday," Hester replied. "Please don't let me forget to bring a pie for her mother."

"Only if you make one for us, too," Will said, leaning heavily on his cane. "I need to go sit down."

As the group made their way to the house, they heard voices coming up the road. Pausing, they looked to see Miss Lilly and a young woman approaching.

"Good afternoon, Miss Lilly," Hester said, changing direction to meet up with the pair.

"Good afternoon, Miss Hester, Mister Van Wycks, Mister Voss. This is my niece, Esther. She's come to live with me."

"Pleased to meet you, Miss Esther," Michael said.

"Welcome," Kent said.

Will hobbled forward and held out his free hand. "Willem Van Wyck."

Esther looked at her aunt.

"Go on, child. They're not like those folks in the city."

The young woman hesitantly held out her hand. "Esther Todd."

In a move that would shock many, Will did not merely give her hand a gentle squeeze but brought it to his lips. "Welcome to Palenville, Miss Todd."

"Miss Lilly, shall we leave out extra eggs for you now?" Michael asked.

"I would be most grateful, Mister Van Wyck. I'm afraid I have nothing to offer you 'cepting some sewing if Miss Hester wishes."

"That won't be necessary," Will said as he took a step back, his eyes still on the young woman standing before him. "Always happy to share. Are you a seamstress, too, Miss Todd?"

"I can, but not as well as Aunt Lilly," Esther said. "I was a maid for a family in Boston."

"Boston? I hear that is a fine city," he said. "How nice that you have moved here. I'm sure your aunt is happy to have you."

"Oh, I am indeed, Mister Van Wyck," Lilly said. "It's been so lonely in that little house all by myself."

"I'm Hester."

"Pleased to meet you, Miss Van Wyck."

"Miss Hester, please."

Esther nodded. "Miss Hester."

"And he's Mister Van Wyck," Will said, pointing his thumb at his uncle. "I'm just Will."

"Mister Will."

"Um, Hester was going to make some pies tonight. Perhaps you would care to come by tomorrow and have some? Certainly it's been too long since you've visited, Miss Lilly."

Hester raised her eyebrows at her cousin. "Well, yes. Miss Lilly, perhaps you and Esther might come by tomorrow afternoon?"

"That would be lovely, Miss Hester. Thank you."

"Yes," Kent said, smirking at Hester. "You're making pies tonight. I don't know how I forgot."

Will grimaced. "I am most sorry, but I must go sit down now." He gave the young woman a smile. "From the war."

"Please, do not let us keep you," Esther said. "Such a brave man. Auntie?"

"Thank you again," Lilly said. "We'll call upon you tomorrow afternoon."

"I'll make sure a peach pie is waiting for you, Miss Lilly," Hester said.

The women continued on their way as the Van Wycks entered the house. Once inside, Hester hauled off and smacked Will's arm.

"I'm making pies tonight?"

Will sat in his chair. "You like making pies."

"I'd like an apple one if you're taking requests," Michael said.

Hester smiled and shook her head. "Peach for Miss Lilly, apple for you." She looked at Will. "I know you want blueberry. I can't make a huckleberry because I need to save those for Mrs. C." Walking to the cupboards, she pulled out several pie tins. "I suppose I should make one for Griet, as well."

"I'd like rhubarb," Kent said. "Since you're making pies tonight."

"I think that was right neighborly of you, Will," Michael said. "You are right. It has been too long since Miss Lilly has been here for something other than picking and planting time." He dropped his hand on Kent's shoulder. "You and I have some lumber to move. Best get it done now before supper."

"All right, Uncle Michael."

As soon as the door closed behind them, Hester turned to face Will. "What do you think you're doing?"

"Being charitable to our neighbors."

"You kissed her hand."

"Never thought you had something against coloreds."

She crossed her arms. "I don't."

"Ain't we supposed to treat coloreds the same as us? Why shouldn't I kiss her hand? I've kissed Mary's hand. I've kissed her mother's hand."

"Have you ever kissed Miss Lilly's hand? Or Miss Sally's?"

"Um, no. But they ain't as pretty as Miss Esther is."

Hester turned back to her pie tins. "Don't you go getting any ideas, Willem Van Wyck. That sort of thing might happen in those big cities but the mountain folk won't ever allow you to take a liking to a colored woman."

She looked at the amount of tins before her, then reached into the cupboard and pulled out another one. "Miss Lilly herself would take a frying pan to you if she thought you were thinking about her niece like that."

"I'm just being nice," he said. "Do you want help?"

She smiled at him. "Since this was your idea, yes. You can cut up the apples and help roll out all the dough." She walked past him on the way to the root cellar. "In fact, you can make the dough. All of it."

He chuckled. "I reckon I should."

Chapter Thirty-Four

Hester placed the rolled canvas into the hinged wooden box. "It is so hard to believe that another summer has ended."

"It seems to go by faster with each year," Mary said.

"We shall soon blink and be old women." Hester closed the box, making certain to engage the latch so it would not pop open during the journey to Gramercy Park. "I am amazed how much Erik has grown in just these past few weeks."

"Much as I have," Mary said, patting her rounded hips. "I barely fit my dresses anymore."

"Oh, dear, your mother will just have to take you shopping as soon as you get home."

Mary laughed. "I swear, we barely unpack from our trip and she is having Old Jack ready the carriage."

"To be fair, I believe Judith has grown at least two inches this summer. Especially on top."

"If the boys buzzing about her, as bees to a flower, is any indication. I believe her bosom is larger than mine."

Hester stood in front of her and looked down at said bosom. "Yours are still larger."

"Have you been looking at my sister's chest?"

"Oh, no," Hester said, putting her arms around Mary's waist. "One Chandler woman is enough for me."

"We just dressed," Mary said softly, though her hands roamed Hester's back. "I'm not certain I could handle another trip to the moon and back."

"We have less than two hours before the carriage arrives. Should we find out?"

"They do say it is better to try and fail than to not try at all."

"Is that so?" Hester smiled slyly. "I think that in five years, I have yet to fail when it comes to giving you pleasure."

"Pleasure beyond words," Mary said, gently nudging Hester toward the door. "Certainly I have never failed in that department, either."

"Most certainly," Hester agreed, reaching behind herself to open the studio door. "Most certainly."

"I do believe our goodbyes are much better now than when we were little girls and cried each time."

"You still make me cry," Hester said, backing up as they went down the hallway toward her bedroom. "It's just a different cry and for a much different reason."

Mary spent her time on the train back to the city rereading the entries in her diary from the summer. Every so often she would close her eyes and remember the things that did not make it on paper, all of them involving Hester.

Upon arrival at home, Mary was pleased to learn that Shakespeare's *The Taming of the Shrew* was opening at her favorite theater the next evening. Her mother had a meeting and her father simply refused to suffer through one more play by the bard, leaving her with no choice but to beg Judith to accompany her. After initial protestations, both from Judith about not wanting to go and from their mother about the propriety of two young ladies going off by themselves, Mary finally won out. It did, however, require her to owe her sister a huge favor to be collected in the future.

The rain was just beginning to fall when the carriage pulled up in front of the Chandler's brownstone. Judith exited first, followed by Mary. The said their goodnights to Old Jack before the groomsman pulled away.

"Thank God that's done," Judith groused.

"You weren't complaining during the play."

"I was sleeping," the younger Chandler said. "I wish Mother or Father would have chaperoned you."

"I wish no one would chaperone me," Mary said. "Goodness gracious, I'm twenty-three. When will I be treated as an adult?"

"I don't believe that we'll ever be treated as adults until we're married and living in our own homes," Judith said.

Mary nodded. "For all of Mother's talk about women having equal rights, I doubt they would make Tobias have a chaperone if he wanted to go out for an evening."

They walked up the steps as another carriage pulled up. Pausing, the women turned to see who would possibly be coming to their home at such an hour. He was bearded and his hair longer than when they last saw him, but there was no doubt who it was.

Mary blinked in surprise, then squealed with delight. "Tobias! Tobias!" She ran to him and engulfed her big brother in a fierce hug. "I love you. I never thought I'd see you again. Oh, Tobias!" It was when she let go that she saw the cane. She moved to let Judith embrace him, as well.

"I'm afraid it's permanent," he said, adjusting his balance and grimacing. "So, too, it seems, is the pain."

"Oh, no!"

"Are you home for good?" Judith asked.

Tobias nodded. "Not much use for a soldier who can barely walk."

"Let's go inside," Mary said. "Mother and Father will be so happy to see you."

"Would either of you have money for the carriage? I told him that I would pay him when we arrived."

"I do," Mary said, walking to the carriage and taking care of the fare along with a healthy bonus to the driver for bringing her brother home.

Leaning heavily on his cane and with his sisters on either side, he took the steps one at a time until they reached the door.

"Don't tell them," Mary said, her handle on the knob. "Let's surprise them."

Tobias smiled. "I like that idea."

Judith entered first. "We're home," she announced.

Their parents were in the parlor. Gideon was sucking on his pipe and reading a book, while Elizabeth seemed to have been resting, waiting up for their daughters to return.

"Did you enjoy yourselves?" their mother asked.

"I did," Mary said from the foyer as she shed her coat. "I believe Judith would rather have had her toenails pulled out."

She helped Tobias from his coat, then reached up and ran her fingers through his messy hair, though it did little to help. "We did find something special that we brought home with us."

"Oh?" Gideon asked. "There is no room on the walls for any more paintings."

"Oh, no," Judith said with a smile. "This is breathing."

"Bre-Judith? You didn't bring home one of those stray animals, did you?"

With that, Tobias stuck his head around the wall. "Is that what I am, Mother?"

"Oh!" Their mother brought her hands to mouth as tears filled her eyes. "Tobias?"

"Son!" Gideon dropped the book and pipe without a care and bolted to his eldest child. "My boy!" He grabbed him in a bear hug so fierce that the cane clattered to the floor.

Sobbing uncontrollably, Elizabeth ran to her son. Never had Tobias been so smothered with kisses from his mother. Gideon released his hold, so his wife could hug her son, but kept his hand on Tobias' shoulder.

"Oh, Tobias!"

It took only moments for the noise to bring Daniel from his room, followed by the robe-covered Sally and Bessie from their upstairs quarters. Mary recovered the cane and put it back in her brother's hand.

"I will put on some tea," Bessie said, tears streaming down her face.

"I would love some coffee, please," Tobias said.

"Here, let's get you off that leg," Mary said, gesturing toward the dining table.

While Tobias took his usual seat on the side near his father's end of the table, his mother took Daniel's seat, insisting on sitting next to her long-lost son. During the next two hours, Tobias filled them in on what had happened. He knee had healed completely the first time but a month ago he was involved in a skirmish with rebs and the butt of a rifle to the side of that knee proved to be too much. The doctors said there was nothing more they could do for him, gave him a cane, and a ticket home.

It was past midnight when the family finally retired to their beds. Mary knew that on this night, for the first time in more than three and a half years, her mother would sleep well.

Chapter Thirty-Five

Hester's smile could not have been wider as the train pulled into the station. A happier Monday had not been seen in years. All about, the news of the union victory buzzed through the air with an energy that nearly crackled. Newspapers were passed around the ladies' car proclaiming that peace had come at long last and praising General Grant and the fine soldiers of the union army. Some were calling it the miracle of Palm Sunday. Others declared it the inevitable result of President Lincoln's decision to free the slaves. No matter which opinion prevailed, the result was the same. The horrible war that had cost so many their lives was now finished and the house divided would become whole again.

"The Lord has finally answered my prayers," a woman said to Hester. "Now, my son can return home."

Hester smiled. "My family will be most pleased to have my cousin Hendrik return, as well."

"My son will never return," another woman said sadly. "He was taken at Gettysburg."

Hester took the woman's hand in her own. "I'm so sorry for your loss. My cousin Martin was killed at the Battle of Cold Harbor last year," she said.

"Such a terrible price our nation has paid for this," another woman said. "But now it's finally through."

"Yes," Hester agreed. Gathering her carpetbag, she stepped off the train. As expected, a jubilant Mary waited for her.

"It's so wonderful to see you," Mary said as they embraced. "And on such a momentous day. Wait until you see Tobias. He'll be so happy to see you."

"Look at all this," Hester said as she admired the red, white, and blue bunting draping the entire roofline of the train station.

"Wait until you see the city itself," Mary said as Old Jack took Hester's bag and they loaded into the carriage. "I've never seen anything such as this in my entire life."

Hester could not help but smile as the coach made its way toward Gramercy Park. Flags hung from near every home while patriotic bunting draped from the upper windows of several businesses. In the distance, the sound of two hundred guns firing in victory rose above the din of the crowds, though just barely. Old Jack had difficulty maneuvering through the streets as so many people crowded them in spontaneous celebration.

"I've never seen so many people at once," Hester said.

"Isn't it just wonderful?"

Unable to contain their joy, both at seeing one another and at the long awaited news, they slid the curtains to allow some privacy from the crowds and properly reunited after more than six months of separation with kisses that lasted until they were almost to the Chandler brownstone.

Mary's room had changed little since the previous time Hester had visited, save for more of her paintings adorning the walls.

"I made room on the dressing table for you," Mary said as she walked to the window. "Also in that middle drawer."

"Thank you."

Mary smirked and pulled the heavy draperies to cover the window. "We should also change before dinner. Here, let me put the lock on."

"Lock?"

"It's new," Mary said, sliding the iron bolt into place. "I grew tired of Judith bursting into my room unannounced and insisted that I deserved some privacy."

"Oh," Hester said quietly, letting go of the nightgown in her hand and walking to Mary. "Yes, you most certainly deserve some privacy."

"We deserve some privacy," Mary corrected, pulling Hester down for a kiss. "Much privacy."

"Yes. The kind of privacy we had when we were in Albany."

"Exactly." Mary's nimble fingers made quick work of the top button of Hester's dress. "That kind of privacy."

"Hmm. Let me help you." Hester reached for the buttons but Mary stopped her.

"I don't want help," Mary said, guiding Hester's hands down. "I like to undress you." She kissed the bare cleft of cleavage. "I love seeing you."

"Oh, Mary."

"I love you, my Hester Pester." She guided them to the bed, engaging their lips in heated kisses. "I love you and I missed you so much."

"Mary. My Mary."

It took little urging on Mary's part to get Hester to lie back on the bed. "I'm going to love you now," she said as she slid her hand up Hester's thigh. "And again tonight when we go to bed." She pressed against the damp cloth covering Hester's most intimate area. "And again in the morning before everyone awakes."

But that was not to be as there was a jiggle of the handle, followed by an insistent knock. "Mary? Let me in."

Both women sprang up and straightened out their dresses.

"Just a minute, Judith. We're changing."

"Well, hurry up. I want to tell Hester about Finn."

"Finn?" Hester inquired as the footsteps retreated.

Mary turned around to allow Hester to finish with the buttons. "Finn O'Malley."

"O'Malley? Oh, dear!"

"Exactly."

Mary removed her dress, then selected a simpler one to wear for the afternoon while Hester changed into one of her two best dresses, the one she called the theater dress. "He's as Irish as can be and Father is absolutely against her being courted by him." Mary pulled the dress over her head. "Which is why she is probably making time with him."

Hester fastened the buttons but quickly ran into a problem. "Um, I don't think this one is going to fit."

Mary growled and pulled the dress back off. "I was hoping," she said as she selected another dress. "I swear I'm getting bigger every day. That dress is only three months old."

Hester put her arms around Mary. "You're still the most beautiful woman I've ever met," she said, punctuating it with a kiss on the back of her love's neck. She let go so Mary could find another dress.

"And you still fit the same clothes you wore when you were sixteen."

Hester wisely did not point out that she had since grown a few inches, something Mary stopped doing at seventeen. Fortunately, the dress still appeared respectable, though her old shoes were rather tight.

Minutes later, they were all gathered in the parlor, Daniel kindly sitting on the floor to allow everyone else to have a seat. Hester found herself sandwiched between Mary and Judith on the sofa.

"Has there been any word from Hendrik?" Mrs. Chandler asked.

Hester shook her head. "Nothing since his letter we received in October thanking us for sending him paper and how he was looking forward to the war ending so he could return home and meet his nephew."

"It is so sad that he had to learn of Martin's death from a letter."

Hester nodded. "Griet and I have written to him several times but there has been no response. I do so wish the army was better about delivering the mail."

"It would be quicker to for us to walk to the battlefield itself and hand deliver than depending on the post," Mary said. "Do you know it took two months for Tobias' last letter to arrive from when he wrote it?"

"It seemed to take as long to get them at times," Tobias said. "I would get one letter only a week after it was sent and then others took so long that I would receive two or even three at once."

"At least we no longer have to worry about that," Elizabeth said. "Tobias is home and soon Hendrik will be back with his family, as well."

"I will pack extra cigars this time and we will have one of those afternoons at your uncles just like we used to," Gideon said. He sniffed the air. "Tobias, tomorrow I will take you to the tobacconist and get you some quality tobacco. What you've been smoking smells rotten."

"At least he doesn't smell like fish," Daniel said.

"Finn works on the pier hauling fish," Mary said quietly to Hester.

"I told you not to mention his name around me," Mary's father said. "I've already resolved that matter."

"I'm almost eighteen. I'm an adult now, Father," Judith said, her tone making it clear that she did not consider the matter resolved. "Finn is a good man."

"Now, see here! No daughter of mine is going to be setting her sights on a ruffian who works at the pier and no doubt spends what little pay he gets in a saloon," her father said. "I'll hear no more about it."

He reached for his pipe. "There are plenty of fine young men from the northern part of the city for you to choose from. No need to go scraping the bottom of the fish barrel."

"Mister Chandler, we do have company," Elizabeth said. "Perhaps this is a matter best left for another time."

"Hester is practically family," he said as he filled his pipe. "Have we not sent her Christmas and birthday presents these past few years?" He took a puff. "Certainly I would rather spend time with her than anyone from your family."

Hester bowed her head, trying hard to hide her smile. Mary had written quite the lengthy letter about her Grandmother Franklin's previous visit and the verbal battles that ensued between mother-in-law and son-in-law.

"I believe we should get ready for dinner," Mrs. Chandler said, promptly standing up and leaving the room.

Gideon tapped his pipe into the tray and looked at Hester. "That, my dear, is my wife's way of saying that I am in trouble. If you will excuse me. I believe Old Jack will be here within half an hour."

Later that night, Hester limped all the way to the bed. "Please, help me get these off."

When the stockings were removed, Mary gave a low whistle. "Hester, your feet are so red and there's blisters."

"They're too tight," Hester said.

"Why didn't you say anything? We could have gone shopping this afternoon."

"I don't have the money to spend on shoes that are too nice to wear at home and I didn't want you to buy them for me," Hester said, painfully moving her toes.

"Well, you most certainly are not putting those on again," Mary said. "Tomorrow you'll wear your regular shoes and we'll go buy you new ones." She pointed a finger at Hester. "No arguing."

"Yes, Mary Berry."

"I'll Mary Berry you," Mary said, rising to her feet and climbing on top of Hester, forcing the younger woman flat against the bed.

"I like it when you Mary Berry me," Hester said, lifting her head to plant a kiss on the tip of Mary's nose. Sinking her fingers into the blonde tresses, she pulled her love down for a gentle kiss.

"I don't believe we'll need nightgowns tonight," Mary said between kisses.

"They'll be in the way," Hester agreed, her hands caressing Mary's generous curves and full hips through the dress. "Just like your dress is right now."

"I'll take care of that," Mary said, pushing back into a standing position. She slid the lock on both the bedroom and washroom doors, then removed her dress and chemise. Hester quickly removed her clothing, then knelt down and helped remove Mary's shoes.

As soon as Mary extinguished the lamp, they made love. Sometimes their repeated warnings to one another to be quiet caused giggle fits, which only served to make their special time together, as it was their laughter, rather than their sounds of passion, that earned a warning admonishment from Mary's mother.

"I wish we could take another trip to Albany," Hester said two hours later, her fingers drawing lazy circles on Mary's bare shoulder. "It was so wonderful. Just you and me, acting as if we belonged together. No one knowing us, no one caring if we were alone together."

"Two sisters visiting a sick brother."

Hester propped herself up on one elbow and used her free hand to cup Mary's cheek. "I used to dream about us really being sisters." Her hand slipped lower, stopping just above Mary's breast. "But if you were my sister, I would not be able to touch you like this."

"Touch me again," Mary whispered, arching her back.

"I thought you were tired?" Shifting position, Hester dropped her lips down to kiss the soft underside of Mary's breast. "I do believe I heard you say that I wore you out." She smiled when she felt Mary's fingers glide through her hair.

"I seem to have taken some sort of elixir," Mary said.

"Hmm, I wonder where you found this magical elixir of yours."

"Actually, the elixir is yours," Mary said.

"You make your own elixir, as well," Hester said, her hand slipping under the blanket to trail down Mary's body. "I do believe you are making some of that elixir right this moment."

Mary cupped Hester's cheeks, gently pulling their faces together. "How is it possible to feel so much for another person the way I do for you?" she asked with all earnestness. "I love you so much that there are times I just weep from the force of it."

She shook her head. "I'm not explaining myself well."

"Yes, you are," Hester said. "I cannot imagine two other people in this whole world that love as deeply as we do. All the songs, the poems, the stories of great love, they just don't seem enough to tell how I feel for you."

"They can't," Mary said. "They're just words and there are no words to describe what we have between us."

Agreeing that words simply would not do, Hester shifted and brought their lips together, conveying with her body what her voice could not.

Chapter Thirty-Six

Hester rolled, her arm automatically curling around Mary's curvaceous form. With a contented sigh, she snuggled closer, burying her face into the soft, blonde hair.

"I love this," Mary said softly, her hand moving to rest over Hester's.

"I wish I could wake up this way every morning."

"As do I."

Hester's hand traveled upward until it found a soft swell. "It's still early," she whispered, kissing the back of Mary's neck.

"We have to be very quiet," Mary warned as she rolled onto her back. Their kiss quickly became passionate with Mary pulling Hester atop her. Daniel's heavy footsteps pounding down the hall along with his shouts broke the moment, causing them to separate as he jiggled the knob, then pounded on the door.

"Daniel!" Mary admonished as both she and Hester worked to bring their breathing under control.

"The President's been shot!" the teen shouted.

"What?"

"President Lincoln! He was shot last night!"

"Oh, dear Lord!" Hester said, gripping the bedsheets tightly.

"Mother is downstairs crying," Daniel added.

"We shall be there in a moment," Mary said, already throwing the blankets back and rising from the bed.

They used the washroom and dressed quicker than ever before.

"I don't understand," Hester said as she pulled her boots on. "Why?"

Mary shook her head. "The war is finished. It doesn't make sense." She slid the bolt and opened her bedroom door. "It has to be a mistake."

But it was no mistake. They entered the living room to see Mary's father slumped forward in his chair, his elbows on his knees, a deep sadness on his face.

"Father?"

"Our president has been assassinated," he said somberly. "They say...they say Mrs. Lincoln was there with him."

"The poor woman," Mary's mother said, her eyes puffy and her face red. Hester went to her, kneeling down and hugging Elizabeth.

"I can't imagine this," Hester said.

"Daniel, go find out more," his mother said. "Their little boys. Those poor little boys."

In the distance, Hester heard Judith's sobs and the deeper voice of Tobias trying to offer her comfort. Mary came and took Hester's spot, allowing her mother to sob against her shoulder. Uncertain what to do, Hester went into the kitchen.

There she found Bessie and Sally wiping their eyes. "Pardon me, Miss Hester," Bessie said. "Is there something I can get for you?" Even as she spoke, the tears rolled down her face. "I'm sorry, I just can't stop crying."

Hester hugged her. "I know. It's all right, Miss Bessie. It is."

"It's just not right," the servant said. "It's just not right."

Hester guided her to the small table. "Please. I'll make some tea."

"Oh, no, Miss Hester," Sally said. "We should be doing that for you."

"I think, with this news, I would feel better to do be doing something." Hester lifted the pot, judging there to be enough water in it, and set it upon the stove.

"He was such a good man," Sally said.

Bessie nodded and continued to sob. Hester opened cabinets in search of the proper cups.

"Please, Miss Hester," Bessie said as she rose from the chair. "It just ain't right for you to be doing it."

She opened the next cabinet and pulled down cups and saucers. She even managed to get the tray out before the grief overwhelmed her again and she leaned against the counter and could not stop the tears from coming.

Hester and Sally guided her back to the chair. After that, Hester finished the task and prepared the tea.

"I should take it out," Sally said. "Please, Miss Hester. It just won't look right, you understand?"

Hester hesitated, then nodded. She followed Sally into the dining room.

The rest of the morning was spent reading and rereading the account in the paper. Hester did her best to offer comfort to the women around her, making several trips into the kitchen where Sally and Bessie remained. Of everyone, Bessie was the most distraught and completely unable to pull herself together. Sally showed Hester where the ingredients were and assisted her with making something for everyone to eat.

Making a decision usually reserved for her parents, Mary sent Daniel to fetch Old Jack and have him bring the carriage. Once he arrived, she told Bessie to go to her sister's home for a few days and insisted that it was acceptable with the family.

The beloved servant started to protest, but then nodded. Hester and Tobias went along for the ride. Hester to comfort Bessie, and Tobias in case anyone thought to question why a colored woman was riding in such a fine coach. Especially in a part of the city that carriages of that caliber were never seen. No one was certain what the mood of the city was and since the draft riots, no one wanted to take any chances. Tobias even brought along his revolver, just in case.

Where less than a week before, the city had been bright and cheerful, absolutely exuberant in mood, it was clear as the carriage moved along, that the exact opposite was now true.

By noon, the sky over the city had joined in the somber mood, turning as dark as the black buntings draped on every building and coach. It was no surprise when the rain started, forcing most of the women and children back inside or under the protection of overhangs and awnings. Many men, however, remained where they were, letting the water soak their skin and clothes. Not a single one moved with any haste, the shock still far too great to yet comprehend. Even the horses seemed to understand the great loss and plodded along with a casual gait.

The newspaper boys, usually shouting in an attempt to sell their papers, no sooner showed up on a corner than Hester saw a line of people handing them money and cleaning out their stack without a word.

Hester had not been to this part of the city before, finding it even more bustling and crowded than downtown. The coach turned onto a street full of houses, all built against one another. Large numbers of people of varying shades of color filled the roads and steps. Black cloth, some buntings, some simply robes or coats, were draped wherever possible.

The coach stopped in front of one such house where several people were gathered. Tobias stepped out first, then helped Bessie down. A woman came and hugged Bessie, nodding when Tobias explained that he would call for her in a few days.

On the way back to the Chandler residence, Tobias had Old Jack stop so he could pick up copies of all the papers. He also stopped and purchased a small bottle of rum.

"On a day such as this," he explained as he removed the top, "I do believe this is called for. I trust you will say nothing to my family."

"Of course not," Hester said.

He gave a small smile, then took a several short swallows. "This is better than what we had during the war. I swear, sometimes we were drinking pure liniment." He took another swallow. "We probably were."

He stared out the small window not covered with black drapery. "Look at them." The bottle returned to his lips. "Lost. Knowing they have to move forward but not knowing how."

"It is a terrible shock," Hester said.

"Indeed. Wake up one morning, all safe in your bed, hardly a care in the world, filled with the idea of glory and patriotism." He shook his head and took another swig. "Then the truth sets in and you're killing boys no older than you. Smoke everywhere, can't even think for the smell of gunpowder and blood. Just shoot and shoot and pray that you'll be alive when it's all finished."

Hester leaned forward, putting her hand on his good knee. "Will was there for only one battle but he wakes up with nightmares."

Tobias gave a small smile and shook his head. "It's been so long that I don't know what sleep is without nightmares." He shook the half empty bottle. "This helps." He patted her hand resting on his knee. "I do appreciate you not telling anyone, including Mary."

"Your sister does believe that anything other than the communal wine is a sin," Hester said as she sat back. "I think it is best to keep this between us."

"Like the jug in your uncle's barn."

Hester's eyes widened. "How did you know about that?"

"Martin and Hendrik showed me," he said. He continued to stare out the window. "I thought my eyes were going to fall out the first time I took a drink of it." He smiled softly at the memory. "The boys certainly had a good laugh at me." The smile faded. "I wish Martin was here now." He raised the bottle to his lips and took a healthy swallow.

The rest of the ride uptown was quiet, save for the sound of the horses clopping along the road. When Old Jack opened the carriage door, he took the empty bottle and hid it within his coat. Hester wondered if this was a regular occurrence between them.

Taking two cigars from his pocket, Tobias lit one and handed the other to Jack before reaching in and helping Hester exit the coach. He then reached in and collected the pile of newspapers he had purchased.

Hester wondered if Tobias was using the cigar to cover the smell of the spirits on his breath. As it was, when they went inside, he complained of being tired and went to his room, not to come back out until called for supper.

During the meal, the conversation centered on the tragedy. Tobias insisted this would bring them back into war while his father disagreed and swore that President Johnson would never allow that to happen. Hester had no opinion to offer, her focus more on wondering what her family was doing and when Hendrik might be returning home.

"What do you think?" Mary asked once they were settled in bed.

"About what?"

"Will the war still be through, or do you think they'll go after the confederates for this?" She rolled to face Hester.

329

"I don't know." Rolling onto her back, Hester stared up at the ceiling. The pale orange of the lamp cast an eerie glow. "I can only hope that we've been at war for so long that no one will want to see it continue. I want Hendrik to come home."

"He will," Mary said. "Soon. He may even be there already."

Shifting onto her side, Hester snuggled up close to Mary, putting them in their usual sleeping position of nestling like spoons, with Hester's arm around the older woman's belly.

"I hope he is," she said softly. "It's time to start moving forward again with our lives."

"Yes," Mary agreed, covering Hester's hand with her own. "Our lives. Our future. Together."

As they went to sleep that night, content in one another's arms, both women were certain that indeed, only happiness could possibly lie ahead of them.

OTHER BOOKS BY BL MILLER

Accidental Love
Court of Love (German)

OTHER BOOKS BY BL MILLER AND VERDA FOSTER

Crystal's Heart
Graceful Waters
She's the One

OTHER BOOKS BY BL MILLER AND VADA FOSTER

Josie & Rebecca: The Western Chronicles

www.blmillerauthor.com

About the author

BL Miller

BL loves animals and currently lives in upstate New York with three cats. A self-described romantic mushball, she spends her free time writing lesbian fiction, hiking, and playing on Facebook.